When she entered her bedroom, all thoughts of sleep vanished at the sight that met her eyes. Framed in her open window was the window of Daniel's bedroom. In that room, a lamp was lit and Lily could see Daniel clear as day. He was undressing.

Fascinated, she watched as he removed his shirt. The light spilled over his bare chest, and the sweat of the hot summer night glistened on his skin. Her throat went dry. The only undressed man she'd ever seen had been her husband, and he had not looked like this, like a wall of sinew and muscle and power. Without his expensive jacket, without his tie and white linen shirt, Daniel seemed even more dangerous, more predatory than before. He reached for the flap of his trousers, and she made an inarticulate sound of shock.

Hearing the sound, he paused and looked up to find her watching him. He smiled at her; a heated, knowing smile. "Sure you don't want a pair of opera glasses, sugarplum? You'd get a better view."

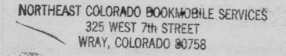

Sleepless in Shivaree

LAURA LEE GUHRKE

Breathless

SONNET BOOKS
New York London Toronto Sydney Tokyo Singapore

This book is a work of fiction. Names, characters, places and
incidents are products of the author's imagination or are used
fictitiously. Any resemblance to actual events or locales or persons,
living or dead, is entirely coincidental.

An *Original* Publication of POCKET BOOKS

A Sonnet Book published by
POCKET BOOKS, a division of Simon & Schuster Inc.
1230 Avenue of the Americas, New York, NY 10020

ISBN: 0-671-02368-3

First Sonnet Books printing July 1999

10   9   8   7   6   5   4   3   2   1

SONNET BOOKS and colophon are trademarks of
Simon & Schuster Inc.

Front cover illustration by Bradley Clark

Printed in the U.S.A.

To my mother, Judy Guhrke.
It might not sound poetic, but you are the
emotional glue that holds our family together
with such strength and resilience.
I love you, Mom.

Breathless

❖ 1 ❖

Atlanta, Georgia, 1905

DANIEL WALKER LOVED a good fight. He loved the law. He loved to win. In fact, Daniel loved winning most of all.

He rose to his feet. He folded his arms across his chest and stared at the short, cherubic-faced man on the witness stand for a long, thoughtful moment, as if trying to decide how best to approach him. It was an act, of course. Daniel knew exactly what he was going to do. He just hoped it worked.

He walked toward the witness and watched the other man swallow nervously at his approach. It was a common reaction. Daniel was six feet three inches tall, weighed two hundred pounds without his clothes, and had shoulders wide enough to block a doorway. He was fully aware of how intimidating his size could be, and before he was done, he was going to intimidate the hell out of George Duvet.

"Mr. Duvet," he began, "tell me about the mysterious woman in red the newspapers have been talking about. What do you know about her?"

Hugh Masterson, a public prosecutor for the city of Atlanta, was on his feet. "Objection! That woman is not relevant. Mr. Walker is trying to cloud the issue by using the romantic speculations that have been generated in the press."

Daniel had expected this. He turned to Judge Rayner. "What is brought up on direct may be refuted on cross."

Hugh stared at him. "I never brought up the woman in red on direct."

"But he did, Your Honor. He asked Duvet about the effect the press was having on him during the trial. If the woman isn't relevant, how could she affect his state of mind?"

Judge Rayner turned to Hugh. "You did ask the question."

"Well, yes," the prosecutor admitted. "But . . . but . . . it was only a passing reference. . . . I mean . . . that is, I never intended . . ." His voice trailed off helplessly.

"You opened the door, Mr. Masterson," the judge reminded him. "You can hardly blame Mr. Walker if he uses it. Your objection is overruled."

The opposing attorney glared at Daniel as he sat down, but there was nothing he could do. Daniel responded to his opponent's anger with a careless smile, but he was fully aware his plan could easily backfire on him. If Duvet didn't fall for it, Daniel knew his entire defense strategy would fall apart, he would lose the case, and Tom Rossiter would hang.

"Once again, Mr. Duvet, tell me about the woman in red."

"I don't know anything about her."

"Was she there that night?"

"I never saw her."

Daniel glanced at the back of the courtroom, where Josiah stood waiting for the signal from him. He nodded slowly, and his law clerk left the room. Daniel returned his attention to the witness.

"You never saw her?" He put just the right amount of derision in his voice. "The newspapers have been discussing her for weeks. They have reported that she was there that night. Was she there, George?"

"I don't know. I didn't see her, I tell you."

"But maybe she saw you. Did she? Did she see you kill Amelia Rossiter?"

"No!" Duvet burst out. "I went to the warehouse that night to go over the accounts, and I found Amelia there. I never saw the woman in red—" He broke off as the doors to the courtroom opened and a tall blond woman in scarlet silk walked in. Murmurs of astonishment rippled through the packed courtroom as she moved with Josiah to stand at the back of the room, in plain view of the witness stand.

George Duvet stared at the woman, and his hands began to shake. He broke out in a sweat. It was exactly the reaction Daniel had hoped for. He resumed his cross-examination. "The truth is, Mr. Duvet, that you killed Amelia Rossiter, didn't you?"

George Duvet shook his head. "No, no. I didn't kill her. I—" His voice broke. "I loved her."

Daniel nodded. "Yes, of course you did. And that's why you killed her. You found out she had no intention of leaving her husband." He leaned closer, and his voice hardened. "She played you for a fool, didn't she, George? And that enraged you. So, you killed her."

The witness looked away, refusing to meet his eyes. "No. It isn't true. I never—"

"You can't lie to us. We know all about it." He pointed to the woman at the back of the room and leaned closer to the witness. "She knows. And she can tell everyone, George," he murmured. "She can tell everyone what she saw."

"That's impossible!" Duvet burst out. "She wasn't there when I—"

"When you what, George?" Daniel asked softly. "When you killed Amelia? When you strangled her with your bare hands?"

Hugh jumped to his feet and pounded the table before him with one fist. "Objection! The witness is not on trial!"

Everyone ignored him. Daniel leaned over Duvet, watching the beads of sweat roll down the man's face. He knew now that he was going to win. He could feel victory, smell it, taste it. "When you had your hands around her throat, did her face turn blue? Did she gasp desperately for air? Did she—"

"She lied to me!" Duvet shouted. "She was using me. She told me she wasn't going to leave Tom. She laughed at me. Nobody laughs at me. I had to stop her from laughing. I had to stop her. I never meant to kill her."

With those words, chaos broke loose in the courtroom. Daniel stepped back with a long, slow breath of relief, watching without pity as Duvet began to sob. He glanced over his shoulder at the girl in the scarlet dress, and she gave him a slight nod in return. Then she slipped out the doors and was gone. He turned to the judge, who was pounding his gavel in a futile effort to quiet the crowd. Over the din, he was forced to shout. "Your Honor, I move that the charges against my client be dismissed."

Judge Rayner nodded. "Your motion is granted, Mr. Walker. The case against Tom Rossiter is dismissed. Bailiffs, take Mr. Duvet into custody."

Journalists rushed out of the room, hoping to get the story in the evening newspapers that the woman in red had come to court prepared to testify, the prosecution's lead witness had confessed on the stand, and that the murder charge against Tom Rossiter, the son of one of the most powerful men in the state, had been dropped. And Daniel Walker, successful attorney and future candidate for the Georgia senate, had just won another case.

He turned to his client. "It's over, Tom."

The young man still looked dazed by the sudden turn of events that had set him free. "I can't believe it. I reckoned I was going to swing on a rope for sure."

Before Daniel could respond, a heavy hand clapped him on the shoulder, and he turned to Tom's father. "Thank you, Daniel, for saving my son," Will said and shook his hand with intense relief and gratitude. "I won't forget this."

"I hope you mean that," he answered, "because I'm counting on your support when I run for office."

"You've got it," the other man promised. But Daniel could feel the hostile stare of Hugh Masterson boring into his back, and he knew his seat in the Georgia State Senate was by no means assured. Hugh continued to glare at him as he and his client received the congratulations and thanks of Tom Rossiter's family, friends, and business associates.

Daniel could see Josiah pushing his way through the crowd surrounding him, but it was not until Rossiter and his entourage departed that his law clerk could reach him. "You did it," Josiah said, shaking his head.

"I never thought you'd get Duvet to confess. Even when I brought the girl in, I still didn't think you'd pull it off."

"There was never a doubt in my mind," Daniel answered, tongue in cheek. Josiah's brows rose in response to that statement, and Daniel chuckled. "Thank God he broke down and confessed," he muttered under his breath to his clerk. "I don't know what I'd have done if he hadn't."

"Congratulations," Hugh Masterson's voice cut in. "Even if it was pure luck."

Daniel turned to face the prosecutor, grinning in the face of the other man's obvious hostility. "Don't pout, Hugh," he admonished. "I won, you lost, and luck had nothing to do with it."

"The press has been trying to locate that woman for weeks. Where did you find her?"

Daniel glanced around to make sure no reporters were within earshot, then leaned closer to the district attorney. "In my imagination," he answered in a low voice.

Stupefied, Hugh stared at him. "What do you mean?"

His grin widened. "I mean, she doesn't exist. I invented her."

Realization dawned in Hugh's eyes. "You son of a bitch," he said and swung, punching Daniel in the face.

Pain shot through his left cheekbone, but Daniel took the blow without flinching. With his greater size and weight, he could have responded with a much more effective punch of his own, but he did not do so. He recognized the other man's fury for exactly what it was. "Sour grapes, Hugh?"

The prosecutor eyed him with contempt. "Trust you to pull some kind of trick to win."

"Trick? I don't know what you're talking about. Your lead witness lost his head on the stand and finally told the truth about what happened. I prefer to call that justice."

"I will have you disbarred."

Daniel knew it was an empty threat. "For what?"

"You fabricated a witness out of whole cloth."

"Ah, but I didn't. She wasn't a witness. I never intended to put her on the stand, and she never testified. The newspapers saw her visiting the police station and my office regularly and going to see Tom in jail. Everything they have reported about her has been pure speculation. She never spoke to them, and I told them nothing untrue."

"It was all innuendo."

Daniel shrugged. "Whatever works to keep an innocent man from being hanged."

Hugh scowled. "You've always been the golden boy with the newspapers. What will it do to your political ambitions when I tell the press what you did?"

"Tell them whatever you like. I did nothing unethical, and you know it. Besides, I doubt the press will pay much attention to such trivial accusations. They'll be too busy writing headlines about how one of Atlanta's public prosecutors punched Georgia's next senator in the face."

"You're not a senator yet," Hugh said furiously. "One of these days, you're going to fall on your ass. I just hope I'm there to enjoy it."

"I hope so, too," Daniel agreed. "God knows, I've enjoyed watching you do it for years."

Masterson's hand curled into a fist, but he did not

try to hit Daniel again. Instead, he marched out of the room without another word.

Josiah, who was still inexperienced enough to be in awe of prosecutors, also watched the other man leave. "I can't believe he actually hit you."

"I can. Poor Hugh. He doesn't like losing, especially to me."

"You'd think he'd be used to it by now." He studied Daniel with a worried expression. "You'll have a black eye."

Daniel touched his throbbing cheek with a grimace. "Probably. But it was worth it." He picked up his leather portfolio and started for the door.

Josiah followed him. "Are we going back to the office?"

"Yes," Daniel answered as they walked out the front doors of the courthouse. "I have something to do first, so I'll meet you there."

The words were barely out of his mouth before he caught sight of the luxurious carriage standing at the curb. It was a fine summer afternoon, the carriage top was down, and Daniel could plainly see the man seated inside. The man beckoned to him, and Daniel paused on the courthouse steps. He turned to Josiah. "On second thought, why don't you just go home? See your wife. How is Muriel, by the way?"

"Fine," Josiah murmured absently, gazing at the carriage. "Baby's not due for over a month." He turned to Daniel. "You're meeting Calvin Stoddard?" he said in surprise. Even Josiah, who did not move in the high social sphere that Daniel did, recognized the man universally acknowledged to be the wealthiest, most powerful man in the state of Georgia.

"The very same."

Josiah let out a low whistle, suitably impressed. "First Will Rossiter, now Calvin Stoddard. You're moving in high circles these days, sir."

"So it would seem. Go on home. I'll see you tomorrow."

His young law clerk knew better than to ask questions. He turned away, and Daniel walked toward the carriage. Calvin swung the door open, and he jumped inside.

"Congratulations." Calvin grinned and offered him a cigar.

Daniel accepted it. "You heard?"

"Of course. A few minutes ago, reporters were running out of that courthouse like it was on fire. I'll bet Will was pleased."

"Happy as a clam in mud. Wouldn't you be if your son was acquitted of murder?"

"Indeed I would. Where can I drop you off?"

"Magnolia Street."

The mention of a street in Atlanta's most notorious prostitution district caused Calvin to raise an eyebrow, but he nodded to his driver, and the carriage jerked into motion. "Celebrating?" he asked.

Daniel laughed. He lit his cigar and leaned back. "No. Business."

"Good. It wouldn't do for a future senator to be seen in an alley with his pants down. Especially if I've given him my backing."

Triumph flooded through Daniel at those words, and it was a sweet sensation. With Calvin Stoddard's support, he would win his senate seat hands down. "So you're endorsing my candidacy?"

"That depends. I have a case for you to handle on my behalf."

"I see. There's a catch."

"Isn't there always?" Calvin shrugged. "Don't worry, Daniel. It's nothing to compromise your legal ethics."

"I'd be more worried if you gave me your backing without asking for anything in return." He met the other man's inquiring gaze and his voice hardened. "I make it a policy never to owe anybody a favor."

"Very wise of you. In politics, it's a bitch when people call them in."

"Exactly."

Calvin took a puff on his cigar. "Then you'll take a case for me?"

"That depends," he answered, throwing Calvin's own words back at him with a smile. "What are you accused of doing?"

"Me? Nothing. I have a business partner, however, who has a bit of trouble. A very beautiful and charming business partner."

"I see." Daniel made it his business to know everything about men like Calvin—men who had power, men he needed on his side—and he knew Calvin had several partners who could fit the description of beautiful and charming. "Which one?"

Calvin laughed. "You're from Shivaree, aren't you?"

The mention of Daniel's hometown gave him the answer to his question. "Is this about Helen Overstreet?"

"You know her?"

"Shivaree is a small town."

"It's also big business, and that business has dried up. The Shivaree Social Club is closed."

Daniel raised an eyebrow at the news. The Shivaree Social Club was famous, or infamous, depending on your point of view, because it was the most notorious gentlemen's club in Georgia. "Has Helen been arrested?"

"No, and that's where you come in. Some woman in Shivaree managed to convince Judge Billings to slap an injunction on the place a few days ago, closing it down. I want that injunction overturned."

Daniel suspected he knew which woman was responsible. A picture flashed through his mind of a slender, fiery redhead who could wreak more havoc than General Sherman. "Why not just reopen under another name someplace else? Isn't that what you usually do when something like this happens?"

"Usually, yes. But the Shivaree Social Club is very well known if a man wants to have a good time. Men from all over the state go there. Helen and I have spent years building its reputation and profits have never been higher. I don't want to lose that if I don't have to, especially since they can't prove anything."

The eyes of the two men met in tacit understanding of the rules of the game. Innocence was always presumed.

"No charges have been brought?" Daniel asked.

"None."

"The judge simply closed the place on Lily Morgan's say-so?"

"How do you know it was Lily Morgan?"

"Stands to reason. Every year, she goes down to the Jaspar County Courthouse and files for an injunction against the Shivaree Social Club. Every year, Judge Billings turns her down. What's different this year?"

"I don't know. Helen didn't give me any details. I want you down there as soon as possible. Helen and I are losing money every day that injunction is in place."

"Since no one has been arrested, and nothing has been proven in court, it shouldn't be too difficult. I'll go down there tomorrow and file a motion with Judge Billings to have the injunction overturned for lack of evidence."

"Excellent. If you manage to win this case for me, there are many things I can do for you."

"All you need to do is endorse my candidacy for the senate." He gave Calvin a cheeky grin, and added, "I won't even charge you my usual exorbitant legal fees."

"From a lawyer, that's a first."

Daniel glanced around, realizing they were very close to his destination. He gestured to the corner. "You can drop me off here."

Calvin tapped his gold-capped walking stick on the floorboards, and the carriage came to a halt. He gave Daniel a speculative glance. "I'd love to know what brings a man like you down to Magnolia Street."

Daniel did not enlighten him. "Thank you for the ride," he said and jumped down from the carriage. "I'll take the train to Shivaree in the morning."

The carriage went on. Daniel waited until it turned at the corner and disappeared, then he walked into a nearby alley. The girl in red silk was waiting for him there.

"Thanks, Pearl." He handed her a twenty dollar bill. "Well done."

The twenty-one-year-old prostitute who really wanted to be an actress hiked her skirt high enough to reveal a long and shapely leg in a black silk stocking. She slipped the money into her garter and, without lowering her skirt, she looked up at Daniel, giving him a smile far too practiced for a young and pretty woman. "Care to spend the night celebrating?"

Many men would have taken her up on her offer, but Daniel did not. As Calvin had reminded him, future senators had to be careful. Besides, Daniel preferred to celebrate each victory by preparing for the next one. He shook his head. "I have work to do."

Pearl sighed and lowered her skirt. "All work and no play," she admonished, turning to go. "You know where I am if you change your mind."

Pearl left him for more promising prospects, and Daniel went back to his office. He worked until midnight, then he went home.

Home was a luxurious mansion on fashionable Courtland Avenue. In it, there was everything that a wealthy and successful man could want. There were silver and crystal, monogrammed sheets and damask draperies, hot water taps and gas lighting. There were servants to see to his every need. Quite an achievement for a man whose father had been a Cracker sharecropper, whose strongest childhood memories were the pain of an empty belly and a razor strap, and whose bed until the age of sixteen had been a dirt floor.

Today, he had won a very important case and the backing of two very powerful men. He was well on his way to being a senator, well on his way to having the power he had always wanted, and the realization filled him with a profound satisfaction. Success was sweet indeed.

When Daniel entered the house, it was dark and quiet. He paused in the marble-tiled foyer, and in that brief moment, all his exaltation vanished with a suddenness that startled him. In the silence, he felt a sense of disappointment. There was no one waiting to share in his victory and celebrate it with him.

It was a feeling so unexpected, so ridiculous, and so unlike him, he ruthlessly shoved it aside. He lit a lamp, walked into his study, and poured himself a drink. He told himself it didn't matter that he drank it alone. Today, he had achieved the greatest success of his career, and to Daniel, success was the only thing in life that mattered.

Shivaree, Georgia, was a small town. From Jacob Cole's purchase of a pair of thoroughbreds from up in Calhoun to Mary Alice Billings's fashionable new bonnet shipped all the way from Paris, anything and everything that happened in Shivaree was fair game for gossip.

Until the Shivaree Social Club had closed down a few days before, plenty of handsome men in expensive suits had always been passing through, and such men didn't usually cause much of a stir. Everybody knew what they came for. But when one man in particular got off the train—a tall man with light brown hair, green eyes, and a charming smile, a man whose face was very familiar to the folks around Shivaree—it didn't take long for word to spread that Daniel Walker was back in town. And folks immediately began wondering what Lily Morgan was going to do about it.

Talk was the lifeblood of a town like Shivaree, since there wasn't much else to do but work, and who wanted to do that? North of Atlanta, south of Calhoun, Shivaree was an important stop on the railroad line, partly because of its lumber mill and two cotton mills, and partly because, for some obscure reason nobody could remember, it was the Jaspar County seat. Of course, it also had the Shivaree Social Club, which until last week had been the most famous whorehouse

in the entire state of Georgia. These things gave
Shivaree a lot to talk about.

It was also the kind of town where ladies of quality
sat on their verandahs in the late afternoon, sipping
lemonade and watching for any sign of a story to tell.
Dovey McRae was one of those ladies. Her widowed
sister Densie Stuart had moved to Shivaree from
Charleston last summer to live with her, and the two
women had taken up the useful hobby of bird-
watching with the use of opera glasses. Because Dovey's house had a clear view of the train station, the
sisters saw Samuel Hardesty standing on the platform
as the eleven o'clock from Atlanta pulled in, and the
minute they saw Daniel Walker get off the train,
carpetbag in hand, they couldn't wait to spread the
news.

They dropped their opera glasses and headed hell
bent for leather to tell their best friend, Sue Ann
Parker, all about it. Sue Ann and her husband ran the
Shivaree Hotel, which was right across the street from
Samuel's house, and Daniel was bound to stay with
Samuel, and Samuel lived right next door to Lily
Morgan. With a situation like that, exciting things were
bound to happen, and Sue Ann would be able to see
everything that went on.

Lily found out about Daniel Walker's return a little
later than some. She wasn't part of Shivaree's gossipy
inner circle, partly because she didn't cotton much to
peering into people's lives with opera glasses, and
partly because she was one of the gossip circle's
favorite subjects. A body could get downright breathless listing all the scandalous things about Lily
Morgan.

For one thing, she was modern, which to the ladies

of Shivaree was almost as great a sin as being born north of the Mason-Dixon line. She had red hair and wore pink. She played band music on her piano and opera on her Victrola loud enough to wake the dead. She refused to wear gloves, even to church, and it was rumored she didn't wear corsets, either. She had a statue of a naked man in her foyer. It was said that her own family wouldn't receive her. Worst of all, she was *divorced*.

Opinion was divided as to whether she was just a bit on the wild side or completely devoid of morals, and the question was hotly debated at the ladies' sewing circle and the men's barbershop. But just about everybody in town agreed on two things: Lily Morgan was a scandalous woman, and Lily Morgan just didn't act like a librarian.

Because she wasn't among the first to hear the gossip, Lily was completely unaware of Daniel's return until Amos Boone came running into the library to tell her.

"Lily!" he cried as he burst through the front doors. "Lily, where are you?"

The shouting caused her to climb hastily down from her perch on a ladder in Nonfiction, where she was putting books back on the shelves. She ran to the railing and looked down from the mezzanine. "Hush, Amos," she admonished, frowning down at the young man, who was weaving his way clumsily between the heavy oak reading tables at an all-out run. "Don't shout."

Amos was a giant, standing over six foot five without his boots. He was nineteen years old, but he had the mind of a child. He was honest, never made moral judgments, and believed implicitly whatever anybody told him. Because his own parents were dead, Lily and her friend Rosie Russell had sort of adopted him as a younger brother. He lived in the basement of the library and did janitorial work there in exchange for the rent, an arrangement Lily had made for him. He ate his meals at Rosie's Cafe. Most folks agreed he was a few peaches short of a pie, but Lily and Rosie didn't care. He was their dearest friend.

"Where have you been all day?" she asked him in a teasing voice. "Having ice cream over at Rosie's, I'll bet, while these shelves needed dusting."

Amos took her words to heart, looking up at her with a stricken expression. "I'm sorry, Lily, but I was helpin' Rosie unload all those tins from Atlanta. And then she gave me an ice cream, and that's when he came in, and Rosie sent me over here to tell you."

"He?" Lily leaned her forearms on the rail and smiled. "Who's in town that's got Rosie in such a lather on my behalf? Is it Alvis Purdy, that flashy book salesman from Missouri who chases me around the library every month waving his money around?"

Amos shook his head. "No, ma'am. It's Daniel Walker."

Lily's smile vanished. Daniel Walker, that bottom-feeding, scum-sucking lawyer who had ruined her life, was back in town. A sick lurch twisted her stomach. "Are you sure?"

Amos nodded vigorously. "Yes'm. Arrived on the eleven o'clock train." Staring anxiously up into her face, he asked, "You all right, Lily?"

Lily scarcely heard. She was remembering all the scandal and shame, the humiliation and pain of her divorce from Jason five years ago, and the man responsible for dragging her name through the mud. Daniel

Walker. Oh, how she hated him. Her fingers curled around the carved wooden railing in front of her so tightly her hands began to ache. "How does Rosie know about this?"

"He's over at the cafe having dinner. Rosie said she would have come to tell you herself that he was in town, but with it bein' noontime, the restaurant's mighty crowded, so she couldn't get over here."

"What is he doing here?" she asked. "Did Rosie say?"

Amos closed his eyes, and his face puckered up as he tried to remember. "Somethin' about Helen Overstreet hirin' him to get the Shivaree Social Club reopened."

"What?" Lily straightened away from the rail. "Of all the stupid, idiotic ideas—" She broke off, too angry to continue.

"Rosie said you'd be mighty upset."

"Upset doesn't begin to describe it." That den of sin and corruption had destroyed her marriage, and after five years of trying, she had finally succeeded in having it shut down. Now Daniel Walker, that conniving, morally bankrupt scoundrel, was here to undo all her hard work. That thought ignited Lily's temper, which was easily sparked at the best of times. She marched down the staircase and out of the library, her anger growing with every step she took across the square to Rosie's Cafe. Amos followed in silence.

It was midday, and the cafe was crowded. Daniel was leaning on the counter at the opposite end of the room talking to Rosie when Lily came in. Samuel Hardesty stood beside him.

Lily halted in the doorway, right next to the sign on the wall that said NO SWEARING, NO SMOKING, NO SPITTING, and she felt the impulse to do all three.

Instead, she stared at Daniel's back, sizzling with the anger she made no effort to hide. She felt gazes light on her, one after another, and heard voices fade to nothing. She stared at Daniel Walker and watched him slowly turn around to see what was causing the sudden silence.

Of course he had to look exactly the same, with that tall, brawny body and those eyes as dark a green as the Georgia pines. He still had that thick hair the golden brown color of tupelo honey. And he still had that smile—a smile that could make him innocent as a schoolboy or wicked as the devil, depending on what he wanted to make you believe. Even the dark smudge of a shiner beneath his left eye couldn't detract from the face of a man too handsome for his own good. Lily wondered who had hit him. Whoever that man was, she wanted to shake his hand.

With the force of a tornado, the sight of Daniel brought back all the anguish he had caused her. Why, oh why, couldn't he have lost his hair and gone to fat? Why couldn't he have lost a couple of those perfect white teeth in whatever fight had given him that black eye? Why couldn't he have just stayed away from Shivaree for the rest of his miserable life?

Lily lifted her chin, meeting his gaze squarely. She took satisfaction in watching his smile fade, but he did not look away. For a long moment, most of Shivaree stared at them and they stared at each other, until Lily couldn't stand it any longer. She began walking toward him.

Her hot temper had always been a sore trial to her, and from the time she'd been a little girl, she had worked very hard to keep it under control. With every step closer to Daniel, she vowed again not to let her temper get the better of her, so by the time she reached him, she was in complete control of her emotions. She knew exactly what she was doing when she slapped him across the face.

Without a word, she turned on her heel and walked out of the cafe, thinking that this time she'd given the town a scandal shocking enough to leave them breathless.

÷ 2 ÷

DANIEL REALLY WISHED people would stop hitting him. Despite the stinging slap Lily had given him, the pain didn't stop him from admiring the luscious curve of her hips as she walked away. He sure did like those fashionable, tight-fitting skirts.

Despite the view she offered on her way out the door, Lily Morgan had dealt him quite a wallop, and he hoped this business with the Shivaree Social Club wouldn't take long. More than a day or two around Lily, and he might not get back to Atlanta alive.

Everyone in the cafe was staring at him, and the place was quiet as church at praying time. Daniel decided it was best to make light of the matter. "I wonder how she really feels about me."

Laughter broke out, relieving the tension, and Daniel turned back around. He tossed some coins on the counter. "Thanks for the dinner, Rosie," he said with a smile to the slender brunette who stood on the other side. "Your quince pie is good as ever."

"Mighty kind of you to say so. How long you staying?"

"I'm not sure," he answered. "Is it safe to walk your streets?"

Rosie glanced at Samuel, then back at him. "Lily's got her reasons for how she feels, Daniel, don't you think?"

"Now, Rosie," Samuel broke in, "it's not all Daniel's fault, you know."

"Maybe, but I'm not the one who needs convincin' of that." Rosie slid the coins off the counter and into her apron pocket.

"I don't think Lily could be convinced water's wet if I'm the one trying to do it," Daniel told her. "She's a fire-eater, Rosie."

"She's not as tough as she seems."

Daniel already knew that, but it didn't make him like her any better.

Rosie grinned suddenly. "She does play the piano like a savage, though."

"What do you mean?"

She nodded to the man beside him. "Are you staying with Samuel?"

"Yes'm."

"Then you'll find out."

At suppertime, he discovered what Rosie meant.

"Tarnation!" Beatrice shouted, slamming a bowl of black-eyed peas onto the dining table with enough force to send several flying into the ham gravy. The housekeeper's face, round and black as a billiard eight-ball, scrunched with displeasure, and she plunked her hands on her wide hips. "She's at it again, Mr. Samuel!"

Stephan Foster's "Camptown Races" was being pounded out on a piano in the house next door. With the weather being so hot, everybody was leaving their windows open, and the window of Lily Morgan's parlor was right next to the window of Samuel's dining room, making the volume of the music high enough that shouting was necessary. Daniel glanced across the table to Samuel. "Lily Morgan?" he yelled.

"Who else?" the other man yelled back.

Beatrice stuck a finger in each ear. "It isn't so bad when she plays something pretty. But this kind of music is a sore trial."

"Does this happen often?"

Samuel shrugged. "When she gets a bee in her bonnet about something, we get band music. This time," he added with a grin, "I think you're the bee."

"Mr. Daniel, isn't there something you can do?" Beatrice asked. "If you could get her to stop this piano playing, I'd sure appreciate it."

The idea of tweaking Lily's tail appealed to him immensely. "Anything for you, Beatrice. I'll go over and have a little talk with her."

Samuel laughed. "Talk to her? You? Sure you wouldn't rather have me do it? Might be safer."

"No, I'll do it. It's my fault she's in such a stir." He left the house and walked the few short steps next door. He tugged at the bellpull, but Lily had already begun to pound out "Oh! Susanna," and he doubted she could hear the bell. He opened the door and walked in just as she began singing along with the music in a faulty soprano.

Because he and Jason Morgan had been boyhood friends, Daniel had been in the Morgan mansion many times, but he had barely taken one step inside the house before he saw something completely unfamiliar. He came to an abrupt halt. Beside him in the foyer was a life-size sculpture of Michelangelo's *David*, no fig leaf to shield his attributes, and a lady's straw bonnet tipped jauntily over his eye. Daniel knew Jason would never have approved of such a thing in his house, which was probably why Jason was gone and David was here.

From his position in the foyer, Daniel could see other signs of Lily's flamboyant personality. A Victrola stood on a teakwood cabinet beside the doors leading into the parlor. Though it was July, a potted fern hung with Christmas ornaments rested atop the matching teakwood cabinet beside the study. Before him a set of stairs with a broad, polished stair rail led to the upper floors. A small, square pillow rested atop the flat newel post, and Daniel knew it was meant for comfort when sliding down the banister. He couldn't help grinning as he crossed the foyer and walked into the parlor. Lily might be a pain in the ass, but she was unique.

Absorbed in her music, Lily did not notice when Daniel walked into her parlor. Playing Foster always made her feel better. There was something about pounding out music at a furious pace that released anger and tension. As she played and sang, Lily's nerves stopped jangling, and she actually began to regain a calm and serene state of mind. Then *he* showed up and ruined it.

It wasn't until the hateful man was standing right next to her that she realized he had actually entered her home. Her hands hit the keys with a discordant clang, and she jumped to her feet, knocking over the piano bench in her agitation. "What are you doing in here?" she demanded, sidestepping the overturned bench and turning to face him. "Get out of my house."

"I did ring the bell first." Daniel glanced at the immense grand piano that took up half the room. "I reckon you didn't hear it."

Lily was a tall woman, but Daniel topped her by a good seven inches. She had to tilt her head back to look him in the eye. She felt her newfound serenity slipping away, and she began to take deep breaths. "What do you want?"

"I'm here to request that you play your piano more quietly."

"What's wrong, Daniel? Don't you like a bit of music with your supper?"

"Music, perhaps. We wouldn't mind at all if you played something pleasant. Not raucous band music badly done."

She ignored the insult. "I will continue to play anything I want on my piano, in my house," she declared, not caring one bit that Samuel and Beatrice were watching them through the open windows. "Furthermore, I'll play as loudly, as often, and as badly as I please. And I don't care whether you like it or not."

"You will care if I pursue litigation against you."

"You'll sue me?"

"Without a second thought, sugarplum."

She scowled at the endearment. "I always knew Shakespeare had the right idea."

"Shakespeare?"

" 'Let's kill all the lawyers.' "

"Can we kill all the bad musicians, too?" he asked hopefully. When she sputtered and stammered, trying to think of a scathing reply, he held up one hand in a conciliatory gesture. "C'mon, Lily. Let's call a truce. I know you're still angry about what happened—"

" 'Angry' is a definite understatement, Daniel. And I don't want a truce with you."

"How long are you going to hold this grudge?" he asked. "Can't you ever just forgive and forget?"

"Forgive, no. Forget, yes. I'll never forgive you for the way you ruined my life, but I will forget about you the minute you get out of Shivaree and go back to Atlanta."

"Then I'll be able to make you a happy woman. I'll be taking the evening train back tomorrow night after Judge Billings grants my motion to revoke that injunction you've finally managed to connive him into signing."

"I heard that's why you're here." She folded her arms across her breasts. "He's not going to revoke it. He has no reason to change his mind."

"Want to bet on it? I don't know how you persuaded him to sign it in the first place, but once I make my legal argument and formally contest the injunction, he'll have to revoke it. You cannot close a business without cause, and there is no proof that Helen Overstreet or her employees have committed a crime."

"So, you are representing Helen Overstreet?" She stared at him. "Honestly, the depths you sink to never cease to amaze me. Divorces, brothels . . . is there anything you won't defend if there is money involved?"

"I didn't handle Jason's divorce from you for money," he snapped before he realized that it had taken her less than a minute to provoke him beyond endurance. Lily could make a man lose his temper faster than a boy could lose his virginity. Daniel took a deep breath and forced himself to say calmly, "It wasn't the money. Jason was my best friend."

"Really? If you and Jason were such good friends, why didn't you come to our wedding? Why didn't you ever come visit us here in Shivaree?"

"It's hard to go to a wedding in Birmingham when you're clerking for a judge in Atlanta," he answered coldly. "Jason understood that I couldn't get away for even a day the summer he got married to you. As for my not coming to visit, I don't have many fond memories of my childhood here, and Jason knew that. He always preferred to come to Atlanta to see me."

"Of course he did." She smiled, but there was no humor in it, only bitterness. "In Atlanta, Jason could go out and do all the things he didn't dare do in Shivaree while his father was alive, like get drunk and visit prostitutes. He had no respect for our marriage whatsoever."

"Even if that's true, his marriage to you was none of my business until he asked for my help to dissolve it."

"I see. His adultery was acceptable to you, but mine was not?"

"I never saw Jason with a prostitute, or any other woman for that matter, when he came to Atlanta. But during the divorce proceedings, I did see Henry Douglas. I know all the details of your affair with him, and I know how much pain Jason felt at your unfaithfulness."

Lily clenched her hands into fists. "Henry Douglas lied to you. I did not commit adultery, but Jason did. Many, many times. At first, he went to Atlanta, using his visits to you as an excuse, so that his father wouldn't know about his wild behavior. But after his father died, he made no effort to hide anything. He started being unfaithful in a place much closer to home—the Shivaree Social Club."

"I don't suppose you might have driven him away by being a shrewish, cold, and nagging wife?"

"Is that what he told you? That's just like Jason, to lay the blame on me rather than himself. He was such a coward." She took a deep breath, then went on, "Since you profess to have been such a good friend of his, do you know where he is? Have you heard from him? I'll bet you haven't. I'll bet he didn't even write to you after he left this town. He sure didn't write to anyone else. Why would he? He never cared about anyone but himself."

Daniel looked away. She was right about the fact that Jason had never written to him, but he was damned if he'd acknowledge it to her.

"You might have been Jason's friend, Daniel," she said, "but you never really knew him. You never knew him at all."

It was a long moment before he spoke. "I am not in Shivaree to reminisce about the past with you," he finally said, turning his head to look at her, careful to keep his voice flatly impersonal. "I am here to represent the interests of the owners of the Shivaree Social Club."

"Well, in case you didn't know," she said in the tone of a schoolteacher to a particularly slow pupil, "prostitution is against the law in the state of Georgia."

"Thank you for pointing that out to me, but there has been no evidence presented in a court of law to prove that the Shivaree Social Club is a house of prostitution."

Lily made a sound of contempt. "Social club, my

eye. It's a cathouse and everybody knows it, including Judge Billings."

"What people think they know and what can be proven with evidence are two different things."

She laughed in disbelief. "And I suppose those fancy painted ladies are just there for conversation?"

"Possibly. I don't know. I've never been there. All that concerns me are the interests of my clients. That's my job."

"So you just do your job, and damn the consequences." She shook her head in disbelief. "You play with people's lives, and you don't even consider what happens as a result. How do you manage to sleep at night?"

"You are only saying that because I represented Jason in the divorce. If I had represented you, your feelings would be different."

"But the result was the same. My husband spent his nights with prostitutes and spent his money on gambling and drink, and those things were more important to him than his own wife. I cannot allow other women to suffer the same fate. I will fight you with everything I've got. I will do everything I can to make sure the Shivaree Social Club stays closed."

His eyes narrowed. "Don't try it, Lily."

"Or what?" she shot back. "You'll ruin my reputation?"

"I'll make your life hell."

"Too late. You did that five years ago."

His mouth tightened for a moment, then he said, "You provided me with the ammunition. Don't blame me if your own love affair came back to haunt you."

"I did not have an affair!"

"So you've always said, but I don't believe you any more now than I did then."

"I don't care what you believe." She looked at him with loathing. "I hate you, Daniel Walker."

"I know." If she didn't know he was a swine, she might have thought there was a hint of regret in that reply. He turned away. "But I don't lose a lot of sleep over your opinion, sugarplum."

"If you want me to play music that's pleasant, then you better stay out of my sight," she shouted after him as he walked out of the parlor. "And I'll keep that cathouse closed—you just watch me," she went on as his footsteps crossed the foyer. "And don't call me sugarplum!" she added just before the door slammed behind him.

In the aftermath of his departure, the sudden silence in the house was deafening. Memories of that awful day in court five years ago began flashing through Lily's mind. She sank down on the horsehair sofa and closed her eyes, trying to blot them out, but she could not. She remembered the shocked murmurs when Jason told everyone she was an adulteress. She remembered all the contemptuous stares directed at her when Henry Douglas had admitted to being her lover, and she wondered again how much Jason had paid him to lie. Most of all, she remembered Daniel Walker twisting her words, tripping her up, putting the worst possible interpretation on everything she said, making her appear to be guilty even though she was innocent.

She covered her face with her hands. Her marriage had been ruined by Jason's nights of debauchery at the Shivaree Social Club, not by some fictitious affair that her husband and Daniel Walker had invented. Her supposed liaison with Henry Douglas had proclaimed her an adulteress, but Jason's countless nights with prostitutes had been regarded as just a bit of harmless fun. How unfair life was.

Lily rose to her feet, resolute. Daniel Walker was not going to succeed in getting the Shivaree Social Club reopened. Not as long as she had an ounce of strength to stop him.

Despite Lily's threat, she stopped playing her piano, and Daniel and Samuel were able to finish their supper in quiet. Afterward, the two men adjourned to the study for cigars and brandy before Helen Overstreet arrived at nine o'clock to meet with Daniel.

The moment Daniel entered the study, he noticed that the bookshelves lining the walls were nearly empty. "What happened to all your law books?"

Samuel handed him a glass of brandy, then poured another for himself. "I donated them to the library," he answered. "I would have given them to you, but you already have a legal library far more extensive than mine. And since I don't practice law any longer, they were just gathering dust. Lily was happy to have them."

"She still run the library?"

"Yes. Does it very well, too."

The two men settled into a pair of comfortable leather chairs and lit their cigars. Samuel leaned back in his chair, blew three smoke rings toward the ceiling in rapid succession, and said, "It's sad, though."

"What is?"

"The library. Most people don't even use it. Lily is an excellent librarian, but she's got some pretty controversial books in there. It caused quite a stir last year when she refused to take them off the shelves."

"Controversial?"

Samuel leaned forward as if he had a secret to tell. "Dirty books," he whispered, struggling to keep a straight face.

Daniel didn't even try. He grinned. "Really? What, like pornography?"

"Some might think so, but really, the books in question are excellent. *Candide*, for example. The women really went on a tirade about those books, Dovey especially. As you know, where Dovey goes, the others follow."

"Saw Dovey sittin' on her porch when we walked here from the station." Daniel looked at the older man, and his grin widened. "When did she take up bird-watching?"

Samuel laughed. "An ideal hobby for Dovey, don't you think? Anyway, getting back to Lily, between her divorce and her adamant refusal to take those controversial books off the shelves, most folks don't want to be seen anywhere near her library, or her. She's become quite the outsider around here. Unfortunately, she makes the situation worse by deliberately provoking Dovey and her friends."

Daniel nodded with understanding. "Yes, I saw the statue in her foyer."

"Exactly. She's such a scandal in this town, most folks won't even speak to her."

Daniel straightened in his chair. "You never told me this."

"The subject never came up. When I see you, Shivaree gossip isn't usually what we talk about." He swirled the brandy in his glass and took a swallow.

"Besides, I didn't really think you'd be interested in Lily Morgan's life or what became of her."

There was a hint of censure in the older man's voice, and Daniel immediately got his back up. "Jason asked me to represent him in his divorce from Lily because she was cheating on him. You know as well as I do how much I owed Jason after what he did for me. I wouldn't have gone to college if he hadn't loaned me the money for tuition. We both know you couldn't have afforded to send me."

"I understand your reasons for what you did, but you don't seem to have ever given a thought to Lily's side of the situation."

"Lily was not my friend for over twenty years," he answered, exasperated. "If she is given the cold shoulder by the town, she should have thought of that before she took Henry Douglas as her lover. And from what you've told me, she hasn't made much of an effort to change that. It isn't my fault."

"I didn't say it was. Why are you being so defensive?"

"I'm not being defensive, dammit!"

"If you say so." Much to Daniel's relief, Samuel changed the subject. "Why don't we talk about how you got that black eye instead?" he asked. "Why do I get the feeling there's a good story behind that?"

Daniel laughed and told him what had happened the day before, summing up the tale with the words "When I run for the senate, I don't think Hugh is going to vote for me."

The older man chuckled. "I should imagine not." He paused, and his amusement faded to a serious expression. "You still plan to run for election, then?"

"Of course. That's why I took this case for Calvin

Stoddard. With his backing, I can go very far in politics."

Samuel did not reply, and Daniel glanced at him sharply. "You don't approve."

"Does it matter whether or not I approve?"

Daniel was astonished by the question. "Of course it matters. If it weren't for you, I wouldn't be a lawyer. Hell, I might not even be alive. You gave me the first job I ever had, you were the father my own father refused to be. Your opinion means a great deal to me. Don't you want me to be a senator?"

Samuel sighed. "When I look at you, I don't see a senator. I see a boy, abused and half-starved, with eyes too hard for a ten-year-old."

Daniel's jaw tightened. "Do we have to talk about those days?"

Samuel paid no attention to that. "I remember how I caught you rummaging through the garbage bins behind my house for a meal because your daddy was always too drunk on cheap moonshine to give a damn. You connived a chicken dinner out of me that day, as I recall, and somehow managed to get a paying job to go along with it. You've always had charm enough to tempt the saints, and that charm could probably get you just about anything, including a senate seat, if that's what you want. As for me, all I want is for you to be happy."

Daniel looked away. He did not want to talk about the boy he had been. "I'm fine. Any time you want to reassure yourself of that, come to Atlanta for a visit. You hardly ever come anymore."

Samuel took a puff on his cigar. "That's because I don't like your house."

Daniel frowned in puzzlement. "What's wrong with it? It's a beautiful house."

"And it's filled with beautiful things, but it's an empty house. There's nobody living in it but you, and you're never there anyway."

"I have six other people living there."

"Three maids, a housekeeper, a butler, and a carriage driver don't count. You're thirty-four, Daniel. It's time you found a good woman, got married, and had some children to fill that big, empty house of yours. A good woman is a prize more worth winning than all the law cases and elections in the world."

Daniel smiled. "Been worryin' about me, old man?"

Samuel had seen Daniel work magic on a jury with that smile, but it was a smile that did not reach his eyes, and Samuel was probably the only person who could recognize the difference. "Don't try to use your charm on me, Danny, just because you don't like what I'm saying. Yes, I'm worried about you. I'm worried about the ambition that drives you."

"What's wrong with being ambitious?"

"Ambition is a harsh mistress, Daniel, because she's insatiable. No matter what you do, you can never satisfy her. No matter how successful you become, she'll never let you think it's enough. I don't want you to get to the top of the mountain and realize there's nowhere to go but down."

"Getting a bit maudlin, aren't you?"

Samuel ignored that. "I remember the first day you ever went to school. You were working for me by then, and I had finally managed to convince you to go to school. The other children laughed at you and teased you mercilessly because you were almost eleven years old and didn't know how to read. Didn't even know the alphabet, as I recall."

Daniel stiffened. "I don't see what that has to do with anything."

"I could tell how much their teasing hurt you," Samuel went on as if Daniel had not spoken, "but you never cried. You just marched into my office after school that day, pulled the biggest, fattest law book off the shelf, and told me you weren't going back there until you could read every word in that book, until you could prove to all of them that you weren't stupid, until you could show them all that you were just as good as they were. You're still doing it, you know."

"I don't know what you're talking about."

"You don't have to prove anything, Daniel. Not to the world, not to Jason, not to me, not to yourself."

"Just what do you think I'm trying to prove?"

"That you're not the loser your daddy was."

Daniel rose to his feet so abruptly, brandy spilled over the side of his glass. "That is ridiculous. I'm running for the state legislature because I love the law and that is where Georgia laws are made. Maybe I'll even become a congressman in Washington. Politics is a way I can truly have some influence and make my mark on the world."

Before Samuel could reply, a knock sounded on the door and Beatrice entered the room. She immediately choked. "Oh, good Lord," she muttered, waving her hand in a futile effort to clear the smoke. "It'll take me a week to air this room. Can't y'all smoke those foul things outside?"

Both men shook their heads, a reaction that made the housekeeper scowl more fiercely than before.

"That woman's here," she said with a snort of contempt, her opinion of Helen obvious.

"Thank you, Beatrice," Daniel said, ignoring the look of censure directed at him. "Bring her in here."

Beatrice *humph*ed and left the room. Moments later, Helen came in. At a glance, no one would ever assume Helen Overstreet was the owner of a men's club. She was not young, flirtatious, or beautiful. With her dove-gray dress and her bun of black hair, she might perhaps be taken for a respectable middle-aged widow. In reality, she was a shrewd, hardheaded woman of business. She was also a woman who understood men. That quality was what made her a success.

She greeted the older man with a nod as he stood up. "Hello, Samuel. Are you working on this case, too?"

"No." He drained his glass of brandy. "I don't have to. I'm not running for senate."

Helen looked from one man to the other. "What on earth does that mean?"

"Nothing," Daniel answered. He gave the other man a pointed stare. "Samuel was just leaving."

Samuel lifted his hands, palms out in a gesture of surrender. "I've had my say." He put out his cigar and left the room.

Helen crossed the room and studied him for a moment. "You've become quite a handsome man," she said with the ease of a woman accustomed to complimenting men. "Quite successful, too, from what Calvin tells me. I'm glad he hired you to handle this matter." She stepped back and took a glance out the window at the darkened street outside. "I shouldn't stay here too long. Both you and Samuel are respectable men."

"Then let's get down to brass tacks." Daniel pulled out a chair for her in front of Samuel's desk, then circled to the opposite side and sat down facing her. "How did this happen?"

Helen leaned back in her chair. "Didn't Calvin tell you?"

"I'd like your version. I know that every year, on the anniversary of her divorce, Lily Morgan goes down to the courthouse and files a motion with Judge Billings for an injunction to close down the Shivaree Social Club, and every year he turns her down. But this year, he granted that motion and closed the club. Why? What's different this year? Why, suddenly, has he decided to rule in her favor?"

"The good judge remarried several months ago."

"Yes, I know. I had my law clerk send them a silver tea service. What does that have to do with anything?"

Helen laughed. "Daniel, you are obviously not a married man."

He got the point. "I suppose his new wife is not the type to overlook a man's need for outside companionship?"

"Exactly. Lily Morgan made sure the judge's wife knew where her husband used to spend his evenings. As a result, Judge Billings has developed a late-blooming case of morality. It won't last, of course," she added with the cynicism of her experience. "But I can't afford to wait around for him to get tired of matrimony. Calvin and I are losing money every day that injunction is in place."

"When I represented Jason Morgan in his divorce, I had no idea Lily would blame the Shivaree Social Club for the failure of her marriage. And I certainly never would have thought Judge Billings would side with her. He's sown many wild oats at the social club himself."

Helen shrugged. "If it hadn't been Lily Morgan, it would probably have been someone else." She frowned thoughtfully. "In truth, I'm not sure I wouldn't feel the same if I were in her place. Hell hath no fury like a woman scorned, you know. And Lily Morgan is a woman with a lot of fury."

Daniel thought of the slap he'd received earlier in the day and wholeheartedly agreed. "But the fact remains that Judge Billings cannot ignore the law. Once I present my motion, he will be forced to either reverse the injunction or have the sheriff bring formal charges against you and your girls."

"Do you think it will come to that?"

"Not if I can help it." Daniel pulled a sheet of notepaper toward him and picked up a pen. Dipping it in the inkwell, he glanced at the woman across the desk. "If I'm going to handle this case, there are things I need to ask you." He paused, and their eyes met. "You own and operate a social club, and you have ten women working there, is that right?"

"Yes."

"And these ladies are there to provide companionship and entertainment to the gentlemen who visit?"

"Yes. Drinks, card games, music, dancing."

"Within the state of Georgia, have you or any of your employees been convicted of prostitution?"

"No."

"Good. That makes it easier. I will be meeting with Judge Billings tomorrow afternoon to present a motion that the injunction be revoked for lack of evidence and that you be allowed to resume normal business operations."

"Thank you, Daniel."

He thought of Lily, and the determination in her brown eyes.

I will fight you with everything I've got.

"Don't thank me, Helen," he advised. "I haven't won yet."

"You will. From what I have heard, you usually do." Helen rose to her feet, and Daniel followed suit. They left the study, and he walked her to the front door.

"Let me know what happens at your meeting with Judge Billings," she said as he opened the door for her.

"I will."

She paused in the doorway and smiled at him over her shoulder, an unexpected pirate smile. "You might also tell the judge that Corrine misses his visits. She's always been his favorite."

Daniel laughed, wondering what Billings would do if he presented an argument that if the club were a house of prostitution, then the judge himself should be in jail for participating in an illegal activity. "Helen, are you suggesting I blackmail a judge with his past misdeeds?"

"Only if his wife isn't in the room."

Lily could not sleep. Thoughts and memories and emotions were all churning around inside her, making sleep impossible. She lay in the dark, trying to think of what she could do to stop Daniel from getting that cathouse reopened, but all she could do was relive the past. All she could hear was Daniel's voice badgering her on the witness stand, trapping her, throwing accusations of adultery in her face as a roomful of people watched. She had been able to tell from their faces how unbelievable her stuttering denials of those accusations had sounded. It had been the most humiliating experience of her life. Now he was back, and she could feel the same rage and frustration she had felt then.

Lily closed her eyes, concentrating on the chorus of cicadas and frogs outside her open window as she slowly forced the past away. Frustration and rage had not helped her five years ago and they would not help her now. What she needed was a plan.

The idea came to her with sudden, unexpected force. "Of course," she murmured. "How simple."

Tossing aside the sheet, she rose and walked to her vanity table. Fumbling in the dark, she lit the lamp, then took it downstairs to the secretaire in her parlor. From the center drawer she retrieved paper, quill, and ink, then sat down. Quill in hand, she began to write.

The letter was brief and specific, taking only moments to complete. She blotted the paper, put it in an envelope, and closed it with sealing wax. She would have Amos deliver it for her in the morning. Satisfied with her handiwork, she took the lamp and went back upstairs, feeling much better now that she had decided what action to take. She also felt incredibly sleepy.

But when she entered her bedroom, all thoughts of sleep vanished at the sight that met her eyes. Framed in her open window was the window of Daniel's bedroom at Samuel's house. In that room, a lamp was lit and Lily could see Daniel clear as day. He was undressing.

Fascinated, she watched as he removed his shirt. The light spilled over his bare chest, and the sweat of the hot summer night glistened on his skin. Her throat went dry. The only undressed man she'd ever seen had been her husband, and he had not looked like this, like a wall of sinew and muscle and power. Without his expensive jacket, without his tie and white linen shirt, Daniel seemed even more dangerous, more predatory than before. He reached for the flap of his trousers, and she made an inarticulate sound of shock.

Hearing the sound, he paused and looked up to find her watching him. He smiled at her; a heated, knowing smile. "Sure you don't want a pair of Dovey's opera glasses, sugarplum? You'd get a better view."

His words brought her to her senses. Horrified, Lily ran to her window, thinking only to close it, to draw the curtains, to shut him out and shield herself from the mortification she felt at having been caught watching him. But before she could fulfill her intention, his voice stopped her.

"I wouldn't do that if I were you," he advised. Belt unbuckled, trousers half undone, he walked toward her. "In this weather, your room'll get awful hot."

She averted her eyes from his naked chest and reached up to close her window.

He lifted his arms, curling his hands around the sash of his own window. Between his upraised arms, he stared at her, and his smile widened. "What's wrong, Lily? Are you shutting your window because you're afraid I'll breathe the same air you do?"

She met his gaze across the short distance that separated them. "I didn't know leeches could breathe."

He didn't get angry at the insult. Instead, he laughed. "You're a worthy opponent. I don't think I've ever met a woman with a quicker wit than you. If you'd been a man, there's no telling what you might have accomplished."

"If I'd been a man, I'd have called you out in the fine

old Southern tradition five years ago and shot you. That would have been a fine accomplishment." She slammed the window shut and closed the curtains.

Daniel was right, of course. Within minutes, the room became suffocatingly hot. She desperately wanted to open the window again, but she didn't want to give him any victory, no matter how small. So, she waited in the dark as her bedroom became an oven, listening to the clock on her dressing table tick away the minutes. When the clock chimed the quarter hour twice, she got out of bed and walked to the window. He was sure to be asleep by now. She slipped the curtains open, and as quietly as possible, she raised the sash.

"Told you so," a sleepy male voice murmured.

Lord, she hated him.

❖ 3 ❖

THE FOLLOWING MORNING, Daniel received word that Judge Billings would be able to meet with him at three o'clock in the afternoon, and he arrived at the Jaspar County Courthouse exactly on time.

The judge's clerk rose to greet him. "Mr. Walker? The judge is in chambers." He gestured to the closed door behind him. "He has someone with him, but he is expecting you, and he instructed that you go right on in."

The clerk knocked on the door, then opened it for Daniel to step inside. He did so, but came to an immediate halt at the sight of the woman seated before the judge's desk, a woman whose glorious red hair and bright pink dress made her unmistakable even before he inhaled the delicate scent of lily blossom cologne. She turned her head to give him a suspiciously sweet smile over her shoulder. He should have known.

There was a glimmer of triumph in the glance Lily gave him. No doubt she was here to prey on the moral sensibilities of the judge. It wouldn't do her any good

44

since Daniel had the law on his side, but he did admire her persistence.

"Daniel, please join us." Judge Billings stood up and leaned across the desk to shake his hand warmly. "I believe you already know Lily Morgan."

"Yes, indeed," he said, returning her smile with one of his own. "We are well acquainted."

"Mrs. Morgan sent me a note this morning asking to see me about the matter of the Shivaree Social Club, and since you and I were going to discuss that very situation, I responded to her request with an invitation for her to join us. I hope you don't mind."

"Not at all." He sat down and set his leather portfolio beside his chair. "It's good to see you again, Lyndon. It's been a long time."

"Too long, Daniel. How are you? Still practicing in Atlanta, I hear. By the way, thank you for the wedding present. Mary Alice loves that tea service."

"I'm glad." Daniel glanced at the woman seated beside him, and he took a great deal of pleasure in seeing some of the complacent confidence fade from her expression.

She looked from him to the judge and back again. "You two know each other?"

"Of course," Daniel answered. "We've known each other for years, haven't we, Lyndon?"

"Yes, indeed. We first met when I was on the bench in Atlanta, long before I came to Shivaree," the judge informed her. "I was the presiding judge on Daniel's very first case. He came into my courtroom straight out of law school, filled with idealistic zeal, wearing a cheap suit, and carrying a stack of case law. Argued very well on behalf of his client. And also used some pretty unorthodox strategy to get himself out of jail, as I recall."

Daniel in jail? Her curiosity got the better of her, and she couldn't help asking, "What happened?"

"My client had been charged with petty theft," Daniel explained, "and the police found the stolen watch in his room. When the prosecutor asked in court for the evidence to be admitted, I objected on the grounds that the police had not obtained a warrant for the search, and therefore, the watch could not be admitted into evidence."

"But didn't the watch prove his guilt?" Lily asked.

"Lyndon thought so. He overruled my objection at first, so I argued with him, citing the Fourth Amendment of the Constitution, which protects people against illegal search and seizure. I cited several similar cases to back up my objection."

"With both the Constitution and case law on his side, I was forced to sustain his objection. His client was acquitted."

"The thief went free?" Lily asked, incredulous. "But he obviously stole the watch."

"It doesn't matter," Daniel told her. "The police cannot violate the Constitution."

"Daniel's right." Judge Billings added, "but Lily, you can take comfort in the fact that even though the thief went free, Daniel went to jail. During our argument in open court, I cited him for contempt. He didn't have the money for the fine, so he spent the next two days behind bars."

"Only two days?" she murmured. "What a pity."

"On the third day, Judge Billings disallowed the fine," Daniel said, "and they released me."

"Only because you sent me a motion from the jail,"

the judge reminded him. He turned to Lily. "It stated that I should disallow the fine because if it weren't for my pigheaded refusal to listen to him when he was obviously right, he wouldn't have been cited in the first place."

"And you agreed to that?" Lily asked in surprise.

"Only because I admired his gall," the judge said, chuckling.

It was on the tip of her tongue to assure him gall was something Daniel possessed in abundance. The memory of the previous night suddenly came back to her, of how he had stood right there in front of her window, practically naked and not at all ashamed of it. She remembered how he had smiled when he'd caught her watching him, a smile that had told her he had enjoyed her discomfiture.

Sure you don't want a pair of Dovey's opera glasses, sugarplum? You'd get a better view.

Oh, yes. Daniel had plenty of gall.

"Enough reminiscing," the judge said, putting an end to Lily's recollections of the evening before. He leaned forward in his chair and cleared his throat. "I have to be in court in less than an hour, so let's get started, shall we?"

He glanced at Lily. "I already know your views on the subject of the social club, and you have made some very persuasive arguments over the past few years in favor of closing it down. Those views finally brought me around to your way of thinking, and convinced me that a gentlemen's club is definitely not good for our community. That is why I closed the place. However, Mr. Walker is here to challenge my decision." He turned to the other man. "Daniel, I am sure you have a motion prepared?"

Daniel pulled a document from his portfolio and gave it to the judge, who began to read it. "I am moving that the Shivaree Social Club be reopened on the grounds that it never should have been closed in the first place."

Judge Billings looked up from the document. "Are you arguing that I made an improper decision?"

"Not at all," Daniel answered with a smile that oozed so much charm, Lily felt sick. "What I am saying," he went on, "is that you made a decision without the benefit of legal argument, either for or against the closure. And I am asking that you reconsider."

"The decision has already been made," Lily broke in. "Why should—"

"That will be quite enough, young lady," the judge cut her off. "No more interruptions, if you please." He returned his attention to Daniel. "What legal argument are you using to support your motion?"

"There is plenty of case law to support this position, sir. *People* v. *Holleran*, for one. In that case, a judge in Tennessee refused to close a riverboat gambling establishment because there was no evidence that the women who worked for the club supplied entertainment of a, shall we say, 'carnal nature' to the guests. That is exactly the case here."

"Just because a judge in Tennessee didn't have the good sense to see what was right under his nose is no reason why we should follow that example," Lily argued. "What difference does it make what a judge in Tennessee does?"

"Because, Mrs. Morgan," Daniel answered, "in law, precedent is everything. If you were an attorney, you would know that."

She ignored the jibe. "Even if the precedent is flawed?"

"You think being considered innocent until proven guilty is a flawed concept?"

The judge held up his hands to stop the flow of argument before Lily could reply. "I am well aware of the ramifications here, and I don't need the two of you to point them out to me. Daniel's motion is worthy of consideration. However, I would like time to research the law on this issue myself. I am going to table a decision on this for a few days. Come and see me at ten o'clock on Monday."

"In the meantime, can the Shivaree Social Club be reopened?" Daniel asked.

"Until I make a ruling on your motion, the injunction remains in place. The club stays closed."

"But, Your Honor, my client is losing money every day that injunction is in place. Another three days—"

"Won't hurt Calvin Stoddard that much, from what I hear," the judge concluded for him. "Or Helen, either, for that matter." When Daniel started to object again, he said, "I have made a decision, Daniel, and I don't wish to discuss it further at this time. Don't argue with me or I'll have to cite you for contempt. And this time, I won't let you out without paying the fine."

Lily rather liked the idea of Daniel going to jail, but he only shrugged at the judge's threat, and she wondered if there was anything that could shatter his self-assurance. If so, she wanted to be the one to find it.

"These days, I can afford to pay the fine, Lyndon, but I'll let it go for now," he answered. "I hope you don't mind if, before our meeting on Monday, I do some more research of my own."

"I'd be disappointed if you didn't come in armed with at least twenty more cases to cite," the judge answered. He pushed Daniel's motion aside, and turned to Lily. "Mrs. Morgan, you are welcome to join us on Monday to hear my ruling."

"Mrs. Morgan is not a lawyer," Daniel objected. "There is no need for her to be present at that meeting."

"Maybe not," Billings answered, "but I'm the judge, and that means I get to make the decisions."

Daniel was fairly certain Judge Billings would grant his motion when they met on Monday, but being fairly certain had never been good enough for him. He stopped in at the telegraph office to send a telegram to Josiah, informing his secretary that he would be delayed in his return to Atlanta, then he headed for the Jaspar County Municipal Library. Lily was already there when he arrived.

She was seated behind a huge U-shaped desk in the center of the main floor that faced the double doors of the entrance. In front of her was a typewriting machine, which she was busily using. Other than the rapid, steady click of her typing, the place was quiet as a tomb. No other people were about.

She glanced up when he entered, but immediately returned her attention to her work. Daniel circled the room, scanning the shelves as he walked, his boot heels tapping on the hardwood floor in time with her typing. He kept one eye on her as he moved about the room, and it amused him that she never once glanced in his direction.

Five years had not changed her much. Lily had

always had a beautiful figure, and although she was thinner than he remembered, she still had a body that made a man's brain stop working. That body, along with skin like rich cream and eyes the dark brown of caramelized sugar, made her a beautiful woman. And that hair. God, what a stunning color, like her temperament, like cinnamon and cayenne and honey all mixed together. No wonder Henry Douglas had lost his wits and had an affair with her.

He remembered the first time Jason had come to see him in Atlanta about obtaining a divorce. She might look as hot as red pepper, he had said, but she was cold to him in bed. Cold, shrewish, and hell to live with.

Daniel studied her covertly from across the library, and not for the first time, he found himself skeptical of that assessment. Hell to live with, maybe. That he could believe. But cold? From the moment he had first laid eyes on her, Daniel had never been able to see it. In fact, he had suspected that her coldness had more to do with Jason's abilities as a lover than Lily's character. Her subsequent adultery had confirmed his suspicion. Obviously, Henry Douglas hadn't found her cold. Either way, it hadn't mattered to Daniel as an attorney. A cold wife was not grounds for divorce, but adultery was.

As if she could feel him watching her, Lily turned her head to look in his direction, and Daniel quickly resumed his perusal of the library. He had more important things to do than speculate about the past.

It did not take him long to determine that Lily had made the library an excellent one. There was a wide variety of books, docketed precisely in accordance with the Dewey system and placed on the shelves with a precision that would make an army drill sergeant proud.

Initially, the library had been built by Jason's father ten years after the war and donated to the town. Ever since her marriage, Lily had taken a passionate interest in the facility, and her position there as librarian had been guaranteed as part of her divorce settlement. Given the charges of adultery against her, it had not been necessary to make any financial provisions for her, but Daniel had insisted that Jason do so. He knew how easily a divorced woman could become destitute, and he had insisted on some financial support for her. Since Jason himself had been administrator of the library and trustee of its funds, Daniel had arranged for her employment there as a condition of the divorce, as well as requiring Jason to provide her with a generous monthly allowance.

Halfway around the room, Daniel had not found what he sought. The card catalog did not list Samuel's law books. The main floor of the building appeared to be devoted to fiction. He glanced at the stairs that led up to the mezzanine, then left and right to the wings that flanked the building, and he decided not to go wandering all around looking for what he needed. He approached Lily's desk, halted directly in front of her, and cleared his throat. "Pardon me, but I need some assistance."

She kept typing.

He leaned over the desk until his face was inches from hers. "Ignoring me won't make me go away," he whispered.

She whipped the sheet of paper out of the machine so fast that if he hadn't pulled back she would have hit him under the chin. She set the paper to her left, then inserted a fresh sheet and resumed her typing without saying a word. Daniel decided to get her attention another way.

He lifted the item she had just finished typing and turned it over to read what was written there. He whistled.

"'A scandal in our town that must be stopped,'" he quoted in pretended horror. "I'm shocked."

He had her attention now. She had stopped typing, and was frowning at him. He continued to read aloud. "'A meeting to discuss the issue will be held at the library Saturday night at seven o'clock. Refreshments will be served—'" He broke off and looked at her. "Are you going to bring that heavenly cream cake of yours? You know the one with the butter cream frosting? I think that's taking unfair advantage, Lily. You bribe the men in this town with that cake, they'll be picketing in front of Helen's place and sending letters to the judge for sure."

"I tried to bribe you with it once, as I recall. It didn't work."

He remembered that day. She had come to him in Atlanta, armed with cream cake and protestations of innocence, hoping to convince him to halt the divorce proceedings. "No, it didn't work," he agreed. "But it was a mighty fine cake," he added, smiling.

She snatched the paper out of his hand. "I'm glad you find all of this so amusing. I doubt you'll be laughing when you lose."

"I was complimenting you. I truly loved that cake."

"I'd be happy to make another one for you," she answered sweetly, "if this time I can put arsenic in it." She resumed her typing.

He rested one hip on the edge of her desk. "Why are you going to all this trouble?" he asked. "Wouldn't it be easier to have these printed on a press?"

"I prefer to type them myself."

"You mean Joe Gandy over at the newspaper refused to print them for you," he guessed.

She let out an exasperated sigh and stopped typing. "Don't you have anything better to do with your time than bother me?"

"As a matter of fact, I do. I came to use the library. I understand that Samuel donated all his law books when he retired, but I can't find them in your card catalog."

"I haven't had time to docket them yet."

"I'd like to take some back to my room tonight to study. Where would I find them?"

"You can't take them out. You don't have a library card."

Unperturbed, he sat down opposite her at the desk. "I'll get one."

Their gazes locked over the typewriting machine between them for a full five seconds before she looked away. She finished typing her announcement and set it aside. Then she opened a tin box on her desk, pulled out a blank card, and placed it in the machine. Hands poised over the keys, she looked at him. "Name?" she asked innocently. "Last name first, please."

Daniel realized that until the matter of the Shivaree Social Club was resolved, Lily was going to do whatever she could to make his life difficult, even something as trivial as a library card. That was fine with him. He'd play her game. "Walker," he answered. "W-A-L-K-E-R. First name is Daniel," he went on before she could ask. "Middle initial is J."

She typed the information onto the card at a much slower pace than she had typed the announcement for her meeting. Thirty excruciating seconds went by. Daniel knew that because he counted them in his head with growing impatience.

She paused. "What does the J stand for?"

"Jeremiah," he answered. "J-E-R-E-M-I-A-H."

Lily typed, then paused again. "Address?"

"Eighteen Courtland Avenue, Atlanta, Georgia."

She smiled, and he found that highly suspicious. When Lily smiled like that, she was up to something. A cat with five courses of canary couldn't look happier.

"I'm sorry," she informed him with mock sorrow, "but if you live out of the Jaspar County limits, you cannot have a library card. Do you have a local address?"

This was getting ridiculous. His patience began to run out. "Samuel Walker's house at Twelve Main Street," he answered through clenched teeth. "Shivaree."

She typed, paused, looked at him. "And have you been in continuous residence there at least thirty days?"

Daniel's control finally snapped. "You know damn well I haven't!" he shouted.

"Then you can't have a card. And don't yell in my library."

"Of all the stubborn, hardheaded women—" He let out his breath slowly, until he was once again in control of his temper. He held up his hands in a gesture of defeat and stood up. "Fine. Then I'll read the books here. Where are they?"

"You don't have time. The library closes at five o'clock."

He yanked his pocket watch from his waistcoat and glanced at it, then turned it so that she could read its face. "I have fifteen minutes. Where are the books?"

"Nonfiction." She pointed to the mezzanine. "Up there."

"Thank you." He tucked his watch back in the pocket of his waistcoat and went upstairs. He found what he sought, but fifteen minutes wasn't long enough to find much. He'd barely read through one case before she called to him that his time was up.

"I'll be back tomorrow," he promised as he came down the stairs and approached her desk.

"Tomorrow is Saturday," she informed him with obvious pleasure. "With the exception of the meeting at seven o'clock tomorrow night, we will be closed. You can come back at nine o'clock Monday morning."

That gave him only one hour before they were scheduled to appear once again before the judge, but he didn't seem upset. He shrugged. "I'll be here. Don't set fire to the library before then. Arson is a crime, you know."

"By Monday, I won't have to," she answered. "I'll have the people in this town on my side by then, and I think the judge will listen to them."

"I doubt it." He paused beside her desk, and began to count off the reasons. "First of all, most of the men in this town like the Shivaree Social Club because it brings wealthy men from Atlanta into the town, and I can easily persuade the men around here to make their feelings known to the judge. Second, most of those who would be in favor of keeping the Shivaree Social Club closed are women, and I don't think the judge will pay much mind to what a bunch of women have to say, since they don't vote to keep him in office.

Third . . ." He paused, and his expression softened slightly as he looked at her. "Forgive me for being blunt, but it isn't likely that the women of this town will be all that willing to listen to you."

She was not going to let him see how much that hurt. She stood up, lifted her chin, and looked him in the eye with all the pride she possessed. "We'll just see about that, Daniel Walker. We'll see."

"I reckon we will." He turned away, and Lily watched him as he walked out of the library. He was an arrogant, immoral liar, and she hated him for it. But at that moment, she realized that it was the times when he told her the truth that she hated him the most.

The following morning, Lily began her battle campaign. Daniel might be right that she had no influence with the women of Shivaree, but she had no intention of standing meekly by, hoping the judge would rule in her favor on Monday. If she could get the women of the town to come to her meeting that night, they might persuade their menfolk to tell the judge they wanted the Shivaree Social Club to stay closed. To get the women on her side, she had to go visit them.

Her usual attire of flamboyant colors would serve only to antagonize the disapproving matrons of the town, so Lily donned a severely styled, terribly boring dress of Havana brown poplin and a plain bonnet of ecru straw. She searched through all the drawers of her house until she found the calling cards she hadn't used for five years and stuffed a handful into her reticule. She even remembered to wear gloves. Her corset, however, stayed in the attic where it belonged.

Five years ago, calls had been a simple and pleasurable pursuit. Back then, she had been a married woman with a handsome, successful husband and an impeccable reputation. Though not born and raised in Shivaree as Jason had been, she had been accepted by the community because Jason's father had run the bank and been one of the most influential men in the county.

Now, all that was changed. Now, she was that scandalous divorcée. She knew her task would not be easy, but she refused to let that stop her. She had right on her side. Armed with a handful of her typed announcements, a purse full of calling cards, and the courage of the righteous, Lily set out to make calls on the ladies of Shivaree.

Two hours later, her courage was gone and she was at Rosie's, drowning her sorrows in a double chocolate soda. Rosie stood across the counter from her, and Amos was mopping the floor nearby, both of them listening to her tale of woe.

"They wouldn't even receive me," she said, slumping forward in discouragement, propping her elbows on the counter. "Not one of them."

Rosie pulled up a stool on her side of the counter and sat down opposite her friend. "Well, what did you expect?" she asked gently. "Honey, you've been thumbing your nose at the women of this town for five years, doing all the outrageous things you could think of just to shock them. It's no wonder they aren't listening to you."

Daniel's words all over again. It hurt just as much the second time around. "I thought you were on my side."

"I am on your side. But I don't like seeing you set yourself up to get hurt."

"I'm on your side, too, Lily," Amos piped up.

"That's right kind of you, Amos," she said, turning to give the boy a smile. But that smile faded when she returned her attention to Rosie. "But it's the women-folk I need on my side the most."

"You can't change five years of defiance in one afternoon."

"I didn't think I had to. I hoped those women would welcome the chance to shut down that awful place."

"They might, but you've got to win them over."

"I can't do that if they won't even speak to me." She looked at her friend hopefully. "Can't you talk to them, Rosie?"

"I'll try." Rosie gave her a rueful smile. "But I doubt they'll listen to me. I don't rank all that high on Shivaree's social register myself. Not since Billy left, anyway."

The eyes of the two women met over the counter in mutual understanding. Billy Russell had been foreman at the lumber mill, and when he had helped himself to the payroll and run off for parts unknown, Rosie had been left behind to face the humiliation. But that had been eight years ago, and Rosie had rebuilt her life alone. Lily had been married then, and with Jason's father in charge of the bank, she had managed to persuade her father-in-law to loan Rosie the money for the restaurant. Since then, Rosie had regained a modicum of respectability while Lily had lost every shred of hers. But Rosie had never forgotten the favor, and she had stood up for her friend many times since then.

"You ever hear from him, Rosie?" Lily asked, breaking the silence.

"Billy?" She shook her head. "If I did, I'd tell the

nearest U.S. Marshal about it right quick, and Billy knows it. You ever hear from Jason?"

"No. He's out West someplace. That's all I know." She took a deep breath. "What am I going to do? Without the support of the women in this town, there's no way to put pressure on the judge. He'll probably grant Daniel's motion and reopen that cathouse."

"Why is it called a cathouse?" Amos asked, pausing in his task to look at the two women with a puzzled expression. "Do cats live there?"

The two women exchanged glances, then Rosie said, "No, Amos. A cathouse is an evil, sinful place where some men go to play cards, drink spirits, and . . . um . . . talk to bad women."

Amos frowned, clearly puzzled. "Bad women? Why?"

"The women there are not nice women, Amos," Lily explained. "They do sinful things."

"Are you sure?" Amos eyed her with skepticism. "Maybe they aren't really bad."

Lily sighed, looking at him. She had no intention of explaining the concept of prostitution to Amos. "It's just a bad place, that's all," she said.

"That's why you wanted to close it down?"

"That's right." Lily returned her attention to her problem. "I thought this time I had succeeded, but then Daniel came along, and now I haven't got a chance. The result is a foregone conclusion, and Daniel knows it."

"I think," Rosie said slowly, "that's probably the thing that upsets you most."

"It's not just me being ornery, you know." Lily took a long pull on her soda. "I'm not just trying to get back at Daniel Walker."

"Of course not," Rosie agreed mildly, but there was a teasing smile to her lips. "He has nothing to do with it."

"He doesn't. I've been trying to close that place down for five years, and you know it." She saw her friend's smile, and she couldn't help laughing a little. "All right, all right, I admit I would find a great deal of satisfaction in watching him lose for once. The snake."

"He's not all bad, you know."

"Oh, yes he is. You should have seen him yesterday, sitting there with the judge, laughing about old times, and talking about the law, so smug, knowing I don't know the first thing about precedents and motions and evidence."

"Maybe you should. What about hiring your own lawyer to speak with the judge?"

Lily was appalled by the very thought. "I wouldn't pay money to any of them. Wolves at lambing, all of them."

"Perhaps, but one of the wolves would be yours."

"I had a lawyer five years ago, and what good did it do me?" She shook her head. "No, thank you. Besides, I don't see what a lawyer could do to help me now. I only have two days. So what can I do?"

Rosie was silent for a moment, then she said, "I can think of only one thing, but you won't like it."

"What?"

"Go see Dovey."

"That vicious old cat? Not a chance."

"I know how you feel, but if you could get her on your side, the other women would follow. She has a lot of influence, you know."

"It'd be like walking into the lion's den." She gave

her friend a feeble smile. "It's Daniel who's supposed to do that, not me."

"Maybe so, but in this case, Daniel doesn't have to. You do, if you want to win the fight. Go see Dovey."

She knew Rosie was right; that if she could win Dovey over, she might be able to rally the other women of the town to her cause. But as she thought of the town's biggest gossip, the woman who had spread more rumors and said more cruel things about her than anyone else, she shook her head. "I can't," she whispered miserably. "I can't go to Dovey with my hat in my hand, asking for her help. It would be too humiliating."

"All right, then. Accept that you've already lost, and let the judge grant Daniel's motion to get that place reopened. Let other women worry about where their husbands are at night. It's not your problem anyway. Give up without a fight. Let Daniel win. Again."

That idea was even more humiliating than going to Dovey McRae. Agonizing over such a horrible choice of options, she groaned. "Isn't there an easier way?"

"Nope."

Lily pulled on the straw, sucking up the last luscious drops of her soda. "If I'm going to do this," she said, giving in to the inevitable, "I'm going to need liquid fortification." She shoved the glass toward her friend. "Make me another soda."

"You'll get a stomachache."

"What difference does it make? Going to see Dovey is going to give me a stomachache anyway. Give me another."

"You better not," Amos advised, speaking with all the wisdom of personal experience. "If you have another one of those, you'll probably throw up."

Rosie smiled. "I don't think throwing up on Dovey will convince her to help you."

"I see your point." Lily rose to her feet and picked up her bonnet. "All right, I'll go into the lion's den." She set the hat on her head and shoved in her hat pin, then she frowned at both of them. "But if I come back bloody, I want another chocolate soda."

✦ 4 ✦

WHEN IT CAME to news, Western Union was nothing
compared to Dovey McRae. She was standing by her
parlor window when Lily opened the gate and approached her front door. Lily saw the lace curtains
move, and she realized with a feeling of dread that
Dovey already knew how she had spent her morning
and had been expecting her arrival. She tapped the
brass door knocker, fully prepared for her knock to go
unanswered, almost hoping it would.

But the door opened, and Lily was forced to face the
woman who had been instrumental in ostracizing her
from everyone in town. Dovey stood in the doorway,
arms folded across her immense bosom, her expression one of intense scorn, and Lily did not miss the
flash of satisfaction in her eyes. It was galling.

Dovey stared her down without speaking, her spine
rigidly straight, whether due to the strongest whalebone corset in the Sears, Roebuck catalog or her
inflexible temperament, Lily wasn't sure. Moral indig-
nation radiated from her like a match on fire, and Lily

wanted to run before she got burned. She swallowed
hard and stood her ground, trying to figure out what to
say now that she was standing here. She could cheer-
fully have killed Rosie for persuading her to do this.

Over Dovey's shoulder, she could see Densie hovering and fluttering in the background like a hen who
believed the fox was about to enter the chicken coop.
"Hello, Densie," she said pleasantly, grateful for the
distraction. "Are you enjoying Shivaree now that
you're living here?"

Being spoken to so boldly by the town's most
infamous woman had the poor creature nearly jumping out of her skin. "Oh, oh," she stammered, lifting
one hand to her heart. "Why, yes, yes, I am. Thank
you, Lily. Of course, it's much cooler in Charleston
than it is in Shivaree this time of year, but—"

"Densie, that's enough," Dovey cut in. She leaned
slightly to one side, blocking Lily's view of her sister.
"Neither of us has anything to say to you. Please
leave."

Lily ignored that. "Dovey, I'm here because—"

"I know why you are here, young woman, and you
are wasting your time."

Lily felt very conspicuous, standing on the other
woman's front verandah. She could almost feel the
stares of Mariah McGill and Louisa Richmond, Dovey's neighbors across the street, boring into her back,
knowing they were probably peeking through their
window curtains to see what would happen. She
shifted her weight uncomfortably. "Dovey, you and I
have had our differences in the past, but I was hoping
we could let bygones be bygones and work together to
see that that sinful social club stays closed. I'm sure

you already know Daniel Walker is here to get the place reopened. Perhaps we could sit down inside and discuss this situation?"

"Let you in my house? Never." Nobody could look down her nose better than Dovey McRae. "Even your own family in Birmingham won't receive you. If they won't, why should I?"

During the walk from Rosie's Cafe to Dovey's house, Lily had sworn to herself at least ten times that no matter what Dovey said, she wouldn't let it affect her, but the reminder of her own family's abandonment was more painful than she would have thought possible. She swallowed hard, determined not to let Dovey see how much it hurt. "Because the enemy of my enemy is my friend," she answered calmly. "You and I both know it's an immoral, sinful place. You can't possibly believe it should be allowed to reopen."

Dovey made a sound that reminded Lily of a cat sneezing. "Ladies do not discuss such subjects—but of course, you are not a lady, so that doesn't stop you."

Lily let the insult pass and tried again. "Not talking about it won't make it go away, Dovey. That place is a disgrace to our town."

The older woman's eyes narrowed. "You think I was born yesterday? I know why you're doing this, and it has nothing to do with your concern for the town."

"What do you mean?"

Dovey smiled with the complacency of someone absolutely convinced she knew the truth. "You're trying to get that place shut down because you think fighting for something good will make everyone think that we were wrong about you. That you are really a moral, Christian woman. Well, it'll never happen. All the good works in the world won't change what you are."

Lily instantly became defensive. "And what am I?"

"A shameless, sinful Jezebel."

"Why?" she demanded before she could stop herself. "Because my husband divorced me or because I refused to turn a blind eye to his philandering?"

"If you had kept your husband happy and comfortable in his own home, he wouldn't have gone to a place like the Shivaree Social Club in the first place."

The same old accusation thrown in her face. The same unfair assumption that Jason's infidelity was her fault, and her own infidelity, which had never really happened, was also her fault. The same incredible belief that a wife was solely responsible for happiness in the home, and if the home wasn't happy, she suffered in silence and told everyone it was. The same disapproval that had caused her family to disown her, all her friends but Rosie to ignore her, and her community to turn on her. Lily thought she had come to terms with the infamous role of a scarlet woman, but the truth was that she had not. It still hurt, terribly, like a raw, open wound that would not heal.

"Why don't you pull out all the stops, Dovey?" she suggested rashly, before she could stop herself. She knew she was defeating her whole purpose in coming here, but she was too frustrated to care. "Why don't you say that if I had not taken Henry Douglas as my lover, Jason wouldn't have divorced me? Isn't that what you believe?" Her voice broke and she felt the mortifying sting of tears in her eyes. "Isn't that what everyone believes?"

"I see that you at least acknowledge your own sinful

behavior, even if you are not ashamed of it." Dovey sighed and shook her head. "When I saw you coming up the walk, I foolishly hoped that perhaps time had made you repentant. I am sorry to say that is not so."

"You're not sorry at all. What you really mean is that you wanted me to grovel," Lily shot back. "Well, I wouldn't dream of giving you the satisfaction. Jason was the one whose behavior was sinful. I have done nothing wrong, and I refuse to stand here and be insulted by you. I'll close that place down, and I'll do it without your help."

She turned away, blinking back the tears of frustration and helplessness. As she walked home, she held her head high and told herself that it didn't matter what people thought of her. She knew the truth, and people could believe whatever they liked. She didn't care. And she wasn't going to cry because small-minded old biddies like Dovey McRae insulted her.

She marched inside her home, slammed the door, and promptly burst into tears.

The women of Shivaree had a sewing circle that met twice a week, but when a man wanted to know what was going on in town, the best thing he could do was get a haircut and a shave. Daniel had gotten a haircut only the week before, and he usually preferred to shave himself, but as long as Lily was on the rampage, he figured he'd better learn as much local gossip as possible. After sending another telegram to Josiah, asking for the case law he hadn't had time to find at the library, Daniel headed for Nate's Barber Shop.

The news of his meeting with Judge Billings had arrived before him, and when Daniel walked in, the tiny barbershop was crowded. Half a dozen men were there, already engaged in a heated discussion of the subject.

"It don't matter to me," Jacob Cole was saying when Daniel walked in. "I can't afford to go there anyway."

"That isn't the point," Nate Jeffries answered. He waved his shaving brush under Jacob's nose. "We can't let the women decide what we do."

"My wife already does," Jacob answered gloomily as the barber continued to cover his face with shaving soap. "I just do what she tells me. It's easier that way."

Nate made a sound of contempt. "You're a sissy."

"And you're not married."

The half dozen men in the barbershop laughed at that, including Daniel. "Afternoon, boys," he said and sat down in an empty chair near the door to wait his turn.

"Afternoon, Daniel," a chorus of voices replied, and he was immediately inundated with questions.

"Do you think the judge is going to let the Shivaree Social Club reopen?" Ezra Richmond asked, turning to spit in a brass spittoon.

"We'll find out on Monday," he answered.

"Is it true Lily Morgan was there when you met with the judge?" asked Tobias McGill.

"Yes, and she's determined to persuade him to keep that injunction in place. If you boys want the club to reopen, you've got to let the judge know how you feel about it. And remind him that you're the ones who are going to vote on whether or not he keeps his job in November. I hear he's being contested for his seat."

Nate paused in the act of scraping the razor over Jacob's face. "Well, it don't sound like we got much to worry about, then. We just tell the judge we want it to be open. Right?"

Daniel was beginning to feel as if he were standing on the courthouse steps with a group of journalists. "That's right, Nate. But you've got to know that Lily Morgan plans to get the women all riled up about this."

Nate chuckled. "I wouldn't worry none. The womenfolk of this town ain't going to listen to her."

Tobias laughed. "My wife sure didn't. She came callin' this mornin' and my Mariah sent her packing. So did most of the women around town."

Ezra spoke again. "I heard she was calling a meeting at the library tonight. Puttin' up announcements all over the place."

"She wanted me to print 'em for her," Joe Gandy put in.

"Did you?" Tobias wanted to know.

"Hell, no. She had to type them all herself."

"She tried to put one of 'em up in here," Nate said with a snort. "I sent her off with a flea in her ear, that's for sure."

All the men laughed except Daniel. Somehow, he didn't find the conversation around him very amusing. He remembered what Samuel had told him about how Lily was now an outsider in her own community. He was now seeing the proof of that with his own eyes, and it made him strangely uneasy. He told himself that he'd taken Jason's case for good reasons, he'd done his job, and he'd done it well. The fact that Lily was now ostracized by the women around Shivaree was her own fault, and not his concern. But those facts didn't stop a vague stirring within him of the one emotion a good attorney could not afford: guilt.

Tobias turned to Daniel as the laughter died down.

"Samuel says you're goin' to run for the Georgia senate. That true?"

"Well, now, that depends," he answered. "Y'all goin' to vote for me?"

"Are you makin' jokes? 'Course we are," Tobias assured him, his words followed by a chorus of affirmation from the others. "You got the governor to get that railroad line to come straight through Shivaree, and that sure was a blessing. Why, half the men in town wouldn't be working if it weren't for you."

"My business has doubled since then," Nate put in. "So's every other business in town." He tugged the apron away from Jacob's chest. "You're done," he told him and beckoned Daniel forward as Jacob stood up.

Daniel glanced around. "You boys were here first," he said, but they all shook their heads.

"They're just here shootin' the breeze," Nate told him and patted the back of the chair. "Shave and a haircut?"

"Just a trim." Daniel sat down in the chair and grinned at the barber. "And try to keep my ears on straight."

Nate laughed and set to work. "I'll do my best."

It was gratifying to know that the men of his own hometown were planning to vote for him, but Daniel wasn't really here for confirmation of that. "So, Lily's having a hard time gettin' the ladies to come to her meetin' tonight?" he asked, bringing the subject back to what he really wanted to learn more about. He had to find out what the hurricane in pink silk was up to.

Before anyone could answer his question, Scotty Fisher entered the barbershop, the grin on his face wide enough to get the attention of all the other men in the room. *"Oo-ee!* I think it's war all over again," he announced, and he began to laugh as the other men fired questions at him.

"What do you mean, Scotty?"

"What's up?"

"War? What you talkin' about?"

"I mean the war between Lily Morgan and Dovey McRae," Scott answered, sticking his thumbs under the chest straps of his overalls and leaning one shoulder against the doorjamb. He shook his head as he went on, "You should've seen 'em. Nose to nose on Dovey's front porch, firing cannons like it was Fort Sumter. It was a sight to see, boys."

"Who won?" Daniel asked. Dovey was a formidable woman, but he figured Lily could more than hold her own. In fact, if this catfight were up for wagering, he'd put his money on Lily.

Scott did not answer his question. He obviously wanted to tell the story in his own way, and in his own good time. "Well, you know I do the gardening for old Dovey," he continued, "so I was standing right there, trimming back the oleander bushes by the porch, so I heard the whole thing."

All the men nodded impatiently. Tobias said, "Yeah, Scotty, we know you do old Dovey's gardenin'. What happened?"

"Well, Lily was trying real hard to be cordial at first, I'll give her that. Talking about how maybe they could work together to shut down the social club and all. She was bein' real pleasant. But Dovey wasn't having any. She said that if Lily's own family wouldn't receive her, she wouldn't receive her either. Then she started in on Lily being a sinful, shameless woman, and how she was only doing this to try and regain her reputation."

Daniel stiffened in the barber's chair at the news that Lily's own family would not receive her. She came from the highest echelons of Birmingham society, and Daniel knew enough about her family to be sure that if they did not receive her, the reason had to be her divorce.

The consequences that divorce would have for Lily had never occurred to him. Once again, Daniel felt that vague uneasiness in his gut.

Scott went on with his story. " 'Course Dovey sayin' that put Lily's back up. She got mad, and just out and out confessed about her and Henry Douglas. Bold as brass, she was. Practically admitted they'd been lovers and didn't even act like she was ashamed of it!"

Shocked murmurs rippled through the barbershop, but Daniel knew it wasn't because of Lily and Henry, since that was old news. The blatant way she confessed her guilt after five years of denying it was the part that shocked them.

Daniel wasn't shocked, but he was a bit surprised. Lily had always denied her guilt, so why would she admit it so freely now? It certainly wouldn't gain her any points with Dovey. On the other hand, there was that temper of hers, and Lily did tend to shoot off her mouth when her temper was in charge.

"Well, it's 'bout time she admitted it," Jacob Cole said, seeming to sum up the general feeling of all the other men in the room. "Nobody ever believed her sayin' they was just friends. 'Specially when Henry admitted it was true about the two of them."

Nate snorted as he set aside his scissors and picked up a shaving mug. "Friends, my eye. If a man and a woman are friends, it only means one thing. She wasn't taking those long walks in the woods alone with Henry for nothing," he went on as he added a bit of water to the shaving cup in his hand and began stirring up a lather.

"She made a fool outta Jason Morgan, good and proper," Tobias said. "I don't hold with divorce, myself, but you can't really blame him for wanting to set her aside. I don't wonder he left town after that humiliation."

"Well, Dovey's right about one thing," Ezra said, and paused to once again spit a stream of tobacco juice into the spittoon. "Lily's a scarlet woman, for sure and for certain, and it won't do her no good to take the high moral ground now."

There were more nods of agreement among the men.

Nate stopped stirring up lather in the cup and laughed. "Shoot, Lily Morgan oughta be workin' at Helen's place, not trying to shut it down."

An image flashed through Daniel's mind of Lily dolled up with rouge on her face, sitting in the infamous red velvet parlor of Helen's, smelling of sex and cologne, and he didn't like the image. He yanked off the apron Nate had laid over his suit and stood up.

"Don't you want a shave, too?" Nate asked in surprise.

"No, thanks, Nate. Not today." He tossed two bits on the chair. "Keep the change," he said and abruptly left the barbershop, wondering why on earth he should care what people said about Lily Morgan.

A woman could cry only so long before her nose stopped up and her throat hurt and her self-pity ran out. Lily's crying spree was over in about fifteen minutes. She used her handkerchief, dried her eyes, and took stock of her situation. She decided it wasn't very promising, but she couldn't quit now. She had called for a meeting, and she was going to have it, even if nobody came.

She went into her kitchen, rolled back her cuffs, donned her apron, and began to prepare her special Italian cream cake, one of the few things involving her that Jason had actually loved. It was the cake that always won the blue ribbon at the fair, and people said it was as sinful as she.

Jason. After five years, she didn't think of him much anymore, but sometimes he stole into her thoughts: when she made cream cake, or when she cleaned out the attic and found another item of his that she'd forgotten to throw away, or when she occasionally dusted the master bedroom that she no longer slept in—a bedroom she'd slept in alone many nights during her marriage.

She poured cake batter into pans, stoked the fire in the stove, and put the pans in the oven. While she waited for the cake to be done, she wandered around the house, unable to find something to do that would take her mind from thoughts of the past.

Sometimes, she'd thought of leaving this town, making a new life for herself somewhere else, but where could she go? She certainly couldn't go home to her family. They'd slam their doors in her face.

There was also Amos to consider. As long as she ran the library, he had a job, and she wasn't certain whoever took her place would let him keep it.

There was also the fact that she had very little money of her own. She didn't own the house, she merely leased it from the bank. It had been sold to a group of investors along with all the other assets of the bank when she and Jason had divorced. As part of the settlement, her former husband had promised to provide her with a monthly income, but once the papers had been signed and all the Morgan assets had been sold, he had left for parts unknown, and his money had left with him. That was fine with her, since she had never wanted his money in any case. As for her family, she wouldn't even consider the idea of turning to them. Even if she had asked them for help or money, they would never have given it. But a lack of money made the possibility of starting a new life elsewhere very risky.

Nonetheless, Lily knew all those reasons to stay were really excuses. The main reason she'd never left Shivaree was that it had always seemed like running away. The idea that a group of petty, vicious, closed-minded women could intimidate her into leaving was a galling one, and always caused her to change her mind whenever she considered the idea of leaving Shivaree. She'd be damned before she let the old cats like Dovey drive her out. The more they tried, the more she'd dug in her heels, determined to stay. Her pride was at stake.

Besides, if she left Shivaree to escape her reputation, she doubted it would do any good. No matter where she went, the fact that she was a divorcée would eventually catch up with her, and she'd spend her whole life running from one town to another. Running away never solved anything. Lily knew that from bitter experience.

One of the reasons she had married Jason in the first place had been because she had really wanted escape; she had been running away from the suffocating life into which she had been born and raised.

She had loved Jason, yes, with all her girlish notions

of that emotion. Too full of romantic ideals; too young to really know what love was; too concerned with pleasing her domineering father, who had approved of his youngest daughter marrying a wealthy banker's son; and too ready to rebel against the stifling life of a Birmingham debutante, a debutante who had been an utter failure in that role. With two blond, beautiful older sisters, Lily had felt like the ugly duckling of the family: too gawky, too tall, and too outspoken to make a successful debutante. Jason had been a handsome, charming young man in his final year at the University of Alabama, and to Lily, he had seemed like the answer to a prayer. To her family, he had seemed like the only man she could get, and more than worthy of their embarrassingly outspoken daughter.

Even your own family won't receive you. If they won't, why should I?

Dovey's words went in like jagged knife blades, reminding her of all the letters she'd written that had been returned unopened by her mother, her father, and her sisters. She was a divorced woman now, and her respectable, wealthy family—a family entrenched in Alabama society—had never forgiven her for that. She didn't even try to communicate with them anymore. To them, she was dead. To her, they were lost forever.

Dwelling on the past was futile, and Lily firmly pushed thoughts of her family out of her mind. She removed the cake from the oven, and while it cooled, she played her piano to drown out memories. She whipped up a butter cream frosting, finished the cake, and headed for the library.

Three hours later, she was trudging home again, trying to console herself with thoughts of the six hefty slices now missing from her cake. Rosie and Amos had come, bless their hearts, armed with quince pie and lemonade. Reverend Jones, the Baptist minister, and Reverend Ogilvie, the Methodist minister, had also come with their wives. Despite her divorce and her subsequent reputation as a sinful woman, Shivaree's two ministers had refused to condemn her. Though many in their congregations felt otherwise, both men had always treated her with respect and a true Christian spirit of kindness.

Both clergymen also supported her efforts to shut down the Shivaree Social Club. At the meeting tonight, both men had promised scorching sermons on the subject the following morning, but as Lily trudged home, she was inclined to think that not even the threat of eternal damnation could overcome the town's animosity toward her and their indifference toward her cause.

Daniel knew without being told how Lily's meeting had turned out. Music from her piano floated up to him through the open window of his bedroom—soft, delicate music that was unfamiliar to him. It was the most melancholy tune he'd ever heard, and he figured that was a pretty good indication of what the result of her meeting had been.

He got out of bed, pulled a chair over to his window, and lit a cigar. He sat in the dark, listening to her play. Behind the sad melody, bits and pieces of the gossip he'd heard that afternoon echoed through his mind, gossip that bothered him more than he cared to admit.

When the song ended, she went upstairs. Through the closed curtains, he saw her silhouette against the lamplight of her room as she undressed. Though she was only a shadow against the curtain, he could see her long legs, curving hips, and small waist. A jolt of pure lust shot through him at the sight. A gentleman probably would have looked away, but Daniel figured a man could miss most of the pleasures in life by being a gentleman. Besides, turnabout was fair play. Hadn't she gotten an eyeful of him the night before?

The view didn't last long, however. She pulled a nightgown over her head, a nightgown that effectively shielded her silhouette from his observations.

He watched her take down her hair. He had never realized how erotic it could be to watch a woman do that. He couldn't see the brilliant fiery color as she took out pins and let it fall down her back, but he could imagine it.

She's cold to me, Daniel. Cold as ice.

Jason's words came back to him, words that might seem a contradiction to Lily's subsequent adultery, but Daniel could see how both situations were true. She must have found something in Henry Douglas to spark her passion, something that Jason had lacked. To ignite a woman's desire, a man needed the right kind of persuasion. Daniel wondered what kind of persuasion lit a fire in Lily Morgan.

Suddenly the curtains of Lily's window were yanked back, interrupting Daniel's train of thought. She frowned at the sight of him sitting by the opposite window. "I knew you were out there. I could smell the cigar. Have you been waiting for me to get home so you could gloat?"

"No. The music woke me, so I thought I'd sit here and listen to it." She obviously hadn't realized yet that he'd done more than listen to her music, and he spoke quickly to distract her before she figured it out. "But I heard about the altercation between you and Dovey today."

She bristled at that. "How did you find out about Dovey? Did you go to the ladies' sewing circle this afternoon?"

"No. Barbershop."

"Same thing. And they say women gossip. Men are just as bad."

He wondered how long it would take before her curiosity got the better of her. He didn't have to wait long. Only a few seconds passed before she dragged a chair in front of the window and sat down. She propped her elbows on the sill. "Well?"

He pretended not to understand. "Well, what?"

"What did they say about me?"

"They said Dovey sent you packing good and proper."

Lily thought about that for a moment, then acknowledged the truth of it with a nod. "For once the gossip seems accurate, then."

"They also said you lost your temper."

She made a face. "My cross to bear, I'm afraid."

Daniel took a pull on his cigar and blew the smoke out slowly. "You played right into her hands, you know."

Puzzled, she stared at him. "What do you mean?"

"Dovey probably provoked you on purpose. She wanted you to lose your temper so she could feel superior to you, so she could reassure herself that everything she thought about you was the truth. She pulled your chain, and you let her do it."

"I suppose you would have handled it differently?"

"Yes, but then, I've made a career out of that sort of thing. Part of being a good lawyer is leading a person where you want them to go by using whatever technique would work with that person."

"And what would have worked with Dovey?"

"You can't strong-arm Dovey McRae," he said. "With a woman like that, you've got to use charm and tact. Flattery would help, too. If you could do that, she'd be butter in your hands."

To his surprise, a slight smile tilted the corners of her mouth. "Why, Daniel Walker," she murmured, "are you giving me advice?"

He shrugged. "Maybe."

"Why? We're adversaries. Why would you help me in any way?"

Daniel didn't know the answer to that question himself. Perhaps because advice from him would cause her to do the exact opposite. Or perhaps it was really because he didn't like what he'd heard people saying about her. "I like a challenge," he answered smoothly. "I wouldn't want to win too easily."

"Don't worry," she assured him with spirit. "You won't."

That made him chuckle. He leaned his elbows on the windowsill. "You are one determined woman," he said. "Have you always been the type to go against the tide?"

"I'm afraid so." The warm breeze caught her hair, sending one long corkscrew curl across her face. She pulled it back. "I never intend to, but it always happens."

"So it would seem." He paused, then said, "I'm sorry about your family disowning you after the divorce."

His words seemed to astonish her. "I almost think you mean that."

"I do mean it." He paused, then said, "Believe it or not, I know what it's like when your family doesn't care about you. My own father—" He broke off. He didn't want to talk about his old man. "Anyway, I'm sorry."

"Divorce or not, perhaps my estrangement from my family was inevitable," she admitted. "I truly wanted to be an accomplished, sweet, and dutiful daughter, but I wasn't very good at it. I was willful and outspoken, and I was always the one who blurted out the awkward truths nobody else talked about. When I was eight, in front of a roomful of guests, I asked my cousin Lila Mae, who was sixteen and unmarried, why she was getting so fat."

Daniel threw back his head and laughed. "You, speak your mind? Why doesn't that surprise me?"

Lily shot him a rueful glance. "It wasn't funny. Lila Mae got shipped off to some school in Mississippi the next day. I was the first person who had noticed that she was pregnant, and when I blurted out the question, everybody else suddenly noticed it, too. That caused quite a scandal in the family. I was always doing things like that. From the time I was a little girl, the biggest question in my family was What on earth are we going to do about Lily?" She paused, then said softly, "The final answer was to pretend she died."

He felt that uneasiness again, that stirring of guilt. His lips tightened and he looked down, staring at the grass far below. "I had no idea that would happen."

"And if you had known?"

He lifted his head. "I'd have done it anyway," he admitted. "Because Jason was my client, and it was his interests I represented. He was also my friend. You, I barely knew."

"And now you represent the interests of people like Helen Overstreet and Calvin Stoddard, even though you know they are breaking the law?"

"It is my job to represent my clients to the best of my ability. Anything less would be a betrayal of everything I believe in as an attorney."

"I see," she said, but he could tell that she didn't see at all. She rose to her feet abruptly. "It's late. I'd better get some sleep."

She reached up to draw the curtains, and dressed as she was in a thin, white lawn nightgown, the silhouette of her body was clearly outlined by the lamplight behind her.

He grinned. He was coming to like the view from this window.

Lily caught that grin and paused in the act of drawing the curtains to frown at him. "What are you smiling about?"

His grin widened. If only she knew. "Nothing, sugarplum. Nothing at all."

Though she could have no idea of the thoughts running through his mind, she might figure out just what the lamplight behind her revealed to his gaze, and he'd lose any chance of seeing that view again. He quickly diverted her attention. "Lily, I'm defending the social club because it's my job. But I'm curious about your motives for starting all this. Closing down the Shivaree Social Club won't give you what you want, you know."

She stiffened and pulled back from the window. "What do you think I want?"

"What you had. What you lost. The respect of your family, social standing, your reputation."

"I didn't lose them. You took them from me. You and Jason. But that shouldn't bother you," she added. "As you said, you were just doing your job."

She yanked the curtains closed, crawled into bed, and put out the lamp.

It was very late, and only the sound of frogs and cicadas disrupted the quiet stillness of the night. He knew he ought to go to bed, but he did not move. He sat in the dark, and Lily's words whispered to him in the sultry summer night: *You were just doing your job.*

They were words he had told himself many times before, but from her lips they were an accusation, bringing with them that disquieting sense of guilt, and he felt a ripple of doubt in himself. It was a feeling alien to him, and he didn't like it. Before the feeling could take hold, he ruthlessly shoved it aside. Guilt and self-doubt were luxuries that a successful attorney and aspiring politician could not afford. Besides, he had done nothing wrong. He had done his job, and dammit, there was nothing wrong with that.

❖ 5 ❖

THE TELEGRAM FROM Josiah arrived at Samuel's house just past eight on Monday morning. In it, he had outlined seven more cases Daniel might wish to use in his meeting with the judge. He also asked when Daniel was planning to return to Atlanta, informing him that several of the men backing his bid for the state legislature wished to meet with him as soon as possible, including Calvin Stoddard. Daniel knew men like Calvin did not like being put off. He walked over to the telegraph office and sent a reply to Josiah that he would return on Tuesday afternoon. He told his secretary to set up a meeting for that evening at a time and place of Calvin's choosing.

He then left the telegraph office. By nine o'clock, he was waiting at the front doors of the library when Lily came to open the building. Neither of them spoke as he followed her inside. He went up to the mezzanine, found the law books that contained the cases Josiah had outlined in his telegram, and skimmed through them, taking notes on the ones that best served to

85

strengthen his argument. He could sense Lily watching him as she pretended to sort books and dust shelves, but she said nothing.

Just before ten o'clock, both of them walked to the courthouse, side by side. Daniel cast a sideways glance at her, and noticed there was something different about her today. It took him a moment to realize she wasn't dressed in her usual vivid colors of fuchsia or purple. She was wearing a plain, almost demure dress of pale green. And she was actually wearing gloves.

"I love the green," he told her, "but I'm surprised. Isn't a crimson dress and bright pink bonnet more your preference?" he asked her. "Why this change in wardrobe?"

She did not look at him. "I thought it would be wise to dress conservatively, for a change."

"I see. Every little bit helps, is that it?"

"Absolutely," she told him. "Even though I'm sure to win hands down, of course."

He grinned. "I told you before you'd have made a fine lawyer. You're even beginning to sound like one."

"Don't insult me."

Daniel laughed. Lily might be one stubborn, hard-headed woman, but he found that he was enjoying their verbal duels. He never knew what she was going to do next, and that made things interesting. *Besides,* he thought, falling back a step to appreciate the subtle sway of her hips as she preceded him up the courthouse steps, *I love to watch her walk.*

News always traveled fast around Shivaree, and quite a crowd had gathered around the courthouse. People were obviously curious to hear what the judge would say. Daniel knew the women's interest in the issue had been piqued, not by Lily's futile round of calls, but by Reverend Jones and Reverend Ogilvie, who had both delivered stinging sermons on the Shivaree Social Club the morning before.

As he entered the courthouse, Daniel was given shouts of encouragement by several men in the crowd behind him, and more than one assured him Judge Billings knew how they felt about the idea of closing down the club.

He could not see Lily's expression since she preceded him inside, but he suspected from the rigid set of her spine that the comments of the men were causing her to grind her teeth. He followed her down one of the long hallways to Judge Billings's chambers. The judge was ready to receive them the moment they arrived.

He wasted little time on preliminaries. "I have researched the law on this issue, and have considered it in light of Daniel's motion. No judge likes to admit that he has ruled in error, but in light of the law, I am forced to admit that very thing. Daniel, you don't need to present me with all that case law under your arm. I'm going to grant your motion that the Shivaree Social Club be reopened."

"But Your Honor," Lily protested, "you can't possibly—"

"I'm not finished yet, young lady, so kindly hold your tongue. I am acutely aware that establishments such as the Shivaree Social Club can negatively affect a town. I am allowing the club to stay open temporarily, but I am reluctant to decide on its permanent place in our community. I am not willing to make such a monumental decision for the people of Shivaree. Therefore, I'm going to make this as simple and fair for everyone as possible. I'm going to let the town decide."

"But there is no precedent in law for such a ruling," Daniel objected.

"Well, then," the judge responded with a beaming smile, "I guess I'll be making new law, won't I?"

Daniel groaned. "I hate it when judges do that."

Lily interrupted this discussion of legal technicalities. "Judge Billings, what do you mean by letting the town decide?"

"I mean, we will put it to a vote. I will write a referendum, asking the citizens to vote on whether or not the Shivaree Social Club should be allowed to continue its existence."

"But that's not fair at all," she protested. "Only men can vote."

He considered her point for a moment, and Daniel spoke quickly before the judge could decide. "The law in Georgia is very clear. In this state, women cannot vote. Allowing them to do so in this matter would be impossible. Besides, the men of this town are perfectly capable of deciding what is best for their wives and children."

"You would say something like that," Lily interjected, glancing sideways to give Daniel a look of exasperation. "Because you know the men will vote to keep that den of iniquity open, and that will certainly not result in what is in the best interests of their families."

Daniel started to refute her argument, but Judge Billings held up one hand to stop him. "Don't bother, Daniel. I'll save you the trouble. The women are excluded from voting."

"But that will make it impossible to gain a fair decision!" Lily cried. "And since the two of you are so concerned about precedent, there is precedent for allowing women to vote. Women vote in Wyoming—"

"But not in the South," the judge interrupted her. "Here in Georgia, our ways are much more traditional than in the uncivilized West. And I will certainly not demand that our Southern gentlewomen do anything so contrary to their feminine natures."

Lily made a sound of outrage, but the glance Judge Billings gave her said clearly that further argument would be futile, and she forced herself to speak in a matter-of-fact tone of voice. "Then I will just have to show the men of this town why voting to close down that wicked place is in their best interests, won't I?"

"Good luck," Daniel said, smothering his laughter with an effort.

"The referendum will be presented for a vote on July twenty-four," the judge went on. "That gives each of you exactly fourteen days to present your arguments to the people of Shivaree." He leaned back in his chair and folded his hands. He smiled at both of them. "I love the democratic process, don't you?"

"A vote, of all things." Lily paced across the rug in front of her fireplace as she related the events of that morning to Rosie. "Of all the incredible ideas. What was the judge thinking?"

Rosie leaned against the back of the horsehair sofa and watched as Lily wore out the rug. "Well, from his point of view, it's pretty smart. I mean, he can tell his wife he did all he could, but the law is law, and console her with the notion that letting the people decide is the fairest thing he could have done under the circumstances. Either way, he can tell her that it was the will of the people. The men certainly won't hold it against him at election time, and his wife can't very well disagree with the democratic process."

"You mean, either way it goes, he wins."

"Exactly."

"I can't get the women to talk to me, so I can't persuade them to influence their husbands to vote against the issue. Nothing has changed. In fact, it's worse. So, now what do I do?"

Before Rosie could reply, a brisk knock was heard at her front door. "It's probably Daniel Walker, come to gloat," Lily predicted darkly.

But the person standing on her front porch when she opened the door was not Daniel. It was Mary Alice Billings.

Astonished, Lily stared at the elegant young woman whose ethereal blond beauty reminded her of her own two sisters, and she couldn't think of a thing to say.

"Mrs. Morgan?" the woman said with a warm smile. "I am Mary Alice Billings."

"Yes . . . yes . . . I know," she stammered. "I know who you are."

A full five seconds went by, then the woman cleared her throat. "May I come in?"

"Oh, of course." Lily could have kicked herself for her lack of manners, but the fact of the judge's wife calling on her was so incredible, she was finding it hard to assimilate.

She opened the door wide and Mary Alice entered the house. The judge's wife paused a moment in the foyer, eyeing David and his bonnet askance, and though Lily had often enjoyed an amused chuckle over the scandalous sculpture, she suddenly wanted to consign Michelangelo's masterpiece to the cellar. Her cheeks heated with embarrassment, and she hastily led Mary Alice into her parlor. "This is my friend, Rosie Russell," she introduced. "Rosie, this is Mary Alice Billings."

"We have already met. Hello, Mrs. Russell."

Rosie appeared to be as astonished by the woman's arrival as Lily was. She looked at Lily, who returned her questioning gaze with a helpless shrug.

Mary Alice glanced around. "Perhaps we should all sit down?" she suggested gently.

Lily blushed, realizing she had once again forgotten her manners. "Please, do have a seat," she said, indicating one of a pair of chintz armchairs. The judge's wife sat down and Lily took the matching chair opposite. Rosie sank back down on the sofa.

"Would you like tea?" Lily asked. "I don't have a maid, but I can easily—"

"No, please don't go to any trouble. I would like to get directly to the point of my visit, since there isn't any time to be lost."

"Time to be lost?" Lily repeated. "I don't understand."

"We only have two weeks if we are going to persuade the men of this town to shut down that horrible, sinful brothel."

Dumbfounded, Lily stared at her. "You mean, you are offering to help me?"

Mary Alice smiled in the face of her astonishment. "That is exactly what I mean."

Lily wriggled uncomfortably in her chair. "Forgive

me, Mrs. Billings, but are you sure you know what you're doing? I mean, you are . . . I am . . . I mean . . ." She was stammering again. She took a deep breath, and spoke bluntly. "I shouldn't think a lady of your background would wish to be seen associating with a woman like me. It might hurt your reputation."

Mary Alice was obviously capable of being as blunt as she. "Why? Because you are divorced? That doesn't worry me in the least. In fact, I find your stand on this issue of the Shivaree Social Club especially admirable in light of the lack of support you have received. You are a woman of courage and conviction, Mrs. Morgan, and those are qualities I have always admired. As for your supposed love affair, that is your own business."

She leaned forward in her chair and smiled, a smile that held charm and a certain amount of childlike stubbornness. "Besides, I am a bit hot under the collar about this issue myself. When I learned of my husband's decision this morning, I decided it was time I made my own feelings on this issue publicly known. I understand why Lyndon did what he did, but I do not agree with his decision. Therefore, I am here to offer you any assistance I can."

"How does the judge feel about this?" Rosie asked curiously.

"Well, when he finds out, he'll be none too pleased, I imagine," Mary Alice answered serenely. "But that won't be for a while. He left town this morning. Circuit court, you know. And he won't be back until after the vote. Besides, Lyndon doesn't worry me. I can sweet-talk him into forgiving me later."

Lily sighed. "You may find it won't be worth the trouble. I am beginning to accept that trying to shut down the Shivaree Social Club is a losing battle. My efforts have proven ineffectual so far."

Mary Alice's lovely blue eyes opened wide. "Oh, you mustn't give up now."

"But what else can I do?"

The other woman's smile became conspiratorial. "I think you should make arrangements for another meeting at the library. It's the perfect place, don't you think?"

"What good would it do?" Lily asked. "I tried once already, and most of the women in town slammed their doors in my face. How on earth am I going to get them to come to such a meeting?"

"You leave that to me. I will call on all the prominent ladies of our community and invite them personally. I am a distant cousin of the governor. I am the daughter of a prominent businessman, and I am the wife of a judge. They wouldn't dare slam their doors in my face." She rose to her feet. "Would this evening at seven o'clock be an acceptable time?"

Lily and Rosie also stood up. "I think seven o'clock tonight would be fine," Lily answered. "But do you really think any of the women will come?"

"They'll come," Mary Alice assured her. "Believe me."

"Even if they do come," Rosie spoke up, "do you really think we can succeed?"

"With every woman in town on our side?" Mary Alice smiled complacently. "The men haven't got a chance."

Beatrice had moaned and groaned so much about the smell of cigars in the house that Daniel and Samuel were forced to enjoy one of their favorite after-supper pastimes on the front porch. As it turned out, that was a blessing for Daniel because from there, he was able to see the stream of ladies who filed past Samuel's door and down the street, and he suspected that they weren't all just out for an evening stroll.

"What do you think is going on?" Samuel asked. "The ladies' sewing circle meets on Tuesdays and Saturdays, and today is Monday, so it can't be that. I haven't heard of a social or any other event happening tonight. So what are they all doing?"

Daniel had an uneasy notion it had something to do with Lily. "I don't know," he muttered around the cheroot clamped between his teeth, "but I think I'd better find out."

He leaned forward in his chair, bringing it back down onto all four legs, and removed the cigar from his mouth. "Evenin' ladies," he called out to Mariah McGill and Sue Ann Parker as they passed by. "Looks like y'all have some kind of party goin' on tonight." They paused at the front gate, and he gave them his most charming smile. "I see that pie in your hands, Miz McGill, and everybody knows you make the best pie in Dixie. If that's what's bein' served, I'm devastated that I wasn't invited."

She fluttered a bit at the compliment. "That's right kind of you, Daniel," she called back, "but it's not a party. The ladies are just having a little social get-together, that's all. And I'm sure the men wouldn't be interested in a bunch of us gettin' together for gossipin'."

"Little social get-together?" he repeated under his breath as they walked on. "And I'm Abe Lincoln back from the grave." He shook his head. "I wonder how she managed it."

"Who?"

"Lily, of course. I think she must've got her meeting after all."

Samuel shook his head. "Can't be. I know what happened Saturday night, and I know that only six people were there. There's no way she could have changed the minds of all those women in so short a time."

"I'm beginning to think Lily could move the world if she set her mind to it." Daniel rose to his feet. "She is one stubborn woman."

"Where are you going?" Samuel asked as he started down the porch steps.

"To hear a little gossip," he answered, and disappeared around the corner. He suspected the ladies were headed for the library. He cut across Ezra and Louisa Richmond's back garden so that he wouldn't be seen, and he arrived at the library from the back side.

Lamps had been lit inside the building, the windows were open, and the voices of ladies floated to him on the still night air, confirming his suspicion. Daniel put out his cigar so the smell would not drift inside and give away his presence outside the window. He settled himself comfortably on the ground, sure he'd hear some pretty interesting and useful conversation.

"Ladies, I think we should get started," Mary Alice suggested, raising her voice to be heard above the chatter in the room. Gradually, the voices faded to silence and the two dozen women present set aside their empty pie plates and teacups and settled themselves in the chairs Lily had arranged in rows facing the podium where the judge's wife now stood. Once she had their attention, Mary Alice spoke again.

"I'd like to thank all of you for coming. I invited you here because of a very serious issue in our town. But before we discuss it, let us take a moment for prayer, because quite frankly, ladies, we shall need the Lord's help in this cause."

All the women followed her suggestion and bowed their heads. After a moment, Mary Alice continued her speech. "All of us know about the Shivaree Social Club. All of us know it is a place of drinking, gambling, and sin. Most of us have turned our heads and ignored the problem, hoping it would go away. I, myself, have been guilty of that."

She paused for breath, and her gaze met Lily's. "But one woman has faced the truth that the Shivaree Social Club will not go away on its own. One woman has been brave enough to speak out. One woman has been strong enough to fight. That woman is Lily Morgan. Mrs. Morgan, would you be so kind as to come up here and speak to these ladies?"

Lily didn't move. She felt Rosie nudge her gently in the ribs, but she also heard the whispers of astonishment and disapproval ripple through the crowd of women. Sudden terror gripped her, twisted her insides, and left her unable to rise from her seat. She hadn't realized Mary Alice would expect her to lead this meeting, to stand in front of women who had eyed her with contempt and gossiped about her behind her back. But everyone was watching her, including Mary Alice. The judge's wife gave her a gentle nod of encouragement, and Lily stood up, her heart pounding. What if they insulted her? What if they turned their backs and walked out on her? Horrible visions multiplied in her imagination during the few steps it took for her to reach Mary Alice's side.

Behind the podium, Mary Alice gave her hand a reassuring squeeze and stepped away, leaving her alone to face the hostile stares of women who for five years had been her enemies. Even Dovey McRae was there, seated in the front row and looking as tense and dangerous as a lioness ready to spring.

Lily swallowed hard, took a deep breath, and said, "Thank you for coming. I know this is a delicate and difficult issue. But I also know that as long as that brothel exists, men will continue to go there. They will continue to spend their hard-earned money, not on their families and their homes as they should, but on cards and drink and painted ladies. Boys will continue to sneak onto the grounds and peek in the windows. All across the country, women are fighting this, and so must we. They are winning the battle. So can we."

She paused. She did not look at Dovey, but she did gaze past her to study the other faces in the crowd. Some women were nodding their heads, others looked skeptical, but none of them had turned their backs on her yet. Encouraged, she went on, "All of you know by now Judge Billings has decided that the town—meaning the men—shall vote on whether or not to keep the Shivaree Social Club in our community. Reverend Ogilvie and Reverend Jones have already spoken God's word on this issue in their sermons yesterday, and as Christian women, our duty is clear. We must persuade the menfolk to vote to close it down."

More heads were nodding in agreement. "I have

been studying what women in Kansas and other states have done to eliminate these dens of iniquity, and their success speaks for itself. Ladies, we must make our feelings known. We must overcome feminine delicacy and speak out. We must tell the menfolk just how strongly we oppose the presence of the Shivaree Social Club. If we can get it closed down, other towns in Georgia may even follow our example."

Nearly all the women in the room were nodding their heads now. But Lily was not able to end her speech and escape unscathed. As expected, it was Dovey who attacked. "That's pretty fine talk, Lily, but coming from you, it's mighty hypocritical. We've heard you playin' that brothel music on that piano of yours many times. Who are you to talk?"

Murmurs of agreement rippled through the room. Lily cast a pleading glance at Rosie, who spoke up. "A song is just a song, Dovey. The women who work at the Shivaree Social Club and the men who go there are the ones who deserve our anger. Men go to the social club to drink, play cards, and commit sinful acts with painted women. They are at the heart of the problem, not Lily's piano playing."

Lily watched Dovey turn, prepared to spill her venom at Rosie, and she spoke quickly before the other woman could attack her friend. "Ladies, it is no secret that my husband, Jason Morgan, was one of the most frequent customers of the Shivaree Social Club. He spent nearly every evening there, he drank spirits until he could barely make his way home, he gambled away hundreds of dollars, and he committed adultery many times with every one of the sinful women who work at that club." Her voice broke, and she paused until she could once again speak clearly. "I know from bitter experience just how painful and destructive places like that can be."

The ladies did not look convinced, nor particularly sympathetic. Dovey must have sensed the tide was turning in her favor, and she faced Lily with an expression of intense scorn and condemnation. "That's as may be, but it doesn't alter what you are." She pointed her finger accusingly and declared, "Lily Morgan, you are an adulteress and a divorcée, and in my book, that makes you a bigger sinner than any man in this town!"

The murmurs of agreement grew stronger, and wild visions of being pelted with blackberry pie in her own library flashed through Lily's mind. She felt the familiar, instinctive urge to fight, to defend herself. She opened her mouth to give Dovey a scathing reply, but before she spoke, Daniel Walker's words came back to her.

She pulled your chain, and you let her do it.

Lily realized Daniel had been right. She decided to take his advice to heart. She wasn't going to argue, or lose her temper, or try once again to deny the accusations of adultery. She was not going to let Dovey pull her chain again. If charm, tact, and flattery would work on Dovey, Lily was prepared to use all three, even if it galled her. "Dovey," she said, giving the other woman her full attention, "I think I speak for everyone here when I say that having you at this meeting is such an honor."

Two dozen women stared at her, dumbfounded by such an unexpected turn of events. Dovey opened her mouth as if to speak, then closed it again, unable to think of a thing to say. Lily gave her a beaming smile. "You are the social leader of this town. Everybody respects your opinion. You are a woman who doesn't just talk, but acts as well. Why, if it hadn't been for you, the Baptist church never would have gotten that brand new bell. And everybody knows we wouldn't have a volunteer fire department if it weren't for you."

"I am always happy to lend my assistance to a worthy cause," Dovey answered stiffly, bewildered by praise from such an unexpected source.

"Exactly," Lily said, pressing her advantage. "Why, I just don't know where this town would be if it weren't for you. And it is very astute of you to point out that I am not the appropriate person to lead this fight. But if you were to take charge of this battle against sin and corruption, there's no way we could lose. You have such a brilliant knack for getting things done."

Lily thought perhaps she had gone too far, but to her amazement, Dovey began to look less like a lioness ready to attack, and more like a house cat who'd found the cream pitcher. Lily went on, "We have to elect officers for the Shivaree Temperance Society, and I'm sure that you would be the perfect woman to run for president."

"President?" Dovey considered the bait being dangled in front of her, and Lily glanced at Mary Alice, hoping the judge's wife would follow her lead.

Mary Alice was as clever as she was beautiful. She walked over to Dovey and said, "My dear Mrs. McRae, we cannot win without you. Please say you will lead us in this fight to stamp out liquor and licentiousness in our community."

Just as Daniel had predicted, Dovey melted like butter in the sun. "Why, of course," she said, with all the majesty of a benevolent queen, "if you think I can help in any way."

Rosie spoke up, nominating a slate of officers for the Shivaree Temperance Society that named Dovey as president; Mary Alice as vice-president; Lola Ogilvie, the Methodist preacher's wife, as treasurer; and Lily as secretary. This slate of officers was accepted without debate, and voted into office unanimously.

Lily concluded the meeting with one final speech. "Ladies," she said, "there is an enemy among us, and that enemy is less than a mile away. We must march in the street, we must hand out pamphlets, and we must fight that enemy with all our strength. We must dedicate ourselves to the cause of ridding our town of sin and corruption. We must make it clear to the menfolk that we will not stand for a brothel in our community!"

Her emphatic words, combined with the prayer and hymn that followed, had a potent effect. The ladies of Shivaree marched out of the library with the words of "A Mighty Fortress Is Our God" ringing in their ears and determination to wage a war against liquor resounding in their hearts.

It had not been Lily's intention to make temperance the issue. For her, the fact that the Shivaree Social Club served spiritous liquors was not as sinful as the carnal activities that went on there. But shortly before the meeting, as they had discussed the evening's agenda, Mary Alice had pointed out that prostitution was a subject that ladies of refinement would not be willing to bring out in the open. Making temperance the focus of their efforts would add momentum to their cause and gain them the support of the local women. Lily watched the ladies file out of the library, relieved that her own reputation had not affected the outcome of the meeting, and grateful that she had heeded Daniel's advice. It was amazing how much a bit of flattery could accomplish.

Rosie thought so, too. "I have never seen anything like that in my life," she declared, laughing. "Watching the way you buttered up Dovey, I practically fell out of my chair. She followed your lead like a lamb to the slaughter."

Lily wasn't sure how long that would last. She turned to Mary Alice. "I hope you don't mind that I suggested she be president. I know we had agreed that we would nominate you—"

"Nonsense." Mary Alice waved aside her concern. "I don't care who's president, so long as we succeed. And Dovey will be a far better president than I. Nothing pleases a woman like that more than being in charge. Making her the president was divine inspiration."

"All of this is really due to you," Lily told her. "Without you, we wouldn't even have had our first meeting."

"I may have gotten them here," Mary Alice answered, "and my public show of support for you may have helped, but your determination and persuasion are what did the trick. You behaved with courage under fire." She smiled and confessed in a low voice, "I would have wilted under Dovey's stinging remarks and run away."

"Me, too," Rosie added. "I was amazed at how well you handled her."

Lily knew that it was due to Daniel that she had managed it. Daniel Walker might not know it, but because of him and his offhand advice, the ladies of

Shivaree were now on her side. Under the circumstances, Lily figured that was quite appropriate.

Daniel walked around to the front of the library and watched as the women left the building. "Evenin', ladies," he said, giving his most gallant bow as they passed. "Hope y'all enjoyed your little party." Their returning glances ranged from girlish blushing to ladylike politeness, but Daniel knew trouble was brewing. He gave Rosie and Mary Alice Billings a smile as they departed, then he went inside.

Lily was putting chairs back in their original places when he walked in. She glanced at him, but she did not pause in her task. He leaned back against a bookcase and watched her for a moment. "So you've pulled out the heavy guns," he finally said.

She shoved a chair into place. "I don't know what you mean."

"Dovey McRae and Mary Alice Billings."

"Both those women are just as determined as I to shut down the Shivaree Social Club. By the way, thank you for the advice about Dovey. It worked like a charm."

"With your contrary nature, I hoped that my advice would make you take the completely opposite tactic," he told her.

A wry smile tilted her lips. "You thought it would make me strong-arm Dovey some more?"

"No. I thought the idea of buttering up Dovey would be too galling for you and that you'd give up."

"Either way, it didn't work."

He sighed. "Unfortunately." He paused a moment, then said, "Lily, I don't think you realize what you're in for, stirring up the town this way. Wouldn't it be best if you gave up now, before it's too late for you to back out?"

She passed him and slid another chair beneath one of the long oak tables. "Back out?" she repeated. "Why on earth would I want to back out?"

"Because this issue is going to divide the town, and I don't think you have any idea just what that means. Things will get pretty ugly, believe me. I'm not sure you can handle it."

"You talk as if I'm helpless."

"You? Helpless?" He laughed. "God help any man who thinks you're helpless. What you are, sugarplum, is dangerous."

That caught her attention. She halted and looked at him in surprise. "Dangerous?"

"Yes, ma'am. You are a woman with a cause. And nothing is more dangerous to a man's happiness and peace of mind than a woman with a cause."

She sniffed, unimpressed, and resumed her task. "Somehow, Daniel, your happiness and peace of mind don't concern me much."

He chuckled. "I don't doubt it." He studied her for a moment as she moved about the room, and his momentary amusement faded. "Lily, I want to be serious now. Stop fiddlin' with those chairs and listen to me for a second. There is something you deserve to know about me before we wage this war you're so determined to fight."

Lily gave a long-suffering sigh and crossed to his side of the room. She faced him with a resigned expression. "What?"

He folded his arms across his chest, and she watched a shadow cross his handsome face, a fleeting glimpse of the ruthless and determined man that existed beneath the surface of Southern-boy charm. "I won't fight fair," he told her. "I won't play nice."

She was not going to let him intimidate her. She shook her head, and a wisp of hair came loose from the knot at the back of her head, tickling her cheek. "Tell me something I don't already know."

"I'm warning you, Lily. I will do whatever it takes to win."

What more could he do to her than he already had? She lifted her chin. "So will I."

He shook his head, and the shadow passed. "No, you won't," he said softly. "And that is the difference between us." He lifted his hand to her face, his fingertips grazing her cheek. She froze beneath that unexpected touch, breathless, unable to move, as he pushed back the loose tendril of hair and tucked it behind her ear.

He let his hand fall away, but her skin tingled where he had touched her, and she felt oddly unsteady, as if she'd been spinning on the carousel at the fair. It was ridiculous that a man she despised could make her feel giddy just by touching her cheek. Dismayed and irritated with herself, she sucked in a deep breath, trying to regain her equilibrium, reminding herself of how arrogant he was. Why, he was talking as if he knew her better than she knew herself. "I don't know what you mean."

"I mean that, to win this battle, I have the one essential quality you lack: the killer instinct."

"You don't think I have it?"

"No, I don't. You're too softhearted."

Astonished, she stared at him. "It was only a couple of days ago that you said I'm stubborn and hard."

"Hardheaded," he corrected her. He smiled and

leaned close. "A hardheaded, softhearted woman," he murmured.

He could work magic on women with that smile of his. "What you're really saying is that I can't win *because* I'm a woman."

"Not at all. I've known a lot of hard-hearted women. This isn't about gender. It's about the willingness to find and exploit the deepest weakness of your opponent. That is something I am perfectly able to do if I have to. You should know that better than anyone."

The reminder of her humiliating experience five years ago made her cheeks heat, but she had learned her lesson. She did not respond with defensiveness. Instead, she tilted her head and gave him a speculative glance. "I think I can find your weaknesses easily enough," she said, hoping she sounded as arrogantly confident as he.

"Perhaps you'll *find* them," Daniel said, "but you'll never use them against me. It just isn't in you. And that's why, in the end, I'll always be able to defeat you."

She forced herself to give him a smile that was serene and complacent, even sweet. "If you say so, it must be true. You are usually right."

He slanted her a suspicious look from beneath his thick lashes. "Why is it that when you start smiling, I expect a knife in my back?" he asked ruefully.

Her smile widened. "Then maybe you should watch your back," she suggested.

"With you, sugarplum, I can't afford to do anything else." He walked away, but his voice floated back to her. "I've warned you. Don't come cryin' to me if you end up battle-scarred."

"You're the last person in the world I'd cry to, Daniel

Walker," she called back as he disappeared out the door.

When the door closed behind him, she stared at it for a long moment. Her skin still tingled from his touch, and she lifted her hand to her cheek, feeling rather bemused. She had always considered herself immune to the charms of Daniel Walker, but she suddenly feared that maybe she wasn't immune after all.

THE NEXT MORNING, tempers were pretty testy at the barbershop, giving Daniel a good indication that his warning to Lily the night before was coming to pass even faster than he had anticipated. The men were downright hostile.

"You shoulda heard Mariah last night when she came home from that meeting," Tobias McGill was saying when Daniel walked in. "She started in on me the second she walked through the door, and didn't stop. Nag, nag, nag about the social club, all night long."

"I went and slept in the barn," Jacob Cole admitted forlornly. "Quieter out there."

The men paused in their complaints long enough to nod in Daniel's direction. "Mornin', Daniel," they chorused, then immediately returned to the subject at hand.

"I told Louisa I wasn't goin' to put up with no naggin'," Ezra said in a decisive voice.

"So what happened?" Nate asked.

"She threw a pie at me. And when I went out to the pump to wash off all them damn blackberries, she locked me out of the house."

All the other men in the room eyed him with empathy.

"Women!" Tobias rubbed his eyes, which were red. From lack of sleep, was Daniel's guess. "They're the very devil, aren't they?"

The question elicited an immediate flood of decisive agreement.

Tobias turned to Daniel. "You're Helen's lawyer. Can't you do something about this?"

All the men in the barbershop fixed expectant gazes on him. Daniel decided to try logic and reason. "Listen, boys, we all know the social club brings men with money into this town. If it closes, the local businesses will suffer. The hotel, the general store, the livery stable, even this barbershop, depend on the money those men bring with them. We've got to stand firm."

"That's right," Nate agreed. "We have a lot riding on this. Are we going to let the women ruin it?"

"That's easy for you to say, Nate," Jacob answered. "You don't have a wife constantly naggin' you."

There were murmurs of agreement from many of the other men, and a debate began.

"We can't let the women tell us what to do."

"But I don't go to Helen's anyway. It might bring some money into the town, but it really is a sinful sort of place."

"Sinful? What's wrong with a man having a bit of fun from time to time?"

Hostile voices grew louder until the men were practically shouting at one another.

Daniel jumped up on a chair and raised his voice to be heard over the grumbling men. "Boys, boys, listen to me for a second. The women were all het up last night after their little meeting, but they'll calm down. By dinnertime, they'll probably have forgotten about the whole thing."

The words were barely out of his mouth before a faint rumbling was heard outside. The sound grew gradually louder, and the men began exiting the barbershop to see what was going on. They gathered on the wooden sidewalk, dismayed by the sight coming up the street that was causing all the ruckus.

At least three dozen women were marching up the middle of Main Street, their voices raised in song and their high button shoes thumping against the hard-packed dirt of the street. Two tambourines carried by Lily Morgan and Rosie Russell at the front of the group kept time with their steps. Dovey McRae and Mary Alice Billings led the way, holding a huge banner between them that matched the song they sang. It read LIPS THAT TOUCH WHISKEY SHALL NEVER TOUCH MINE."

They passed the group of dismayed men on the sidewalk and turned the corner at the newspaper office, obviously headed for the Shivaree Social Club, located a quarter mile past the train station.

Tobias came up beside him. "What was it you were saying about the womenfolk calming down?"

Under his breath, Daniel muttered a curse.

That afternoon, Daniel left for Atlanta. He was a bit reluctant to leave with Lily and her cohorts marching in the streets, but he didn't have a choice. He had other cases to work on, and more important, he had to see

Calvin and the other men who were planning to back his legislative race. Besides, he would be gone only a week. Let the women march up Main Street and sing their hymns and have their meetings. He'd be back in plenty of time to countermand any negligible effect they might have.

His carriage was waiting at the Atlanta train station when he arrived, and his driver took him straight to his offices. When he walked in, Josiah was there, looking worried. But that didn't concern Daniel overmuch; Josiah always looked worried.

The law clerk followed Daniel into his office, and the two men spent the day going over pending cases, Daniel delegating everything he possibly could to Josiah. He then went home, bathed, changed into evening clothes, and arrived at the Lexington Hotel at precisely eight o'clock.

The Lexington was the most prestigious hotel in Atlanta. Cut crystal chandeliers, carved mahogany woodwork, comfortable leather chairs, and the best bourbon the South had to offer made the Lexington impressive, but what really counted were the private smoking rooms. It was behind the doors of these rooms that million-dollar deals were made, laws were written, and destinies determined.

In one of these private rooms, five of the state's most influential and powerful men waited for him. Calvin was there, of course. Also seated at the table was Will Rossiter, owner of half the lumber mills around Atlanta, whose son owed his life to Daniel. Richard Darnell, the cotton king of Macon County, and Travis Cooper, who bought most of Richard's cotton and turned it into calico, were also present. Harley West, owner of Atlanta's second largest newspaper, completed the group. Like Calvin, all of these men had money invested in saloons, brothels, gambling houses, and the manufacture and sale of spirits.

They greeted Daniel warmly, but he sensed some reserve. He put on his most charming, easygoing facade, but he wondered how long it would be before they got to the matter of the Shivaree Social Club.

Calvin spoke first. "You know how politics work, Daniel. How the voting goes can be manipulated. In the factories and mills, we persuade the owners you're the one who would best represent their interests. They tell the ward bosses you're our man, they tell the workers, and the workers vote for whomever we pick. Same with the landowners. We persuade them, and they tell the sharecroppers. In order for us to convince the businessmen and landowners in this district that you are the perfect man to send to the state senate, we have to set you up properly."

Daniel gave the men around the table an innocent look. "You mean I'm not perfect just the way I am?" he drawled. The question elicited some chuckles, but Daniel felt uneasy.

"We think you'll make a fine legislator," Calvin assured him. "You're handsome, you're popular, and you handle the journalists very well. You know how to persuade people to your way of thinking and, well, most folks just plain like you. After you get your feet wet in the Georgia legislature, we'll set you up to become a senator in Washington. One day, you might even be President of the United States."

"I'm honored, gentlemen, but I'm waiting for the other shoe to drop. What is it?"

The five other men glanced at one another, but it was Richard who spoke. "We have some concerns."

Daniel spread his hands wide and leaned back in his chair. "I'm listening."

Richard spoke bluntly. "You've got to get yourself a wife. The sooner the better. Unmarried men aren't popular candidates."

He felt a prick of instinctive rebellion, but he smothered it. He had no intention of gaining his goals through marriage, but these men didn't have to know that.

Richard cleared his throat and pushed a piece of paper across the table toward him. "We've come up with a list. Any of these fine young ladies would be ideal as the wife of an aspiring politician. All of them have powerful families and impeccable backgrounds."

Daniel picked up the list. "Yeah, but are any of 'em pretty?"

As expected, all the men laughed. He folded the list without even reading it and put it in the breast pocket of his evening jacket. He glanced at the group of men around the table. "Gentlemen, if that's the only thing you're worrying about, put your minds at ease. I'll get married just as soon as I can. But this isn't a choice to be made lightly. As you've pointed out, this is a decision that needs careful consideration. So y'all will have to give me a bit of time to look around for the right woman."

"That isn't the only thing, Daniel." Calvin drained his glass of bourbon, then refilled it from the decanter on the table. "This matter of the Shivaree Social Club is getting out of hand. When I sent you down there, I'd hoped we could handle it quick and keep it quiet."

Daniel let out his breath slowly, and he decided nonchalance was his best tactic. "It'll be over in a couple of weeks," he assured the men at the table. "By election time, everyone will have forgotten about it."

"Everyone except the men in the Republican Party," Travis pointed out. "You can bet whoever they put up as a candidate will remind everyone about it."

Daniel looked at Calvin. "You hired me. Do you want me to drop the case?"

"No." Calvin shook his head. "It's too late for that, but we have been discussing a new approach to the problem. We all know what this is going to come down to. If those temperance people have their way, things will get mighty ugly in this state, and it'll be a lot of trouble for nothing."

Daniel thought about his father, who would have sold his soul for one more drink, and he nodded with understanding. "Passing a law won't stop people from drinking. Kansas is proof of that. People there are making their own whiskey. Hell, bootlegging has become an industry all its own out there. If anything, this temperance movement is making people drink more."

"Exactly. But we don't want to make our money on bootlegging."

"As your lawyer, Calvin, I'm mighty glad to hear it," Daniel answered dryly.

The other man grinned. "Keeping prohibition out of Georgia is important to us." He gestured to the other men at the table, and went on, "We might be able to resolve this in a different way. Get those men in Shivaree to vote to keep Helen's place open, and maybe we can keep prohibition out of Georgia long enough for you to get into office. Then we can work on the Georgia legislature from the inside and maybe keep prohibition out of the state altogether."

Daniel glanced at the men around the table. "I assume you are already making your feelings known to the legislators who aren't up for reelection this year?"

Richard gave him a tight smile. "Of course. But keeping the Shivaree Social Club open would be an important victory. It would show those legislators that temperance is a vocal minority in this state, not an important voting block."

Calvin leaned forward and met Daniel's gaze across the table. "We have a lot riding on this, Daniel. Keep the Shivaree Social Club open."

"I understand." Daniel downed the last of his bourbon. "I'll do whatever I have to do," he assured them. From the pleased expressions on their faces, he knew that was exactly what they wanted to hear.

When Daniel got off the train in Shivaree six days later, Samuel was waiting to greet him. His boots had barely hit the platform before the older man was at his side. "Thank God you're back," Samuel said with fervent relief. "This has been the longest week of my life."

"Why? What's been going on around here that's got you in such a stir?"

"It's not just me, Daniel," the other man answered as the two of them walked out of the station and headed up Main Street. "The women are up in arms, the men are furious, and the whole damn town is in an uproar. I've been asked at least a hundred times when you were comin' back to straighten out this mess."

Daniel shrugged. "I know it's inconvenient, having

the women marching all around, naggin' the men and singin' hymns, but it's nothing to get all het up about."

"That's easy for you to say," Samuel replied through clenched teeth. "You haven't been here. The women aren't just marching and singing anymore. They've gone on strike."

"What?" Daniel came to a halt on the boarded sidewalk and turned to Samuel, who halted beside him. He was uncertain he'd heard correctly. "What do you mean?"

"I mean exactly what I said. They've gone on strike. They're not cooking, or cleaning, or sewing, and there isn't a married man in this town who's slept in his own bed this past week."

Daniel let out his breath in a low whistle. Lily had been busy. A strike, of all things. He felt a grudging hint of admiration.

"So, what are you going to do about this?" Samuel demanded. "You've got to do something."

"I intend to. I intend to have something to eat." He pulled out his pocket watch. "It's almost dinnertime, and I'm hungry. Let's go over to Rosie's and discuss this over a plate of ham steak, biscuits, and gravy." He grinned and clapped Samuel on the shoulder. "No man should have to deal with a bunch of angry women on an empty stomach."

"You don't understand," Samuel began, but Daniel resumed walking up the street, and Samuel muttered a curse of pure exasperation. "Fine," he agreed coldly, and fell into step beside the younger man. "By all means, let's go to Rosie's. Maybe then you'll start to take this thing seriously."

Daniel thought of his meeting in Atlanta and his promise. "Believe me, I am taking this very seriously," he assured Samuel. "But I'm hungry, and I always think better on a full stomach."

They arrived at Rosie's Cafe, but they had barely walked through the front door before they were stopped by Rosie herself, who stepped in front of them. "Sorry, but y'all can't come in here."

Daniel frowned, glancing past her to the roomful of women and children who filled the restaurant. "Why not?"

For an answer, Rosie pointed to the printed sign on the wall that proclaimed NO SWEARING, NO SPITTING, AND NO SMOKING. Beneath those words, a new rule had been added, handwritten in bold red ink: AND NO MEN.

Daniel gave her his most charming smile. "Now, Rosie," he said coaxingly, "you can't do that."

She folded her arms across her breasts, unmoved. "This is my place, Daniel. I own it free and clear. I can do anything I want. The only men allowed through those doors are Amos, Reverend Ogilvie, and Reverend Jones."

Daniel decided the best thing to do at this point was give in gracefully. He turned to Samuel. "Let's go home, then. I'll have Beatrice cook me up something to eat."

Samuel shook his head. "I'm afraid not. The minister over at the colored Baptist church has been giving his congregation the same sermons that Reverend Ogilvie and Reverend Jones have been giving their congregations. Beatrice is on strike, too. I've been living on canned beans and salt pork ever since you left. So's every other man in this town. And I have to warn you, most of the men are starting to feel like this is all your fault."

Daniel felt his temper flaring up, and his anger was

going in the same direction it always seemed to be going these days—straight toward a stubborn, red-headed librarian. Lily might have eyes like brown sugar and a body beautiful enough to stop a streetcar, but she could create more havoc than a hurricane.

Barely a week ago, he had assured five of Georgia's most powerful men that he would keep the Shivaree Social Club open. If some journalist got hold of this story, it wouldn't be long before it was filling up newspaper pages all over the state. Not only would he look like a complete fool to the men backing him for the legislature, he'd be labeled a depraved, Godless home wrecker who advocated card-playing, drinking, and prostitution. He had to counteract the damage or he could kiss Calvin's support and his political ambitions good-bye.

Daniel turned on his heel and left the restaurant. He paused on the sidewalk outside and reached into the breast pocket of his jacket for a cheroot. He bit off the end and spit it into the gutter, then lit the cigar. He looked at Samuel, who had followed him outside. "You'd better wait here."

"Why? Where are you going?" Samuel asked.

"And you'd better plan on practicing law again," he answered and clamped the lit cheroot between his teeth. "Because when I strangle that woman, you'll have to defend me."

For the first time in five years, the library was crowded. Since most of the women in town weren't busy weeding their gardens or churning butter or hanging up the washing, they had time on their hands, and they were putting it to good use. Women who weren't at Rosie's enjoying a five-cent dinner cooked by somebody else were in the library with their children, showing them the books, reading to them aloud, and having a wonderful time.

Lily had already pushed all the tables and chairs against the walls to make more room on the main floor and she had taken down the sign that read QUIET, PLEASE. The noise in the building was deafening, but she didn't care. Most families, if they owned any books at all, had only a Bible, and most of these children had never seen books of any other kind outside the schoolroom. The picture books and the atlases were in the most demand, and she had pulled every single one off the shelves. Now the women and children were sitting in groups on the floor going through them, their rapt expressions showing how fascinated they were by places and things they had never seen.

Lily stood on the mezzanine, leaning on the railing as she watched the hum of activity down below. It was really remarkable the way her whole life had turned around in the past few days. Women who had not spoken to her in years were now doing so. Many women who had not set foot in the library since all that fuss the previous year over the "dirty books" were seated with their children on the floor below.

Lily was once again a welcome presence at the ladies' sewing circle, and doors were no longer slammed in her face when she made calls. Apologies did not come easy to most folks, but several of the ladies did confess being sorry they'd misjudged her. Those women too proud or embarrassed to actually give her an apology managed to convey their regret over their harsh judgment of her in other ways— Louisa Richmond sent her twin sons over to weed Lily's garden, Mariah McGill lent her some dress patterns, and Eliza Cole complimented her Italian cream cake at least three times at the last meeting, insisting on having the recipe. Even Dovey's attitude toward her was changing. Though too stubborn and proud to ever apologize, she was treating Lily more like a colleague and less like a pariah.

It wasn't all smooth sailing, though. There was still some stiffness, there were still some awkward moments. Lily knew the tentative friendship she had developed with the other women in town during the last few days was extremely fragile. If she didn't watch her temper and her tongue, that friendship could vanish in a heartbeat. In a new spirit of cooperation, she had tactfully moved the books that had caused all the fuss to shelves in an obscure back corner, too high for children to reach—a compromise that didn't make her feel as if she had given in to censorship, but seemed to satisfy the mothers of Shivaree.

This temperance business was helping Lily to regain her respectability, and it felt so good. The loneliness and isolation of the past five years was easing away, and Lily had no intention of messing that up.

She felt exhilarated by all the activity, but as she gazed down at the groups of mothers and children on the floor below, she couldn't help feeling a hint of envy. She had desperately wanted children of her own, but in the entire time she and Jason had been married, she had never become pregnant. Not once. During the fifth and final year of her marriage, Doc Wilson had told her that some women just couldn't have children, and if she hadn't become pregnant after five years of marriage, she probably never would. The doctor didn't know, of course, that Jason had hardly exerted any effort in that direction, although he had seemingly had the energy for any number of prostitutes.

The opening of the front doors caught her attention, and when she saw Daniel Walker standing in the doorway, a lit cheroot in his hand and a thunderous expression on his face, all thoughts of Jason went out of her head.

Daniel caught sight of her standing up on the mezzanine at the same moment she saw him, and he began walking toward the stairs. He moved slowly at first, negotiating his way carefully amid the groups of women and children on the floor. But when he reached the stairs, his long legs took them two at a time. Anger emanated from him like a Georgia heat wave, and Lily felt the wild impulse to run for cover, but there was nowhere to go. She had no choice but to face him down.

The room was quiet by the time he reached her. Even the children seemed to sense the sudden tension in the air, and all the gazes in the room were lifted to the pair as if the mezzanine were a stage.

A man made of six feet and three inches of solid muscle who looked furious enough to chew nails was an intimidating thing. So much for thinking he had charm. Her heart began hammering in her chest, but Lily stood her ground with as much bravado as she could muster.

She seized on the lit cigar in his hand as a reason to take the offensive. "You can't smoke in here," she said coldly. "If you must smoke that thing, kindly do it outside."

His response was to blow smoke in her face, making her choke. "*Kindly?*" he repeated through clenched teeth. "Somehow, I don't feel *kindly* at this moment,

Lily. What I feel is the overwhelming desire to pitch you over this railing."

She waved aside the smoke as best she could, and looked him in the eye. "Go ahead," she dared even though her voice shook. "I'm sure that would impress everyone."

"And give me a great deal of satisfaction, I assure you. The only reason I won't is because those children down there might get hurt."

"Why should that stop you? If you cared about the children, you'd be on my side. You'd be fighting to close down the Shivaree Social Club."

"The club brings money into this town. Wealthy men from Atlanta come to Shivaree just for the purpose of going to that establishment."

"What a wonderful thing for a town to be famous for," she shot back sarcastically. "We should all be proud."

"Like it or not, the social club has brought Shivaree to the attention of some very wealthy men. They realized this town was an excellent location for a railway station, two cotton mills, and a lumber mill. Half the men in this town wouldn't have jobs if it weren't for those wealthy men. What happens to the children of this town if their fathers lose their jobs because those men decide to close down the mills?"

"I doubt the closure of the club would cause those men to shut down their mills now," she answered, dismissing his words with a shrug. "They have too much invested. And if that awful place closes, fathers would be home with their wives and children at night, not out gallivanting with painted women and spending their wages on drinking and gambling."

"It might surprise you to know this, but most of the

men in this town *are* home with their families most
nights. Or used to be, until you messed up their lives.
Unlike your former husband, most of the men who live
around here enjoy being at home with their wives.
And knowing you, I can't blame Jason for wanting to
be anywhere else."

Lily felt the impact of his words like a punch in the
stomach. "That's a mean, unfair thing to say," she
whispered.

"I get a helluva lot meaner, believe me. And I
already warned you I wouldn't fight fair."

She wasn't going to let his ruthless remarks get to
her. She drew a deep, steadying breath. "You're just
angry because I've beaten you at your own game. You
underestimated me, I outmaneuvered you, and you
don't like it."

"Maybe so, but I never make the same mistake
twice. And the game isn't over yet." He took a pull on
his cigar. "You insisted on this little war, sugarplum,
and I'm damn well going to win it. When it's all over,
believe me, you'll regret the day you started it."

With that, he turned and walked away, leaving Lily
feeling as bruised and battered as if the war had
already taken place and his prediction had already
come true.

❖ 7 ❖

DANIEL KNEW THAT if his words to Lily were going to be more than just an empty threat, the first thing he had to do was talk to the men. Somehow, he had to persuade them to stand their ground for seven more days.

He strode back down Main Street, stopping briefly at the barbershop, the dry goods store, the general store, the post office, the newspaper office, and every other business he passed on his way, announcing that he was calling for a meeting of his own in the town hall at quarter past five that afternoon.

Word spread, and at the appointed hour, Daniel stepped up onto the platform normally used by the town council and faced a crowd of unhappy men.

"Quiet down, boys," he shouted to be heard over the voices of the men. "Listen up."

His words had little effect, and he nodded to Sheriff Trusedale, who stuck his pistol out the open window and fired one shot in the air.

That did the trick. The men instantly fell silent and

faced Daniel. Their hostile stares and belligerent scowls told him they looked perfectly capable of lynching him if he couldn't persuade them otherwise.

"Seems to me," be began, "the womenfolk have dug in their heels over the social club. They're thinking they can use blackmail to get us to vote to close it the way they want. We can't let them do that."

"That's easy for you to say, Daniel," Jacob Cole shouted. "You don't have a wife nagging you. And you're staying at Samuel's place. I've been sleeping in the barn all week. And whenever I see my wife, all she does is harp at me."

His words opened the floodgates of resentment, and complaints began flowing from all sides of the room.

"Same with me. My wife won't even speak to me, 'cept to tell me I'd better vote to close that place down."

"I've hardly seen my children all week."

"My wife locked me out of the house."

"Mine, too. Put my clothes and my shaving kit on the front porch with a note that told me not to bother comin' home until this vote was over and the Shivaree Social Club was closed down for good."

"You think that's bad? My wife didn't even bother to leave me any clothes before she locked me out. I've been wearing the same pants and shirt for five days."

"Well, my wife took all the food in the house and all the vegetables in the garden and gave the whole passel to Rosie for the women to eat. My cupboard's bare as a baby's behind."

"Mine, too!"

"My girl, Annie, told me not to bother come callin' again until the club was closed. We was plannin' to get married next spring. She said that's off if the club stays open."

"No great loss, Cyrus," another man commented. "Being married is hell."

"Boys! Boys!" Daniel shouted over the din. "Listen to me for a second. Now, I know it's hard, with the women bein' so stubborn. But it's only one more week. If we can just hold out that long, everything will be fine. After we vote to keep the Shivaree Social Club open, the women will know they've lost, and y'all will be right back home again. I bet we'll never hear another word about it."

"That may be true, Daniel," Tobias shouted from his seat near the back. "But in the meantime, we've got to eat. None of us knows how to cook, and Rosie ain't lettin' us eat at her place. What do we do about that?"

"I know how y'all are feeling," Daniel answered. "Believe me, I know. I tried to have dinner at Rosie's today. Got as far as the front door. But I've come up with a solution to that problem. Come tomorrow morning, Rosie's isn't going to be the only place a man can get a meal. Helen's got a fine cook over at her place, and she's going to be offerin' you men five cent meals, just like Rosie's been giving the women."

"Helen's really goin' to do that?" Travis asked.

Daniel hadn't discussed this idea with Helen yet, but if it would help to keep her place open, Helen would go along with just about anything. "Yep. Starting tomorrow morning you boys can eat your meals at the club."

Daniel saw the expressions on the men's faces change from anger to relief, and he figured he'd better wrap this up before another round of complaints started. He needed to end the meeting by getting the men fired up, so they would have the determination to hold out until the vote on Tuesday.

"You men know what's happening here. The women are trying to force us to do what they want. If y'all let your wives do that, what's next? No tobacco? No admirin' a pretty girl walking down the street? Do we want to be like Kansas, with women telling the men what laws to make? Next thing you know, they'll be wanting to vote. If we let the womenfolk get away with this, they'll be tryin' to blackmail y'all with this same stunt every time they want something from you. Is that what you want?"

"No!" all the men shouted together, clearly appalled by that idea.

"Are we going to let them tell us how to vote?"

"No!"

Daniel took a deep breath and fired his final shot. "Don't let your wives blackmail you. Vote the way you think is right, and to hell with what the women think."

The men cheered their approval and stormed out filled with determination, but Daniel knew a man could get mighty lonely sleeping alone at night, and he hoped their determination was strong enough to last another week. Keeping their bellies full would help, and he knew he had to talk to Helen about the promise he'd made to the men. Helen was sure to agree, and Calvin would certainly foot the bill for the extra food. Daniel just hoped Helen's cook wouldn't walk out in a huff at the idea of feeding over ten dozen men two or three times a day for the next seven days.

* * *

Despite Daniel's attempt to intimidate her, Lily proceeded to do what she had done each of the seven previous evenings. She marched. Along with about four dozen other women, she paced back and forth in front of the Shivaree Social Club, a sign in her hand and a chant of protest on her lips.

From the outside, the most famous whorehouse in Georgia didn't look like any such thing. Built by Hiram P. Amberly of Connecticut, one of the many wealthy Yankee carpetbaggers who had invaded Georgia after the war, it was an immense mansion in the antebellum style, designed and built to accommodate Hiram's extravagant lifestyle and many servants, with a parlor and ballroom big enough to entertain his fellow carpetbaggers. Oblivious to the venomous hatred of the locals, Hiram had stayed twenty years, long enough to make a second fortune and produce twelve children. Then he and his family had gone back up north where they belonged. The house had been sold and resold, but had finally been purchased by Helen Overstreet and Calvin Stoddard, who had obviously seen the potential for their decadent business in a luxurious house with thick carpets, a huge parlor, and ten bedrooms.

But the women of Shivaree knew all of those bedrooms were now being put to a use that Hiram Amberly had never imagined. And while they found it fitting that Hiram was probably turning over in his Connecticut grave at what his home had become, it didn't alter their determination to close the place down.

Before the front gates that led onto the grounds, the women marched back and forth, holding torches for light and singing the songs of temperance, moving out of the way only when the carriages Helen's customers rented from Jacob Cole's livery stable pulled into the long lane leading up to the house.

As Daniel had pointed out to Lily only that afternoon, most of the men who came to the Shivaree Social Club were not locals, but wealthy men who came from Atlanta, spent an enjoyable evening at the establishment, slept off the drink at the hotel, and returned to the city the following morning. It was a ninety-minute trip each way by train, but from the number of men that came through the gates, it was obviously worth the trouble. All the ladies standing outside couldn't help but wonder why.

The long lane leading to the house prevented any of the women from taking a peek through the windows, but during their nightly vigil when lamps illuminated the interior, Dovey and Densie's opera glasses were put to good use, and all the women of Shivaree knew there were ostentatious crystal chandeliers, scarlet-red wallpaper, and paintings of naked women. If the activities were as sinful as the decor, the Shivaree Social Club might just as well have been built in Sodom.

"Oh, my goodness!" Louisa Richmond gasped, opera glasses perched on her nose. She leaned over the wrought-iron railing that bordered the wide expanse of front lawn. "A woman is dancing right on top of the piano. And she's taking off her clothes."

"I see her." Densie began to shake like a terrier left out in the cold as she peered through the other pair of glasses, and Lily hoped the timid little woman's heart wouldn't give out from the shock. "And all the men are watching her. Oh, how sinful."

"Ladies, please," Lily said for perhaps the tenth time

that evening, "put those things away. We aren't here to participate in this wickedness, you know."

"I know, I know," Densie answered without lifting the opera glasses from her nose. "But . . . oh . . . it's quite scandalous. Lily, don't you want to see?"

"No, I don't." She reached out and snatched the glasses from the older woman. "And neither do you. You're as bad as the schoolboys who come sneaking around here at night to peek in the windows."

"Lily," Densie wailed, "give them back."

"I won't. We're not here to watch what goes on in there. We're here to prevent it."

"You're as curious as the rest of us," Dovey said, taking her opera glasses back from Louisa. "You just won't admit it."

For the past seven nights, Lily had resisted temptation. She had staunchly refused to take a peek through the opera glasses, telling herself that she didn't want to see even a hint of the activity inside that house. But Jason had spent many an evening in there, doing his best to spend the fortune his father had accumulated, and she had often wondered about the temptations that had beckoned him to this place. She might never get another chance to find out.

She lifted the glasses in her hand for one—just one—quick peek.

The sound of wagon wheels on the road had her guiltily jerking down the glasses, and she glanced in the direction of the sound to find Daniel Walker driving a wagon up the road toward the group of women gathered at the entrance to the estate. The wagon was filled with barrels and crates of food. Two other men were perched on top of the pile.

Lily tucked the glasses into the pocket of her skirt, hoping Daniel hadn't seen her peeking through them, but the knowing grin on his face as he pulled the wagon to a stop only a few feet from where she stood told her he knew exactly what she'd been doing.

"So, you've taken up bird-watching, have you, sugarplum?" he drawled.

She did not dignify that comment with anything more than a scowl.

"And at night, too," he added. "See anything interesting?"

"Enough to justify everything I've said about this place," she answered tartly. "Why are you here? For an evening's entertainment?"

"It's a tempting idea, but no." He started to turn the wagon into the lane leading to the house, but he was forced to halt again because of the women who blocked his path. "Ladies, I need to get past y'all. Would you kindly stand aside?"

Lily moved to the head of the group and faced him down, only a dozen feet from the noses of the horses who pulled the wagon. "We will not."

In the dimness of the moonlit night, she could only imagine the dangerous glint to his green eyes, but she did not imagine the determination in his voice when he said, "Lily, if you don't stand aside, I'll be forced to put you out of the way."

She folded her arms across her breasts, widened her stance, and did not move. He inched the wagon forward slowly, his gaze never leaving hers. As the horses drew nearer, other women moved out of the way, until only Lily remained.

He braked the wagon, let out an exasperated sigh,

and jumped down. He walked toward her, and with every stride he took, her inclination to step back grew stronger, but she did not move.

He halted less than a foot in front of her, his wide chest a wall that blocked her view of anything but him. He was so close, she could smell the luscious combination of shaving soap and bay rum on his skin. He was so close that when she lifted her chin to meet his gaze, she could see the reflection of the torchlights in his eyes.

"Are you going to make me use force?" he asked quietly.

Though her heart was pounding and her throat was dry as a desert creek bed, she was not going to let him intimidate her just because he was big and arrogant and far too handsome for his own good. "I reckon so," she answered, but she was mortified that her brave answer came out in a breathless whisper.

Daniel smiled, an angelic choirboy smile, and she found that highly suspicious. She knew he was capable of anything, but she could not back down.

He leaned down, and his lips brushed her ear as he spoke. "Sure you don't want to save us both a lot of fuss, and just move out of the way?"

She shivered. "No."

"Fine. If that's the way you want it, sugarplum." He moved so fast, she had no chance to escape. He seized her wrist with one hand, while with the other he reached into his pocket. Two seconds later, she found herself handcuffed to the wrought-iron rail that surrounded the property.

"Daniel!" she shouted as he walked away amid the hoots of laughter from the two men in the wagon and the shocked gasps of the women gathered nearby. She tugged against the steel that fastened her to the rail, but her effort was futile and all she accomplished was bruising her wrist. "Let me out of these handcuffs right now."

He jumped back into the wagon. "I promised Sheriff Trusedale I'd give the handcuffs back, but he told me he didn't need 'em, so I guess they're yours to keep." He snapped the reins, turned the wagon into the lane, and started toward the house, causing her to wonder if he intended to leave her trapped there forever.

She watched along with the other ladies as Daniel drove the wagon around to the back of the house and disappeared from view. It didn't take more than a minute for Lily to figure out what Daniel was up to. Helen had a cook, and entertainment to go along with it. So much for thinking the men would miss their wives' cooking. She hated to admit it, but Daniel had won that round. She just had to figure out how to win the next one. Frustrated, she tugged uselessly at her handcuffs and wished Daniel Walker at the bottom of the nearest swamp.

When the wagon came back around the side of the house and down the lane toward them about an hour later, she was so relieved, she stopped cursing him. All she felt was glad that he was coming back, so he could let her out of these silly cuffs. But the wagon turned out of the lane and started back down the road without stopping.

"Daniel!" she cried.

The wagon halted and he stood up, turning around to look at her. "Hell's bells," he swore. "I almost forgot." He reached into his pocket for the key, but instead of jumping down from the wagon to release her, he remained where he was, tossing the key in the air, then catching it in his hand. He repeated the motion several times, his speculative gaze never leaving hers.

No one spoke, the silence lengthened, and Lily finally could not stand it. "Daniel, let me out of these things," she demanded, tugging hard enough against the handcuffs to rattle the railing.

"Say please," he said. "Just once in your life, try to be polite to me."

She opened her mouth to tell him to go to hell, but the steel was scraping her wrist raw, and it was dark, and there were snakes out here. She hated snakes. Especially the two-legged kind. She scowled at him, and through clenched teeth, she said, "Please."

He immediately tossed the key toward her, and it landed in the dust at her feet. As Louisa unlocked the handcuffs that chained her to the railing, she watched the wagon head on down the road, and she knew his words to her that he would not fight fair had not been an idle threat. She wondered what else he was capable of doing, and she realized the answer was just about anything.

By the time she got home, Lily was bone weary. Seven days of marching and singing until late at night, managing the library with its crowds of women and children during the day, and grueling battles with Daniel Walker were taking their toll. She entered her front door, lit the lamp on the hall table, and went toward the kitchen, thinking only of a cup of tea and a good night's sleep. But when she entered the kitchen, all thoughts of tea or sleep vanished from her mind.

There was a sheet of paper nailed square in the center of her kitchen table. She walked toward it slowly, feeling nothing but a numbing sense of shock as the lamp in her hand illuminated the hand-printed words written on it.

STOP MEDDLING WITH THE SHIVAREE SOCIAL CLUB OR YOU'LL REGRET IT.

It was unsigned, but whoever had written it had been inside her house. He could still be here, waiting for her. Hairs rose on the back of her neck at the realization. She whirled around in a circle, holding the lamp high, but she could see no one else in the room. She backed up against the nearest wall, listening, but the only sound she could hear was her own rapid breathing.

Someone had invaded her home, someone had threatened her, but who could it be? She could imagine no man she knew doing something like this. No man but one.

Lily jerked the note away from the nail that held it to her table and marched out her back door. She circled to the front sidewalk, crossed the narrow space that separated her house from Samuel's, and pounded on the brass door knocker of his front door.

When Beatrice answered her knock, Lily wasted no time on preliminaries. "Tell Daniel I need to speak with him right now," she said through clenched teeth.

The housekeeper took one look at her face and nodded. She opened the door wider for Lily to step inside, then she went in search of Daniel, who appeared a few moments later. "Well, I'll be damned," he murmured, crossing the foyer to stand in front of her. "To what do I owe the honor of this visit?"

"Don't bother to pretend you don't know why I'm here," she said in a voice shaking with anger. "I've always known you were a cad, but I never knew just how low you could go. Until now, that is."

"Evenin' to you, too, Lily," he answered easily, no sign of guilt in his eyes or his voice. "If this is about what happened earlier tonight, I'm real sorry I had to put those handcuffs on you. But you kind of brought it on yourself, don't you think?"

"I'm not talking about those handcuffs." She held up the paper in her hand. "I'm talking about this."

He actually managed to look as if he didn't know what she was talking about. A slight frown pulled his brows together. "What is it?" he asked, his drawling voice suddenly sharp.

If he wanted to pretend, that was fine with her. "What do you think it is?" she countered, rustling the paper between her fingers. "Take a guess."

"Not a love letter, from the sound of it."

"Hardly. I doubt you would write one, especially to me."

He took the note from her hand, read it, then looked at her again, still betraying no sign that he had anything to do with writing it. But Lily was certain Daniel had no problem with lying if it suited his purpose, and she eyed him coldly. "Did you really think this note would stop me?"

"You think I wrote it?" The frown etched lines of anger deeper into his face. He glared at her, and she could see a tiny muscle working at the corner of his jaw.

"You said you wouldn't fight fair," she reminded him. "I guess you meant it."

"Lily, you ought to know me well enough by now to

know that when I threaten you, I do it to your face. I don't write notes."

She studied him for a long moment, telling herself not to believe a word he said, but she could see no sign of deception. Doubt crept into her mind for the first time. "If you didn't write it, then you must have a pretty good idea who did," she finally said. "I heard about your little speech in the town hall tonight. Which of the men did you get riled up enough to threaten me?"

"If any man there tonight reacted to my words by leaving you that note, I have no idea who he was."

She didn't want to believe him, and yet, his words did have a ring of truth. Now that she was calmer, now that the shock and anger of finding the note had faded somewhat, she could assess the circumstances more clearly, and she was forced to admit he had a point. He might handcuff her to a railing, but he really wasn't the sort of man to threaten her with a note. Which left open the question of what sort of man he really was. Beneath the Southern-boy charm was the ruthless lawyer. What was beneath that? she wondered.

"Where did you find it?" he asked, interrupting her thoughts. "On your front door?"

She shook her head. "No. It was nailed to my kitchen table."

"It was inside your house? Did they break in?"

"No. It wasn't necessary. I don't lock my doors. No one does around here."

"No one but half the women in town," he answered with a touch of wry humor. "C'mon."

He took her hand and started for the door with her in tow.

"Where are we going?"

"I want a look through your house."

"Whoever put that note on my table is probably long gone," she pointed out.

"Probably, but humor me. I want to be certain."

Lily made no argument. To tell the truth, she was quite relieved that he was having a look through her house to make sure the intruder wasn't still lurking in some dark corner, waiting for her, although never in a million years would she have asked Daniel for his help or admitted that she needed it.

With Lily following behind him, Daniel went through the house from root cellar to attic, searching every room. He looked in the armoires and under the beds, opened old storage trunks, and looked behind drapes. But the intruder, whoever he was, had fled. They ended their search in the kitchen, where Daniel took a look at the nail that had been driven into her table. "I'll take the note to the sheriff tomorrow and tell him what's happened."

"You will?"

Unexpectedly, he smiled at her. "Well, you wouldn't get anywhere with Trusedale. Because of you, his wife tossed a mattress in the front yard and told him to sleep there from now until the vote. Mosquitoes have been his best friends ever since, so he's a bit testy when it comes to you. He'd be more likely to try and find out who wrote that note if I took it to him."

"Why would you do that?" she asked skeptically. "We're on opposite sides, remember? We're enemies."

"Yeah, but I like you anyway."

The comment was too flippant to believe. "Sure you do," she answered, "that's why you handcuff me to railings."

He pulled out a chair from the kitchen table and sat down. "I'd heard you and the other ladies were marching out at Helen's, and I kind of figured you'd get in the way. Having those handcuffs seemed like a good idea. I had to lay in some food for Helen's cook so she could feed those men."

"Lucky for you, Helen's got a cook," she countered dryly, taking the chair opposite his at the table. "If it was left up to those painted dolls over there, the men would starve. There's only one thing Helen's girls know how to do and cooking isn't it."

"Oh, I don't know about that." He gave her a grin. "That all depends what they're heatin' up."

She couldn't help it. That grin was so wicked, she couldn't help a responding smile of her own. "You really are a devil."

He stared at her in pretended astonishment. "Is that a smile I see threatening your face? Careful, Lily. You might start to like me, and that could ruin all the fun we're having."

"Don't bet on it," she answered with spirit. "Liking you would rank right up there with visiting Nate to have a tooth pulled."

Daniel chuckled. "I have no doubt."

After a moment, his laughter faded. "From what I hear, you're getting what you wanted out of all this."

She didn't think he was referring to the closure of the social club. "What do you mean?"

"I heard you've become a regular member of the ladies' sewing circle again. And no woman in town has slammed her door in your face lately. It seems you've regained your respectability."

"Not yet. A scarlet reputation doesn't disappear overnight. But at least I'm starting to feel as if I have friends again. Eventually, I might regain my respectability. I hope so."

"I never thought convention and respectability were that important to you."

She stiffened in her chair. "You have no idea what it's like to lose your reputation, your husband, your marriage."

"Was your marriage so wonderful, then, that losing it was so devastating?"

He was too clever, he really was. His shrewd gaze studied her, and she knew he would see through a lie instantly. She didn't bother to invent one. "It wasn't so much that my marriage was wonderful. It was, I imagine, typical of most marriages. But what you don't seem to understand is that it was all I had."

"And would you take Jason back, if he came running to you now?"

"No."

"Well, then, it seems your troubles will soon be over. You'll eventually regain your respectability. Someday, you might even marry again."

The very idea was horrifying. "Even if there were some man out there willing to flout convention and marry me, it wouldn't matter. I will never marry again. I will never put myself in a position of subservience again, of knowing my husband is being unfaithful and being expected to simply tolerate it like a good little wife until he decides to cast me aside."

"Not all men are unfaithful to their wives."

"I know. But all the same, I'd rather not risk it." A new thought struck her, and she tilted her head to one side, studying him across the table. "Why haven't you ever married?"

"Why should I?" he countered with a shrug. "Marriage is not always a desirable thing for a man."

"Or a woman, either."

He acknowledged the truth of that with a nod. "Does this mean you and I are in agreement about something?" he asked with a smile.

"I guess so. Who'd have thought it?" She yawned, suddenly realizing how tired she was.

Daniel noticed that yawn and rose to his feet. "It's late. I'd better go."

She also stood up and led him to the front door. He reached out to open the door, but suddenly paused, his hand on the knob. He turned to look at her. "Lily?"

"Yes?"

He let go of the door and turned to her. "Do me a favor," he murmured and reached out to cup her cheek in his hand. "Lock your doors from now on."

At the touch of his hand, Lily froze. Unable to move, she felt the calloused tips of his fingers slide up her cheek, across her temple, and into the knot of hair at the back of her head. Pins fell and her hair came tumbling down, tangled in his grasp.

"I hate you," she reminded him, trying to catch her breath as she felt him pull her closer.

"Yeah," he agreed and tilted her head back.

Frantic, aware of his intent, she added, "You hate me. Remember?"

"I don't hate you." His mouth came down on hers before she could reply, effectively cutting off any contradiction she might have made. She felt his mouth open against hers, and his tongue lightly grazed her lips. Lily felt her knees buckle as if there were no strength in them, and she curled her hands into the folds of his shirt to keep herself from falling.

Daniel's fingers tightened in her hair. He pulled her lower lip between his teeth, tasting her like a piece of candy, and she felt herself melting against him. Her mouth opened, her tongue touched his in response, and the whole world caught fire.

Then, just as suddenly as it began, it stopped. Daniel let go of her and stepped back, shoving his hands into his pockets. Even through the haze of her stunned senses, she could hear his harsh breathing in the stillness.

That kiss left her dazed and breathless, and though he was no longer kissing her, she could still feel his mouth on hers. She pressed her fingers to her lips, and looked at him, too shaken to speak. She had only been kissed by one other man in her life, and Jason had never kissed her like that—open, hot, and lush.

"Believe it or not," Daniel said, his voice a bit unsteady, "I have never hated you." His gaze traveled down the length of her and back again, pausing a second or two at her mouth. "Now, I don't think I ever will."

Abruptly, he turned away. Yanking open the door, he walked out of her house without a backward glance. "Remember to protect yourself," he called out. "Lock your doors."

Lily stood in the doorway and watched him go, relieved, disappointed, confused. There was a dizzying, weightless sensation in the pit of her stomach, and she knew she had to be going out of her mind. What would have happened if Daniel hadn't stopped? She knew the answer to that, and it was mortifying to realize that a man she thought she despised could make her feel other passions as well. She knew that he could have done anything he wanted to her, and she would have let him. That thought frightened her, and made her feel very, very vulnerable.

"I'll lock my doors, Daniel," she whispered, watching him walk away, "but who's going to protect me from you?"

❖ 8 ❖

THE FOLLOWING DAY, Lily found herself wishing for Daniel's presence to protect her, but not from men who wrote threatening notes. No, Lily needed Daniel's protection from flashy book salesmen.

Alvis Purdy loosened his bow tie and eyed her with lecherous intent between the bookshelves, snapping his chewing gum between his teeth. "Sure I can't sell you some Funk and Wagnall's Encyclopedias this month?"

"No, thank you." Lily wished she could tell him what to do with his encyclopedias. But she was waiting for a big shipment of new books from New York, and if Alvis got mad enough, she might not get her books until Christmas.

She decided running away was her best option. She dodged around the bookshelves, and she actually managed to get to her desk without Alvis getting his hand anywhere near her body. She grabbed her letter opener and faced him across the desk. Even though the way he looked at her always made her want to go take a bath with lye soap, she knew Alvis was basically harmless. Nonetheless, she felt much better with her silver letter opener in her hand. If he got fresh, she'd skewer his hand clean through, books or no books. *That'd teach him to keep his hands to himself,* she thought and smiled, picturing it.

Alvis, of course, misinterpreted that smile. "I hear there's a dance comin' up in Calhoun next week," he said, leaning closer to her across the desk. "I could rearrange my schedule to be down that way. How about we go, girly, you and me? I got a brand new automobile to take us there, and I got the money to show you a real good time." His gum snapped again.

"No, thank you." Lily began opening her mail, wishing someone, anyone, would come through the front doors. Even Dovey would be a welcome sight just now.

He watched her for a moment, then he straightened his celluloid collar, cleared his throat, and tried again. "Now, you got no call to stick your nose up the air with me, you bein' a dee-vor-say and all. We both know gals like you want a bit of fun now and again, and you'd have a lot of fun with me, girly."

Lily set her jaw. Her hand tightened around her letter opener. "I doubt it."

"You and me could go to that dance, and afterward, we'd find us a nice hotel, and . . ." He winked at her. "You know."

One more word, just one, and she was going to let him have it.

He started to reach across the desk, and she jumped back, out of reach. He circled her U-shaped desk, and before she could escape, he had her trapped within the confines of her desk.

"Come on, honey," he said, laughing as he took a step toward her. "We know you're a loose woman who likes a good time. And nobody could show you a better time than me."

Lily decided she'd had just about as much of Alvis Purdy as she could stand. She lifted her letter opener threateningly. "Alvis, if you don't get out of my library this instant, I swear, I'll—"

"What the hell is going on here?" another man's voice interrupted, and Lily glanced past Alvis to see Daniel striding across the library toward them.

"Afternoon, sir." Alvis quickly stepped out from behind her desk and away from her. He turned to Daniel. "I was just having a visit with Miz Morgan, is all," he explained. "We're old friends."

Daniel looked Alvis over, and the expression on his face clearly showed his opinion that the book salesman was something that had just crawled out from under a rock.

Beneath the narrowed gaze of the man twice his size, Alvis started squirming just like the worm that he was. Lily thoroughly enjoyed watching Alvis squirm, and she almost burst out laughing.

Daniel frowned down at the man almost a foot shorter than he and folded his arms across his chest. "Why don't you go visit somebody else?" he suggested.

"Sure, sure." Alvis laughed nervously. He tipped his hat to Lily. "I'll be here for a few days, Miz Morgan, if you change your mind about those Funk and Wagnall's," he said and beat a hasty retreat out the front doors.

Lily chuckled. "Thank you. I thought sure I was

going to have to run him through." She brandished her letter opener like a sword.

"I take it that means that for once in your life, you're glad to see me?" He turned his head to look at the door where Alvis had departed. "Who was he, anyway?"

Lily thought of what had happened the night before, and she felt her cheeks heating with embarrassment at the memory. She did not want to explain Alvis Purdy to Daniel, especially after last night. Instead of answering his question, she asked one of her own. "What are you doing here? More law research?"

"Not this time. I came to tell you I spoke with True about that note left in your house. He was reluctant to do any investigating, which is not surprising, given how his wife has been treating him because of you and your temperance cause. But he said he'd look into it." Daniel folded his arms and leaned one hip against her desk. "Aren't you going to answer my question?"

She should have known she couldn't divert Daniel so easily. "Alvis Purdy. He's a book salesman."

"He acted like he knew you pretty well."

The cool tone of his voice dismayed her. Now he was thinking exactly what everybody else, including Alvis Purdy, thought of her: that she was a loose, immoral woman. After the way she had responded so wantonly to his kiss last night, what could she expect him to think?

"Alvis would like to think he knows me very well," she answered, her voice as cool as Daniel's had been. She figured she might as well tell him the truth, and let him make what he wanted of it. "He comes into town, flashes his money around, tries to sell me some new books, makes improper advances toward me, and leaves in a huff when I spurn him. It happens every month, like clockwork."

"I see." His gaze fell to the letter opener still in her hand. "And you feel you need a weapon to defend yourself?"

She shrugged. "With Alvis, it's probably not necessary. But better safe than sorry."

"And how many other women in town are subjected to this man's pawing behavior?"

"I believe I am the only one. Alvis thinks a divorced woman is easy pickings."

"Damn." Daniel let out his breath in a slow sigh. "I was afraid you were going to say that."

The next four days were tense ones in Shivaree. A heat wave rolled in on Wednesday, along with its usual stifling humidity. Temperatures climbed into the high eighties, and the tempers of the townspeople escalated with each degree their thermometers rose. The humidity and the tension made the air thick enough to cut with a knife. Quarrels among friends, domestic disputes, and street brawls kept Sheriff Trusedale constantly busy and cursing the Ladies' Temperance Society. By Sunday, nearly every resident of Shivaree had been in at least one heated argument on the subject of the Shivaree Social Club.

The strategy of the women to close down the place by boycotting their domestic responsibilities began to take a heavy toll on the men. More and more of the menfolk began to believe that Shivaree didn't really need Helen's place anyway, and asserting their male authority became less important with each day that passed. Though Daniel did what he could to boost their flagging spirits, he couldn't stop men from missing their families, and as much as he wanted to, he couldn't hog-tie Lily to a tree until the vote.

Lily had her own set of problems. Most of the women were beginning to complain about the effect the boycott was having on their children. Some of them defected and returned to their wifely duties— sometimes willingly, and sometimes because their husbands used force to make them do so. And though Sunday's sermon in each of Shivaree's three churches condemned spiritous liquors, licentiousness, and gambling, and denounced Helen Overstreet as the spawn of the devil, the Shivaree Social Club continued to do a booming business. Men from out of town had always been the mainstay of her clientele, and they didn't care what Shivaree's preachers had to say. In addition, many local men who had never set foot inside Helen's before were now doing so, partly because they couldn't get a hot meal anywhere else, and partly because they wanted to show their wives who was boss. The fact that Helen had dropped the price of a half-hour's entertainment with one of her girls to two bits, served bourbon at ten cents a shot, and lowered the entry stakes on the poker tables also helped a lot, since more local men could now afford to go there.

Neither Lily nor Daniel could predict how the men would vote when it came down to it, and both of them did what they could to ensure success for their side.

But murder took the situation completely out of their hands.

It happened Sunday night, round about midnight. By one o'clock Monday morning, Amos Boone was in jail. By four that morning, Lily was at Samuel Walker's house.

"What the hell?" Daniel muttered, waking out of a sound sleep to the loud pounding on the front door and the calling of his name. He fumbled in the dark for matches and lit a lamp, then jerked on a pair of trousers. He went downstairs, making it to the front door just ahead of Samuel.

When he opened the door, he found Lily standing there, fist raised to knock again. "Finally!" she cried at the sight of him and lowered her hand. "I thought I'd have to set the house on fire to get you out of bed."

"Lily?" Still half asleep, he rubbed one eye with the heel of his hand, not quite able to assimilate a visit from her at this ungodly hour and wondering if perhaps he were dreaming. It was still pitch-dark, and the silence outside told him even the local roosters weren't up yet, but he knew this couldn't possibly be a dream. If he were having a dream about Lily, she sure as hell wouldn't have any clothes on. "Mite early for calling, isn't it?"

"Maybe. I don't know what time it is." She took a deep breath, glanced at Samuel standing behind him, then returned her gaze to Daniel. "One of the girls at the Shivaree Social Club was stabbed to death last night."

If her intention was to shock Daniel fully awake, she succeeded. He stared at her in astonishment, but he could tell she was stating a fact. Even in the glowing lamplight that spilled through the doorway, her face was pale and she was shaking. He grabbed her arm and pulled her inside. "Could you make some coffee?" he asked Samuel and took Lily into the parlor.

She sank onto the edge of the chintz-covered sofa, and immediately burst into tears. In Daniel's mind, it was an action so uncharacteristic of her that he was startled. To him, Lily had never seemed the type to dissolve into tears. "Tell me everything."

Lily regained control of herself with an effort and fumbled in her pocket for a handkerchief. She blotted her cheeks and dried her eyes, then glanced at him. "I'm sorry," she said. "I didn't mean to lose control like that. It's just that I saw her."

"Who?"

"Corrine Hughes. That poor girl. She had blood all over her. Her own blood." Lily's face crumpled, and he could see her tears threatening to fall again. He thought of the man who'd left her a threatening note, he thought of Alvis Purdy pawing her in the library, and suddenly, a fierce desire to protect her washed over him, and he wondered if he were going crazy. Despite the way she'd kissed him the other night, she still hated him. He figured he must be out of his mind to start getting all protective about a woman who had given him one hell of a wallop the first moment she saw him back in town. Abruptly, he got to his feet and crossed the room to the liquor cabinet.

He poured two fingers of bourbon into a tumbler and took it to her. "Here."

She refused it with a shake of her head. "I'm fine. I don't need any spirits."

"Humor me. Drink it anyway."

"I'm the secretary of the Shivaree Ladies' Temperance Society. What would people think?"

"Who's going to know?" he countered. "Besides, when did you start caring what people think?"

"Believe it or not, I always cared."

Despite her words, he did not take the glass away.

He simply continued to hold it out to her until she finally accepted it. She swallowed the bourbon in two gulps, two coughs, and a shudder.

He took the glass from her hand, watching as a hint of color came back into her cheeks.

"Feel better?"

"Yes," she gasped past the burning in her throat. "Thank you."

He set the tumbler on a nearby table, then sat down beside her. "How did this happen and how did you see her?"

"Sheriff Trusedale's wife came and got me after they arrested him."

Daniel didn't interrupt her to ask who had been arrested. He'd interviewed enough upset witnesses to know she would get to that in her own good time.

"We were headed for the jail," she went on, "and the men were taking the . . . the body to Doc Wilson. You know the doctor's place is right across the street from the jail. Anyway, they were carrying her inside for a . . . a . . ."

She paused, groping for the right word. He supplied it. "Autopsy."

"That's it. My wits are so scattered, I can't think straight." Lily paused and looked at him, her eyes wide in horror and shock. "She had a blanket wrapped around her, but you could see the blood soaking through it everywhere. Oh, my God." She caught her lower lip between her teeth to stop its trembling, lowered her head, and was silent for a moment. Then she looked up at Daniel once again. "He didn't do it. He couldn't have done such a thing."

"Who?"

"Amos."

He stared at her. "Sheriff Trusedale arrested Amos Boone?"

Lily must have sensed his surprise. "I know. I couldn't believe it either. As if Amos could kill anybody."

"True must've had a reason. What evidence does he have?"

She did not answer, and Daniel knew from her silence that there must have been plenty of evidence to warrant arresting Amos. "Tell me how this happened."

She sighed. "He was at the social club. I'm sure he went there because . . . well, because . . ."

"He wanted a woman?"

"He was curious!"

"Fine, have it your way. He was curious. Then what happened?"

"I don't know. The sheriff won't even let me see him." Her voice rose, trembling and panicky. "He's probably scared out of his wits, and True won't even let me see him. Why can't I see him?"

Daniel cupped her cheeks in his hands. His fingertips caressed her temples. "Easy," he said softly, sensing she was still on the verge of hysteria. "I'll talk to True about that. I'll see that you get visitation rights while Amos is in jail."

Her brown eyes softened with gratitude. "Thank you."

Once again, he felt that unexpected desire to protect her. His arms slid around her, but she immediately stiffened, and he reluctantly let his hands fall to his sides. Yeah, he was definitely going crazy to think Lily wanted or needed protection. He stood and took a safe step away from her. "Lily, there were probably two dozen men at Helen's. Why did the sheriff arrest Amos?"

"He was in her room. The sheriff said something about finding him in the closet. He had blood on his clothes, and they arrested him. That's all I know." She looked at Daniel expectantly. "So, now what happens?"

"They'll schedule an arraignment first. Probably in two weeks or so, when Judge Billings gets back. They'll convene a grand jury, and if they get an indictment, Amos will be tried for murder."

She shook her head. "That's not what I meant."

"What did you mean?"

"What are you going to do about this?"

"Me? Nothing."

"What do you mean, nothing? You've got to defend him."

He shook his head, dismayed. "Oh, no. I'm going back to Atlanta tomorrow. I've got matters there that require my attention."

"Like campaigning for the senate?"

"Exactly."

"Amos will be hanged."

He conceded that with a nod. "Possibly."

"But he didn't do it."

"How do you know?"

The question had her jumping to her feet. In her agitation, she began to pace. "I know Amos. Besides, he told the sheriff he didn't do it."

"Of course it's not possible he could be lying."

"He didn't do it," she said stubbornly. Pausing in

her pacing, she looked at him. "You've met Amos. Do you honestly believe he could do such a thing?"

"It doesn't matter what I believe. What matters is what a jury would believe."

"How about the truth? Or is that too straightforward for you?"

He took a deep breath. "Lily, find some other lawyer. I'm not taking this case."

"Oh, yes, you are." She jabbed a finger in his direction accusingly. "This is all your fault anyway."

"My fault?"

"If you hadn't come down here and got the injunction overturned, that horrible place would be closed, and that girl would still be alive. Don't you feel any responsibility?"

"No," he said bluntly. "I don't."

"And just when I was starting to believe you had a heart."

He started to speak, but she forestalled him. "I know, I know, you just do your job. I see. And then you leave, and you never see the consequences of what you do. You have no conscience."

There it was again. That phrase. *You just do your job.* He was coming to hate that phrase on her lips. "Besides my conscience, which you are sure I don't have, is there any reason why I should get involved in this?"

"Because Amos is innocent. Because this is your hometown. And because you are the best lawyer there is. Amos deserves the best."

He was startled by the compliment, even though the look on her face told him it was grudgingly given. "Thanks, but no thanks."

"Why not?" she countered.

Her chin lifted. She looked at him as a tigress protecting her cubs might look, and Daniel knew he had trouble on his hands. He recognized that look. He almost feared it. Because when Lily lifted her chin and looked at him with those accusing eyes, when she had a cause to fight for, Daniel's plans went awry, and his life got complicated.

"If it's money," she said, "I'll find a way to pay your fees. I don't have much money, but—"

"Money has nothing to do with it," he interrupted her. "I told you, I have other obligations."

"You mean Amos isn't important enough to warrant the attention of a big lawyer like you."

"That's not it at all."

"I think it is. If the man sitting in that jail cell was Calvin Stoddard, or some other rich, powerful man, you'd drop your other obligations quicker than a hot potato."

There was enough truth in her words that they stung. But he was damned if he'd let her see it. He stood up, facing her without expression. "I'm not going to defend Amos Boone. I'll talk to True, and see that you get to visit him while he's in jail, and I will give you a list of several excellent attorneys who, I am sure, would be quite willing to take his case."

Their gazes locked in silent combat for a full five seconds before she finally gave up. "Fine," she said and turned away. "I can see you've made up your mind. I guess I'll have to find some other lawyer."

She turned away, then paused to glance back at him over one shoulder. "But if you're going to refuse your help to someone who needs you, the least you can do is look him in the eye when you do it."

With that parting challenge, she started for the door. Daniel watched her go, and something she had said a few minutes before suddenly came back to him. "Hey, Lily, wait a second."

She paused again and turned toward him. "Yes?"

"What did you mean when you said you didn't have much money? Jason was required to pay alimony—quite a generous sum, as I remember. What do you spend it on?"

"I don't spend it at all," she answered, and Daniel suddenly got a sick feeling in his gut. "Jason sold all his assets," she went on, "packed his bags, and left. All his money left with him. Alimony agreement or not, he never paid me a dime."

She left, and this time Daniel didn't stop her. He raked a hand through his hair and leaned back against the nearest wall.

All this time, he'd thought her financially secure. All this time, he'd thought she had done just fine for herself out of the divorce.

No, he contradicted himself with brutal honesty, the truth was that he hadn't thought about her at all. *Hell.*

The sound of footsteps jerked him out of his thoughts. He opened his eyes as Samuel entered the room, a tray of cups in his hands. "Here's the coffee," he said and paused, glancing around. "Where'd she go?"

"She left." Daniel briefly outlined what Lily had told him about the murder and the reason for her visit.

"They found him in the girl's closet?" Samuel let out a low whistle. "This is a fine kettle of fish. So, you're not taking the case?"

There was no censure in Samuel's voice and no condemnation in his eyes, but Daniel felt a prick of guilt. He immediately became defensive. "I have other cases," he said.

"Mm-hmm."

"I have obligations in Atlanta."

"True."

"Amos isn't my responsibility."

"Uh-huh."

With each murmured agreement, Daniel's guilt increased. "Damn," he muttered and straightened away from the wall. He strode past Samuel out of the room.

"Where are you going?"

"I'll be back later." He yanked the front door open.

"I thought you weren't going to take the case."

"I'm not. I'm just going down there to see what's going on."

He walked in the direction of the jail, telling himself with every step that he was not going to get involved. He'd fulfill his promise to Lily and get her in to see Amos. Then, when he got back to Atlanta, he'd find another lawyer to take the boy's case. A good lawyer.

Even at half past four in the morning, news traveled fast around Shivaree, and a crowd had already gathered outside the jail when he arrived. The sheriff's deputy, Bobby Tom Thayer, kept stalwart watch at the doorway to keep the onlookers outside.

"Mornin', Daniel," he greeted. "Guess you heard?"

He nodded. "Mind if I go in?"

Bobby Tom stood aside, and Daniel walked into the sheriff's office. Lily and Rosie were there, pleading with the sheriff to let them see the boy, while True, an unlit cheroot clamped between his teeth, stood in front of the closed door that led to Shivaree's two jail cells, his feet planted and his arms folded across his chest, unmoved by their entreaties. All three glanced up as Daniel entered the room.

"Ladies." He greeted the two women with a nod, then walked over to Sheriff Trusedale. "I'm here to see Amos."

The sheriff reluctantly stood aside and Daniel walked into the back room. Through the iron bars, he could see Amos huddled on a bunk in one corner of his cell, curled up like a depressed animal in a cage. He turned to True, who had followed him. "I'd like to be alone with Amos for a few minutes."

"What?" True yanked the unlit cigar from between his lips. "I can't do that, Daniel. He's a killer."

"How do you know? Did you see him kill anybody?"

"Might as well have. He's dead bang guilty."

"Nobody's guilty until the trial's over and the verdict comes in," Daniel pointed out. "And I want some time to talk with Amos alone. I'm a lawyer, and I have the right to do that, True. You know it. I'll give a shout when I'm done."

"But what if he comes at you?"

"Through the bars?"

"He could. He could grab you by the throat. What if he kills you?"

"Then you'll know he's dead bang guilty of killing somebody, won't you?"

Reluctantly, the sheriff left the room, closing the door to the office behind him.

During Daniel's conversation with the sheriff, Amos had not lifted his head, nor had he given any other sign that he was aware of what was going on. He remained utterly still, his forehead resting on his knees, his arms curled protectively around the back of his head. Daniel crossed to the iron bars that separated him from the young man in the cell and sat down on the visitor's chair.

He waited for several minutes, but Amos did not move. Finally, he spoke. "Amos? It's Daniel Walker. You remember me, don't you? Lily asked me to come and see you. She's worried about you. So is Rosie."

There was a long silence. Then, the sound of his voice muffled by his arms, Amos spoke.

"I want to go home."

"I know, but you can't go home just now. Do you understand why?" When Amos didn't answer, he went on, "People think you killed that girl, Corrine Hughes."

The mention of the girl's name caused Amos to finally lift his head. He did not look at Daniel, but instead stared unseeingly past him as if at something in the distance. "She was always nice to me," he said.

"You knew her?" Daniel was startled.

The boy nodded slowly. "She used to walk in the woods. I seen her throwin' bread around for the birds. She liked birds. We talked sometimes. Rosie and Lily said she's one of those bad women, but they didn't know her. She wasn't bad. Least she didn't mean to be."

Daniel wasn't sure if the fact that Amos knew the girl would help or hinder the case against him, but if he were going to find Amos a lawyer, he'd better learn all he could. "Can you tell me what happened last night?"

Amos remained silent. He was obviously scared, and probably in shock, and Daniel decided perhaps the best method of approach was to guess at Amos's actions, and see what response, if any, he got from him. "Amos, I'm going to tell you what I think happened, and you can tell me where I go wrong. All right?"

As if in a trance, Amos continued to stare at the wall beyond the bars of his cell and did not reply.

"You went to the Shivaree Social Club last night. You went to visit Corrine because she was . . . your friend. You went upstairs and entered her room. Is that right?"

Amos said nothing.

"Did you see anybody in the room?" Daniel asked. "Besides Corrine, I mean? When you went up to her room, did you see anybody coming down the stairs? Did you see anybody in the hall?"

Amos remained utterly still, completely silent. At this rate, getting the truth out of him was going to be like pulling teeth, but the young man's silence only reinforced Lily's contention that he was innocent. Murderers were usually eager to talk, to tell what they knew or to establish their alibi or make you believe they hadn't done anything wrong. Daniel's instincts told him Amos hadn't killed that girl. But when it came to getting him to tell what had happened, Daniel was at a loss. "Amos, did you do it? Did you kill Corrine Hughes?"

Amos simply looked at him, the picture of acute misery, reminding Daniel of a whipped puppy, but he still did not answer, and Daniel deliberately raised his voice. "Did you kill her? Yes or no. Did you kill her?"

Amos flinched, scooting back against the wall, his arms curling protectively over his head, a gesture that Daniel knew, that he recognized and remembered. Far too well. "No," Amos whispered.

Sheriff Trusedale came running in, Lily right behind him. Staring at Amos, Daniel barely noticed them.

"I heard you shout," the sheriff said, halting beside him. "You all right?"

Daniel ignored them both. He kept his attention on Amos. "Amos, if you didn't kill her, why did you hide in the closet?" he asked, but Amos made no answer. He had withdrawn into a private world of his own, and Daniel knew he would get no more information right now. He rose from his chair and turned to the sheriff.

"Well?" True asked him. "Are you satisfied now?"

"No. I'll be satisfied when the trial's over and Amos is set free."

The sheriff's heavy eyebrows climbed halfway up his forehead. "You're not really goin' to be his lawyer, are you?"

Over True's shoulder, Daniel caught sight of Lily watching from the doorway. "His daddy was a drunk," she said, "who beat him. Amos used to hide from him in a closet."

Daniel let out his breath in a low, slow sigh, remembering his own hiding place beneath the front porch. He could hear his daddy's drunken voice, and the whistle of a razor strap.

Come outta there, you little piss–ant, or I'll really beat the shit outta you.

Daniel closed his eyes for a moment and fought against the memory, struggling for control until he could blot it out. When he opened his eyes, Lily was watching him.

He told himself he couldn't afford to let personal feelings interfere with his career. He told himself Calvin would be furious with him if he took the case. He told himself all the reasons why he could not help

Amos. But when he looked into Lily's eyes, all those reasons dissolved, because despite what she might think, he did have a conscience.

Without taking his gaze from Lily, he answered the sheriff's question. "Yes, True," he said heavily. "I'm going to be his lawyer."

✦ 9 ✦

LILY WAS STUNNED by Daniel's words. While he argued with the sheriff about allowing Amos to have visitors, she watched him, trying to figure out what had made him decide to defend the boy after all. She had seen his face when she'd mentioned Amos's daddy, and his expression had been undefinable. Pain and rage and something else, something like fear. Try as she might, she could not imagine Daniel afraid of anything, but she was sure she had not been mistaken. Whatever the reason for that expression on his face, she was grateful that he had changed his mind.

After Daniel had finally bullied True into giving her and Rosie visiting rights with Amos, he left the jail. Rosie had already left the sheriff's office to open the cafe, and Lily knew her friend would want to know as soon as possible that Amos could now have visitors. But she decided to follow Daniel instead, wanting to thank him for his change of heart.

"Forget it," he answered curtly and turned away from her, shouldering his way through the crowd of people gathered around the jail. Folks began asking him questions, but Daniel didn't answer them. He kept his gaze fixed straight ahead, oblivious to their curiosity.

Dawn was breaking as Lily followed him through the crowd. On the boarded sidewalk, she fell in step beside him. There were questions she wanted to ask, too, but when she slanted a sideways glance at him, the tight line of his mouth did not bode well for getting any answers. Lily wondered if perhaps he were angry with her for getting him involved, but she told herself that didn't really matter. He was going to help Amos, and that was what counted.

They walked in silence for several moments, until it dawned on Lily that she had no idea where they were headed. "Where are we going?" she asked.

"I don't know where you're going," he answered, "but I'm going to take a look at the scene of the crime."

"Can I go with you?"

"No."

Lily felt a keen sense of disappointment. "Why not?"

"It's not a garden party, Lily. When you came to Samuel's a couple hours ago, you were looking about ready to faint from seeing her body. Her room won't be any prettier."

"I can handle it." She put a hand on his arm and both of them halted. He turned to face her, and she said, "Daniel, I can handle it. I want to help, and two heads are better than one. I might notice something you'll miss."

"I doubt it. You'll probably be too busy vomiting in the hall."

"I won't."

He studied her face for a moment. "All right, but the girls aren't going to be real friendly toward you, so keep your mouth closed and let me ask the questions. All right?"

She nodded earnestly, and the two of them walked the quarter mile to the Shivaree Social Club.

The inside of the mansion was as opulent and decadent as Lily's one peek through Dovey's opera glasses had promised. The foyer was Italian marble, the parlor was carpeted in red and papered in gold, and the music room contained a grand piano far more elegant and expensive than Lily's own. But it was the women who drew her attention. Half a dozen of them were lined along the staircase looking down silently on the foyer where Daniel and Lily stood, and she took a long look at them.

They were beautiful women, all of them, Lily noted in some surprise. She would have expected a life of sin to have taken a toll and made them look hard, even ugly. But then, men probably wouldn't have paid as much for ugly women, she supposed, and in a place like this, Calvin Stoddard would want the best-looking women he could get. She also observed with some sadness that all of them were very young.

She turned her attention to Daniel, who was speaking with a man even larger than himself, a huge black man with a shaved head who topped Daniel by a good two inches, and who she discerned from their conversation was the butler. "So," Daniel was saying, "you're sure he didn't move from that parlor until Helen told him he could go up to Corrine's room?"

"Yes, sir," the man answered. "I'm sure."

Helen Overstreet appeared at that moment, coming past her girls down the stairs. Lily knew who she was, of course. Everyone did. The girls who worked for her never went into town, but Helen sometimes did, ordering supplies from Ezra Richmond's mercantile or taking letters to the post office. She greeted Daniel politely. Lily she did not even acknowledge.

"Helen, is there someplace we can talk?" Daniel asked her.

She nodded and led the way down a hall toward the back of the house. Daniel made a beckoning gesture to Lily, and they followed Helen to a study. The madam circled a mahogany desk and sat down behind it, gesturing that Daniel should take one of the chairs facing it. She glanced at Lily. "Is there some reason she's here?" she asked Daniel coolly.

"Lily is assisting me with some things. She stays, Helen."

The madam did not argue, though Lily could feel the woman's hostility.

Lily took the chair beside Daniel, and she remained silent while he asked the questions.

"Tell me your movements that evening," he said. "What were you doing?"

Black eyebrows lifted elegantly. "Am I a suspect?" she asked. "I thought they arrested that boy."

"They did. I'm his lawyer."

The black brows rose higher. "Does Calvin know about this?"

"Not yet."

"That explains why you're still alive," she said, her voice wry. "He'll kill you when he finds out."

"Not if my client didn't do it," Daniel answered. "Now, tell me your movements, Helen. I need to know what was going on last night."

"I was in the music room with some of our guests

when the boy arrived. That was about eleven o'clock. Mathias showed him into the parlor to wait and rang the bell to Corrine's room to let her know her next guest had arrived."

"Bell?"

"Yes. Each room is wired to its own bellpull in the foyer downstairs. The girls also have bellpulls in their rooms. That way, Mathias can tell each girl her next guest is here, and she can ring back to indicate she's ready for that guest to come up."

Daniel nodded. "Go on."

"Ten minutes went by, and I noticed the boy was just sitting there. I went upstairs to Corrine's room. Her last guest had already departed, and I told her to speed things up, since she had someone waiting. She said she was almost ready, and I went back downstairs. Five—"

"Wait," Daniel interrupted. "Did you see Corrine?"

"I spoke with her through the door."

"I see."

"Five minutes later," Helen continued, "I saw Mathias send the boy upstairs. An hour later, Mathias came into the music room and told me the boy had not come down, that Corrine's next visitor had arrived, and that she would not answer when Mathias rang the bell to her room. I went upstairs and knocked on her door, but there was no answer, so I went in. And I found her."

For the first time, Lily saw a trace of emotion cross the madam's face, a hint of shock and distaste, but no grief. "I immediately went downstairs and asked Mathias to go for the sheriff."

"It was True who found Amos in the closet, I understand?"

"Yes. He arrested him and took him to jail. They also

took the . . . body away and locked the room, taking the key. The room has been untouched since then."

Daniel nodded. "What kind of girl was Corrine Hughes?"

"Does it matter?"

"It might. Tell me about her."

Helen shrugged. "I don't become friends with these girls, Daniel. They simply work for me."

"You must have formed some kind of impression about her," he persisted.

"She was fairly typical of the women we employ. Although she did have a certain quality of innocence that made her seem naive."

Watching Daniel, Lily saw him give the madam a skeptical look. "Naive?" he repeated.

"That was part of her allure. Innocence." Helen's expression hardened into cynicism. "Some men like that illusion."

An image flashed through Lily's mind of the body she had seen wrapped in a bloody blanket, and she was repelled by the madam's cold description.

Daniel stood up, and the two women followed suit. "I think that's all for now," he said. "I'd like you to give me your statement in writing, Helen. Everything you've told me. Also, I'd like statements from your girls and Mathias on their movements."

"The sheriff already requested that information."

"Good. I'll get it from him, but I also want something else. I want to know what men were here last night. All of them."

Lily could tell the madam was not pleased by the request. "Is that necessary?"

"Very necessary. Don't make me force you and the girls to give depositions."

The madam gave him an acquiescent bow of her head. "I'll get you a list."

"Good," Daniel said. "I'd like to see Corrine's room."

"You'll have to get the key from the sheriff," she replied as she preceded them out of her office. "I no longer have access to that room."

Helen led them back to the foyer, but when they got there, Mathias informed the madam that the sheriff had returned and was now up in Corrine's room with Doc Wilson, making a trip back into town for the key unnecessary.

Helen led them up to the second floor, down a narrow hallway past a series of bedrooms to the one at the end of the hall. Beyond Corrine's room was another set of stairs. Daniel paused, staring at the stairs for a moment, then he turned to Helen. "Where do those go?" he asked.

"Down to the kitchen, up to an attic." She gestured to the doorway facing the stairway, then turned around, walked past Lily, and departed the way she had come. Daniel entered the bedroom. Lily started to follow him, but she paused in the doorway, one hand pressed to her mouth at the sight that met her eyes.

A large bed stood against the far wall, its sheets rumpled and splashed with large blotches of reddish brown. More blood stained the wood floor, and flies were gathering, their buzzing the only sound. The room had a sickeningly sweet smell, a combination of blood and cologne that Lily found overpowering, even from the doorway. She pressed a second hand to her mouth, fighting desperately not to fulfill Daniel's prediction and vomit. But she remembered the sight of the girl's body, and she stared at the bed, horrified by what had occurred in this room.

Sheriff Trusedale and Dr. Wilson were there, evidently having arrived while Lily and Daniel were in Helen's study. Both men were standing near the bed, and they glanced up as Daniel entered the bedroom.

The sheriff frowned at the sight of him. "Hell, Daniel. What are you doing here?"

"You can't kick me out, True. I've got a right to see the crime scene."

True jabbed a finger toward Lily, who was hovering in the doorway. "She doesn't."

"She'll stay out of the way." Daniel took a step backward and muttered over his shoulder to her, "Don't prove me wrong."

He glanced around the room. It was not as opulent as the downstairs, containing only a double four-poster, a nightstand, a washstand, and an armoire. There was a closed door at the opposite side of the room. "That the closet where you found Amos?"

"Yep."

"Where's the murder weapon?"

"He had it on him when I arrested him. A knife."

Daniel crossed to where the two men were standing beside the bed. He glanced at Doc Wilson. "Blade width match the wounds on the body?"

"Yes. And there are traces of blood on the blade. In my opinion, the knife Amos had in his hand is the knife with which she was stabbed."

Daniel nodded thoughtfully. "What kind of knife is it?"

"It's an ordinary kitchen knife. The handle matches some others in a drawer downstairs."

At those words, Daniel turned and gave the sheriff

his full attention. "If Amos did it, how'd he get the knife?"

"The knife could've already been in the room," True countered.

"For what? Protection? Most prostitutes keep a gun very close at hand. Corrine probably did, too." Daniel jerked open the top drawer of the nightstand and pointed out the tiny, pearl-handled pistol that lay there. He stared at it thoughtfully for a moment. "It didn't do her much good," he added and shut the drawer.

The sheriff shrugged as if the knife wasn't particularly important. "Amos could've got the knife out of the kitchen before he went upstairs."

"No." Daniel shook his head. "According to Mathias, Amos came in the front door, waited in the parlor for a while, then went straight upstairs. He also told me that he put Amos in the parlor, then rang the bell to Corrine's room. Fifteen minutes later, Helen sent Amos up to her. Mathias swears Amos sat there and didn't move for those fifteen minutes."

True rubbed a hand over his unshaven jaw. "There's a set of back stairs leading to the bedrooms from the kitchen. He must've come down those stairs and got the knife after Helen sent him up to Corrine's room."

Daniel made a sound of contempt that clearly indicated his opinion of that theory. "Right. He goes upstairs, sees Corrine, and is overcome by the desire to kill her, so he says to her, 'Hold on. I'll be right back,' then he runs down the back stairs which, of course, he knew led to the kitchen, grabs a knife out of a drawer, goes back upstairs, and kills her. Then he hides in the closet and stays there waiting for you to show up and arrest him."

Lily held her breath, realizing that Daniel was already making the arrest of Amos look ridiculous. He was already preparing Amos's case.

Sheriff Trusedale blustered a little. "Well, Daniel, Amos isn't all there, you know. And murderers are stupid. That's how they get caught."

Daniel returned his attention to the nightstand. Next to a hurricane lamp lay an open book. "A Bible," he murmured. "Open to Ezekiel." He frowned. "A prostitute with a Bible?"

"Believe it or not, lots of the girls have 'em," True told him. "I asked. Miz Overstreet said it's quite common."

The sheriff's words triggered something in Lily's mind, something she knew was important, but for the moment, she could not think what it was. She frowned at the nightstand, thinking hard, but the harder she tried, the more elusive the idea became.

Daniel also stood lost in thought for several moments, then he took another look around the room. "I think I've seen all there is to see here. Doctor, I'd like a full report on that autopsy."

"You'll get it," the doctor promised him, and Daniel walked toward the door.

He stopped at the sight of Lily's face, and he put a hand on her elbow to turn her around. "You're lookin' a bit peaked there, Lily. We'd better go."

She wanted to tell him peaked didn't even begin to describe the sick feeling in the pit of her stomach. She preceded him down the stairs, hand still over her mouth, hoping she didn't make a fool out of herself and fulfill Daniel's prediction by throwing up. As they went down to the first floor, she heard him mutter something under his breath. He said, "Whoever did this is one sick bastard," and she was in complete agreement with that assessment. The moment they got outside onto the verandah, she came to a halt. Her stomach was churning and she grabbed the nearest column for support, sucking in deep breaths of air to rid herself of the cloying smell that had permeated Corrine's room.

Daniel grabbed her elbow and dragged her over to the wrought-iron bench at one end of the verandah. "Sit down," he instructed her. "Put your head between your knees and take slow breaths."

She did as he bid her, and after a few minutes of breathing fresh air, the nauseous feeling began to subside. She lifted her head and found him kneeling in front of her. The fact that he was so close reassured her. It made her feel safe.

"I told you that you wouldn't like it," he said, but his voice was gentle, and the look he gave her was not without sympathy. "Are you all right now?"

She nodded, but it wasn't until they had walked halfway down the lane that she felt her stomach returning to normal. "Now what happens?" she asked him as they approached the edge of town.

"I'm going to try to get somebody to feed me some breakfast."

Her insides twisted again, and Lily pressed a hand to her stomach. "How can you eat after that?"

"I'm used to it. I've seen murder scenes before. You should eat, too. Believe me, you'd feel better if you did."

"I don't think I can," she said faintly. "I'm not hungry."

"I am. Maybe I can sweet-talk Rosie into making me something to eat."

"I wouldn't worry. You prove Amos didn't kill that girl, and Rosie'll let you eat at her place for the rest of your life," Lily predicted. "Probably for free."

The cafe was empty when Daniel and Lily arrived. Evidently, most folks had decided all the excitement was to be found at the jail. Rosie heard the bell over the door jangle when they walked in, and she came running out of the kitchen. "Well?" she asked Lily eagerly. "Is he going to do it?"

Lily nodded, and Daniel gave a long-suffering sigh. "Against my better judgement," he muttered. "Rosie, I'd appreciate some breakfast."

"With what you're doing for Amos," she answered, "I'd give you the moon if I could."

"Forget the moon. How about a cup of coffee, fried eggs, ham steak, biscuits, and plenty of gravy?"

"Coming right up." She glanced at her friend. "You want the same, Lil'?"

She shook her head violently at the suggestion. "No. I don't want anything to eat."

"Yes, she does," Daniel said. "She'll have some dry toast and tea. Don't argue with me," he added as she opened her mouth to protest. "Trust me. If you eat a little, you'll feel much better."

Lily didn't argue the point. While Rosie made breakfast for them, she returned her attention to the matter at hand. "What are you going to do next?"

"I'll be taking the morning train to Atlanta."

"Atlanta? Why?"

"I wasn't just making excuses when I said I had other cases," he told her. "I also have to tell Calvin Stoddard what has happened. During the train ride, I'd better figure out how to explain that I'm planning to defend a man accused of murder who, if he did it, also managed to shut down the Shivaree Social Club at the same time."

Lily nodded in agreement, but she felt no sense of triumph. "The vote is today. In light of what's happened, the men are bound to vote for closing it down."

"Exactly. And since the social club is one of Calvin's most profitable ventures, I doubt he's going to be all that happy about this."

"While you're in Atlanta, what do you want me to do?"

"Nothing."

"What do you mean, nothing?" She stared at him in dismay. "I have to do something to help Amos."

"Fine. You've got visitation rights now, so go see him in jail. Try to get him to tell you what happened, if you can. You might be able to get more information out of him than I did last night. Also, try to keep his spirits up, and see that he gets three good meals a day. Jailhouse food is usually pretty foul. And don't go jumping to his defense every chance you get."

She started to speak, but he interrupted her. "Lily, this is important. Listen to me, now. People are going to talk. You know that. Some of them will say things— unkind things—about Amos. Because he's been arrested, some people will have a preconceived idea that he's guilty. You won't help him by being his guardian angel and defending him to anybody that makes a nasty comment. All you'll succeed in doing is making them even more convinced of his guilt. I'll see to it that whatever jury is picked thinks differently by the time the trial is over. That's my job, not yours. Keep your mouth shut. Can you do that?"

Just on principle, she never liked admitting that

Daniel was right. But she knew that in this case, Amos's life could be at stake. "Yes. I can do that."

"Good."

"But, Daniel, isn't there anything I can do? You'll need help with the case." She leaned forward eagerly in her chair. "Can't I help you prepare his defense? Every lawyer has a secretary or assistant or something."

"A law clerk. And I already have one of those."

"What do law clerks do?"

"Forget it, Lily. You're staying out of it."

"But Amos is important to me. He's my friend."

"Now, that's something you can do. Tell me about Amos. How did you and Rosie become so attached to him?"

Lily thought about that for a moment, trying to find a way to explain. "Amos is nineteen years old, but in many ways, he is a child. When his daddy died, he was only fifteen. He had no one to look after him."

"No relatives?"

"He's got some cousins here in Jaspar County, but—" She broke off and met Daniel's gaze across the table. "They didn't want him. Rosie and I couldn't just stand by, so we sort of adopted him. Maybe it's because neither Rosie nor I has children of our own, and we both wanted them."

"And, like you and Rosie, Amos is an outsider."

Lily drew in her breath sharply at the shrewd guess. Daniel always seemed able to cut to the heart of any situation. That was probably why he was such a good lawyer, but sometimes it was very disconcerting. "Yes," she answered. "Rosie and I both know what it's like to be an outsider. Because of that, we are very protective of him. He's like family to me. That's why I want to help."

At that moment, Rosie brought their breakfast, and it wasn't until she had set down their plates and returned to the kitchen that Daniel spoke again. "I understand your reasons, Lily, but this is not a matter for amateurs. I'll be back from Atlanta tonight, and I'll be bringing my law clerk with me. Josiah is very good at what he does. He graduated near the top of his class from law school at Old Miss, and he is an excellent law clerk. As you said earlier, Amos deserves the best possible defense. As his lawyer, it's my job to see that he gets it."

That was an argument she could not refute. She lowered her gaze to the toast on her plate to hide her disappointment. "Doing nothing is very hard for me," she said quietly.

"Yes, I know." He reached across the table and slid his fingertips beneath her chin. He lifted her face to look into her eyes. Though his touch was gentle, his expression told her arguing with him about this would be useless.

"I want your word," he said. "Aside from talking to Amos, promise me that you won't say or do anything about this case while I'm gone."

"I promise," she said, and she meant it. But she thought of standing idly by while poor Amos sat in that jail cell, and she knew it was the hardest promise she had ever made.

Daniel left on the early train to Atlanta. While he was gone, Lily found that she had plenty to do after all. Mayor Thayer called an emergency town meeting, and Lily attended that meeting, along with all the other women of the Ladies' Temperance Society. After much debate, it was decided that the vote on the referendum of the Shivaree Social Club would proceed as scheduled.

At five o'clock, the polls were closed, and after the votes were counted, Dovey convened a meeting of the Ladies' Temperance Society to officially announce the results. As Daniel had predicted, the vote was a foregone conclusion. In reaction to the brutal murder the night before, the men resoundingly voted to close the establishment for good. Though their goal had been achieved, there was very little celebration among the ladies. It was a shocked and subdued group of women who were gathered in the library that evening. Only Rosie, who was taking turns with Lily keeping Amos company at the jail, was absent.

Talk about the events of the last few days swirled around her, but Lily paid little attention. She wondered how Daniel was doing in Atlanta. What if Calvin Stoddard forbid him to take Amos's case? Lily thought about that, but she thought about that hard, uncompromising look in his eyes yesterday, and she couldn't imagine Daniel letting anybody forbid him to do anything. He was no pushover. After all, she vividly remembered how he had slashed her to pieces during her divorce testimony five years ago. But she also remembered the feel of his arms around her and the way he could touch her, and she wondered how a man could be so tender in some ways, so ruthless in others.

"Lily," Dovey's voice broke into her thoughts. "I heard that Daniel Walker is going to defend that boy. Is it true?"

She forced away thoughts of Daniel's touch and nodded. "It's true."

The older woman shook her head, her disapproval obvious. "That's a shame. Daniel Walker is a man who could go far in the world. Too bad he's wasting his time on a murderer."

"Are you so sure Amos is a murderer, Dovey?" Lily asked before she could stop herself.

Dovey's heavy dark eyebrows rose in surprise. "Well, of course. He always was a very odd boy. Always had a look in his eyes that I didn't like." She turned to her sister. "Isn't that so, Densie? Haven't I always said that?"

Densie nodded so emphatically that Lily knew Dovey had never said any such thing. "Yes, indeed," Densie agreed. "And you have such good instincts about people. Why, Amos would be capable of anything."

Sue Ann Parker had to put in her two cents. "Well, I know he talks to himself all the time," she said. "Just the other day, I saw him mopping the kitchen floor at Rosie's, and he was chattering away, and nobody else was in there." Sue Ann cast a triumphant look around the room as if that was definite proof that Amos was a murderer.

"He came into the store yesterday afternoon," Louisa Richmond said. She leaned forward in her chair and looked at the expectant faces that turned in her direction. "He bought a packet of sen-sen."

Shocked murmurs rippled through the room. Everybody knew what that meant. Sen-sen was a breath sweetener, and a man supposedly bought it only if he had sinful things on his mind.

Lily opened her mouth to fire off a scathing reply, but she remembered what Daniel had told her, and her own promise. She bit down on her lip and turned away in frustration. She walked over to a table at one side of the room where pitchers of lemonade and plates of cookies had been laid out. She paused beside Mary Alice, who was standing at the refreshment table sipping lemonade with Annie Horsley, the local schoolteacher.

"Sen-sen," Lily muttered, rolling her eyes. "A packet of sweets, and he's a murderer. By the time they're through, somebody will have seen him walking the streets with a knife and foaming at the mouth."

"If it makes you feel any better, Lily, I don't believe for a moment that he did it," Annie spoke up. "There's no way he killed that girl."

Eliza Cole, a disgusted expression on her face, joined them. "Can you believe those cackling hens?" she said, gesturing to the circle of women at the other end of the room. "All of 'em sayin' they always knew Amos was a murderer. It is just ridiculous to think of Amos Boone killing anybody."

"Lily and Annie were just saying the very same thing," Mary Alice said and turned to Lily, giving her an understanding smile. "This must be very hard for you, dear. I know Amos was your friend."

"He still is," she answered staunchly.

"Of course." The judge's wife laid a hand on her shoulder. "If Daniel is defending him, then I'm sure you have nothing to worry about. Lyndon has told me he is a fine attorney. But if Amos didn't do it, who did? Does Daniel have any idea?"

Lily shrugged, knowing she could not discuss the case. "I never know what Daniel thinks," she said truthfully. "He is a difficult man to understand."

"Lawyers always are." Mary Alice gave her a rueful look over her glass of lemonade. "Believe me, I know. Don't even try to figure him out."

That was probably good advice. Daniel was relentless and cynical, yet he could also be devilishly charming. Ruthless, but also capable of tenderness. He could defend the innocent, but he could also defend the guilty with equal determination. He was a complex man, and she wondered if she would ever understand him. She also wondered why on earth she wanted to. That was the most bewildering thing of all.

❖ 10 ❖

THERE ARE SOME days in a man's life when he knows he'd have been better off if he'd stayed in bed. By the time evening rolled around, Daniel knew it had been one of those days. Calvin was furious at the turn of events that had shut down his club and was even more furious with Daniel for choosing to defend the man accused of doing it. The only reason Calvin had not withdrawn his support for Daniel's senate race on the spot was the fact that he had already given his support of Daniel's candidacy publicly and could not back out without some explanation to the press.

Nonetheless, Daniel had found it necessary to do some pretty slick talking. He had insisted the boy accused of the crime was innocent, but what had pacified Calvin was Daniel's declaration that he intended to find the man who had really murdered Corrine and shut down the club.

To add to Daniel's troubles, Josiah wasn't able to come back to Shivaree with him to assist with the case since Muriel's baby was due any day. And, to top it all off, a ton of work had piled up in Daniel's absence, he lost track of time, and ended up missing the evening train back to Shivaree. Forced to hire a carriage to take him back, he didn't get to Samuel's house until after midnight. He let himself into the darkened house, lit a lamp, and went straight upstairs, thinking only of a good night's sleep.

When he entered his room, he was not surprised to find Lily awake and sitting by her window with a book. In a high-necked white nightgown, with her long hair loose, any other woman would have looked demure, even sweet. But not Lily. The glow of the lamp caught the fiery lights in her hair and the shadows of her shape beneath her gown, and made a lusciously tempting picture that banished any connotation of demure and sweet. It was a mighty fine sight for a man to see just before he went to bed, even if it was through a window. Any thoughts of a good night's sleep vanished from his mind.

She's cold. Cold as ice.

Daniel was beginning to think that either Jason must have been out of his mind or had no idea how to kiss a woman. Jesus, if that kiss they had shared in her foyer the other night had gone on one second longer, he might have ended up staying for breakfast. He had ended that kiss because of some stupid idea of his legal ethics and not making love with his opponent. But now, appreciating how the sweat of a hot July night made her nightgown cling to her body, Daniel felt a jolt of pure lust rock his body, and he wanted to kick himself in the ass for being an idiot. If they were back in her foyer again, legal ethics could go hang, because Lily Morgan was about as cold as a house on fire.

"Waiting up for me?" he asked, tossing his carpetbag and portfolio on the bed. He removed his suit jacket and loosened his tie, then walked to the chair by his own window. When he sat down, he suddenly remembered how tired he was. He leaned back in his chair and closed his eyes.

He heard Lily set her book aside. "Bad day?" she asked him with sympathy.

"Hellish."

"What happened? What did Calvin Stoddard have to say?"

"Before or after he stopped cursing a blue streak?"

"After."

"He told me that if Amos is innocent and I'm determined to defend him, then I'd better find the son of a bitch who really killed one of his girls and shut down his club."

"Wouldn't you try to find the murderer anyway?"

"Only if it's necessary to my case. I'm no Pinkerton man or U.S. Marshal. I'm a lawyer. All I'm required to do is establish reasonable doubt as to my client's guilt. That might be enough to acquit Amos, but Calvin isn't going to be satisfied with that."

"I see." She was silent a moment, then she asked, "Did you bring your law clerk back with you?"

"No, I didn't."

"Why not?"

"His wife is going to have a baby any day, and Josiah doesn't want to leave her alone just now. So he's staying in Atlanta, and handling things for me there on other cases."

"So you still need a law clerk?"

The question had hope in it, and Daniel opened his eyes. He lifted his head from the back of his chair to look at her. "You can just forget it." He watched her eyes widen innocently, but he wasn't fooled for a second. "The answer is still no. You are not going to assist me with this case."

She immediately changed tactics. "You're just being stubborn. It makes perfect sense for me to help you. I'm a librarian, and I know how to do research. And, I'll have you know, I'm also quite intelligent."

"Your intelligence is not the issue. You are too emotionally involved in this case to be objective."

"And that is an accusation men always throw at women, even when it isn't true."

Daniel closed his eyes again, wondering what he had done in his life to deserve a stubborn, single-minded redhead who refused to take no for an answer. Something awful, he was sure. "Did you wait up for me just so that you could aggravate me and put a fitting end to a thoroughly horrendous day?"

"I wanted to let you know what happened while you were gone."

"They voted to close," he guessed.

"Yes."

"That must have made the Ladies' Temperance Society very happy."

"That's not a very nice thing to say," she admonished. "No one was celebrating, believe me." She paused, then added, "You were right about one thing."

"That does occasionally happen," he drawled, "but it's gratifying to hear you admit it. To what are you referring?"

"Some of them were talking as if Amos's guilt was a foregone conclusion. You should have heard some of the things they said."

"I'm more concerned with what you said, Lily."

"You would have been very proud of me," she assured him. "I about bit my tongue off to keep from speaking my mind today."

"You bite your tongue off? I wouldn't be that lucky."

He heard the rustle of paper, and he was not surprised when a rolled-up wad of it came flying through the window and landed on his chest. He chuckled and brushed it aside, but he did not open his eyes.

"This isn't funny, Daniel. Some of those women already had Amos tried, convicted, and hanged."

"Of course. That's human nature."

"Doesn't anything ever take you by surprise?"

"Very little."

"You're fortunate, then," she said with a sigh. "The more I know of the world, the more the behavior of the people in it shocks me."

"This from a woman who has a sculpture of a naked man in her foyer."

"I did that to shock everyone else," she confessed, and he suddenly understood that her outrageous behavior was a protective shell to cover her hurt at being ostracized. "But," she went on, "I'm continually amazed at the way people always think the worst about other people."

"That's because you have such high expectations."

"I do not."

"Yes, you do. You think you can change the world, and it's always a shock when you discover that the world doesn't want to be changed."

"Have you always been such a cynic?"

"Yes. Have you always been such a do-gooder?"

"Yes."

They both laughed at the fundamental difference between them. He opened his eyes, and met her gaze through the window. Their laughter faded to silence as he looked at her. "You really want to help Amos, don't you?"

"Yes."

He knew that Judge Billings would schedule a short trial date when he returned. He also knew that he wouldn't be able to get everything done by himself, especially if he had to figure out who really killed the girl. He would need help. He suspected that no matter what he did, he wouldn't be able to keep Lily out of it anyway, and maybe she could get more information than he could get by himself. Taking those things into account, he figured the best thing he could do was make sure she was under his control. "If I make you my clerk," he said, "do you think you can continue to keep your mouth closed and your temper in check?"

She straightened in her chair. "I can," she answered. "I will do whatever you think will help Amos."

"Tomorrow, I'm going to see Amos again and try to get a statement. So far, he hasn't told me much."

"He's scared of you."

"I know," Daniel said heavily. "But I need a coherent statement from him of what happened. Maybe you can help me with that."

"I went over to see him several times yesterday, and he wouldn't talk to me, either. I talked on nineteen to the dozen, and he didn't say a word."

"Lily, I've got to get a clear statement from him if I'm going to put together any kind of defense."

"I'll try. Anything else you want me to do?"

He gave her a hard stare. "If I agree to let you assist, we do things my way. You take orders from me without question, and you don't do anything I don't specifically tell you to do. Understood?"

She nodded earnestly. "Understood."

"All right then. You're my clerk. Tomorrow, I want you to come with me to question Amos."

"You won't regret this."

Daniel studied her for a long moment and did not reply. Damn, she was beautiful. With the way she could kiss, she made his thoughts turn in a dangerous direction, and he knew the decision to make her his clerk was one he was regretting already. Through half-closed eyes, he looked at her clinging nightgown and her tumbled hair, and he felt again that jolt of desire. So much for getting a good night's sleep.

The following morning, Lily went with Daniel to visit Amos at the jail. The boy was lying on the bunk with his back to the bars, and he glanced over his shoulder as they came in, but at the sight of them, he turned away once again to stare at the wall.

Lily pulled the visitor's chair close to the bars and sat down, hoping they could get him to talk. With Amos's disinterested reaction to their arrival, the prospect did not look promising.

"Amos?" she began. "We've come to visit you. Won't you at least turn around and talk to us?"

He did as she asked, but he would not meet her eyes. Instead, he kept his gaze glued to the floor.

Daniel brought another chair in from the office and sat down beside Lily. "Amos, I'm going to be your lawyer. I'm going to represent you during your trial and prove to the judge and the jury that you didn't kill Corrine. Do you know what a trial is?"

"That's where they decide if you did something bad."

"That's right. You're accused of killing Corrine, and we both know you didn't do it, but we have to make sure the jury knows it, too. Amos, you're going to have to tell me everything you remember about that night. Okay?"

Amos glanced at Lily. "I don't want to talk about it."

"I know how you feel," Daniel said. "But Amos, I have to know what happened. If I don't, people will think you killed Corrine and they'll hang you. I'm not going to let that happen, but you have to help me."

Amos resumed staring at the floor and did not reply.

Daniel studied the boy's lowered head for a long moment, then he turned to Lily. "I've got some work to do. Why don't you talk to Amos without me, and I'll meet you over at the library this afternoon." He rose to his feet. "Take good notes," he added and left the room.

Lily tried to do as Daniel had asked. For three hours, she sat there asking questions, getting information little by little. She noted down everything Amos told her, and when Daniel met her at the library late that afternoon, she had some information for him, but she wasn't sure how coherent it was.

"I was hoping he would do more talking without me there," Daniel said as he sat down at one of the tables. He retrieved a sheaf of notes from his portfolio and set the leather case on the floor beside his chair. "Was I right?"

Lily took a seat opposite him. "He didn't say all that much, but I did get some information. He said—"

"Wait," Daniel interrupted her, and glanced around the library. "Is there anyone else here?"

She shook her head. "I don't think so."

Daniel pulled out his pocket watch and checked the time. "It's after five o'clock. Why don't you make sure no one's left in the building, then lock up?"

"All right." She rose from the table, locked both the front and back doors, and walked through the building to make doubly certain they were alone. She then returned to the table and sat down next to him. "Everything's locked, and no one's here," she assured him. "I even locked the windows."

"Good."

"Do you really think someone would eavesdrop on us?"

"You never know," he answered. "I know how many busybodies there are in this town, and how they love to gossip." He leaned back in his chair and turned his head to look at her. "So, what did Amos tell you?"

"He went to the social club because Corrine invited him to come visit her."

"She offered him her services?"

"No. I don't believe that."

"Lily, open your eyes. She probably invited him there. Amos may be a bit slow, but even he would know what that means. Especially after hearing people talk about it being a bad place and how bad women work there. Don't you think he's capable of sexual feelings for a woman?"

His plain speaking caused the kiss they had shared in her foyer to flash through her mind, and Lily blushed hotly at the memory. She was suddenly aware of how close to Daniel she was sitting, close enough to feel the heat of his body. She looked away, but her body still tingled with awareness of him, and when she spoke, she could not help stumbling over her words. "Amos wouldn't . . . he didn't go there to . . . to have . . ."

"Sex?" he supplied when her voice trailed away.

She kept her gaze fixed on the notes that lay on the table, not daring to look at him. "Corrine and Amos were just friends. He told me so."

"Right." Daniel laughed low in his throat, making Lily feel even more hot and bothered.

"Can we move on with this conversation?" she asked in vexation. "Do you want to know what Amos told me or not?"

"Fine. What else did he say?"

"I spent half the day with him, and I think I finally got a story from him of what he did that night, but it's pretty meager." She pushed a piece of paper toward him on the table. "There's my notes on what Amos told me. I don't know how complete it is."

Daniel read the lines neatly penciled across half a sheet of paper. "Well, at least what he told you fits in with what Mathias and Helen told us yesterday, which is a good thing for our case. He found her there, dead, when he went into her room. He was frightened, and he doesn't remember touching her, but he must have at least touched the bedclothes, because his own clothes had blood on them. He doesn't remember picking up the knife, but when True opened the closet and found him there, he had the knife in his hand."

"That's what he told me. He must have come in

just after she was killed." Lily frowned thoughtfully. "Wouldn't Corrine's last . . . um . . . customer be the most likely person to have killed her?"

"Perhaps, but in this case, it isn't that simple. While you were with Amos, I read the statements Helen, Mathias, and the girls gave to True. Corrine's last customer before Amos was Ezra Richmond, and—"

"Ezra!" Lily straightened in her chair. "You're joking. The man must be seventy years old."

Daniel threw back his head and laughed at her appalled expression. "Well, what do you think? Seventy-year-old men are immune to the allure of young, pretty women?"

Lily sighed. "I think before this is all over, I'm going to know things about people I never could have imagined. And I don't think I like it."

"If you want to quit, tell me now." When she shook her head, Daniel continued, "I spoke with Ezra this afternoon, and he swears up and down Corrine was alive when he left. Also, Helen spoke with the girl before she sent Amos upstairs, remember?"

"One of them could be lying."

"Possibly, but Helen has no motive as far as I can tell, and Mathias swears that Ezra came back down the stairs without a trace of blood on him. There was so much blood in the room, I can't believe the killer got none of it on himself."

Daniel pushed his own notes toward her. "I copied the statements of Helen, Mathias Waller, and the girls. There's also a list of all the men there that night who the girls recognized."

She took the list and scanned it. "There aren't many."

Daniel gave her a wry smile. "No man is going to

give his name, and these women don't look up their gentlemen callers in the social register. Getting to know a man isn't necessary for what they do."

"I suppose not." She scanned the list again and let out an unladylike whistle that would have had Dovey McRae bristling with disapproval. "Now that the Shivaree Social Club is closed, Helen could make a living on blackmail. Some of the people on this list are very important men."

"Tomorrow, I want you to go see Jeff Parker over at the hotel and get a list of the men who stayed there that night. We might be able to confirm some names, since many of them came to town just for the purpose of going to the social club."

She made a face. "If their wives only knew."

"Don't fool yourself. Most of them do." He met her eyes over the list. "You did."

Lily set down the notes, returning his searching gaze head-on. "Yes. I knew. So did everybody else." She gave him a brittle smile. "But that wasn't infidelity, you know. Just a man having fun. It was so unfair."

"Life ain't fair," he said bluntly. "But I knew Jason pretty well, and if it's any consolation to you, I'd bet my last dollar none of those women at the social club meant a thing to him."

"Neither did I," she whispered. "That was what hurt."

It was a painful and bitter admission, and as the words hung in the air between them, Daniel's discerning green eyes made her feel utterly vulnerable. She shrugged, giving a tiny laugh to pretend she didn't care. "So, you see, you were right."

"Right?"

"You said Jason would rather be anywhere else than with me. And you were right."

His mouth tightened and he looked away. "Forget what I said," he muttered. "I was furious with you when I said it."

That didn't make it any less true, but Lily didn't want to talk about her failed marriage to the man who had broken it apart, especially since she could vividly remember how it felt when that man kissed her.

Lily returned her attention to the list. "Ezra Richmond," she read aloud. "Nate Jeffries, Joe Gandy. It's just as I've always suspected. Not all of these men are from out of town. Some of them are locals, men I've known for years."

"Well, quite a few of them only started going there after Helen lowered her prices, and that was because of your Ladies' Temperance Society."

Lily was skeptical. "And none them ever went down the social club before two weeks ago?"

"Well," he responded with a grin, "at least not very often."

"It's shameful, that's what it is."

"It's reality, sugarplum, and if you're going to interview potential witnesses with that prudish disapproval all over your face, you'll be of no use to me. Pretend you're playing poker, and try not to show your cards, okay?"

"Despite what has been said about me and my sinful ways, I've never played cards. But I get the idea." She schooled her features to an impassive expression. "How's this?"

He grinned. "Not bad. Remind me never to teach you how to play poker." He reached into his portfolio and pulled out yet another handful of notes. "That's Doc Wilson's autopsy report."

She took it and began to read it, but Daniel's voice stopped her. "I'll save you the trouble," he said. "Cause of death was a knife wound to the chest. There were twelve more stab wounds on the body."

Lily shook her head. "Poor girl," she murmured, and glanced down at the coroner's report. "Lord, it's an ugly world."

"Yeah," he agreed, sounding suddenly weary.

Lily gathered up the sheets of paper he had given her and began sorting through them. She could feel Daniel's gaze on her again, and she lifted her head, wishing he wouldn't look at her as if he was trying to read her mind. "Why are you looking at me like that?"

"There's something I want to ask you, and you're not going to like it. But it's necessary that I ask."

"Ask me anything you like, if it will help prove Amos didn't kill that girl. What is it?"

"I want to know how strongly the members of the Ladies' Temperance Society felt about closing the social club. Were any of them fanatical about it?"

She frowned, puzzled by the question. "Mary Alice is what I would call fanatical about temperance. Dovey is fanatical about anything as long as she gets to be in charge of it. As for the others, I don't know. Why?"

He picked up a pencil from the table and rolled it idly back and forth between his palms. "Do you think any of them would be fanatical enough to kill?"

Lily stared at him in dismay. "You don't think . . ." Her voice trailed away at the idea that was forming in her mind, an idea she knew Daniel already had. She swallowed hard, feeling slightly sick. "You don't really believe one of our members would be capable of killing Corrine Hughes just to shut down the Shivaree Social Club?"

"I don't know. It isn't likely, since a knife is usually a man's weapon. But it's possible." Those eyes became harder, like glittering green ice. "When you've been a lawyer as long as I have, you come to realize that given the right motivation, anyone is capable of just about anything. I'm wondering if any of those women had that motivation."

Lily shook her head in disbelief. "You really do think the worst of human nature. Are all lawyers like you?"

"No. Some are worse." He saw her expression and lowered his gaze, frowning at the pencil in his hands. "Being a lawyer doesn't have much to do with it, actually," he murmured. "I don't think I've ever had a very high opinion of people."

Lily propped an elbow on the table and studied him without speaking. He was unlike any man she'd ever known, able to don whatever mask he found useful. She had seen the relentless lawyer who could hammer away at her convictions and twist her words in a courtroom. She had seen the handsome Southern gentleman who could make a woman's heart flutter. She had seen the devil who could tease her, and the concerned man who made her promise to lock her doors at night. But with all that she had seen, she still did not know what sort of man he really was. Maybe he was all of those, and more.

Remembering his words of last night, she said, "If you don't believe in changing the world, why do you want to go into politics? What's the point of it?"

He lifted his head and met her gaze. "Power," he

said simply. "So, rid yourself of any notion that I'm doing it for my ideals. It's ambition, pure and simple."

She straightened in her chair, astonished. "You have no ideals? I don't believe that."

"I don't know why you should be so surprised. If I'm not mistaken, you're the one who said I don't have a conscience."

She bit her lip. "I say a lot of things, but it's usually my temper that's talking, not my head," she admitted. "I didn't really mean it."

"Didn't you?" A faint smile touched his lips, but it did not reach his eyes. "I think you did, so don't apologize. Besides, I lost my ideals before I was ten years old, Lily. It's hard to keep your ideals when your daddy's drunk, your belly's empty, and your backside's raw." He rose to his feet abruptly. "C'mon. I'll walk you home."

Lily put out the lamps and gathered the notes he had given her, then they left the library. Neither of them spoke during the short walk to her house. At her front door, she turned to him and asked the question uppermost in her mind. "If your ambition is so important, why are you risking losing Calvin Stoddard's support to defend Amos?"

Daniel turned away, and she thought he wasn't going to answer her question, but as he crossed the lawn to Samuel's house, his voice drifted back to her on the still night air. "I told you before that power is what counts. I'm not Calvin's puppet, and now he knows it."

That was a logical answer. A cold and logical answer that made perfect sense, given what she knew of him. And yet, Lily didn't believe it for a second. She remembered suddenly the sickened look on his face in the jail when she had told him about Amos's daddy, and his words in the library a few moments before. The truth came to her with startling clarity. "Or maybe you see something of Amos in yourself," she called back to him, "and you don't want him to lose his ideals the way you did."

He paused for only a second, then kept walking, but that second was long enough. Lily knew she had finally glimpsed the man beneath the masks, and her heart ached for the boy he had been, a boy who had lost his ideals to his daddy's belt and who thought power could take their place.

The following evening, Dovey called a meeting to discuss the future of the Ladies' Temperance Society. Lily did not really believe that one of its members could have committed the brutal murder of Corrine Hughes, but she could not help wondering about it as Dovey called the meeting to order. As one of the directors, she took her usual seat beside Lola Ogilvie in the row of chairs facing the members, and while Dovey droned on about keeping the Ladies' Temperance Society as a permanent organization in the community, Lily took that opportunity to study the faces of the women before her.

Sally Jones, the Baptist minister's wife. Annie Horsley, the schoolteacher. Densie Stuart, who couldn't hurt a fly. Rosie, who had the kindest heart of anyone she knew. Mariah McGill, Louisa Richmond, Sue Ann Parker, Eliza Cole . . . Lily's gaze went up and down the rows of chairs, looking at the faces of women she had known for years. Yes, they were gossips with too much time on their hands. Yes, they had been cold to her, some of them had even been cruel, but she just couldn't see any of them killing someone. It was too ridiculous to contemplate. Damn Daniel for putting his jaded ideas in her head. Corrine Hughes was killed by some man, some stranger passing through who was probably halfway to Texas by now.

"Don't you agree, Lily?"

Startled at the sound of her name, Lily blushed, realizing she hadn't paid a bit of attention to what Dovey had been saying. "Oh, yes," she said, nodding emphatically. "Absolutely. I agree with you one hundred percent, Dovey."

"Good." Dovey returned her attention to the ladies seated before her. "It seems the board has unanimously agreed to carry on for a full one-year term of office, even though our goal of closing down the Shivaree Social Club has been achieved. So now this matter needs to be brought before you, the membership, for a vote."

Lily turned her head and stared at the older woman with an ominous feeling, realizing that she had just agreed to sit on this committee with Dovey for a whole year. She could have kicked herself for not paying attention to the business at hand. The only way she would be able to get through a whole year with that woman was to cut her own tongue off. Why on earth did Dovey want to keep the Ladies' Temperance Society going anyway?

"Before we vote," Dovey was saying, "I want to tell you what I feel our goal for the coming year should be. There are two saloons in Calhoun, one in Cartersville, and five in Rome. I have also learned that those three towns have seven—ladies, can you imagine?—seven brothels amongst them. Our duty is clear. We must work with our sisters in other towns to eliminate spirits in the entire state of Georgia."

Her question answered, Lily was dismayed. All she had wanted to do was close down the whorehouse where Jason used to go. She might believe in what they were doing, but she wasn't sure she wanted to be involved in a temperance war through the whole state. How did life get so complicated?

✦11✦

Daniel, of course, was highly amused when she told him of her predicament later that night through the windows of their rooms. "Serves you right," he said, laughing. "After all, no good deed goes unpunished."

She almost threw a pillow at him. "It's all your fault," she complained, folding her arms on the windowsill. "I was so busy wondering if any of the members could be a murderer, that I had no idea what I was agreeing to. And you put that ridiculous notion in my head."

"Why is it that everything unfortunate that happens to you ends up being my fault?"

She laughed, knowing it must seem that way. "Because you are the bane of my existence."

Daniel grinned back at her, unperturbed. "There are times when I feel the same about you, sugarplum. Personally, I think you got exactly what you deserve. A whole year with Dovey."

"Remember what you said about anyone being

capable of murder, given the right motivation? I think I agree with you. A year with Dovey, and I'll have to kill her." She groaned at the thought and lowered her head onto her folded arms.

"Cheer up. It won't be murder. It'll be justifiable homicide, and I'll defend you."

"Thanks," she said, her voice muffled by the crook of her arm. She lifted her head. "I just can't see any of those women stabbing that poor girl. After the meeting, there was a lot of talk about the murder over pie and coffee, but everyone was doing exactly what you and I were doing that night. Sleeping."

"So they say."

She acknowledged the truth of that with a nod. "The Shivaree Social Club is less than a quarter mile away. Anyone could have walked over there in the middle of the night without being seen." She shook her head. "But I still can't picture any of those women committing a murder. Marching through the streets for temperance, yes, but killing? No."

"Either way, I don't think we should be talking about it through open windows where anyone can hear. Let's discuss it tomorrow."

"Some of the women are more fanatical about temperance than I realized. Dovey and Mary Alice, especially. They plan to get women in other towns committed to the cause, and they are counting on my help to do it." Her shoulders slumped dismally. "I think I really opened Pandora's Box on this one."

"You mean all you wanted to do was have your revenge on the Shivaree Social Club, and you didn't plan on devoting your life to the temperance movement?"

Damn him for always being able to discern her motives. How did he always know? "I really believe in what the group is trying to achieve. It's just that a whole year on a committee with Dovey was not something I planned on."

"Why didn't you just say no?"

"It's not that simple." She sighed and propped her chin in her hand. "You wouldn't understand."

A long silence passed, a silence which finally impelled her to speak. "I always wanted to belong, and I never felt that I did. All my life, I've felt rather out of place. I have two older sisters who have always been beautiful, graceful, and charming, and I was none of those things, I'm afraid. They married well, and both of them became leading matrons of Birmingham society. Because I was so impetuous and outspoken, and always getting into trouble, no one expected me to marry at all. When I married Jason and he brought me here, I finally had the opportunity to change all that. I finally had a place where I belonged, I developed a circle of friends, and for the first time in my life, I felt as if I were part of life rather than watching it from the outside. But it didn't last."

Telling him about it was like reliving it, but she took a deep breath and told him the rest. "When Jason accused me of adultery and divorced me, I found myself firmly planted back on the outside. Only, it was far worse than before. Except for Rosie, I lost my friends. I also lost my respectability, and I lost my family. You have no idea how that felt." Her voice wobbled, and she paused. She didn't want pity, especially from Daniel. She lifted her head. "This temperance business puts me back on common ground with these women, and if I can sustain that, I can regain at least a semblance of my respectability. At least people don't turn their backs when they see me coming. I can't quit now."

"I see."

Lily watched Daniel's features harden into the implacable lines she recognized. He leaned back in his chair, moving out of the moonlight and into the shadows of the darkened room behind him. "Did you tell me this to coax an apology out of me?"

"No. But I'll take it if you're offering."

"I'm not. I told you before, I'm sorry that you lost your respectability and your family, but I represented Jason, not you, in the divorce, and as his attorney, it was my duty to represent him to the best of my ability. I'm not going to apologize for doing my job. If you were so concerned about your reputation, perhaps you should not have had an affair with another man." He slid his chair back and stood up, then turned away from the window. "It's late," he said over his shoulder, "and we have a lot to do tomorrow if we're going to prepare a defense strategy for Amos before Judge Billings gets back."

She should have known better than to expect an apology from him, and yet, she felt foolishly disappointed that he had not given her one. She rose from her chair to go to bed, but his voice floated to her through the open window, making her pause.

"Lily?"

"Yes?"

"You were wrong when you said I wouldn't understand. I understand very well what it's like to be on the outside looking in." There was a moment of silence, then he said, "You were wrong about something else."

"What?"

"I saw you once, at a cotillion at your parents' house. I hadn't wanted to go, but Jason had dragged me along with him, even though I wasn't invited. In those days, I didn't move in the same social circle with debutantes and the sons of wealthy bankers. I was only there a few minutes, but I saw you standing in the garden waltzing in the moonlight by yourself. You were wearing some kind of silvery white dress and you reminded me of Shakespeare's Titania, like it was a scene from *Midsummer Night's Dream*. I watched you for a long time."

"You did?" Lily was torn between astonishment that he had been to one of her parents' parties and embarrassment that he had seen her dancing alone. She frowned in an effort to remember that evening, but she could not. Her parents had held many cotillions. "I was probably dancing alone because no one asked me," she said, trying to sound as if it hadn't mattered to her in the least.

"Why on earth not?"

"I told you before, I was not a very successful debutante." She tried to laugh it off, but the laugh sounded hollow even to her own ears. "The only man who ever asked me to dance was my daddy."

"Jason wouldn't dance with you?"

"He never asked me."

Daniel's next words told her he wasn't fooled by her light tone of voice. "That must have hurt."

She should have known she couldn't fool him. "Yes, it did," she admitted. "Of course, later, when I knew him better, I learned that he thought dancing made a man look silly. He never would dance with me. Not even at our wedding." She glanced at the window across from her own, but he was sitting back in the shadows, and she was unable to see his face. "But what was I wrong about?" she asked.

"You were wrong when you said you weren't beautiful. You were. You just never knew it." There was a long silence, then he said softly, "You still are."

Stunned, Lily stood there in the dark for a full minute, unable to believe what she had just heard. Daniel thought she was beautiful. It was an astonishing revelation. But all the compliments in the world could not change the fact that he still believed her to be an adulteress.

She had wasted her breath trying to convince him and everyone else of her innocence five years ago, and she was tired of trying. There was nothing she could say that would change what he believed, and never in a million years would she admit to him how much that hurt. After all, she had her pride.

By the time they met the following evening, Lily had typed all the notes Daniel had given her, and she had copied the names from the register of the Shivaree Hotel.

Daniel had also been busy. He had telegraphed Judge Billings, who was currently adjudicating a case in Calhoun. He received a reply that the judge would be returning to Shivaree on Monday, and would schedule the arraignment of Amos Boone for the following day, with the grand jury to convene the day after. If the grand jury handed down a true bill, a trial would follow.

Daniel also learned that because the public prosecutor for Jaspar County was a third cousin of Amos's on his mother's side, he would not be able to try the case for the People, and a special prosecutor would be brought in from Atlanta. That prosecutor was Hugh Masterson, who had volunteered to take the case. Daniel knew full well what Hugh's reason was for being so magnanimous. Hugh would be out for his blood after the Rossiter case, and that made him even more resolved to win an acquittal for Amos.

When working on a case, Daniel rarely interviewed a witness just once. Experience had taught him that often it was the third or fourth interview that yielded the most valuable information, sometimes because the witness had forgotten certain details or had deemed them too insignificant to mention. So Daniel met with Helen Overstreet again, and he interviewed both Sheriff Trusedale and Dr. Wilson a second time. By the time he met with Lily that evening, Daniel had sorted through all the evidence he had gleaned and had come to several conclusions about Corrine's death.

"There are three possible motives for killing the girl," he told Lily as he paced restlessly around the library, thinking out loud. "The most obvious solution is that one of the men who visited the club that night killed her. I'd better ask Helen who Corrine's regulars were."

"Regulars?"

"Most prostitutes have regular customers, who request them over and over again. If one of Corrine's regular customers wanted to see her, but she was busy with other men, he might have slipped into the kitchen for the knife, then gone up the back stairs, and killed her in a fit of rage or jealousy. Or maybe he isn't a client. Maybe he's just some twisted man who gets his fun by killing prostitutes."

He caught sight of Lily's grimace of distaste and stopped pacing. "Don't get all ladylike and delicate on me now, Lily," he said. "If I'm worrying about your sensibilities, I can't discuss the case with you."

"Sorry," she answered. "But it's so sordid."

"Murder is sordid," he answered shortly and continued to pace. "I want you to telegraph Josiah in Atlanta tomorrow and ask him to find out if there have been any similar murders of prostitutes recently, especially in Georgia."

Lily made a note to do that as Daniel went on, "Another possibility is that one of the people in town became overly zealous about temperance, and killed Corrine in the hope of getting the club shut down."

Lily was as skeptical as ever of that motive. "I think that's just too far-fetched."

"So do I, but it's possible. You'd be amazed at some of the motives I've seen in my career. People can do murder for reasons you or I would think incredibly trivial. But it is unlikely. A knife is not a woman's typical weapon, unless she is acting in self-defense."

"You said that before. Why isn't a knife a woman's weapon? Because it's too brutal?"

"No. Because it's too risky for a woman to use. It's much easier for a man, because a knife is such an intimate weapon."

"Intimate?" His choice of words puzzled her. "I don't understand."

Daniel came over to her. "Stand up. I'll show you." The moment she rose to her feet, he wrapped an arm around her waist and pulled her against him, bringing his free hand toward her as if to slip a knife between her ribs. She caught her breath in surprise at the hard contact of his body, of his thighs pressed to hers, of his forearm against the small of her back, of his fist against her ribs, of his thumb nestled just beneath her breast.

She knew he felt her heartbeat against his hand. He must, it was pounding so hard. His skin seemed to burn hers through the layers of fabric everywhere that he touched her. She completely forgot what they had been talking about, and all she wanted was for him to kiss her again.

"You see what I mean?" he murmured, his breath warm against her cheek.

His hands slid away, and he stepped back, freeing her. Turning away, he returned his attention to the subject at hand, while Lily tried desperately to gather her wits and calm her shaken senses.

"Because of that," he went on, "a knife can be taken from you during a struggle. A woman will usually use poison, or a gun with a low caliber, to commit murder. It's easier to kill with a gun, because you can stand farther away. Poison is even easier."

Lily felt the heat of his body even though he was no longer touching her, and she couldn't seem to catch her breath. She wondered how he could act as if nothing had happened. She swallowed hard, desperately trying to think of something to say. "You said you had three possible motives. What's the third? Robbery?"

Daniel shook his head. "True told me Corrine had thirty dollars in her room. She wasn't robbed. The third possibility is that she was killed for reasons we know nothing about." He looked over at Lily. "See if you can find out anything about her life. Was she married? Did she have any family? Any jealous lovers?"

"Wait," Lily implored, grabbing for paper and pencil. She began writing as fast as she could. "Slow down."

Daniel paused long enough for her to catch up, then he continued, "I think that covers motive. Let's look at opportunity." He strode over to the desk and rummaged through the notes until he found the sketch he had drawn of the ground floor of the club. It was rough and not even close to scale, but it was good enough. With the end of a pencil, he indicated the kitchen area. "Remember those back stairs leading up to the bedrooms from the kitchen? There was a trace of blood on the kitchen floor."

"That's good, isn't it? I mean, that proves the killer escaped that way. If Amos—"

"It proves nothing," Daniel interrupted, shaking his head. "It was the kitchen floor. How often do you cut your finger in the kitchen? The blood could be anyone's. It was only a few drops. Nonetheless, I think the killer probably did leave that way." He tossed his pencil on the table and raked a hand through his hair. "It's getting late. Let's quit for the night."

"Fine with me," she answered. "I'm getting hungry."

"Lord, we never did eat, did we?" He glanced at the clock on the wall. "It's after ten. Sorry I kept you so late."

"It's all right," she assured him as he gathered up the notes and statements spread across the table and put them in his portfolio. "I'll make myself something when I get home." She hesitated, then said tentatively, "If you're hungry, I'll make you something, too."

"Thank you," he answered as they left the library. "I'd appreciate that. Rosie's is closed by now, Beatrice has long since gone home to her family, and I'm not much of a hand in a kitchen."

"At this hour, neither am I," she warned. "Don't expect much more than cold chicken, cornbread, and a slice of pie."

"If your pie's anywhere near as good as that cream cake of yours, it's fine by me. I've always had a sweet tooth."

They made the short walk to her home. When they arrived, she had to dig in her pockets for her key, and Daniel was glad to note that she had taken his advice to lock her doors. They stepped inside, and Lily lit several lamps to illuminate the darkened foyer and parlor, then picked up another lamp. "The kitchen is this way," she said and started for the back of the house.

"Yes, I know. I was in and out of this house many times when I was a boy." He started to follow her, but paused beside the Victrola. "How about some music?" he suggested.

She looked at him over the lamp in her hand and smiled. "I thought you didn't like music with your supper."

Remembering the day he had walked into her house and threatened to sue her for her piano playing at suppertime, Daniel grinned back at her. "I wasn't suggesting band music. I was thinking of something a bit more traditional."

"Opera?" she suggested, and when he agreed, she

handed him the lamp, then opened the Victrola cabinet. She took one of the recordings out of the cabinet, removed it from its paper jacket, and placed it on the machine. She cranked the handle, placed the steel needle on the disc, and the sounds of a one hundred-piece orchestra filled the house.

"C'mon," she said, raising her voice to be heard above the rich tenor of Enrico Caruso as she headed toward the kitchen. "I'm hungry."

He followed her and took a seat at her kitchen table as she began putting together a meal for them. Daniel leaned back in his chair, rested his head against the wall behind him, and closed his eyes, letting the music wash over him like a warm ocean wave. Behind the music, he could hear Lily moving about the kitchen, lighting a fire in the stove, opening and closing the icebox, bringing plates and flatware to the table. When the smell of baking cornbread began to fill the kitchen, he inhaled deeply, savoring the luscious scent. He felt himself falling into a blissful lethargy.

"You're not going to fall asleep on me, are you?" she asked.

He could hear the wry amusement in her voice, and he smiled. Without opening his eyes, he shook his head. "No. It's just that I don't get to do this very often."

"Do what?"

"Listen to opera. Smell home cooking. Relax."

"If you don't have time to relax, eat good food, and listen to music, that means you work too hard."

"Perhaps. I eat out in restaurants most of the time because of my social commitments and schedule. I also have box seats at the Atlanta Opera House, for both the winter and summer seasons, but I almost never have the chance to go."

"Box seats! If I had box seats to the opera, nothing could keep me away."

Eyes still closed, he shrugged. "It's hard to go to the opera in Atlanta if you're working on a case in Chattanooga or St. Louis. I think I'll have to get one of these Victrolas. Then I can have music when I'm home, no matter what my schedule."

"You've got that big, fancy house in Atlanta, and you don't already have a phonograph?"

He opened his eyes. "How do you know what kind of house I've got?"

She turned away to open the icebox. "Jason told me when you built it. He was quite envious."

"Was he? That's rather ironic."

Lily loaded food into her arms, closed the icebox with a swing of her hip, and carried the food to the table. "Ironic?" she repeated as she unwrapped a platter of cold fried chicken. "Why?"

"When we were boys, I lived in a tin-roof shack with tar paper over the windows to keep out the rain. Jason was the banker's son, this house was one of the fanciest in town, and he always had money to spend. Back then, I envied him."

"I see." Lily crossed the kitchen, snagged a quilted potholder from a hook near the stove, and removed a pan of cornbread from the oven. She brought the cornbread to the table, set it on a wrought-iron trivet, then sat down opposite him. "What made you decide to become a lawyer?" she asked, unfolding her napkin.

"Samuel. He gave me a job sweeping floors and

running errands when I was about ten. By the time I was fifteen, I was clerking for him. My father died that year, and I moved in with Samuel until I went to the University of Alabama two years later. Clerking for him was great experience."

He laughed, shaking his head as he remembered those days. "Samuel had clients all over the state back then. Mostly, I wrote briefs on boundary disputes, served subpoenas, and bailed vagrants out of jail, but I loved it."

Lily propped an elbow on the table and rested her chin in her hand, watching him as he set a piece of fried chicken on his plate. "Why did you love it so much?" she asked.

He paused, trying to think of a way to explain. "Samuel taught me that the law was open to all, fair for all," he finally said. "It was something I could believe in, and it didn't matter that my father was a drunken Cracker and we lived in a sharecropper's shack on the south side of the tracks. I wanted to be more than my father was, and I knew that becoming a lawyer was a way out of that life."

He cut two pieces from the pan of cornbread between them, careful not to burn his fingers. "You wouldn't understand that, I suppose," he went on, dropping a steaming hunk of cornbread onto each of their plates and reaching for the butter. "You grew up in wealth and privilege."

"On the contrary," she said, reaching for a piece of chicken. "I understand more than you realize. Even a gilded cage is still a cage. I wanted to escape my life, too. That's one of the reasons I married Jason."

He set down the knife, looking at her in surprise. "You didn't love him? You just wanted escape?"

"I did love him, but I was so young. I was barely seventeen, and at that age, I'm not sure anyone knows what love really means. I thought he could take me away and change my life, make everything right. You mentioned irony before. The irony for me was that I thought I was escaping from a stifling life, and I ended up more stifled than before."

"What do you mean?"

"Jason's father lived with us until he died, and he was very demanding. He told me what to wear, what to buy, what to say, even what to think. I felt like an animal performing in the circus."

"But what about Jason?"

"Jason?" She shook her head. "Jason didn't dare contradict his father. Although when he first brought me here, he did make some effort to be a good husband. For the first year or so. But over time, he became more and more withdrawn, more and more discontented. At first, I could not understand why. It took me a long time to figure out the reason."

"Which was?"

She stared down at her plate, and he thought she wasn't going to answer his question, but after a long moment of silence, she did. "Jason simply did not love me. He married me because his father wanted him to marry me. I came from a family that would enhance the Morgans' social status. Elias Morgan was a banker, and he was rich, but he didn't have a high society background. And he wanted that status for his son. Jason went along with it, but underneath, I think he deeply resented his father for forcing him into a marriage he did not want. He didn't dare express that resentment to Elias, so he blamed me instead. It was easier."

Daniel remembered old Elias. Ruthless, overbearing, and unable to see anyone's point of view but his own, he had always managed Jason's life like a chess game. Daniel knew that what Lily said was perfectly possible. He may have been Jason's friend, but he had also known Jason's greatest weakness—taking the easy way out of difficult situations. And Lily had paid for it.

He looked at her, but she was not looking at him. She was still staring down at her plate. "Three years after we were married," she went on, "I overheard him arguing with his father. It was shortly before the old man died, and I learned that Jason had only married me because I was the girl his father had chosen for him, and that he never would have married me otherwise."

Daniel didn't know what to say. A few weeks ago he might have jumped to Jason's defense, but he was beginning to understand that Jason's side of the story wasn't the only one. "Knowing that must have hurt," he finally said.

"Hurt?" She lifted her face and looked at him then, and somehow, the pain in her eyes hurt him as well. "After his father died, it was as if Jason had been let out of prison. He let things at the bank deteriorate. He started drinking heavily, and he began gambling. He began spending more and more time at the social club. He made no effort to hide the fact that he did not love me, and he blamed me for his unhappiness. Eventually, the situation reached a point where I almost never saw him. When I did see him, it was even worse."

Daniel was startled. "What do you mean, worse?"

"When I did see him, he hardly spoke to me. If I

came into the room, he would walk out. It was as if he wanted to be anywhere else but with me. Nothing is crueler than indifference."

"That's probably true," he conceded her point. "But coldness, indifference, and blame leave little hope of reconciliation."

She seemed to read his mind. "So, our divorce was a blessing in disguise?"

"Maybe it was," he said gently.

"I lost any chance of marrying again or having children of my own. I lost my reputation, my friends, and my family." She gave a hollow laugh. "My marriage might not have been the best in the world, but I paid a high price to be blessed with the loss of it."

Her words brought back to him that sense of uneasiness and self-doubt, and he knew he didn't want to examine the part he had played in what she had suffered. He reminded himself about her affair, but that was no justification for her former husband's treatment of her, especially in light of his own adultery. Daniel felt a sudden rush of anger toward his boyhood friend.

Abruptly, she pushed back her plate and stood up. "For heaven's sake," she said and began to clear the table, "let's talk about something else."

He was quite relieved to do so, and their conversation returned to Amos's case. They resumed their discussion of the identity of the real killer as she washed the few dishes they had used.

"Doc Wilson's report said there were defensive wounds on the body," she remarked, turning from the sink to look at him. "That means there must have been a struggle, doesn't it? If there was a struggle in

Corrine's room, wouldn't someone have heard something?"

"Not necessarily. The piano music is quite loud. Also, the sounds of a fight could very easily be put down to sounds of a much different nature."

She obviously understood his meaning. "I guess . . . I guess so," she stammered, turning away as her face grew hot. She dried her hands on a towel, then crossed the kitchen and began putting the leftover food in the icebox without looking at him.

Daniel grinned at the blush in her cheeks and the way she averted her face to try to hide it. "You *are* easily shocked, aren't you?" he said, laughing. "Lily, Lily, if people only knew your secret."

She was highly suspicious of that grin on his face. "I don't know what on earth you're talking about," she said, shutting the icebox with a bit too much force. "What secret?"

He leaned back, curling his hands around the edge of the counter behind him. "You have a statue of a naked man in your foyer," he reminded her. "You play that sinful band music on your piano, you have copies of shameless books like *Candide*, *Moll Flanders*, and the *Rubaiyat of Omar Khayyam* in that library of yours, and everyone says you don't wear corsets. Practically the whole town thinks you're a wicked, sophisticated woman of the world, but in reality, you're a prude."

"I am not!"

"Really?" he countered softly and straightened away from the wall. "Then why does your body go stiff as a board if a man puts his arm around you?" He began walking toward her. "Why does your heart slam like a trip-hammer when a man touches you?"

Of course he had noticed. Damn him anyway. She could think of nothing with which to refute his contention except another denial. She lifted her chin as he came to a halt in front of her. "I am not a prude!"

"If you say so." He reached out with one hand and glided his finger down her cheek. "See?" he murmured. "You stiffen up like a baby possum when it sees a badger comin' round."

He lifted his free hand and his fingers caressed the sides of her neck as he moved his thumbs back and forth along her jaw. She hated him. She knew she should stop him. She should act outraged and indignant, kick him out of her house, anything except let him do this. But she could not seem to move. Paralyzed by the light caress of his fingers, she saw his lashes lower a fraction as he watched himself touching her with open fascination. "You may be prickly as a thistle on the outside, but inside, you're just plain scared. What is it about men that scares you so much? Fear of getting hurt again?"

Those words were close enough to the truth to provoke her into action. She ducked under his arm and walked away as she denied his words. "I'm not scared of any man. Least of all you."

"Really?" he drawled, clearly disbelieving.

She couldn't blame him. Her hands were shaking. She turned around and lifted her chin, looking him in the eye. "It's late, Walker," she said evenly. "Go home."

He lifted his hands in a gesture of capitulation. "I'm going, I'm going," he said, heading for the back door. In the doorway, he paused and looked at her over his shoulder. "Deny it all you want to, sugarplum, but it won't change a thing." He shook his head in disbelief. "Lily Morgan scared of me. I'll be damned."

With those words, he departed out the back door. Lily leaned back against the counter, drawing a deep breath of relief. She vowed that he would never find out the humiliating truth that she was scared of him because no other man, not even her own husband, had ever touched her like he did.

❖ 12 ❖

THE FOLLOWING EVENING when they met at the library to work on Amos's case, Daniel arranged for Rosie to bring them sandwiches and bottles of sarsaparilla from the cafe, and they ate their supper as they worked. Lily tried to stay focused on the matter at hand, but she found it hard to concentrate. She sat close beside Daniel as they went through witness statements, and whenever his shoulder brushed hers, all she could think about was the feel of his arm around her. Whenever he pointed to something of importance on a particular page, all she could do was stare at his hand and remember the caress of his fingertips against her skin. Depositions and evidence were the last things on her mind.

Daniel seemed to be completely unaffected by what had happened the night before, and she found that rather irritating. She felt as tense and jumpy as a cat on hot bricks, and he was treating her with the casual attention he would give a kid sister.

For six straight hours, they meticulously went over

the statements of witnesses, discussing any scrap of information that might be useful to Amos's defense.

Lily dragged a huge chalkboard up from the cellar, and they used that to outline the movements of the people who were there the night of the murder. It was not an easy task. The statements did not match, making it very difficult to get a true picture. Lily found that exasperating, but Daniel took it in stride.

"Very seldom do witnesses ever agree," he told her. "Ten people can see the same man rob a store, and they will all describe him differently. He'll be young and old, tall and short, blond and dark. It's very common."

Lily stepped back from the chalkboard to stare at the jumble of names and times that she was trying to put in order. "If we can't rely on anyone's statement, it's not possible to know what really happened."

"Sure it is. It just takes time." Daniel leaned back in his chair, also studying the names on the board. "I'd be much more concerned if all their statements matched perfectly. Then I'd smell collusion and an effort to lie. The very fact that their statements don't all dovetail neatly tells me they're essentially telling me the truth."

Lily shook her head in bewilderment, causing a tendril of hair to come loose from the twist at the back of her head. She tucked it behind her ear. "The truth? But if they contradict each other, how can they all be telling the truth?"

"Because it's the truth the way they remember it. Getting back to my example of a man robbing a store, let's say in reality that the man is about fifty years old. An eighty-year-old witness would say he was a young man. A sixteen-year-old girl would say he was terribly old. Both of them are telling the truth. It all depends on your point of view. Truth always does."

She walked around the table to sit beside him and propped an elbow on the table. She rested her chin on her hand, staring at the chalkboard and trying to think. But she had put in a full day's work already, and she and Daniel had been working for hours without a break. She was so tired that all the facts were beginning to blur in her mind, and she was finding it hard to think clearly.

She rubbed her eyes with her fingertips. "Is this getting us anywhere?" she asked. "It seems to me that all we've determined in the last two days is that we can't be sure of the motive, everyone had opportunity, and very few people can provide an alibi, except to say that they were asleep. The only people I'm sure didn't commit this murder are Amos, you, and me."

"Convince Trusedale while you're at it. It'd save us a lot of work."

Lily shook her head in disgust. "As far as he's concerned, Amos did it, and that's it. Case closed."

"Well, True isn't exactly filled with intellectual curiosity. To him, the obvious answer is always the real one, and he never digs any deeper. He's always been like that."

"Then he shouldn't be sheriff."

Daniel shrugged. "Being the sheriff of a town where a Saturday night fistfight is usually the most serious crime of the week, he doesn't need to be very open-minded. Murder isn't exactly a common occurrence around here."

She sighed. "Why do I get the feeling we've got a tough job ahead of us?"

"Cheer up. We're just getting started. We'll figure it out."

She lifted her head and looked at him through the tendrils of hair that had come loose and fallen over her eyes, too tired to even brush them back. "Are you always this confident when you're working on a case?"

"Always." He looked over at her and abruptly stood up. Gathering all the notes, he stuffed them into his portfolio. "C'mon."

"Where are we going?"

"Rosie's. I think you need some ice cream."

"Ice cream?" she repeated. "I don't want any ice cream."

"Yes, you do." Holding his portfolio in one hand, he placed the other beneath her elbow and pulled her to her feet. He turned out the two lamps on the table and led her firmly toward the door of the darkened library. "You are in desperate need of a chocolate sundae with whipped cream."

"You're only saying that because you want ice cream yourself," she said, but she couldn't help laughing. "After all, you're the one who has a sweet tooth."

"I plead guilty. Besides, Samuel has told me that ice cream at Rosie's has become an evening tradition in this town during the summertime."

"It has," she assured him. "Now that the train comes through twice a day, there's always plenty of ice, and ice cream socials have become all the rage around here. Besides, it gives everybody another place to exchange gossip."

"Speaking of gossips, lock the door behind us," he instructed. "Tomorrow, before you open up the library, lock that chalkboard in a closet."

"I will," she promised, turning the key to lock the front door. She put her key ring in her pocket, and they went over to Rosie's. The cafe was crowded, confirming what Daniel had been told. Families and courting couples filled the tables, and Daniel concluded that Shivaree's war between the sexes seemed to be over. Rosie was standing behind the counter talking to Samuel, but when she saw them come in, she immediately came over to greet them. She managed to find them a table for two near the door.

Rosie had barely set a pair of chocolate sundaes before them and walked away when the bell above the cafe door jangled, and more customers came in. Daniel, who was facing that way, glanced over Lily's shoulder toward the doorway. "Mary Alice, Dovey, and Densie just walked in," he told her. "Planning to have Italian sodas and plot how to rid Georgia of saloons and brothels, I'll bet."

The three women paused beside their table. "Evening, ladies," Daniel greeted them. "How's the war on liquor?"

"We are winning," Dovey assured him. "Despite your efforts to stop us, young man."

Daniel placed a hand on his chest, and looked as innocent as a schoolboy in the church choir. Lily quickly lowered her head to hide a smile.

"Dovey," he said, "I admire what y'all are doin', I really do, and if anyone can inspire a man to stop drinking and lead a good Christian life, it's you. But I'm a lawyer, and a man's got to make a living. Calvin Stoddard hired me to represent him." Suddenly, he grinned at her, wicked as the devil. "You should've hired me first."

She *humph*ed at that, but Lily could see by her expression Dovey really didn't bear him any ill will. "You always were a rake, Daniel Walker," she said in a tone almost indulgent enough to be motherly.

"Yes, ma'am," he agreed mildly.

Dovey turned to Lily. "We'll need to have those pamphlets typed by Tuesday. Can you do it?"

"Of course," she answered.

"Excellent. I must say, Lily, you are proving to be quite a good secretary."

"Thank you," she drawled. The slight bite behind the sweetness of her words was lost on Dovey, but behind her, Lily could see Mary Alice holding a gloved hand over her mouth to hide her smile. Densie, as usual, just looked confused. The three women walked away, and Lily returned her attention to Daniel.

"Praise from Dovey," he murmured. "That must give you some satisfaction."

"It does. But, more important, I also have the satisfaction of knowing other women in this town won't suffer the way I did."

He shook his head and took another bite of ice cream. After swallowing it, he said, "Don't fool yourself. Y'all are wasting your time."

She bristled at those words. "Really? What makes you say that?"

"If a man wants to go skirt-chasing, a lack of prostitutes in town won't stop him. This temperance stuff works the same way. If a man wants a drink, he'll find a way to have it." A far-off look came into his eyes, and he glanced past her, letting his gaze rove absently over the crowd. "I used to pour out my old man's whiskey when I was a kid," he murmured. "The only thing that came of it was a whipping for me and a daddy who got even meaner than he already was. It didn't make him stop."

He brought his gaze back to hers. "You pass a law that says it's illegal to drink, people will do it illegally. In fact, you'll only end up making things worse. You'll add to the graft and corruption already present in the police departments of the cities because bootleggers will bribe the police to look the other way, you'll lose the income from taxes on liquor, and people will drink more than they ever did when it was legal. People, I'm afraid, are like that."

"And maybe all this is just your cynical nature talking."

He shrugged. "If you want proof, look at Kansas. They passed a temperance law, but when I went there on a case a few years ago, there were places all over town where a man could get a drink. They weren't any harder to find, and several local policemen were downing shots of whiskey and pints of beer right along with the rest of them. Like I said, just because it's illegal, that doesn't mean people won't do it."

Lily thought about that for a moment. "But if you take that argument out to its logical conclusion, then nothing should be illegal. We shouldn't pass any laws and if that were the case, we wouldn't need lawyers."

He grinned at the jibe. He was really coming to enjoy these verbal duels with her. "There's a difference. The right to drink liquor was legal before, and you now want to make it illegal. You want to change the rules. That's different from laws covering murder, for example, because societies since the beginning of time have condemned murder, legally and morally. And robbery. And assault. And most other crimes.

Prostitution is like temperance. It hasn't always been illegal or morally unacceptable, but it is now, and any policeman will tell you that of all the laws in a state's penal code, prostitution and temperance laws are the most difficult to enforce."

"So, is that why you were so willing to defend a brothel? Because you believe temperance and prostitution laws are wrong?"

"No. What I believe isn't relevant. It's a matter of law. Everyone—whether he is a petty thief, the owner of a brothel, or a nineteen-year-old boy charged with murder—deserves his day in court. I make sure they get it, regardless of my personal feelings."

She shook her head. "I don't understand how you can defend someone if you know that person committed a crime. The Shivaree Social Club is a perfect example. You know—don't tell me you don't, because I shan't believe you—that place was a whorehouse, and prostitution is against the law, which you say you love so much. So, why did you take the case?"

"Because what I know doesn't matter. I am not the one who decides guilt or innocence. That is for juries to decide. It was not up to Judge Billings to close down a business just because he knows the place is a house of prostitution. No charges had been brought against Helen or her girls, no proof of illegal activity was ever brought forward, and there was no just cause to close the business."

She thought about that for a moment, then she said, "All right, I'll accept the idea that you might be able to overlook a whorehouse breaking the law. But what about something like murder? Could you really defend someone you knew was guilty of murder?"

"Lily, again, what I know is meaningless. Our

Constitution specifies that every man is entitled to his day in court, guaranteed a fair trial by a jury of his peers, and my role is to see he gets that day in court. That is how the system functions, and without it, we might as well live in a monarchy, subject to the will and whim of one person. The law has to be applied equally to everyone, or it will not work. Whether I believe him to be innocent or guilty, if I do not defend my client to the best of my ability, I am betraying everything I believe in about law and justice and democracy. That is how I can do what I do."

"That's all very well in theory," she answered, "but I couldn't do it. I couldn't put forth a convincing argument in someone's defense if I was certain in my own heart he committed the crime."

He smiled at her. "That's because you are still thinking that your own opinion is what matters. It doesn't. The only opinion that means anything is that of the twelve men in the jury box."

"So you would never refuse to defend someone even if you were convinced of that person's guilt?"

He shook his head. "I didn't say that. Every attorney has, in his heart, his own ethical line, a line that he cannot cross without jeopardizing his client's case. If I believed in someone's guilt so strongly that I was unable to defend him properly, I would refuse the case. I would also refuse if I were so emotionally involved with that person that my personal feelings would get in the way of doing my job. I have also refused cases where I felt that my client was lying to me or if I caught them lying in court. I will not suborn perjury, and I will not defend someone who lies to me."

She studied his serious face, and she believed him. He meant what he said, and that was the hard part, because that was why she didn't hate him anymore. "Jason lied to you," she said quietly, "and he bribed Henry Douglas to lie."

Daniel started to speak, but she held up one hand to stop him and continued in a choked voice, "And no, I have no proof of that bribe. But Henry, who was about to lose his farm to Jason's bank, was able to clear his debt right after my divorce, sell his farm, and leave town."

She knew from the look on his face that he did not believe her. He did not want to believe her. "Oh, Daniel, I know you have always felt some loyalty to Jason, and I know he was your friend, but face the truth about him. Jason set up my supposed affair with Henry because he knew accusing me of adultery was the only way he could obtain cause for a divorce. He wanted to be free of me, free of this town, free of the responsibility for running the bank, free of the whole life his father had made for him. To do that, he ruined me, he used you, and he lied to everyone."

"Lily—"

"I'm tired." She pushed aside the bowl of melted ice cream and stood up. "I'm going home. No, please don't bother," she added as he rose to his feet to accompany her. "I'd rather go alone, if you don't mind. I'll see you tomorrow."

Lily walked out of the cafe, relieved that Daniel did not try to follow her. She needed to think over what he had told her, knowing it did not fit with what she had always believed about him. She had always thought he had helped Jason to fabricate the evidence against her, and it had been easy for her to blame him. Now, she no longer had that resentment to sustain her, her preconceived ideas were falling away, and she knew

Daniel was not the black-hearted villain she had once thought him to be. And Lily had no idea how she felt about that.

Daniel wasn't wrong very often. When he was, he hated admitting it, even to himself. He watched Lily depart, and for the first time in five years, he considered the possibility that Jason, not Lily, was to blame for her lost reputation.

Jason lied to you.

He sat there, idly sculpting vanilla ice cream and chocolate sauce with a spoon, and thought about Jason. His boyhood comrade, his university roommate, the best friend he'd ever had. Jason had come to his defense on his first day of school in Shivaree and both of them had gotten bloody noses. They'd fallen for the same girl at fifteen, gone to the same university at eighteen, and lost their virginity at the same whore-house when they were nineteen. Jason had loaned him money out of his own trust fund for Daniel to attend university with him so they wouldn't be separated. Without Jason, he wouldn't have been able to go to college at all. He could not remember a time when he had ever caught Jason lying to him. He didn't want to believe Jason had lied to him about Lily. He didn't want to believe Jason had used him. He didn't want to believe he'd been that blind.

"Mind if I join you?"

He looked up to find Samuel standing beside him. "Not at all," he answered, gesturing to the empty chair across the table. "Have a seat."

Samuel sat down. "You're looking mighty low, Danny. Are you worried about the case?"

"Amos's case? No."

"Then what's got you so down in the mouth? You look like you just lost your last friend."

Daniel's mouth tightened and he shoved the bowl of ice cream aside. "Maybe I did, and I just never knew it."

The older man studied his downcast face for a moment before he spoke. "Is this about Jason?"

Daniel lifted his head. "How did you know?"

"Stands to reason. When you came in, you looked like you didn't have a care in the world. Lily says something and walks out, and now you're looking lower than a pregnant ant. If it's not about Amos Boone's case, then it's bound to be something about Jason."

"It is." He leaned back in his chair, staring at the cafe's tin-stamped ceiling. "When he asked me to represent him in his divorce, Jason swore to me that Lily was having an affair with Henry Douglas. I believed him, and I'm wondering now if my faith was misplaced and I made a mistake. A mistake that Lily has paid for."

"You are a lawyer. It's your job to believe your client. What makes you think you were wrong?"

He told Samuel what Lily had said.

"But Henry wasn't the only one who said they were having an affair. Many people here in town said they'd seen Lily and Henry walking in the woods alone together on numerous occasions, and that he some-times came to her house in the evenings, but only when Jason was away."

"I know. I know. It's just that—" Daniel broke off and let out his breath sharply. "It's just that maybe there's more than one side to this story. Maybe what other people saw was harmless. Maybe it was all gossip and innuendo."

"No smoke without fire," Samuel said, and Daniel couldn't help a smile. Samuel loved to talk in cliches. He had at least one for every occasion.

"You mean there wouldn't have been talk if they weren't having an affair?"

"No," Samuel answered, shaking his head. "Rumors can fly even when there's not a bit of truth in 'em. But Lily isn't a stupid woman, and she isn't naive. She must have known there was talk going on. If they weren't having an affair, why did she keep walking with Henry in those woods? Why have him over for dinner with Jason away? Why didn't she stop?"

"She always maintained that they were just friends. Can a man and a woman ever really be just friends?"

"In my experience, no."

"Mine either," Daniel said. "But after the divorce, when Jason left Shivaree and went west, he promised to let me know where he ended up. He never did. We were best friends, and he never did. I haven't gotten a single letter from him. I've often wondered why. Now, maybe I know."

"You're thinking now it's guilt?"

"Maybe. Over the years, I've wondered where he was and what he was doing. But it's as if when he left Shivaree, he put his entire past behind him. Me, Lily, everything. Couldn't guilt explain that?"

"It's possible. We can't ever really know what's in another person's heart and mind. What I'm wondering about is what's in yours. Jason's been gone five years now. Why are you fretting about it all now?"

Daniel rubbed a hand across his forehead. "I can't

help wondering if my loyalty to Jason got in the way of my judgment. I was so ready to believe him, and so ready to disbelieve her. Was I wrong?"

"You're doubting your own instincts. That's only natural." Samuel leaned forward in his chair. "Don't let that get in your way now. You've got a boy accused of murder, and you need to concentrate on that. When that's over, then you can worry about whether you were wrong about Lily."

"I may have ruined an innocent woman's reputation. How the hell do I live with that?"

Samuel did not reply, and Daniel knew his question was one that had no answer.

For the next few days, as they worked on Amos's case, Daniel and Lily spent many hours together. Daniel did not mention the subject of her former husband, and she was grateful. Talking about the past could not change it, and Lily was tired of feeling as if she had to defend herself when she had done nothing wrong. She could insist that she was innocent until hell froze over, but it wouldn't make Daniel believe her.

Alvis Purdy came back into town. The shipment of books she'd been waiting for had been delivered to him in St. Louis—by mistake, he said—but Lily was not fooled. She knew perfectly well that he'd arranged it that way on purpose, just as an excuse to see her, to get her alone, to get fresh with her. She accepted her case of books politely, and when he put his hand in a place it had no business to be, she dumped a bottle of ink over his head and sent him flying out of her library in fear of his life.

Speculation about the murder of Corrine Hughes and the part Amos might have played in that murder continued. Sunday morning, Reverend Ogilvie preached a fine sermon on the important concept of 'judge not lest ye be judged,' but standing outside the Methodist church afterward and listening to what some people were saying about Amos, Lily wondered if she was the only one who had heard it.

Dovey wasn't there to fuel the fire, since she and Densie always attended the Baptist church at the other end of town, but Lily had the feeling similar opinions were being expressed by Reverend Jones's congregation.

Sue Ann Parker and Louisa Richmond were standing close by, talking to Alvis Purdy, and their insulting comments about Amos had her seething.

"Off his rocker, that's what he is," Sue Ann declared, snapping her fan closed and waving it in the air to emphasize her point. "The fact that he killed that sister of Sodom was no surprise to me."

Alvis spoke up. "I hear he was at the Shivaree Social Club that night. They found him in her room, with the knife in his hand and blood all over him. Guilty as can be. They'll hang him for sure and for certain."

"Well, I'm glad he's locked up until then," Louisa put in. "I feel much safer without that lunatic on the streets."

Lily's temper flared. She whirled around to make a scathing comment, but before she could even open her mouth, Daniel was beside her. It was only then that she remembered her promise to him.

"C'mon," he said in a low voice, and he took her by the arm to steer her away. "I think you need to cool off. A good, long walk is definitely in order."

Lily knew he was right, and she stalked away at a rapid pace. Daniel fell in step beside her.

"You promised me you'd keep quiet," he reminded her as they strode along the dusty, rutted road out of town and out of earshot of the gossiping townsfolk.

"I know, I know," she said through clenched teeth. "But it's so hard to stand by and listen to that rubbish. Honestly, some people have minds like compost piles."

"You'll get no argument from me," he answered, following as she turned onto Harlan Road and crossed the railroad tracks. "But Lily, you can't change that."

Still fuming, she couldn't help expressing her anger to him. "Sue Ann Parker hasn't got the sense of a rabbit. She thinks her pecan pie is the best thing under the sun, so she makes it for the hotel guests every single day. Of course, everybody else in town knows it's awful and the guests never eat it, but she keeps on makin' it. Isn't that stupid?"

"Very stupid," he agreed.

"And as for Louisa . . ." She took a deep breath and started again. "That woman's always acted holier-than-thou, looking down her nose at me, acting like she's got the perfect husband, the perfect marriage, the perfect life, when you and I both know it's all a lie. We know where Ezra Richmond liked to spend his time, don't we?"

"Yes, we do."

"As for Alvis Purdy, don't even get me started on that little worm." She fired off several more interesting tidbits about the intelligence of Sue Ann and Louisa and the appalling conduct of Alvis, until her temper had cooled and she had gotten her resentment off her chest.

"Feel better?" Daniel asked when she finally fell silent.

"Yes," she admitted.

"Good. Then can we slow down and walk like civilized people?"

Realizing they were practically running down the road, she laughed and complied with his request. "Sorry. But I was mad as a hornet."

"I can tell. But there's no point in getting all riled up about things you can't change."

"Doesn't anything ever get to you, Walker?" she asked him, exasperated by his easygoing attitude.

"You," he answered and grinned at her.

Remembering the day he'd stalked into the library, threatening to pitch her over the railing of the mezzanine and blowing cigar smoke in her face, she felt herself smiling back at him. "You did look mad enough to spit nails that day in the library."

"Can you blame me? A strike, for God's sake. Of all the things in the world I thought you might do, getting the ladies to go on strike never entered my mind."

"It was pretty clever, wasn't it?" she said gleefully.

"You needn't sound so pleased with yourself," he told her. "In Atlanta, I had a helluva time convincing Calvin you weren't anything to be worried about, and when I came back, I found the whole town in chaos."

"It was only temporary. Things seem to be back to normal now. For everybody but Amos, that is. I wish—"

Daniel came to an abrupt halt, and what she wished was never voiced. Lily stopped beside him and glanced up at his face, but he was not looking at her. Instead, with his head turned away from her, he was staring utterly still as if frozen to the spot. She followed his gaze past the battered wooden fence beside the road, across the weed-choked field to a dilapidated shack about sixty yards away.

It was nestled against the foothills and woods beyond, and it wasn't much to look at. The siding was weathered to a dull gray, the jerry-built front porch sagged in the middle, and the tin roof had rusted to terra-cotta brown. The two front windows were boarded up and the whole place looked like a feast for termites. One swift kick would probably bring it tumbling down. A barn nearby looked to be in equally bad condition, and everything about the place spoke of decay, neglect, and acute poverty.

"Daniel?"

He didn't seem to hear her. Keeping his gaze fixed on the shack, he started down the lane toward it, eventually coming to a halt just shy of the rotted front porch. Lily followed him.

Placing a hand on one of the posts of the porch, he murmured, "My God, hasn't Jack Brody torn this place down yet?"

"Jack Brody went out to Oklahoma three years ago," she answered. "The bank foreclosed on him and owns all his property now. They've had the land up for sale ever since he left, but nobody's even made an offer, so far as I know."

Daniel walked up the two front steps, and the boards beneath his feet groaned in protest.

"Careful," she cautioned him. "You're liable to go right through the floor."

He crossed the porch and did not reply. The front door had long since disappeared, and he halted in the open doorway. Hands raised to rest against the jamb above his head, he stared at the interior. Lily followed, tentatively making her way across the rotted floorboards of the porch, and stopped just behind him. Ducking her head, she peeked under his arm to have a look.

Sunlight filtered into the shack's one room through the cracks between the laths of the siding. The walls had never been painted and were the same dull gray as the exterior. A rusted dry sink stood in one corner, a rope bed with a tattered mattress in the other. Rubbish littered the dirt floor, and the pungent odor of mildew permeated the shack. A huge burned-out log in the center of the room made it clear that vagrants had been through.

"You lived here, didn't you?" she said softly.

"Yeah." He let his arms fall to his sides, and in his hard profile, she saw again that fleeting look of fear and anger. "Home sweet home."

Daniel entered the shack, and she hovered behind in the doorway. In the center of the room, he paused beside the log, looking around him without saying a word. He glanced down at the floor and stiffened, then slowly bent down to pick up whatever had caught his attention. It was a clay jug of dirt-brown.

He held it in his hands, staring down at it for a long time. "Do you know how my daddy used to spend his Sunday afternoons? He sat on that porch out there, drinking rotgut moonshine and cursing out my mama for leaving him while he used his twenty-two rifle to shoot at the birds that perched on the fence at the end of the road, 'cause my mama had a pet parakeet once. So drunk he could hardly stand up, but he could still blow off a bird's tail at sixty yards."

"Your mother left him?"

He gave a humorless laugh. "Do you blame her? She went out for church one Sunday when I was about three years old, and she never came home. I barely even remember her. All I remember is hiding from my daddy every Sunday, clamping my hands over my ears to shut him out and praying to God that my mother would come back for me. But I knew, even then, she never would. When I was about fourteen, Samuel did some investigating and found out that she had died in Memphis about two years after she left here."

"I'm sorry."

"Don't be. It was a long time ago."

She tilted her head to one side, watching him. "Amos always hid in a closet," she said softly. "Where did you hide?"

He was silent so long, she thought he wasn't going to answer her question. Finally, he did. "Under the front porch. My daddy always knew I was there, but he'd leave me alone until I started cryin'. The second I did, he'd drag me out from under there, give me a few good wallops to shut me up, and pass out on that bed over there. He was really something, my old man."

Lily wrapped her arms around her ribs, watching him helplessly, wishing there was something she could say to ease his pain, but all she could do was listen.

"I was a lot luckier than Amos, though. I learned how to fight back. By my twelfth birthday, I was as big as my father. The next time he hit me, I hit him back. That was the last time he ever laid a hand on me. He died when I was fifteen, in that bed. Do you know what his last words to me were? He said, 'I'm dyin' and I'm glad of it, boy, because I'll be in hell. When your mama gets there too, I can wrap my hands around her throat and strangle her, which is what she deserves. I can go on stranglin' her forever.'"

With sudden violence, Daniel threw the jug, and it hit the dry sink with a shattering crash that made her jump. "You son of a bitch!" he shouted as the pieces of the jug fell to the floor amid the rubbish. "I hope you are in hell. May you rot there."

Lily felt sick. She pressed her hand over her mouth, anguished and silent, feeling his pain with no idea how to stop it.

He looked at her suddenly. "It's so hard to get it out, you know."

"What?" she whispered.

"The dirt. It's like a permanent stain. You can build a big, fancy house and hang your university degrees on the wall, but it doesn't change a thing. You can wear a hundred dollar suit and a silk tie, but you've still got the dirt of poor white trash underneath. And it feels like all the washin' in the world won't get you clean. I ought to know. I walked out of this place when I was seventeen years old, thinking I was finally free of that dirt, but it's been seventeen years since then, and I'm still trying to get clean."

Lily couldn't stand it any longer. She crossed the room and put her hand on his arm. "C'mon, Daniel," she murmured and began walking backward, pulling him with her toward the door. "Come out into the sunlight."

He followed her out of the house, and they began walking back the way they had come. Both of them were silent. Daniel walked beside her, lost in the past. Knowing that he would talk about it if he wanted to do so, she did not try to make conversation. They were at her front porch before he finally spoke. "You were right, you know."

In the act of unlocking her front door, she paused and turned toward him. He had not followed her onto the porch, but remained standing at the foot of the steps. "About what?" she asked.

"About why I'm handling Amos's case. Because of his daddy and the lousy life he's had, when he got into trouble, Amos didn't have anyone to help him." Daniel thrust his hands into the pockets of his trousers, looking up at her. "I thought about my daddy, and what a bastard he was, and where I'd have ended up if I hadn't had anyone to help me."

"Samuel?" she guessed.

He nodded. "Yes, Samuel. And Jason."

"Jason?" she said in surprise. "What did he do for you?"

"He was the best friend I ever had. When we were boys, his father didn't want him to be friends with me because I came from the wrong side of the tracks, but Jason actually defied his father's wishes about that. He used to sneak out at night and we'd go do things together. When he went to college, he gave me the money out of his mother's trust fund so that I could go, too. Samuel was just a struggling country lawyer whose clients paid him in hogs and chickens and jars of honey. He couldn't afford to help me get a university education or go to law school. After law school, when I started to earn a decent living, I tried to pay Jason back, but he wouldn't take the money. He just laughed and said he'd call in the debt someday if he ever needed a lawyer. One day, he did. He asked me to help him get a divorce from his wife. I know you despise me for it, but I owed more to Jason than I could ever repay. I could not refuse."

Lily did not know what to say. She looked down at the key in her hands. She wanted to tell him it didn't matter. She wanted to tell him that by helping Amos, she was the one in his debt. She wanted to tell him she didn't despise him anymore.

When she looked up to tell him all of that, he was already gone.

❖ 13 ❖

THE FOLLOWING MORNING, Lily went to the jail to visit Amos. When she arrived, Sheriff Trusedale was not in, and Bobby Tom Thayer was in charge.

"Here to see Amos?" he asked. When she nodded, he gestured to the closed door behind him that led to the jail and continued, "You'll have to wait. Reverend Ogilvie's back there now."

As if in answer to the deputy's words, the door opened and the reverend entered the office. He caught sight of Lily and crossed the room to her, shaking his head and looking discouraged. "I'm afraid I am having no luck keeping Amos's spirits up," he confessed. "I am very worried, Lily. He doesn't say a word, not a word."

"Maybe he will after a while, Reverend," she answered.

"Has he talked with you at all?"

"A little, but it's all quite a shock to him. And he's scared."

The reverend nodded. "Yes, we must have hope and

245

faith. I understand Daniel Walker is defending the boy. That is a blessing. Samuel tells me that he is quite an excellent attorney. I'm glad to see he turned out so well. There was a time when his life did not look so promising."

The image of that shack on Harlan Road flashed through her mind. "No," she murmured, remembering Daniel's rage as he had shattered his father's whiskey jug, "I suppose not."

"I had the misfortune to know Daniel's father. Not well, of course, since Jeremiah Walker was not a churchgoing man, but well enough." The reverend leaned closer to her. "Between you and me, Lily, he was the meanest son of a bitch I've ever run across."

"Reverend!" Lily choked, caught between shock and laughter at the description.

"A vulgar choice of words, I know, and I apologize for speaking them, especially to a lady."

"Don't apologize, Reverend. You are one of the few people in Shivaree who thinks I am a lady."

"That is changing, I hear."

"Perhaps. I hope so."

"I'm very glad to see it." The reverend gave her a smile of encouragement, then reverted to their former topic. "Daniel has done well for himself. I'm confident Amos is in good hands. Does he plan to have the boy testify at his trial?"

"I don't know," she answered. "If so, I hope Amos will be able to handle it." She lifted her hands in a gesture of helplessness. "I just wish so many folks in this town hadn't already convicted him. You should hear the talk."

"I already have." The reverend gave her a pat on the

shoulder. "These things are sent to try us, my dear," he said and departed.

Lily stood there for a long moment, remembering the day before and the look on Daniel's face as he had told her about his father. He and Amos had something in common—abusive fathers. What a horror their childhoods had been. Her own childhood had been awkward, difficult, and in some ways painful, but she could not even imagine suffering what Daniel and Amos had experienced as children.

"Do you want to see Amos, now, Mrs. Morgan?" Bobby Tom Thayer's voice interrupted her thoughts, and Lily turned to him.

"Yes, Bobby Tom. I do."

He jerked a thumb toward the doorway behind him. "Go right on back."

When she walked into the back room, Amos did not acknowledge her. He sat on the edge of his bunk, staring at the floor, and he would not look her in the eye. The visitor's chair was against the wall by the door, and she sat down. "Mornin', Amos."

She began her visit by telling him some of the news around town, carefully avoiding any reference to the trial or the social club. "Mr. Cole got himself another pair of those Morgans he's been wanting. And Agnes Shoup—she's the milliner, you know—got herself a new Singer sewing machine, even fancier than the last one she had."

He did not say a word, nor even lift his head. Lily tried again.

"Rosie's got a new flavor of ice cream over at the cafe. Mint chocolate chip, they call it. Doesn't that sound good? When this is all over, we'll have to go over there and give it a try."

Even ice cream, one of Amos's favorite things in life, could not seem to lift him out of the doldrums. Lily took a deep breath and said, "Amos, I thought we were friends. Don't you want to be my friend anymore?"

The young man shook his head, still refusing to look at her. Lily studied him with compassion, knowing he didn't mean it. "Why won't you talk to me? Are you angry with me? Have I done something wrong?"

Amos didn't answer. He just shook his head again.

"I think I have," Lily continued. "I think that's why you won't talk to me. I didn't know Corrine, and I didn't know she was your friend, and I said unkind things about her. I'm sorry."

A long silence passed, and Lily had just about decided to leave and try again another day, when Amos finally spoke. "She was bad," he mumbled. "All the girls who live at the social club are bad. You and Rosie said so."

Lily remembered her conversation that day in the cafe, and she wished now she could take back her own harsh judgment. "I know that's what we said, but we thought she was a bad woman because of where she lived. Maybe we were wrong. If she was your friend, she must have been very nice."

"She was nice to the birds. She used to put bread out for 'em. I helped her do it a couple of times. Sometimes, we'd sit on a log and talk. It's quiet there. Nobody to bother you. Nice place to talk, the woods."

Lily closed her eyes, remembering the long walks she and Henry used to take, the talks they'd had, and all the silly gossip that had surrounded something completely innocent. Henry had told her how much he loved his farm, and how hard times were when you didn't have money. She had confessed to him her loneliness, and how hard it was to know her husband did not love her. She had thought Henry to be her friend, and she remembered the shock of realizing her friend had betrayed her.

But Lily wasn't here to dwell on the past. She opened her eyes. "Amos, I have to ask you a question. Why did you go to the social club that night?"

He shifted uncomfortably on the bunk. Finally, he said, "She told me to come see her, and I went, even though you told me never to go there. I did a bad thing, and now she's dead."

Lily knew that in Amos's mind, cause and effect were simple and obvious. He had done a bad thing, so his friend was dead. She had to make him understand that was not so.

"Amos, listen to me." Lily leaned forward in her chair, getting as close to him as she could with bars between them. "You did nothing wrong. What happened to Corrine was not your fault. It had nothing to do with you. Somebody killed her. Somebody very bad. It didn't have anything to do with you, and you did nothing wrong. Do you understand?"

Amos did not answer, and she went on, "I've never lied to you, have I?"

"No, ma'am."

"Then believe me. What happened to Corrine was not your fault. The fact that you went there to see her had nothing to do with her death. Do you believe me?"

He didn't acknowledge her words for a long moment. Then, slowly, he nodded his head.

Lily drew a breath of relief. "Daniel is going to prove

that you didn't kill her, but you've got to help him. You've got to tell him everything you know. About Corrine being your friend, about why you went to the social club, everything. Do you understand?"

"Yes'm."

Lily rose to her feet. "I'm glad Corrine was your friend, Amos. I'm sorry I said bad things about her. I'm sorry she's dead."

"I miss her."

"I know." She reached through the bars, stretching out her arm as far as she could, holding out her hand to him. He looked at her hand for a moment, then he leaned forward on the bunk and took it.

"I would have liked to have met her," Lily said. "I wish you had told me about her before."

"I didn't think you'd understand. She was my friend."

"I understand, Amos." She entwined her fingers with his and gave his hand a reassuring squeeze. "Believe me, I understand very well."

Daniel never had trouble concentrating. He had always had the ability to focus on his work, regardless of what else was going on in his life. But tonight, as he sat with Lily in the library going over Amos's case, he found himself unable to think about anything but her.

He remembered the shock and revulsion in her face the day before when he'd told her about his daddy. He couldn't blame her for that. Anyone would be repelled by his father's Sunday hobby. Anyone but himself. He'd seen so many appalling things in his career that nothing really shocked him anymore.

He had told Lily once that very few things in life

surprised him, but when he thought about yesterday, he was surprised by his own behavior. He never talked to anyone about his daddy, not even Samuel. It was a forbidden subject as far as he was concerned, something to be pushed deep down inside and ignored, and the fact that he had told Lily about it yesterday astonished him.

He was also astonished by his explanations to her about Jason and the divorce. Never justify and never explain was a rule Daniel had adhered to all his life, but standing on Lily's front porch yesterday, he had done both, and he had no idea what had possessed him. What was it about her that caused him to break his own rules?

He remembered Samuel's words to him at the cafe, and he knew they made perfect sense. He knew he had to stay focused on Amos's case, and he could not afford to be distracted by thoughts of a woman.

He did his best to push all this emotional rigamarole aside and concentrate on the case, but several times during the evening, he caught himself studying her as she sat opposite him at a table in the library, her head bent over the statements of potential witnesses, and he found himself trying to figure her out.

She was a bewildering bundle of contradictions. She could be courageous on behalf of another and tenacious in a fight, yet she was also scared as hell of a man's touch. He remembered the way she trembled when he had touched her the other night, and he wondered how something as simple as a caress could frighten her. There was something about her, a hint of innocence that a woman who had been married should not have had, a quality of naivete that did not fit with a woman who'd had a torrid affair. Now that it was firmly planted in his mind, Daniel could not rid himself of the notion that her protestations of innocence had been true all along, that perhaps Jason had maneuvered them both for his own selfish ends.

"If I understand you correctly," she was saying, "you don't get to be present when Amos goes before the grand jury."

"No, I don't," he agreed absently, wondering if it could be proven that Jason had bribed Henry to lie about having an affair with her.

"And if they decide there's enough evidence to warrant a trial, they hand down an indictment?"

"Right," he murmured. Hell, if he were taking long walks in the woods with Lily, he wouldn't have had to lie about an affair with her. He would have had one.

"Without you there to represent him, I don't suppose Amos has a chance of being released for lack of evidence?"

"Not a chance in hell." He would have taken her to the old Souther place, on the other side of Allatoona Lake. No one ever went there. The idea of making love with Lily Morgan in the tall grass of a field on the Souther place sent desire coursing through his body.

She looked up and found him watching her. Her brows knitted in a frown. "Daniel, are you listening to me?"

As if from a long distance, her voice recalled him to the situation at hand. "Of course I'm listening. We'll end up going to trial."

His words did not seem to satisfy her. She still regarded him skeptically across the table. "You seem quite distracted tonight. Are you worried about the case?"

"No. I'm fine," he answered. God, she was beautiful. He remembered the exquisite shape of her silhouette beneath her nightgown, and the sweet taste of her mouth, and he wondered how Jason could have left her alone at night and gone off to Helen's.

Did she have an affair with Henry Douglas? A few weeks ago, Daniel had been sure of the answer to that question, sure beyond any reasonable doubt, but now he wasn't sure at all.

"Daniel? Why on earth are you looking at me like that?"

"Like what?"

A delicate flush came into her cheeks, even though she couldn't possibly know for certain the thoughts going through his mind. "Like that. Fierce. Predatory. Like a wolf at the door. I can't explain it."

He couldn't explain it either. He drew a deep breath and forced himself back to the matter at hand. "I'm just tired. Let's talk about Amos. We've got to prepare him to testify."

"Prepare him? How?"

"We've got to make sure his story sounds credible," Daniel answered. He could smell her perfume, the delicate scent of lily blossoms, making it hard for him to concentrate. He stood up abruptly and began to move around the room, putting some distance between them and talking about the case to force away distracting thoughts of her. "Juries are odd. You never know what idea they'll get in their heads, but once the idea is there, you'll never get it out again."

Lily made a sound of frustration and tossed down her pencil. "Then there's no hope. The jury will be locals, and most folks around here are already convinced he did it."

"That's true, but until his arrest, nobody would've thought Amos capable of hurting a fly. The talk that's going around now is only natural, but when those twelve men get in the jury box, I want them to revert to their original opinion of him. But Amos has to help me. He has to tell his story on the stand. How can I do that if he won't talk to me?"

"When I spoke with him today, he promised me he would help you in any way he could."

"Good. I was beginning to think I had a client who wants to be hanged."

"He thought he was to blame for Corrine's death. Amos's daddy was always telling him he was to blame for anything bad that happened to anybody. It's quite understandable that he would blame himself, even though he did not kill her."

"I understand that, but he has to get over it. If the jury sees any hint of guilt on his face, they'll convict him. That's why his testimony is so important."

"Doesn't he just get on the stand and tell the truth?"

"Yes, but a trial isn't just about telling the truth. It's also about the way you tell it. When Amos tells his story, I want the jury to think there's no way he killed that girl." He turned to her. "I want character witnesses, too. Any suggestions?"

"Rosie. She's known Amos since he was born. Jacob Cole would be good, since Amos worked for him mucking out stables when he was fifteen. Oh, and Annie Horsley, the schoolteacher. He never went to school, but he worked for her, too, doing odd jobs. I'd be happy to testify, too, if you think it would help."

He looked her over, remembering the day five years ago when he had cross-examined her during the divorce proceedings, how guilty she had seemed during her testimony, how easy it had been to manipulate her. It had been one of the most successful cross-examinations of his career, but one that he wasn't very proud of. Especially now, when he doubted her guilt, doubted his best friend's word, and doubted his own instincts.

"Do you want me to testify?" she asked, breaking into his thoughts.

"I don't know if it would be worth it. I've seen you testify before, and I know how flustered you can get. Hugh Masterson might easily discredit you on the stand."

"Thanks for the vote of confidence," she answered wryly. "Who is Hugh Masterson?"

"He's an Atlanta prosecutor. Jaspar County's prosecutor is related to Amos, so he asked to be excused from handling the case, and Judge Billings requested a prosecutor from Atlanta. Hugh is that prosecutor."

"And he's good?"

There was no sense in sugarcoating the truth. "Very good."

"If this man could discredit me on the witness stand, what will he do to Amos?"

"That's exactly what I'm worried about. Hugh will try to get him to contradict himself, make it look as if he's lying. I have to be sure Amos is prepared for that and can handle it."

Lily rose to her feet and walked over to the chalkboard, which was propped up against the typewriting machine on her desk. She took a piece of chalk in her hand and began to write.

Daniel leaned against the bookcase and folded his arms, watching as Lily outlined Amos's story on the chalkboard, from the beginning of his relationship with Corrine until his arrest. "There," she said and tossed the chalk on her desk, "that's basically what Amos has to tell them. It's up to you to help him tell it convincingly."

Daniel crossed the room to stand beside her. "Will he be able to do that?"

"I just don't know." Lily faced him, rubbing her palms together to remove the chalk dust from her hands. "Maybe we're fretting about nothing. He might do just fine."

"Maybe, but Amos does not understand the process or the consequences of his testimony. He knows what a trial is, and what a jury does, but the deeper implications are lost on him, and he can't help me put the best face on his testimony for the jury. I'm especially concerned about how he'll handle facing Hugh. If he's scared of me, God knows how he'll react when Hugh starts badgering him."

Daniel scanned the chalkboard. "I have to anticipate every question Hugh's going to ask him and make certain he has convincing answers for those questions. How can I do that if he won't tell me what happened?"

"He's told me the essential facts."

"I know, but he hasn't told me. Besides, I get the feeling Amos is not telling me the whole truth. He's holding something back." He pointed to what Lily had written on the board. "For example, he told you he went to the social club because Corrine invited him to visit her."

"I believe him."

"I know from Helen that he paid a dollar for the privilege. On what Amos earns here at the library, one dollar is a lot of money, and he could have talked with Corrine any time in the woods for free. Why pay money to visit her at the club?"

"Wouldn't Helen expect him to pay?"

"Yes, but if he has to pay, why see Corrine there at all? There's only one reason that makes sense."

"It makes sense to you, but not to me, and I know Amos better than you do. You think he went there for . . . for . . ." She paused, groping for the right words, an expression of acute embarrassment on her face.

"For carnal pleasure," he supplied. "There's nothing wrong with it, you know. Most men have been initiated into sex that way. Including me," he added, watching in amusement as the blush in her cheeks deepened. Lily had a reputation for adultery and shameless behavior, but at this moment, she wasn't living up to it. She looked as if carnal pleasure was completely out of her experience, but Daniel knew that was not true. Just thinking about the kiss they had shared in her foyer was enough to drive him crazy, because it had been a taste, and when a man wanted the whole meal, a taste wasn't enough.

"That's not why Amos went there," she insisted, breaking into his thoughts. "I don't think he had any ideas of that sort. Corrine was his friend, nothing more."

"Right." He turned to face her. "You really believe he used to meet her in the woods, the two of them were completely alone, and he never thought about anything more."

"That's right. Why is that so hard for you to believe?"

"Because I'm a man, and I know how men think."

"Amos is a boy!"

"He's nineteen. And simpleminded or not, he's enough of a man to think about things besides talking when he's with a pretty girl." Daniel leaned closer to her, dangerously close, and caught the scent of lilies. "What about you and Henry?" he asked softly. "I suppose the two of you just talked during your long walks in the woods?"

Her chin lifted and she looked him in the eye. "Yes." Something of his skepticism must have shown on his face. "You still don't believe me."

He lowered his gaze to her mouth. No, a taste just wasn't enough. "Does it matter what I believe?"

"No, it doesn't matter in the least."

"I'll tell you anyway," he replied and lowered his head until his lips were an inch from hers. "I believe that if talking was all that went on between you, Henry Douglas was not only a liar, he was a fool."

Wrapping an arm around her, he pulled her hard against him, and his mouth came down on hers, capturing her lips in a kiss he told himself was merely to satisfy his curiosity. But her lips beneath his were clamped together, her body was stiff as a ramrod, and he knew she'd been expecting him to do this. The first time he'd kissed her, he'd caught her off guard, but this time, she was prepared for the possibility, and she was wrapped in her own defenses. Her reaction was a challenge that Daniel could not let pass by, and his curiosity was no longer the only thing he wanted to satisfy. He immediately gentled the kiss, running his tongue back and forth over her closed lips in a slow caress designed to coax, to persuade, to make her yield to him.

When he felt her body soften in his arms, he released her and brought his hands up to touch the velvety skin of her cheeks as he kissed her. Free now, she could have pulled away, but she did not move. He felt her lips tremble, then her mouth opened with a wordless sound of surprise.

Given what he had been waiting for, Daniel deepened the kiss. His tongue entered her mouth, his hands slid back into her hair. Pins hit the floor with tiny clinking sounds as her hair came down, soft and silky in his fingers. He wrapped the thick strands in his fists as he tasted deeply of her mouth. But it was not enough. He wanted more.

He wrapped an arm around her waist and brought her closer, as his other hand tightened in her hair. He broke the kiss and tilted her head back to slide his lips down the warm, sweet skin of her throat and back again. He caught her earlobe in his mouth, gently grazing the velvety softness with his teeth, and when she moaned, he reveled in the sound. But it was not enough. He wanted more.

Something inside Daniel told him he should stop now, before the desire raging through him like a prairie fire flared out of control. But he could feel every soft curve of her body where she was pressed against him, and he did not stop. *Not yet,* he told himself. *Soon, but not yet.*

His hand left her hair and slid downward between them until his palm covered her breast, embracing the full shape of it. Even through the layers of fabric that she wore, he could feel her nipple harden, and he smiled against her ear as he slid his thumb against her breast in a slow, coaxing rotation that made her breath quicken to soft little gasps. But it was not enough. He wanted more.

Her hips shifted against him, and he shuddered as a jolt of pure pleasure shot through his body. He pressed kisses to her ear, her cheek, her temple, then he pulled back and opened his eyes, wanting to see her face as he caressed her. But before he could enjoy that view, another caught his attention. Over the top of her head, he could see the windows that flanked the back wall of the library, windows where no curtains had been drawn. The lamps in the room were blazing, and there was nothing to hide them from the view of anyone who happened to be passing by. Sanity returned like a splash of icy water, and he wrenched back, breathing hard. He let her go and stepped away, hoping no one had seen them, hoping what he had just done had not further damaged her reputation. He looked at her, wondering if she had come to the same realization he had, but it appeared she had not.

Her hair, the color of burnished copper in the soft lamplight, fell loose around her shoulders in tempting disarray. She was staring at him, her dark eyes wide and startled. Her fingers were pressed to her mouth and they were trembling. Her breathing was rapid, shallow, in perfect time with his own. Daniel knew he finally had the truth, because her reaction told him no other man had ever kissed her this way, not even Jason. Her torrid affair with Henry had been fabricated in Jason's imagination.

"Henry really did lie about having an affair with you," he muttered, watching her eyes. "Jason did bribe him."

She did not reply. She didn't have to. Confirmation was in the way she kissed—like a woman who'd never been made love to properly in her life, by her husband or any other man.

"It seems I'm the one who's been a fool." He turned away without another word and walked out of the library. He was furious with Jason for what he had done to Lily, dismayed at how his best friend had used him, and ashamed of the part he had played in ruining her reputation.

He'd been wrong about a lot of things, but there was one thing about which he was absolutely right. His body ached like hell with frustrated desire, and he'd been right that a taste of Lily Morgan just wasn't enough.

❖14❖

LILY COULD NOT sleep. She lay in bed, her thoughts filled only with him. She could feel the heat of his mouth everywhere he had kissed her, her body tingled everywhere he had touched her, and sleep was the last thing on her mind. Until Daniel, she'd had no idea that kisses could make you burn, make you dizzy, make you breathless. How strange it was that Daniel, who had been her enemy and a man she had once hated, could make her feel that way.

Her own husband had never kissed her like that, bold and lush, caressing her tongue with his own, making her quiver inside. She shivered at the memory, and she did not know whether to be delighted or ashamed.

Lily rolled onto her side. Moonlight spilled down between her house and the house next door, and she stared through her open window to the one beyond. She wondered if Daniel was asleep. She imagined him lying there, the sheet flung back, moonlight sculpting shadows from the muscles of his bare chest. Her throat went dry.

Unable to banish the restlessness inside her, Lily pushed aside the sheet and got out of bed. She went downstairs in the dark, lit a lamp in the kitchen, and made herself a cup of tea. It did not help.

Lamp in hand, she wandered through the house, aimlessly going from room to room. In the parlor, she ran her fingers lightly over the keys of the piano, remembering how her father had paid for the instrument to be shipped from Birmingham because Jason had refused to do so. She fingered the pieces of the chess set, remembering how Jason would not play with her because the first time they had played, she had made the mistake of winning. She opened the hall closet and studied the crates stacked inside, crates filled with wedding presents from her family—the china, the crystal, the silver. All were meaningless now, useless now.

By the end of her first year of marriage, she and Jason had been two strangers sharing the same house, and that was all. Married for five years, but never, in all that time, had Jason kissed her in the way Daniel had done this evening. In fact, until tonight she'd had no idea anyone kissed like that, that a man's touch could light you on fire.

She remembered her return to Birmingham two years after her wedding to visit her family and the conversation she'd had with her sisters about marriage. When she had tentatively broached the subject, confessing how empty and unfulfilled her marriage was, both Hannah and Beth had looked at her in bewilderment. When she had confessed Jason's infidelity with prostitutes, they had taken the news with total complacency. "Well, of course," Hannah had said. "All men do that. The sooner you accept that, the easier things will be."

Beth had advised her to have a baby, as if becoming pregnant were something she could control. Hannah had told her to find "good works" to occupy her empty hours. Both of them had accepted long before that love played little part in matrimony. Neither of them had understood her acute loneliness. They, at least, had Mama, Daddy, and each other for distraction, while Lily, hundreds of miles away and without the support of her family, had only the library and sewing parties to ease her anguish.

Lily went upstairs to the bedroom she and Jason had shared, a room she never entered anymore, a room where dust covered the furniture and memories lay sleeping. She held the lamp high and stared at the mahogany four-poster, remembering the brief, furtive couplings that had always left her oddly empty and strangely disappointed, remembering Jason's coldness afterward that had left her bewildered and unable to understand what she'd done wrong, remembering the nights she had spent alone, waiting for him to come home and wondering why he preferred the prostitutes at the Shivaree Social Club to his own wife, a wife who had truly wanted to make him happy.

Lily thought again of Daniel and the incredible way his kiss had made her feel. She could not help but wonder why a man she had once despised could evoke more passion in her with a kiss than her own husband had ever been able to do, even in the intimacy of the marriage bed.

* * *

Though Daniel did not know it, one person had seen him kissing Lily Morgan through the back windows of the library, and the very next morning, the first thing that person did was tell her best friend all about it.

"Have you lost your mind?" Rosie stared at Lily, shaking her head in amazement. "I saw you kissing Daniel, plain as day. Don't you deny it. Daniel Walker, of all people. I thought you hated him."

"I do," Lily answered automatically, but her friend's raised brows told her how unbelievable that was. "At least, I did," she amended. "I mean . . . I mean . . . oh, I don't know what I mean." She groaned and leaned forward at her kitchen table, burying her face in her folded arms even though it was too late to hide the flagrant truth.

Rosie took a swallow of the coffee Lily had poured for her, and went on, "All the shades up, lamps blazing. It's a good thing those windows face Cole's livery and not the street, otherwise anyone could have seen you. You're lucky it was only me and Jacob's horses."

Lily was mortified. The fact that someone, even Rosie, had seen her kissing Daniel was humiliating. She recalled all the times she had said how much she hated him, and she felt like a hypocrite. Worse, she felt as if she were what many had accused her of being: shameless.

"By the way, how was he?"

Lily lifted her head. "What?"

Rosie was watching her and smiling. "How was he at kissing?"

"Rosie!"

Her friend laughed. "You needn't look at me as if I'd just asked you how it felt to rob a bank. After all you went through with Jason, you could use a little romance. There's nothing wrong with kissing. You just ought to be more discreet about it."

"I won't have to. It isn't going to happen again."

"If you say so."

"I do say so. I've put too much effort into rebuilding my reputation to watch it be shredded again." Lily straightened in her chair and took a sip of her coffee. "I still can't believe it happened at all."

"Neither can I. All I wanted was an evening stroll. You could've knocked me over with a feather when I turned that corner and saw the pair of you through the window. People have been talking, of course, but—"

"What have they been saying?" Lily demanded, interrupting her friend.

"Well, it did raise a few eyebrows when the two of you came into the cafe together the other evening for ice cream. And you have been spending a lot of time together, at night, in the library. Everybody knows you're helping him with the case because of Amos, and of course, everybody knows how you've always felt about him, so most folks don't think anything shady is going on." A mischievous smile tipped the corners of her mouth. "Although I'd bet they wish there was, so they could talk about it. If only they knew what I know."

"Nothing is going on." That sounded ludicrous, given what Rosie had seen. Lily felt herself blushing again, and cursed the fair complexion she possessed that betrayed her embarrassment so easily. "What I mean is, what you saw just sort of happened, and it isn't going to happen again, and I'm upset enough as it is, so let's change the subject."

"All right, but I have one last thing to say first. Be

careful. If it does happen again—" She raised a hand to ward off the renewed protest Lily was about to make. "If it does happen again, make sure you turn the lamps off first. And have Daniel go out through the front door as if he's leaving, then come back around the back way. That's what I always do when Samuel comes over to the cafe after closing time."

"Samuel?" Lily was stunned and it took a moment for her friend's words to sink in. "You are having a love affair with Samuel? You're pulling my leg."

"You needn't look so shocked," she said, laughing. "Samuel is a wonderful man, even if he is twenty years older than I."

"It isn't the age difference between you that shocks me. It's the fact that you are my best friend, and I had no idea of such a thing."

"We're very careful about it. I'm still a married woman, after all." Rosie paused a moment, then she said, "I sometimes think about trying to find Billy. I could get a divorce on grounds of desertion, but Samuel knows what divorce did to you, and he refuses to put me through that. So, our affair is a secret."

"Why didn't you tell me?"

Rosie shrugged. "I guess because of the way you felt about Daniel and all. Samuel has always been Daniel's mentor, you know, and almost like a second father to him. I didn't think you'd understand."

"Oh, Rosie. Of course I understand. I'm the last person in the world who could stand in judgement about someone else. Besides, I've never had anything against Samuel. I've always liked him."

Rosie drew a long breath and let it out in a sigh. "I must say, it feels good to have that off my chest. I've hated keeping that secret from you." She took a swallow of coffee. "So, have you and Daniel come up with the real killer of Corrine Hughes?" Her eyes caught a sparkle of mischief. "Or are you too busy swapping spit to figure it out?"

Lily, in the act of taking a sip of coffee, choked. "Rosie, really!"

"Sorry."

"To answer your question, we have been very busy, though Daniel has forbidden me to discuss the details with anyone. I've been talking to Amos, too, now that he's speaking to me again. How about you? Is he talking with you when you visit him?"

Rosie nodded. "Finally. He was so afraid that we would be angry with him. And he was ashamed. And it sounds silly, but I think he was also blaming himself for her death."

"Yes, I know. It was as if he thought that because he was bad, she died. As illogical as that sounds, you can't blame him for thinking it. After all, his daddy told him all his life that everything bad that happened was his fault."

"Lily, he's very scared."

"I know, but Daniel says he's got to tell the jury about his own movements that night. Why he went there, what he did while he was there, why he hid in the closet, everything."

"That's going to be hard for Amos. Is it necessary?"

"Daniel thinks it is, but he's worried that Amos won't be able to tell his story convincingly. He wants me to help in preparing Amos to testify. He also may call you as a character witness for the boy."

"Of course, I'll help any way I can. But does Daniel have any idea who really killed the girl?"

"He has possible theories, but no real evidence. As

for myself, I think it must have been some man who came to the social club that night."

Rosie nodded. "Somebody insane."

"The frightening thing is how do you know if someone is insane? It's not as if that person would wear a sign advertising the fact. Such a person might seem as normal as you or I."

Her friend looked doubtful. "Do you really think that's possible?"

"I don't know. But it's a frightening thought."

Both women fell silent, contemplating possibilities. When the grandfather clock in the foyer chimed loudly, breaking the silence, Rosie gave a cry of vexation and stood up. "Is it really eight o'clock? I'd better go open up the cafe before rumors start flying that I died or something. Tell Daniel I'll do anything he wants me to do in order to help Amos." She started for the back door of the kitchen, but Lily's voice stopped her.

"Rosie?"

Her friend paused in the doorway and looked back at her. "Hmm?"

"About Daniel." She paused, took a deep breath, and confessed, "He was good at kissing. He was very good."

Rosie didn't look surprised. "As I said, just be careful."

Hugh Masterson arrived on the eleven o'clock train from Atlanta the following morning. Lily knew that because at quarter past eleven, a man she had never seen before strolled into the library with a carpetbag in his hand, a man Daniel greeted with the ease of long familiarity. "Hullo, Hugh," he said, looking up from the notes he had spread out over a table. "About time you showed up."

"When you have a case this cut-and-dried, you don't need to do a lot of preliminary work," the other man answered lightly. He glanced around and chuckled. "Can't you afford an office?"

"With a case this cut-and-dried, I don't need one."

He didn't look like a dangerous opponent. He was shorter than Daniel, balding, and was dressed like a dandy in expensive blue suit, celery-green waistcoat, and blue-green plaid bow tie. Daniel's gray trousers, plain white shirt with rolled-back cuffs, and undone tie stood out in sharp contrast. The difference between the prosecutor and Daniel was like the difference between a peacock and a hawk, and it was hard for her to take the Atlanta prosecutor seriously, but Lily knew better than to judge by appearances. Daniel had said Hugh Masterson was very good. She believed him.

While Lily was making these silent observations, the two men were exchanging their opinions on the case.

"You haven't got squat," Daniel was saying. "My client is a kid who was in the wrong place at the wrong time. That's all."

"Wrong time, my foot. He planned to kill that girl, he did kill that girl, and I'm going to prove it."

"With what?" Daniel countered, laughing. "Your charm and persuasion?"

"That's more than you've got."

Their voices were light and pleasant, almost bantering.

"I have a very strong case," Hugh said. "Amos Boone had motive, means, and opportunity to commit the crime. I can place him at the scene with blood on his clothes and the knife in his hand. And you? What do you have? A client who's half a bubble off plumb."

"You've got motive? What motive?"

"C'mon, Daniel. He was nuts about that girl. They used to meet in the woods. He wanted her for himself, and when he realized what she was, he was enraged and he killed her."

Daniel didn't seem perturbed by that theory. "Well, since, as you put it, he's half a bubble off plumb anyway, and since he was enraged, at least you won't be able to get him for premeditation."

"Intelligence isn't required for that," Hugh answered. "There's such a thing as animal cunning. And jealousy can simmer a long time before it explodes."

Daniel shrugged. "You oughta know."

Instantly, a change came over both men. Something passed between them, an unspoken communication that was primitive and ruthless, something she sensed but did not understand. In the sudden silence that followed Daniel's words, Lily could feel the tension rise in the air until it became almost a tangible thing, suffocating in the hot confines of the library.

One look at Hugh Masterson's face told Lily exactly what he was feeling. *He hates Daniel,* she realized. *Hates him through and through, and Daniel knows it.*

Masterson's body was rigid and tense as he stood across the table from Daniel. Anger and hostility emanated from him, and he no longer made any effort to hide how he felt. In contrast, Daniel was leaning back in his chair, his pose one of careless insolence. It was unnerving, and she realized it was deliberate, calculated to provoke reaction from the other man. She recognized the tactic and knew how effective it could be, for Daniel had used it on her in the past. Lily didn't know quite how she felt about that, but if such a tactic helped Amos in any way, it had her blessing now.

The prosecutor clenched and unclenched his fist around the handle of his carpetbag in perfect rhythm with the muscle twitching at the corner of his jaw. "You're going to lose this one."

Daniel rose to his feet. He was quite a bit taller than Hugh, and the move was an intimidating one. Another tactic, Lily realized. "No, I'm not," he answered, looking down at the shorter man, "I'm going to win. In fact, I'm going to whip your ass." He paused a fraction of a second. "Again."

The two men's gazes locked in silent combat for a moment, then Hugh clamped his lips together, turned on his heel, and walked toward the door. "We'll see," he called back over his shoulder.

"I guess we will," Daniel answered as the prosecutor disappeared through the doorway.

Lily didn't realize she'd been holding her breath until she let it out in a rush. The soft sound was like a gunshot in the silence. Daniel glanced at her, then looked away, but not before she saw the anger in his eyes, a flash of cold and glittering green. She was astonished. She had witnessed the entire scene, she had seen and felt Hugh Masterson's anger, but until this moment, she had not understood that Daniel's feelings were exactly the same.

"What was that all about?" she asked.

"What was what about?" He sat back down and pulled a cigar out of his jacket pocket. Tapping it absently on the table, he looked at her again, his anger masked by an innocent expression.

Lily was not fooled. She waved a hand toward the

door where the prosecutor had just departed. "That. What was going on between the two of you?"

"Oh, that." He shrugged and grinned at her, like a boy who'd just been caught with his fingers in the pie and didn't care one bit. "Just your run-of-the-mill, pretrial pissing contest."

Lily made a grimace of distaste at the profanity. "What do you mean?"

His grin faded. Daniel leaned back in his chair and stared at the door through narrowed eyes. "It's positioning," he explained. "Maneuvering yourself to appear as confident and strong as possible. I told you, a trial isn't just about people getting together to discover the truth. It's a game. All about strategy and tactics. Like chess. That was the first move."

"A game?" Lily couldn't believe what she was hearing. "A game over Amos's life?"

"A game with very high stakes, I admit. But a game nonetheless."

"And one of the first rules is to act as cocky and arrogant as possible?"

Daniel met her eyes and clamped the unlit cheroot between his teeth. The grin came back. "You betcha."

❖15❖

HUGH MASTERSON WASN'T the only man involved in the trial of Amos Boone who came to Shivaree on Monday. Judge Billings returned to town that day, and at that evening's meeting of the Ladies' Temperance Society at the library, Mary Alice confided to Lily how she felt about her husband's return.

"If he's going to behave so boorishly, I wish he'd never come home," she said with a pout. "Honestly, Lily, you'd think I'd been chaining myself to men's washrooms and wearing trousers and scandalizing the world, the way he's carrying on."

The two women were folding pamphlets, and Lily set another one on the pile that lay between the two women on the table. "He's upset about your involvement in temperance?" she asked.

"Upset is not the word. He was furious. He ranted and raved for two hours. He actually forbid me to come tonight. I, of course, could not let that stop me." She slapped another pamphlet on the pile with an almost childish flare of temper. "I don't let him tell me what to do!"

Lily looked at her across the table, at a loss for a suitable reply. She did not want to get embroiled in the other woman's matrimonial woes. "Mary Alice, I'm so sorry. But—"

"I know, I know," Mary Alice brushed aside her words with a delicate wave of her hand. "You tried to warn me that first day I came to see you, but I don't regret a moment of it. I told him that I had to help close that place down, since he refused to do it."

"What was his reaction to that?"

"He did not take it very well. But Lyndon knew I was committed to temperance work before he ever married me." Mary Alice sighed, a frown creasing her forehead. "He got even angrier when I pointed that out."

"I should imagine so," Lily answered dryly.

Dovey bustled over to their table, interrupting their conversation. "How are we doing, ladies?" she asked. "Will all these be ready to be mailed tomorrow?"

"Yes," Lily answered, pausing in her task to look up at the woman who stood beside the table. "But mailing all of these to ladies' societies and clubs all over Georgia is going to cost quite a bit of money. We don't have enough in our treasury to defray the cost."

"Mary Alice has generously volunteered to donate the money for the postage." Dovey moved on to the next table, where Densie, Rosie, and Eliza were addressing the pamphlets to be mailed.

Lily looked at the woman seated across the table. "You're paying for the postage on these temperance pamphlets with your husband's money?" she asked in disbelief. "After his reaction today?"

"Yes, of course," Mary Alice answered serenely. "I'll

just have to overspend my household allowance this month." Her blue eyes opened ingenuously wide, but it did not escape Lily's notice that a glimmer of cleverness showed in their depths. "Why, I just can't keep to a budget." Mary Alice went on, fluttering her eyelashes as delicately as a butterfly's wings. "When I see a delicious new bonnet over in Agnes Shoup's Millinery, budgets and sums just go right out of my head."

"And if he finds out the truth?"

"I guess I'll just have to be as sweet and nice and as good a wife as I can be until he calms down and forgives me. And he will. A gentleman will forgive a woman anything if she goes about it the right way."

"I see." Lily studied the other woman's pretty face across the table, noted the childlike determination in the set of her jaw that belied the lovely smile, and was again forcibly reminded of her own two sisters. Hannah and Beth had been adept at wheedling, flirtation, and flattery to get their way or to be forgiven their transgressions. It had worked on their father, it had worked on their husbands. Though Lily had always known she could never employ such techniques—her own being more along the lines of a bull in a china shop—she had always envied the ease with which women such as Mary Alice, Hannah, and Beth got what they wanted while making you feel as if they were doing you the favor.

After the pamphlets had been folded, addressed, and stamped, the ladies were able to enjoy some of Lily's cream cake and Rosie's coffee, and the talk turned to the biggest news in town, the trial of Amos Boone.

Opinions of the boy's guilt or innocence were just

about evenly divided. Those who felt he was innocent detailed stories of Amos's kindness, while those who thought he was guilty pointed out his odd behavior.

In fulfillment of her promise to Daniel, Lily said nothing, but by the time the ladies left the library to go home, she was at the end of her tether. When Daniel arrived to work with her on preparations for the trial, she informed him in no uncertain terms how big a sacrifice she was making on Amos's behalf by keeping her mouth shut. Daniel, of course, gave her no sympathy.

"It's good for you," he told her.

"Good for me?" She stared at him. "How?"

"It makes you more aware of what you say, and oftentimes, the less said, the better." He set his portfolio on a table, then slid out of his jacket and tossed it over the back of a chair. "How's the fight for temperance going?"

"Very well, I'll have you know. By the time we're through, you won't be able to get a drink in the entire state of Georgia."

"Only in your dreams, sugarplum," he countered, loosening his tie with a tug. "I told you before, you'll never stop people from drinking. But go right on ahead, if it makes you feel better."

"That's just the kind of remark I'd expect from you," she countered with spirit. "Why don't you pat me on the head while you're at it?"

He chuckled as he undid the top button of his shirt. "As much as I love debating with you, I think we need to get some work done. Has Josiah sent you any information on the murder of prostitutes?"

"Yes." Lily retrieved from her desk the information Josiah had sent her and sat down opposite Daniel at the table. "He told me that in the past two years, seven prostitutes have been murdered. That seems like a lot."

"Prostitution is a hazardous profession." Daniel took Josiah's information from her and scanned it quickly. Lily, who had already read it, watched him and waited, knowing how important it was. Four of the women had been shot by customers, and all four men had been convicted of manslaughter and sent to prison. Another of the prostitutes had been beaten to death by her husband, who had then shot himself.

The remaining two prostitutes had been stabbed, and both cases were still unsolved, one in Georgia, and the other in Missouri. Josiah had been thorough. He had included details on both murders, including newspaper articles and notes on the investigation. Both women had been found with Bibles, and it was clear that the deaths were connected.

"Lily, this is great! Do you know what this means?"

"I think it means we've found the murderer of Corrine," she answered. "But how do we prove it?"

Daniel tossed Josiah's notes down on the table and rose to his feet. Lily was becoming accustomed to the fact that whenever he was thinking hard, Daniel liked to pace, and her gaze followed him as he wandered through the library. She had come to respect him, and she realized she actually enjoyed their heated discussions. She had even come to respect his profession, something she never would have thought possible.

She liked watching him. She liked the way his linen shirt stretched taut across his broad back. She liked the low pitch of his voice as he talked to her and yet to himself. She liked the way he moved, with a masculine grace and strength that were somehow fascinating to watch. He reminded her again of a hawk, circling with seeming aimlessness, yet his purpose always in mind.

He was so different from Jason. Her former husband had been charming, too, but Daniel had a strength of will and a sense of purpose that Jason had never had. She thought of the horrors Daniel had endured as a boy, and she realized the kind of strength he possessed came from suffering. Daniel had learned the hard way to work for what he wanted, while Jason had always had everything in life handed to him from the moment he was born. And though they had been boyhood friends, that fundamental difference must have been between them all their lives.

"Ezekiel," he muttered as he walked around the room. "Did you notice that? Obviously, the killer is leaving us his opinion of prostitutes each time."

Lily brought her thoughts hastily back to the matter at hand. "Have you read that passage all the way through? Listen."

She walked over to her desk and picked up a Bible. Daniel stopped pacing around the room and waited as she came to his side, opened the Bible to the appropriate page of Ezekiel and began to read aloud. "'Because thy filthiness was poured out, and thy nakedness discovered through thy whoredom with thy lovers, and with all the idols of thy abominations, and by the blood of thy children, which thou didst give unto them; Behold, therefore I will gather all thy lovers, with whom thou hast taken pleasure, and all of them that thou hast loved, with all them that thou hast hated; I will even gather them round about against thee, and will discover thy nakedness unto them, that they may all see thy nakedness.'"

She stopped and looked at Daniel over the book in her hands. "The inference is obvious."

Daniel nodded. "Some lunatic out there is going around killing prostitutes and thinking that he's fulfilling the word of God. If I can introduce this evidence during the trial, along with the Bible found in Corrine's room, that might be enough evidence to get Amos acquitted."

Daniel's words triggered something in her mind, something she had seen in Corrine's room, something she could not remember, something that she just knew was important. Lily frowned, thinking hard, but the more she tried to figure out what it was, the more elusive it became.

Daniel noticed her sudden preoccupation. "What is it?" he asked.

She shook her head. The vague mist of an idea disappeared with those words. "There's something about Corrine's room that I noticed at the time, but I couldn't quite pinpoint what it was. I still can't."

"Something? What do you mean?"

"I don't know. It was something about the nightstand, I think. Or—" She paused, then shook her head. "No, it's gone. But I know that, somehow, it's important. I wish I could remember."

"You will. It'll pop into your head at the most unexpected moment."

"I hope so." Lily set the Bible on a nearby table. "By the way, if you call Annie Horsley to the stand, she'll be able to testify that Amos can't read. All he knows is the alphabet. This passage would be impossible for him to find. He couldn't have left the Bible in Corrine's room open to this particular page."

"That helps a great deal. And I want you to tell

Josiah to try and dig up more information on these two cases. Anything he can find."

"I already did. He'll have it here in a few days."

"Good girl," he said approvingly.

She frowned at him, but when she spoke, her voice was teasing. "Are you going to pat me on the head again?"

"I wouldn't dream of it."

Suddenly, there was something in his eyes as he looked at her, something that made her catch her breath. There was something in the way his gaze lowered a fraction to her mouth that paralyzed her, hypnotized her. He lifted his hand as if to touch her, and she waited, utterly still, certain he was going to kiss her again, knowing he shouldn't, hoping he would.

He did not move.

Be careful. Rosie's words came back to her. But just now, being careful wasn't what she wanted at all. Anticipation curled in her belly like tongues of fire, and she leaned forward a fraction, until her cheek touched his upraised fingertips.

His reaction was not at all what she was hoping for. His hand jerked back as if he'd been burned. He stepped around her and walked away. "It's late," he said, pulling his jacket from the back of the chair. He shrugged it on. "We'd better get some sleep. Amos's arraignment is tomorrow."

Lily bit her lip, trying to hide the myriad emotions churning inside her. Embarrassment, frustration, relief. Daniel could turn her inside out until she didn't know what she really felt anymore. But as he walked her home, she realized what she felt at this moment was disappointment. When they reached her front door, she unlocked it, then turned to him. In the moonlight, she saw his mouth tighten slightly.

"Good night, Lily," he said and started to turn away.

"Why didn't you kiss me before?" she whispered.

He paused and looked at her. He was silent for a moment, then he said, "I didn't think it was a very good idea. People might see us. You've been working hard to regain your reputation. I don't want you to lose it again."

"When did you become so chivalrous?"

"Hell, I don't know," he murmured. "But if you don't stop looking at me like that, chivalry be damned. I'll kiss you right here on your own front porch until you're on fire. That'd really give this town something to talk about."

"Bragging, Walker?" she whispered.

"Nope." He turned and walked away. "Just being honest."

Daniel closed his eyes and listened. She was in her parlor, playing Beethoven. It was the *Moonlight Sonata,* if he remembered the melody correctly. He leaned on the sill of his bedroom window, letting the music wash over him in the dark. He smoked his evening cigar and tried to relax, tried not to think about what had almost happened tonight.

He'd known when he agreed to let her assist him with the case that she was going to be a dangerous distraction, and he'd been proved right. She was distracting him, and he could not afford that. Amos was what mattered now. He needed to put all his attention and energy to his client's defense. *Get your priorities straight,* he told himself. *Focus on what's important.*

He leaned back in his chair. He had reasonable doubt. He was sure of that now. He had a very compelling alternative to the prosecution's case. What he had to do now was put his facts in order and figure out the best way to present them to the jury.

The music stopped. Daniel opened his eyes. Her curtains were closed, but when light illuminated her window, he could see her silhouette move across the curtains as she went about her nightly ritual, a ritual he knew by now. First, she changed into her nightgown, and though she was out of his line of vision and he could not see her do it, he could sure as hell remember the times that he had. Desire spread through his body.

God, he wanted her.

He took a deep breath and closed his eyes. *Focus.*

He'd put the character witnesses on first, and establish how ridiculous it was that Amos had been arrested. Amos's testimony would be next, and that was probably the aspect of the trial that worried him most, because he knew Amos was not telling the whole truth. He needed to see the boy again, try to discover what he was holding back, and make sure he was prepared to testify.

He glanced at Lily's window, and he could see her silhouette against the curtain, elbows pointed toward the ceiling as she removed pins from her hair. She shook her head, and all that long, thick, fiery hair came tumbling down, and lust hit Daniel with all the force of a tornado.

He shut his eyes. *Focus.*

By sheer will, he forced thoughts of Lily out of his mind again. After Amos's testimony, he would introduce the evidence of the other two similar crimes and present his theory of what really happened at the social club that night. But the first thing he had to do was set the tone of his defense with his opening statement. He concentrated on that, composing it in his mind, reworking it, until he had a rough draft of what he would say burned in his brain.

When he opened his eyes again, Lily's room was dark. He wondered if she were able to sleep. He sure as hell couldn't.

Why didn't you kiss me?

He wanted to laugh at that question. Every time he kissed her, it seemed the only thing he could think about was kissing her again. It seemed as if the feel of her, the taste of her, had been the only things on his mind for weeks, when they were the last things in the world he ought to be thinking about, especially now, when he had to concentrate on Amos's case. It didn't help to know she was feeling the same as he. Dammit, she should have slapped his face, and reminded him of how much she hated him, and how much he deserved it. Instead, she had looked at him with all that desire written on her face, easy to read as a book, easy to take as a piece of candy.

Why didn't you kiss me?

First she didn't care what he thought of her. Then she did. First she hated him. Then she didn't. For God's sake, couldn't the woman at least be consistent? The more he knew her, the less he understood her. She was as changeable and unpredictable as the weather, and it was driving him crazy.

Focus.

But he couldn't, and he finally gave up. He went to bed, thinking sleep ought to be a good enough distraction. But he was mistaken. He dreamed about her, hot and lusty dreams. When he woke up the next morning, he knew that he could ruin the whole case and end any chance of getting Amos acquitted if he couldn't keep erotic thoughts of Lily out of his mind. One way to do that, of course, was to end this torture and make love to her. It was not a solution he was proud of, and his only other option was sheer force of will.

Daniel got out of bed and walked to the washstand. He splashed water on his face. It didn't help, and he tossed aside the towel with a muffled oath. It was barely sunrise, but he threw on some clothes and left the house to go for a walk. He had no idea where he was going, but he didn't care as long as he could free himself of thoughts of her.

He wasn't going to run the risk of losing the case and watching Amos hang. Even though the memory of how Lily had looked at him with all that passion in her eyes was still vivid in his mind, even though his body ached with wanting her, Daniel walked and walked until he had managed to blot out all erotic thoughts of her. Force of will, however, played no part in it. He succeeded by promising himself that he would take Lily Morgan to bed after the trial was over. He had the feeling the trial was going to be a very long one.

❖16❖

When Daniel made a promise, he kept it. Even if that promise was only to himself. During the days that followed, he shoved all thoughts outside of those involving the case from his mind. Amos was arraigned on Tuesday and entered a plea of not guilty. A grand jury was convened, and by Friday, a true bill had been handed down, just as Daniel had predicted. The case was remanded for trial, and Judge Billings scheduled that trial to begin in three weeks.

With only three weeks to prepare, Daniel worked feverishly. He wrote his opening statement, he made notes for his closing argument, and he selected character witnesses to testify for his client and helped them prepare their testimony.

He spent a great deal of time with Amos. Daniel knew his client was afraid of him, but the young man had promised Lily he would cooperate, and he finally told Daniel what had happened that night. When Daniel pressed the issue of why Amos went to the social club that night, the young man finally admitted that he had gone there for exactly the reason Daniel had suspected. Amos begged him not to tell Lily about that, because she would hate him for going to see one of those "bad girls," and he didn't want Lily to hate him.

Daniel promised he wouldn't tell Lily what Amos had admitted, and as a result of that promise, Amos became more comfortable with him, and more trusting. They spent hours together, going over the young man's version of events with painstaking care as Daniel prepared him to testify. Despite the amount of time they spent together, Daniel could not rid himself of a strong feeling Amos was keeping something back. The young man denied it, and there was nothing more Daniel could do. He could only work with what he had.

He decided to add Lily to his witness list after all. She would be able to corroborate Annie Horsley's testimony that Amos didn't know how to read, and Daniel knew corroboration was especially important where evidence was circumstantial.

Josiah sent him more information about the other two prostitutes who had been murdered, and Daniel contacted the sheriffs in both cases, arranging for the two men to testify at Amos's trial.

Under Georgia law, neither the prosecution nor the defense was obligated to divulge any information about their case to the other, but Shivaree was a small town, and secrets were hard to keep. The day before the trial began, Daniel discovered that Hugh was planning to call Louisa Richmond to the stand. When he asked his client what Louisa Richmond might know about him that was damaging, Amos could give him no information.

That night, Daniel discussed the situation with Lily. "I'm sure Hugh will call the sheriff, the doctor, and Helen Overstreet as witnesses, because his reasons for doing so are obvious, but why Louisa Richmond?" He looked at her across the table in the library. "What could she possibly say that would be valuable to Hugh's case?"

"Ezra was there that night," she answered. "Could that have something to do with it?"

"Then why doesn't he just call Ezra to the stand?"

Lily shook her head, lifting her hands in a helpless gesture. "I don't know."

Daniel drummed his fingers on the table, thinking out loud. "I know Hugh, and I'm sure Louisa must have some very powerful testimony. I just wish I knew what it was."

"Amos doesn't know?"

"He says he has no idea."

"Maybe I could ask Louisa."

Daniel shook his head. "Absolutely not. You're working with me, and she's a prosecution witness. That could be construed as witness tampering. You don't talk to Louisa about the case at all. It would be unethical."

She smiled suddenly, and Daniel frowned at her in response. "Did I say something funny?"

"A couple months ago, in my wildest dreams, I never would've thought Daniel Walker would be giving me a lecture on ethics."

"That's because you never really knew me before. You only thought you did."

"True," she agreed, sounding almost surprised. "But, then, you never really knew me either."

He thought he had, but he'd been wrong. He had

discovered that Shivaree's most scandalous woman wasn't an adulteress, but she could sure kiss like one.

He knew his thoughts were heading him into dangerous territory again, and he jumped to his feet. "C'mon. We have a lot more work to do. Turn your chair around so it faces away from the table. I'm going to prepare your testimony and get you ready to face Hugh's cross-examination."

"Already?" she asked, turning her chair as he instructed. "I'm probably not going to testify for several days."

"I know, but I won't have time to prepare you once the trial begins. So let's do it now."

He started out gently enough, going through the questions she would answer for him on the stand, but when he took on the role of the prosecutor, the gentleness gave way to bullying.

"So, Mrs. Morgan, how do you know Amos Boone can't read?"

"Because Amos works for me at the library, and I have taken an interest in the boy," she answered. "I, myself, tried to teach him to read. I was not successful."

"It's a bit convenient, isn't it, that you bring forth this evidence? Isn't Amos Boone a friend of yours?"

"I don't know what you mean by convenient. I am simply stating a fact."

Daniel leaned over her, an aggressive move that made her lift her chin and glare at him. "You are simply stating a fact," he repeated. "You've stated facts in court before, haven't you, facts which were not believed, facts which were proven to be untrue. Why should we believe you now?"

"Really, Daniel," she said, digressing from their rehearsal, "do we have to go into that?"

"Yes, we do, because Hugh very well might."

"My divorce is not relevant," she said rebelliously.

"It is if it enables Hugh to discredit your testimony about Amos not knowing how to read. Lily, I'm not doing anything to you I haven't already done to Rosie, Jacob Cole, and Annie Horsley. You ought to know me well enough by now to know this isn't personal. I'm only preparing you for the hammering Hugh may give you on the stand."

"I know." She rubbed her forehead with her fingertips as if a headache was coming on. "It's just that it brings back some unpleasant memories."

He watched her for a moment without speaking, then he said, "If you're going to take this personally, then I'm not putting you on the stand. Your testimony isn't important enough to warrant having it discredited."

"All right, all right," she said with a sigh. After a moment, she straightened in her chair, forced an emotionless expression onto her face, and gave her answer with cool self-assurance. "I am only saying that I know from my observation of him as his employer and my experience in attempting to teach him, that Amos Boone does not know how to read. That is all."

"Good," Daniel told her. "That's exactly right. State the facts, and don't respond to the implication that you're lying by trying to defend yourself. Act as if you don't care one way or the other whether you are believed, because you know you're speaking the truth."

"I wish I had known that five years ago," she mumbled.

He pulled out a chair from another table and sat down opposite her. "If I had been your attorney, that is exactly what I would have advised you to do about Henry Douglas. When you started defending yourself, I knew I had you."

Lily bent her head. "I knew it, too," she admitted in a small voice. "I just didn't know why. And the more I tried to explain, the more it sounded like a lie. The worst part of it was Jason, sitting there acting like the outraged husband and letting everyone think—"

She broke off, staring at the hands in her lap. Anger shot through Daniel like a jolt of electricity, anger toward Jason, who had so callously abandoned her, and anger toward himself for helping Jason to ruin her.

Daniel knew he could not undo the damage that had already been done, but as he studied her sitting there with her shoulders slumped and her head bent, his anger dissolved into something totally different. Tenderness. He reached out to touch her before he could stop himself. He lifted her chin with one finger to look into her eyes.

"Letting everyone think you were to blame," he finished for her. "And not giving a damn while I slashed your reputation to shreds." His fingertips caressed her cheek, and he wished they could soothe away the hurt. "Lily, I am sorry about what happened, but I genuinely believed Henry's story. Jason was my friend, the best friend I ever had, and the thought that he was lying to me, that he set the whole thing up, never occurred to me. Perhaps it should have, but it didn't. I wish I could make you understand."

"Does it matter whether or not I understand?" she asked.

His thumb brushed across the velvety softness of her

lower lip, and he felt it quiver beneath the light caress. "Yes."

"Why?"

"Perhaps for the same reason you wanted me to believe you weren't an adulteress."

A faint smile lifted the corners of her mouth. "But I wanted you to believe me because I wanted you to realize how wrong you'd been and grovel."

"Forget it," he said. "I realize now that I was wrong about you, and I'm sorry about that. But I'm not groveling, even if you hold the divorce against me forever."

"I don't hold it against you anymore," she whispered and reached up to cover his hand with her own.

Her touch was like a match to powder, and Daniel sucked in a deep breath, trying to hang on to the promise he had made to himself to keep his priorities straight. He jerked his hand back. "We'd better get some sleep," he said and stood up. "The trial starts tomorrow."

Both of them were silent as he walked her home. *Why now?* he wondered. Now, when she didn't hate him anymore. Now, when she understood his reasons. Why now did he feel like a prize bastard? Perhaps because that was exactly what he had been.

The following morning, Lily was at the jail early so that she could see Amos before the trial began. He was dressed and shaved, and his fair hair, still damp, was neatly combed behind his ears. He was dressed in a brand-new dark brown suit, ivory waistcoat, and white linen shirt and looked so handsome in it, Lily's throat constricted with pride.

"Who is this handsome man?" she asked. "I came to

see Amos Boone, and instead, I find some other fella in his place."

As always, Amos took her words at face value. "It's me, Miz Lily," he said seriously. "Don't you know me?"

"Lordy," she said, pretending surprise. "It is Amos Boone! That brand-new suit had me fooled for a second."

"Daniel sent it over yesterday. I've never had a new suit of clothes before." He tugged at the unfamiliar waistcoat. "Does it look all right? I hope I don't tear it or stain it or nothing, 'cause Daniel gave it to me and I got to take care of it."

That was just like Amos. Lily felt a sudden desire to cry. The boy was about to go on trial for his life, and he was worried about his new suit of clothes. She prayed this wasn't the only chance he got to wear it.

"You look mighty fine," she whispered, fighting back tears so Amos wouldn't see how scared she was as she reached through the bars to brush an imaginary speck of dust from his lapel. "You look like such a gentleman."

"Good morning."

Both of them looked toward the doorway to find Daniel standing there. She caught her breath at the sight of him. In his impeccable gray suit, he was devastatingly handsome, but more important, he looked confident and self-assured. Lily was glad of it, for she was scared to death.

"They're getting ready to start," he said. "Fifteen minutes." To Lily, he added, "I need to meet with Amos, and you'd better go. Rosie saved you a seat, and it's a good thing she did. The courtroom is packed."

"I wish I could sit with you and Amos."

"It wouldn't be appropriate."

The bailiff entered the room, handcuffs ready. Lily eyed them with a frown. "Are those really necessary?"

"Judge's orders," the bailiff responded. "Sorry, ma'am."

She looked at Daniel, who shrugged. "I tried. I petitioned Billings, asking that the handcuffs be removed while Amos is in court on the grounds that they would bias the jury against him, but Billings refused. There's nothing else I can do." He jerked a thumb over one shoulder. "Go on. Bobby Tom knows you're on your way, and he'll let you bypass the line at the front doors."

She nodded and walked toward the door into Sheriff Trusedale's office. As she passed Daniel in the doorway, she whispered, "Good luck."

"Luck has nothing to do with it," he told her, "so don't worry. Amos is in good hands. Mine."

"Who's worried?" she quipped, but left the jail sick to her stomach.

Daniel was right about the courtroom. It was filled to overflowing, and those people who had arrived too late to get seats inside were gathered around the front steps. As Daniel had said, Bobby Tom let her into court ahead of the line. She gave Mary Alice a nod of greeting as she passed her on the aisle.

Alvis Purdy was there, too, seated only a few rows behind Mary Alice. She ignored the wink he gave her, and kept following Bobby Tom, but she could feel Alvis's ogling gaze boring into her back as she continued toward the front of the courthouse to take her seat beside Rosie and Samuel.

"What is Alvis doing here?" she muttered to Rosie

under her breath, as she watched Daniel come in from the opposite door, Amos and a bailiff behind him.

"Probably here for the trial," Rosie answered. "Either that, or he's going to propose marriage to a certain librarian I know."

Lily made a sound of disgust. "There's only one kind of proposal on Alvis's mind, and it sure doesn't involve walking down the aisle."

"Oh, I don't know. He was in the cafe this morning, bragging to everybody that he was going to be buying a wedding suit pretty soon."

She groaned. "That man is unbelievable. Did he mention my name?"

"He said a beautiful redhead and, of course, everybody knew who he meant. You marry Alvis Purdy, and I'll have to kill you."

"Before marrying Alvis Purdy, I'd kill myself." She shuddered. "There is something about him that always makes my skin crawl."

"Because he's such a lecher? Or because he wears plaid suits and calls you girly?"

Lily shuddered again, and Rosie changed the subject. "Did you see Dovey and Densie?" she asked, tilting her head back and slightly to the side. "Over there, behind us?"

Lily half rose to her feet and turned her head in the direction her friend had indicated, and saw the two ladies several rows back. Dovey had a picnic basket on her lap and both women were sipping from bottles of lemonade.

"Of all the bad taste," she murmured, sinking back down in her chair. "What do they think this is? The county fair?"

"I guess they're afraid they'll lose their seats when court adjourns for the dinner hour."

"And that would be a tragedy," Lily said tartly. "They might miss some juicy gossip. I'm surprised they didn't bring their opera glasses."

"They did. I saw them lookin' through them earlier."

Lily was given no chance to express her opinion on that, for just then the bailiff called out in a dry, clear voice, "All rise, all rise. The Jaspar County Court is now in session, the honorable Lyndon R. Billings presiding."

From his position at the bench, Billings cast a glance across the packed courtroom over the glasses perched on his nose, his gaze pausing briefly on Amos. Then he sat down, instructing everyone before him to do the same.

The trial began.

Opening statements came first. Daniel had defended enough clients against Hugh Masterson to know the other man's style. He was sure Hugh would begin with a cold, factual preview of the evidence he intended to introduce and would end up sounding like a Baptist minister evoking holy vengeance. He was not disappointed.

Hugh made the most of the damning evidence: Amos's relationship with the victim, his presence at the scene, the bloody clothes, the knife in his possession. He made Amos's relationship with Corrine into something sordid. Hugh contended that Amos had not known she was a prostitute and that when he found out, he killed her in a rage of jealousy. By the way Hugh played up Corrine's background, she might have been the girl next door instead of a prostitute, gone bad solely because of Amos Boone's influence. He then played on the deepest fear of the twelve men in the jury box by predicting that if Amos Boone didn't hang, the womenfolk of Shivaree would never be safe again.

"Gentlemen of the jury," he concluded, lifting his hands and his gaze toward heaven above, "this is a crime so horrendous, so brutal, that God cries out for swift and merciless justice." He turned and pointed at the jurors as if he were in the pulpit and they were his congregation. "God has made you the instrument of His holy justice, gentlemen, and He has placed the sword of justice in your hands. He is confident you will wield that sword with wisdom, confident you will find Amos Boone guilty of the murder of that poor girl, Corrine Hughes, and see that His justice is done."

Daniel waited several moments, then he rose to his feet. He ambled out from behind the table, hands in his pockets, and planted a look of bewilderment on his face. He walked slowly toward the jury, shaking his head like a man who didn't understand what he had just witnessed.

"Whew!" he said, halting in front of the jurors. "That was some speech by Mr. Masterson." He tugged at one ear as if confounded by what he had seen. "You know, I'm an old-fashioned man, and I'm not real familiar with all the new inventions in the world. I've heard of telephones, of course, and I've even used 'em once or twice. Although I don't know quite how they work, I know the sound travels on wires." He shook his head as if sorely puzzled. "I didn't know Mr. Masterson had a telephone with a wire long enough to get all the way to heaven."

He waited for the chuckles to die down, then he went on, "Hugh's talkin' like he, and he alone, can talk to God, and only he knows what God wants you to do."

Daniel placed a hand on his chest, humble as he could be, and went on, "Now, we all know the Lord works in mysterious ways and we can't always know His purpose. What we can do is find the truth. And that is what I'm going to ask you folks to do. Search for the truth."

He paused, then began to walk in front of the jury, making eye contact with each and every one of them. "What is the truth? I don't know if anyone can define it, but we know it when we see it. We feel it in our guts. When we hear it, we recognize it. And I reckon maybe that's the real telephone line to God, the truth that's in our hearts."

Daniel had spent hours outlining exactly what to present in his opening statement, but as he spoke to the jury, he decided not to use it. He decided to end his opening statement right here, and give Hugh no clues as to what his defense strategy would be, and no chance to spike his guns during the prosecution's case. "Gentlemen of the jury," he said, pausing before them respectfully, "Hugh and I are going to present you folks with all the evidence we have, and it will be your job to find the truth. When you search your hearts, you'll find it. You'll know that Amos Boone is not guilty."

When he sat down again, the prosecution called its first witness. "Sheriff Harmon Trusedale."

From the sheriff, the jury learned of finding Amos in the closet with the knife still in his hand, his clothes smeared with Corrine's blood. The knife and the clothes were entered into evidence. Hugh spent half the morning getting all the details from the sheriff on what he had discovered at the social club, what he thought, how he felt, and the impression Amos Boone had made on him when he found him in the closet. Though Daniel objected that the witness was drawing conclusions, Judge Billings overruled him, and by the time the prosecutor had finished questioning him, it was as if True had actually witnessed the murder itself.

It was a common belief among most people that if jurors thought a man was guilty, they wouldn't look him in the eye. Daniel knew from experience that belief simply wasn't true. He studied the faces of the jurors surreptitiously as the sheriff gave his testimony, and he saw by their expressions that those men were already becoming certain of Amos's guilt because they were staring at him in horror, as if they'd never seen him before. Daniel wasn't overly worried, because by the time he had put on his defense, he intended their faces to look a whole lot different.

When Hugh sat down, Daniel began his cross-examination. He rose to his feet and rubbed a hand over his forehead. "True, I'm kinda confused here, so I need to get this straight. Did you see Amos kill that girl?"

"I didn't see him do it, no."

"I didn't think so." He gave the jury a dismissive shrug that made True's chin jut out like a bulldog with indigestion, then he went on, "The knife you found was an ordinary kitchen knife, is that right? From the kitchen of the social club itself?"

"Yes. It matched the ones already there."

"And anyone who passed through the kitchen could've gotten hold of it?"

"I suppose so."

Daniel left off the subject of the knife, and moved on to the piece of evidence most crucial to his defense. "True, when you found the prostitute's body, there was a Bible open on her nightstand, wasn't there?"

"Yeah, I guess there was."

"That Bible was open to a passage from Ezekiel, was it not?"

"Yeah."

Murmurs of speculation by those who knew their Bible rippled through the crowd.

"Thank you. No further questions."

Daniel could tell from the puzzled frown on Hugh's face that the other man was trying to understand the significance of the Bible, and he was glad of it. He vowed that by the time Hugh figured out that the Bible was much more than Corrine's nightly reading material, it would be too late.

Hugh called his next witness. "Mathias Waller."

The huge black man took the oath and sat down in the witness box. From him the jury learned that Amos Boone arrived at the social club around eleven o'clock, asked to see Corrine, and was led into the parlor. Mathias then returned to his position in the foyer. By his questions, Hugh made it clear to the jury that no one left the club with any sign of blood on him, and that Amos, who did have blood on his clothes, never left at all.

Daniel intended to present an explanation of the bloody clothes with Amos's testimony, so there was only one thing to clarify with Mathias on his cross-examination, but it was something that would begin to turn the tide toward reasonable doubt. "Mr. Waller, you testified that you put Amos in the parlor. Could you see him sitting there from your position standing in the foyer?"

"Yes."

"And he did not leave that parlor until he went upstairs, isn't that right?"

"That's right."

"You're sure he never left his seat for a moment?"

"Yes."

Daniel scratched his head as if thinking hard. He paused so long, he could hear people begin shifting impatiently in their chairs. Judge Billings said, "Mr. Walker, did you have another question?"

"I was just wondering about something, Your Honor. Sheriff Trusedale testified that the knife was from the kitchen of the social club. But Amos never left the parlor until he went upstairs, so how'd he get hold of the knife?" He waited for that question to sink into the minds of the jury, then he shook his head as if it weren't all that important. "Never mind. I'm sure we'll be able to find out the truth of that later. No more questions."

The prosecution called Helen Overstreet to the stand. Murmurs of excitement shot through the crowd as her name was announced, and people craned their necks to see the infamous madam of Georgia's most infamous whorehouse as she walked to the witness box. By their reaction, it was almost as if they'd never seen her before. If they were hoping she would testify in feather boas, hennaed hair, and rouge, they were let down. Helen, as always, looked so utterly respectable, that it must have been a sore disappointment to the spectators.

From Helen, the jury learned that Amos Boone had paid for the privilege of an hour with Corrine, and she made it clear that, in her opinion, he knew what he was paying for.

Daniel asked Helen no questions. Instead, he reserved the right to cross-examine her later, and the trial adjourned for the dinner hour.

Emerius Wilson, medical doctor and Jaspar County coroner, took the stand just after one o'clock. His testimony was technical and involved, and Hugh made it even more tedious by dragging it out as long as he could.

Though it might seem to irritate the jury, Daniel knew exactly what Hugh was doing. The prosecutor was stalling so that he could end the day with a powerful piece of testimony that Daniel would not be able to refute until morning. It was a tactic he had often employed himself. He objected once to show the jurors he was on their side, citing relevance and pointing out that Mr. Masterson was putting everybody to sleep. But though Billings agreed and cautioned Hugh to keep it short, the painfully boring testimony went on for over two hours, and there wasn't a damn thing Daniel could do about it, so he made his cross brief and to the point.

"Doctor Wilson," he began, "you have testified that the knife wounds of the prostitute matched the knife found with Amos, but we heard from the sheriff that it was an ordinary kitchen knife from the club itself. Would you concur?"

"I would, yes."

"Other knives matching the supposed murder weapon were found in the kitchen?"

"Yes."

"There was also blood in the kitchen, wasn't there?"

"Yes. On the floor."

"Indicating that the killer escaped through the kitchen and left that blood on his way out?"

Hugh was on his feet. "Objection!"

"Withdrawn." Daniel shrugged and walked away. "No more questions."

"The prosecution calls Louisa Richmond."

Louisa took the stand and was duly sworn. Hugh walked toward her to begin his questions.

"Here we go," Daniel muttered under his breath.

Amos looked at him curiously. "Where we goin'?"

"Never mind."

"Mrs. Richmond," Hugh began, "you and your husband own the local mercantile, do you not?"

"Yes." She lifted her head proudly. "Twenty-six years now."

"Did Amos Boone come into your store on the day of the murder?"

"He did." She cast a baleful glare at the accused. "He had the devil in his eyes that day. I could see it."

"Objection," Daniel said, putting a hint of weariness in that one word, as if to say the witness's comment was too ridiculous for a more strenuous objection. His objection was sustained, Billings ordered Louisa's comment stricken from the record, and Hugh continued his questioning.

"When Amos came into the store, what happened?"

"Well, he bought a packet of sen-sen, and left. I just couldn't understand what that boy would want sen-sen for, so I closed the store and followed him."

"And where did he go?"

"He went to the old church."

"By the old church, you are referring to the deserted building on the edge of the woods that used to be Shivaree's Baptist church?"

"Yes. But then we built the new church and so—"

"And," Hugh interrupted, "when Amos went there, was someone waiting for him?"

"Yes. That girl, Corrine Hughes."

"And did you hear any of their conversation?"

"Well, I wasn't eavesdropping!" Louisa immediately began defending herself. "By the time I got there, they were shouting so loud, I'm surprised half the town didn't hear."

"What were they shouting about?"

Daniel felt a sickening knot begin to form in the pit of his stomach. Amos had told him nothing about any shouting. He'd had a feeling all along Amos had not told him everything, and it looked as if his instincts had been right. He could guess where Hugh was heading with this testimony, and he didn't like it.

"He was telling her that the place she worked was a bad place, and that she shouldn't go back there. He told her she should marry him, and he'd take care of her." Murmurs of the surprised spectators shot through the packed courtroom. "She said no. She had bigger fish to fry, she said. Men who spent money on her, bought her presents."

Louisa turned her head and looked at Amos defiantly, as if daring him to deny her testimony, but Amos wasn't looking at her. He was staring at his hands folded on the table, head hung low, and he looked as guilty as sin.

Daniel nudged him with one elbow and whispered, "Lift your head. Sit up straight."

Amos did so, but still managed to look guilty. He

would not meet Daniel's gaze, and it was a good thing, because Daniel was furious. He looked over his shoulder at Lily, who answered his unspoken question with a helpless shrug. She obviously knew as little about this conversation as he did.

"What was the reaction of the accused when she turned down his marriage proposal?" Hugh asked the witness.

"He got even madder. He told her she better not go back, or there'd be hell to pay. She told him if he wanted to see her again he had to pay for the privilege like everybody else."

"Thank you, Mrs. Richmond. No more questions."

A stunned silence followed her testimony. Daniel's mind raced as he tried to figure out what the hell he was going to do. Amos had told him nothing about this quarrel or marriage proposal. Either Louisa was lying or his client was lying, and either way, Daniel saw his case falling apart.

He couldn't just sit here. People were waiting for him to cross-examine the witness, and he had to ask her something, find a way to break her testimony. Daniel rose to his feet, thinking hard, but the judge intervened. "It is now half past four. We will adjourn for the day."

Daniel drew a deep breath of relief, but his expression did not show it. He switched tactics instantly. "But Your Honor," he protested, knowing he had to act as if he was eager to cross-examine her, that his client had nothing to hide. "I must be allowed—"

"Daniel, I have ruled that we will adjourn," Judge Billings interrupted. "You may begin your cross when we reconvene tomorrow morning at nine o'clock."

He gave an exaggerated sigh. "Very well," he said

and reluctantly returned to his seat. Hugh flashed him a look of triumph as he passed the prosecutor's table.

He moved to stand beside Amos as everyone else rose to their feet for the judge's departure. Through clenched teeth, Daniel muttered to his client, "You and I had better have a little talk."

❖ 17 ❖

Lily could see Daniel's face in profile as he leaned close to Amos and spoke to him. Sitting several feet away, she could not hear what he said, but she didn't have to hear the brief conversation to know what Daniel was feeling.

I won't defend someone who lies to me.

As she remembered his words to her in the cafe, Lily felt a sickening rush of fear. If Daniel quit the case, what would happen to Amos?

She shoved her way frantically through the crowd filing out of the courtroom, getting to the jail as fast as she could. Right now, she didn't care why Amos had lied, all she cared about was preventing Daniel from quitting the case.

She could hear him shouting before she even made it through the front door of the sheriff's office, and she marched right past Bobby Tom, ignoring his protests that she couldn't go back to the jail right now.

"Would you mind explaining to me why the hell you didn't tell me about this conversation?" Daniel demanded, pacing back and forth in front of the bars as she entered the jail.

She glanced past him and saw Amos in the cell, curled up on his bunk with his arms protectively cradled around his head, a heartbreaking reminder of the boy's fear of angry men. Daniel seemed too furious to notice.

He went on, "You told me you went for a walk in the woods, met up with Corrine, and she invited you to the social club. You didn't tell me you proposed to the girl, for God's sake! Or that she turned you down. Or that you quarreled. What, you didn't think it was important?"

He came to a halt and turned toward the boy. "Do you have any idea how this looks to the jury? Now I know what Hugh meant when he said he'd prove motive and intent. You had every reason to be angry, and it doesn't take a lot of imagination to think you would be angry enough to go back there and kill her."

Amos let out a whimper of fear, and Lily couldn't stand it any longer. "Daniel, for goodness' sake, stop terrorizing him."

He gave her a brief glance over his shoulder. "You stay out of this," he told her and returned his attention to his client. "If you had told me, if I had known about this, I could have found a way to refute it. Now, I don't know what to do, and if you don't start explaining to me what really happened, you'll hang, boy. Is that what you want?" Without waiting for an answer, he went on, "I should find you another lawyer. I should petition the judge and hand your case over to somebody else right now."

Hearing exactly what she'd been afraid of, Lily spoke again. "Daniel, you can't—"

"Lily." The one word, softly and quietly spoken, was somehow more dangerous than any shouting would have been. He turned toward her and Lily took an involuntary step back at the anger she saw in his eyes. "Get out of here."

His tone left no room for argument. Slowly, she backed away, but she spoke as she retreated. "You can't quit now. You're his lawyer. You've got to stay on the case."

"Give me one good reason why I should," he demanded through clenched teeth.

"Because he's innocent, Daniel," she reminded him gently. "And you're all he's got." With those words, she departed, knowing she'd done all she could, hoping it was enough.

It seemed like years before Daniel came to meet her at the library, but in reality, it was only a few hours. She jumped up as he came through the doors. "Well?" she asked anxiously.

He set his portfolio on the table, then shrugged out of his jacket and tossed it over the back of his chair. "You can stop fussing like a hen over her baby chick," he said as he began rolling back his shirt cuffs.

A wave of relief washed over her. "You're still his lawyer?"

"For now," he muttered and loosened his tie with a tug. "If I find out he's lied to me again, they won't have to have a trial."

"Why not?"

"Because I'll hang him myself."

He sat down and Lily took the chair opposite him across the table. "So he did lie?" she asked.

"Yes."

"But why?"

"Amos knew from what you and Rosie had been saying that the women at the social club were bad. When he met Corrine that afternoon, he confronted her with it, and they argued, just as Louisa said. He told her she should marry him, and he'd take care of her so she wouldn't have to work there anymore."

Lily smiled. "What a sweet thing to do."

Daniel shot her a wry glance. "Corrine didn't think so. She told him she liked her life just the way it was, wearing beautiful clothes and living in a fancy house, eating shrimp on ice and peaches flambé anytime she wanted it. All for only a few hours a night on her back. Why would she want to give all that up?"

Lily wasn't surprised. "So, Amos went there that night because . . ."

"Because he was determined to make her change her mind," Daniel finished for her. "In a way, you were right about why he went to the social club that night, by the way. Corrine had told him that if he wanted to see her again, he'd have to pay for it, so he got out his savings and went there. He did not go there to have sexual relations with her."

His plain speaking caused Lily to blush, but her embarrassment was beside the point. "Why on earth didn't Amos just tell you about this incident in the old church?"

"Think about it. He knew from you and Rosie that prostitutes were bad, and he must have been humiliated to know she'd rather be a prostitute than marry him."

"Male pride?" She made a sound of exasperation. "Is that all?"

"It's enough," he assured her. "Believe me."

"But who killed her? I feel as if we're no further along than we were before."

"I think we're dealing with that son of a bitch who killed those other two prostitutes. Amos swore up and down to me that what he said before was true, that he came in and found her dead. The problem is, the jury now has a preconceived idea that Amos was so enraged by her refusal to marry him, that he went to the social club that night with the intent to kill her, and that he did kill her. How do I refute that?"

"Amos's testimony might help," Lily suggested hopefully. "If the jury hears the story from his point of view—"

"Truth is its own reward, you mean?" Daniel gave her a cynical smile. "I doubt it."

"You believed him. Don't you think a jury will believe him, too?"

Daniel was silent, and Lily studied him uncertainly. "You do believe him?"

"It doesn't matter what I believe."

"But do you?" she persisted.

He was silent so long, Lily thought he was going to say no, but to her surprise, he nodded. "Yes, I believe him." He rubbed a hand across his forehead. "But whether I believe him or not isn't the issue, and I can't rely on Amos's ability on the stand to convince the jury. I have to show them he didn't do it when they now have the idea of his guilt firmly entrenched in their minds." Daniel lifted his head and looked at her. "If I fail to convince them, Amos will hang."

He looked so tired. For the first time, Lily fully appreciated the weight of his responsibility. He was in charge of a man's life. She now understood that while he thrived on the challenge, he also suffered the doubts and fears that accompanied it. "Maybe you just need a good night's sleep."

He gave a humorless laugh and leaned back in his chair. "What I need is a strategy. I have to cross-examine Louisa tomorrow, and try to undo the damage of her testimony. I have no idea how to do that because everything she said was true."

Lily reached out and brushed back the lock of hair that had fallen over his forehead. "You'll find a way," she said simply, her fingertips grazing his cheek.

His hand seized her wrist, pulled it down. Over their hands, his gaze locked with hers. "I'm not made of stone, you know," he said. "You keep touching me like that, and I swear, we'll really give this town something to talk about."

She jerked her hand away. "Sorry. I didn't mean—"

"Forget it." He shoved back his chair and stood up. "It's just damned hard to keep my mind on the case right now, when you're looking at me like that."

"Like what?" she whispered.

"Like that. There's a phrase for that look. Bedroom eyes. I think you can figure out what it means."

She could and she did. An image of the two of them in a bedroom flashed through her mind, and she shivered suddenly, awareness and anticipation penetrating every nerve of her body, making her tingle. She looked into his eyes and saw what she felt reflected there, an aching hunger for what was out of reach.

He turned away and began to pace restlessly around the room. "When you give me that look, I can't think about anything else."

Lily watched him, astonished by his admission. She could see the tense set of his shoulders, the grim line of his mouth, and she sensed that he was forcing unwelcome thoughts out of his mind, thoughts of her that would distract him from what really mattered right now. The case.

Silence fell between them as he roamed restlessly around the library. But when he passed the staircase, he came to a halt, looking at the mezzanine above. "Ezekiel," he muttered and climbed the stairs. He disappeared from view amid the bookshelves.

"What are you looking for?" she called up to him.

"The Bibles," he called back. "This is a library. You must have some. What happened to the one you had the other night?"

Daniel's words caught something in her memory, that same nagging idea that had been in the back of her mind ever since she'd seen Corrine's room. Something about that Bible.

"Oh, lordy!" she cried, pressing her hands to her head, thinking hard, feeling all the pieces falling into place with abrupt and startling clarity. "Alvis Purdy! Daniel, are you listening to me? Alvis Purdy!"

Daniel walked to the railing and looked down at her. "Who?"

She paid no attention to his question. "Oh, why didn't I see it before?" she moaned. "How could I have been so blind?"

"What are you talking about?"

She looked up at him. "The book salesman. Bibles. Brand new Bibles. The spine was broken." The realizations were flashing through her mind so rapidly, she couldn't get the words out fast enough to make a coherent explanation. "I knew there was something odd in her room. It was the Bible, Daniel. It was the Bible! Don't you see?"

He was staring at her doubtfully, and she knew he did not see at all. She took a deep breath and started up the stairs toward where he stood by the railing, thinking it all out as she spoke. "The Bible was open to Ezekiel because the murderer wanted us to see that passage. But why was it open?" She didn't wait for an answer, but rushed on, "It was a brand-new Bible, and brand-new books don't stay open to a particular page by themselves. The spine had been split so the book would stay open to that page. Being a librarian, I notice things like that. The spine being split is what drew my attention to it." She halted in front of him. "How would a brand-new Bible get into Corrine's room?"

"Because she bought it?" Daniel suggested gently, a tiny smile tilting the corners of his mouth.

Lily saw that smile, but she was too excited to care that he was teasing her. "Or it was given to her. Either way, who would she get a brand-new Bible from? From Alvis Purdy, the book salesman, that's who. He comes into the library every other month on the pretext of selling me books, but what he really does is chase me around. He thinks that because I'm a divorced woman, I'm easy prey. Every time he comes in, he brags about how much money he makes, thinking he can impress me. He was in town the day of the murder. I saw his name on the register at Sue Ann's hotel."

As she spoke, she watched the tiredness in his face vanish, and exhilaration take its place. "All that because of the spine of a book?" he said, laughing out loud. "Only a librarian would notice something like that. Lily, you're beautiful!"

Without warning, he grabbed her by the shoulders and pulled her hard against him. "Absolutely beautiful," he repeated just before he kissed her.

When Lily felt his mouth cover hers, she melted against him without resistance, parting her lips to receive his kiss as she wrapped her arms around his neck. For days and days, this was what she had been waiting for, this fire that raced through her veins and heated her blood. She arched against him with a moan, aching for the feel of his body, hard and lean, against her own.

Before she knew what was happening, he was pulling her down to the floor. He eased her onto her back, his arms sliding beneath her to cushion her from the impact of the hard wooden floor even as he rolled on top of her. The air rushed from her lungs at the overpowering weight of his body, the delicious heaviness of him against her. "Daniel," she gasped, unable to stop the involuntary rotation of her hips against his. "Daniel."

He groaned at the movement, burying his face against her neck. He trailed kisses along her throat, each one making her gasp his name again. He shifted his weight so that he could pillow her neck with his forearm, then he slid one hand between their bodies to reach for the top button of her dress.

"I wasn't going to do this," he muttered, raining kisses over her face as he began unfastening buttons in an unrelenting descent down to her waist. "I swore I wasn't going to do this. Not now. Not yet."

He parted the edges of her bodice and jerked her chemise upward to slide his hand beneath the hem. The thought entered her mind that she should stop him, push him away, but that brief flash of reason disappeared at the touch of his fingertips against her bare skin.

Beneath her chemise, his hand opened intimately

over her breast, his palm cupping the shape of it as his thumb closed against his finger, imprisoning her nipple. He began a slow, coaxing motion of his fingers that tore soft, rasping sounds from her throat with every exquisite caress.

"Lily. Oh, God. Lily," he murmured. A prayer or a curse, she couldn't be sure. "I want you, and it's driving me insane. You know that?"

She hadn't known, but his admission brought her a glorious feeling of joy. He lifted his head to gaze at her, his eyes roaming over her face with a hunger and passion that confirmed his words. Daniel wanted her. It was a revelation to Lily, whose husband had never wanted her at all. She reached up, tangling his hair in her fingers and pulled him down to her breast.

Kiss me there, she pleaded silently, and he did, dampening the fabric that covered her breast, making the thin cotton rasp against the sensitive skin of her nipple with each lave of his tongue. Lily felt herself caught up in the exquisite sensations he was creating, powerless to stop him.

She raked her hands through his hair, thick and silky within her hands. Heat spread through her limbs, hotter with each kiss of his mouth, each caress of his hand. She held him to her, wanting never to let him go, wanting him never to stop. It felt so glorious.

Suddenly, with a muttered curse, he rolled away from her. She cried out in protest, but it was too late. He turned his head to gaze at her for one heated moment, then abruptly shoved away from the floor and rose to his feet.

Lily came slowly out of the sensuous daze he had created, bereft and bewildered by his sudden withdrawal. She sat up, staring at the rigid set of his wide shoulders as he stared at the wall. "You stopped," she whispered. "Why?"

Without looking at her, he made a choked sound that might have been a laugh. "Damned if I know," he said, his voice hoarse, ragged with unslaked passion. "But I know this much. When this trial is over, you and I are going to finish what we've started. You know it, too, don't you?"

"Yes," she whispered, that one word both a consent and a promise. "I know."

❖18❖

THE FOLLOWING MORNING, Daniel had to get Joe Gandy out of bed in order to send a telegram. Joe, who ran the telegraph office as well as the newspaper, grumbled unceasingly as he tapped out the message Daniel wanted to send to Josiah, but he did it.

"Why you want to know about Alvis Purdy anyhow?" the older man asked him, but Daniel ignored the question.

"I'll be in court when the reply comes in," he said instead. "Can you bring it to me there?"

"I'll have Matt do it," Joe answered, referring to his thirteen-year-old son.

"Fine. But Joe, don't you be telling anybody about this. It's legal business."

Joe glared at him indignantly. "You don't have to tell me that, Daniel. I been running this telegraph for nigh on twenty years and I would never—"

"Sorry, sorry," Daniel apologized hastily. "It's just that I don't want to read about this in the *Shivaree Register* tomorrow morning." He paid for the telegram and left before Joe could fire off another testy reply, and he headed for the jail to see Sheriff Trusedale. Over scrambled eggs and coffee, he told the sheriff what he and Lily had figured out the night before. Although True was reluctant to abandon the idea that Amos killed Corrine and thereby admit he'd been wrong, he did agree to keep an eye on Alvis Purdy and make sure the book salesman did not leave town.

Daniel then went to the hotel. He spent an hour with Sue Ann, going over her hotel register. After telling her he was going to call her as a witness that afternoon, and telling her to bring her register with her, Daniel left the hotel and returned to Samuel's. He bathed, shaved, changed into a suit, and was in court two minutes past nine o'clock, just as Judge Billings took the bench and the bailiff called the courtroom to order.

Lily watched Daniel walk in, and she drew a deep breath of relief as she sat down with the rest of the spectators. It wasn't like Daniel to be late. His tie was askew and his hair was wet from his morning bath, giving the impression he was late because he had overslept, but she knew that was not the case, for she had stopped by Samuel's house before coming to court, and he had not been there.

In light of what she and Daniel had realized the night before, Lily was surprised when he took his place beside Amos without looking up into the crowd to see where Alvis Purdy might be. In one of the loud plaid jackets he usually wore, he would be easy to find, but Daniel did not even glance in the direction of the crowd.

Louisa Richmond was still under oath, and she took the witness stand without being sworn again. Judge

Billings informed Daniel that he could now conduct his cross-examination, and as Daniel rose to his feet, Lily wondered what he was going to do. Last night, he had been uncertain, but now he looked his usual confident self. He must have a plan to break Louisa's testimony.

"Your Honor," Daniel told the judge, "I have no questions for Mrs. Richmond at this time. However, I reserve the right to cross-examine her later."

Astonished, Lily stared at him. He was going to let her testimony pass without question? But why? Her testimony was crucial to the prosecution's case, and last night, Daniel had been certain it could ruin his defense. Now he wasn't even going to make an effort to countermand it. Lily knew he must have his reasons, but she could not help wondering what they were.

The prosecution rested, and Lily saw the satisfied smile on Hugh Masterson's face. Daniel, however, did not seem to notice it.

He began his defense with Rosie, who spoke of Amos's benign character. He reinforced her testimony with Jacob Cole, for whom Amos had worked as a boy. Then he called Annie Horsley to the stand. The schoolteacher, young, pretty, and known to everybody in Shivaree as one of the sweetest women alive, would make a good impression.

"Miss Horsley, you are the schoolteacher here in Shivaree, are you not?"

"Yes."

"Has Amos ever been one of your pupils?"

"No."

"Please explain."

"When I first came to Shivaree, I found out that Amos was not attending school, that in fact, he had never set foot inside the schoolhouse in his life. He was about fourteen at that time. I was concerned, and not knowing his family situation, I went to see his father to find out why." Annie's face took on an expression of distaste, conveying more clearly than words her opinion of the late Mr. Boone. "Amos's father informed me that it was no good trying to teach a dog to learn how to read."

"He referred to his son as a dog?"

"Yes."

Daniel waited for the shocked murmurs in the courtroom to die down, then he asked, "What was your reaction to this?"

"I was appalled, but there was nothing I could do. I spoke with Amos but, of course, the boy would not defy his father, and I could not encourage him to do so."

"Thank you. I have no further questions."

It was clear from the puzzled frown on Hugh Masterson's face that the prosecutor had no idea where Daniel was headed with this testimony. He declined to cross-examine the witness, and Annie stepped down from the stand. Daniel then called Lily, who was duly sworn.

"Mrs. Morgan, Annie Horsley has testified that Amos Boone never learned how to read. Can you confirm this?"

"Yes."

"How do you know Amos can't read?"

"Everybody knows. It's common knowledge in Shivaree."

"I see. But do you have personal experience that would verify this common knowledge?"

"I do. When Amos's father died, I knew the boy needed help. I gave him a job working for me as janitor at the library, and I felt it would be a good thing for him to learn to read. I attempted to teach him, but I never got him further than the alphabet."

"Why was that?"

"Amos has a very difficult time with letters. He switches them around. If he saw the word 'was,' for example, he would read the word as 'saw.' Amos knew this himself, and it frustrated him so much, he gave up learning to read altogether. I have tried several times to persuade him to continue the lessons, but he has never done so."

Daniel walked over to the table and picked up a Bible. He entered it into evidence as defense exhibit number one, informing the jury that this Bible was the one found in the bedroom of Corrine Hughes. He opened it and handed it to Lily. "Sheriff Trusedale has already testified that this Bible was found open on the prostitute's nightstand to this passage. Please read it for the jury."

Lily did so, speaking clearly over the speculative murmurs of the crowd.

"Mrs. Morgan, you are the librarian for the Jaspar County Municipal Library. As such, you have a great deal of experience with books. Do you notice anything special about this Bible?"

"Yes." Lily turned to the jury and held the book high so the twelve men seated there could see it. "This Bible is brand-new. There is a printing date of 1905, and the cover has no scuffs or blemishes." Opening it to Ezekiel, she went on, "Although it is clearly brand-new, the covers of this book have been bent back so that the spine was broken."

"What do you think that means?"

"Objection," Hugh called out. "Calls for a conclusion."

Daniel turned to the judge. "Your Honor, this witness is a librarian, and she is clearly qualified to draw such a conclusion."

Billings nodded in agreement. "Your objection is overruled, Mr. Masterson. He turned to Lily. "You may answer the question."

"When the spine of a book is broken apart like this one, the book will stay open to the page of the break."

"Thank you." Daniel turned to Hugh. "Your witness."

Hugh obviously still believed the Bible belonged to Corrine, and did not know what Daniel was driving at with all this testimony and, as Daniel had hoped, he didn't know what questions to ask. Despite her fears that she would be battered on the stand, Lily was excused without cross-examination.

Daniel called his next witness as Lily returned to her seat, glad her part was over. "The defense calls Amos Boone."

This was the moment everyone had been waiting for. The crowd watched the young man as he was escorted by the bailiff from the defense table to the witness stand. Still in cuffs, Amos was forced to raise both hands when he took the oath, giving the jury a clear view of the steel that bound his wrists together, and that view was as devastating as Daniel had predicted it would be. He could tell from the expressions of the jurors that guilt was more firmly entrenched in their minds than ever. But before he was finished, Daniel vowed that was going to change.

He wasted no time on preliminaries. "Amos, we've

heard Louisa Richmond testify that you quarreled with Corrine Hughes on the day she was killed. Would you tell us about that conversation?"

Amos repeated his story, just as Daniel had rehearsed with him the evening before.

"So," Daniel said, "you offered to marry her as a way for her to leave her life as a prostitute?"

"Yes, sir."

"And she refused to marry you?"

"Yes, sir. We fought about it tooth and nail, and that's the truth. She told me she didn't want to marry me because she liked the way she lived, and that made me mad, because it was a bad life."

"So bad, in fact, that you were afraid she'd go to hell, isn't that right?"

"Yes, sir. I told her she should stop being one of those bad women, and maybe she should start going to church."

"And what did Corrine say to that?"

"She laughed, and said she didn't believe in God."

"What, exactly, did she say?"

"No God, no church, no Bibles."

"So, it's pretty unlikely that the Bible found on Corrine's nightstand actually belonged to her, isn't it?"

Hugh jumped to his feet. "Objection! Once again, the defense is calling for a conclusion."

"Withdrawn," Daniel said before the judge could rule. He quickly went on to his next question. "Why did you go to the social club that night?"

"I was hoping to make her change her mind about marryin' me."

"You knew you had to pay a dollar for an hour with her?"

"Yes, sir. Corrine told me that's what I had to do."

"I see. What happened when you got there?"

Amos outlined for the jury how he had arrived at the social club, waited in the parlor, then followed Helen Overstreet's instructions to go upstairs.

They had come to the crucial moment. Would the jury believe Amos's testimony? Daniel mentally crossed his fingers, took a deep breath, and said, "Amos, when you entered Corrine's room, what did you find?"

An expression of intense pain twisted the young man's face. "She was dead," he said simply. "She was lying on the bed, and she was dead. There was blood all over the place." His voice broke on a sob and it took a moment before he could speak again. "I grabbed her and shook her, but she wasn't breathing."

"That's how you got blood on your clothes?"

"Yes, sir. I think so."

"Did you see a knife?"

Amos nodded. "It was lyin' on the floor."

"Did you pick it up?"

"Yes."

"Why?"

"I don't know. I saw it and I picked it up. But then I heard people comin' down the hall, and I was scared. I didn't know what to do. I hid in the closet."

"Why the closet, Amos?"

"I don't want to talk about the closet."

"I know, but you have to tell us about it. Why did you hide in the closet?"

"There was nowhere else to hide."

"Why did you feel you needed to hide?"

"They'd say I was bad, and they'd wallop me. I was so scared, and I didn't want to get walloped."

Daniel took a deep breath. "Like your daddy used to do?"

"Yes, sir."

"Amos, did you kill Corrine Hughes?"

Amos lifted his head proudly, just as Daniel had taught him. "No, sir," he answered. "I swear, I didn't kill her. She was already dead."

There was a long moment of silence, then Daniel said, "Amos, Hugh's going to ask you some questions now." Before he stepped back, he leaned closer and muttered quickly, "You did great. Remember what I told you—don't get rattled. Just tell the truth."

He walked away and drew a deep breath. Amos had done better than he'd expected, but he knew there was still a long way to go. He looked over at Hugh. "Your witness."

To give the prosecutor his due, he tried. He tried hard, but all the rehearsal Daniel had done with his client paid off. Amos, to everyone's surprise, would not back down to Hugh's intimidating tactics. Daniel realized that his client had more character and strength than he would ever have expected.

"You expect us to believe all of this?" Hugh shouted, getting right in Amos's face. "You expect us to believe you just walked in and found her dead?"

"I don't expect nothin'," Amos answered stolidly. "I'm just telling you what happened."

"But that's not what happened. You went there to kill her and you did kill her. Didn't you?"

"No." Amos folded his arms across his chest and glared at the prosecutor. "I don't say what's not true. You're trying to make me say somethin' that's not true, and I won't say it. No matter how much you bully me."

Daniel was proud of the boy. When the crucial

moment came, he'd faced down Hugh Masterson better than most witnesses would have done. He glanced over his shoulder at Lily, who gave him a nod and a smile.

Hugh finally gave up. He walked away, shrugging as if Amos was clearly lying and the jury obviously knew it. Daniel didn't care. While Hugh had been questioning Amos, Matt Gandy had entered the courtroom and handed Daniel three telegrams. One was from Josiah with the information he had requested. The other two were from St. Joseph, Missouri, and Macon, Georgia, and they confirmed what Josiah had discovered. His law clerk had done an excellent job, and Daniel vowed that when he got back to Atlanta he was going to give that young man a raise.

Daniel tucked the telegrams under his notes and called his next witness. "The defense calls Harley Booker, sheriff of Macon, Georgia."

Hugh frowned, clearly uncertain as to the purpose of this testimony, and Daniel's spirits rose another notch. Hugh had no idea what had really happened to Corrine Hughes. Daniel was about to enlighten him.

"Sheriff, last summer there was a murder in Macon, was there not?"

"Yep. A prostitute was knifed to death."

The excited voices of the spectators resounded through the courtroom, and Judge Billings pounded his gavel to quiet the crowd.

Daniel waited until the room was quiet, until everyone was waiting breathlessly for his next question. "When the victim's body was discovered, a Bible was found in her room, is that correct?"

"Yes. It was open to a passage from Ezekiel. Chapter sixteen, verses thirty-five through forty, to be exact."

"The same passage, in fact, that we heard Lily Morgan read for us? The same passage found in the room of Corrine Hughes?"

"Yep."

"Was this murder ever solved?"

"Nope."

"Thank you, Sheriff." He turned to Hugh. "Your witness."

Hugh stood up to cross-examine the sheriff. He was obviously shaken and trying not to show it, but he rallied sufficiently to establish that there was no evidence besides the Bible passage that linked the two deaths. Nonetheless, the damage had been done.

As Daniel rose to call his next witness, he could feel how the atmosphere had somehow changed. Suddenly, there was electricity in the air, and anticipation. Daniel loved it when he felt that shift, that change in the air that told him victory was within his reach. He called Joe Hailey, sheriff of St. Joseph, Missouri, to the stand, and the jury heard of yet another unsolved stabbing of a prostitute. When they heard how a Bible open to Ezekiel was by her side, Daniel knew it was enough to convince them that the deaths of all three prostitutes were due to the same man. When they heard Bobby Tom Thayer testify that he had seen Amos in Shivaree the same night the Macon prostitute was killed, they knew Amos was not that man.

It was time to tell the jury who that man was. Daniel walked to the defense table and held up two documents. "Your Honor, these are telegrams from the managers of the Macon City Hotel and the Jefferson Arms Hotel. I'd like to enter them into evidence."

Billings granted his request, and Daniel called Sue Ann Parker to the stand. "Mrs. Parker, you and your husband run the Shivaree Hotel and Rooming House, do you not?"

"Yes."

"And the night Corrine Hughes was murdered, you had a certain gentleman staying at your hotel, is that correct?"

"Yes."

"Who was that man?"

Prepared for the question, she gave him the name he wanted. "Alvis Purdy."

Heads turned in Alvis's direction, and even from across the room, Daniel could see the sweat that broke out on the book salesman's forehead. He rose from his seat and turned in the direction of the exit, but Bobby Tom Thayer stood in the doorway to block any attempt at escape, and Alvis would have been no match for Bobby Tom. The salesman sank slowly back into his seat.

Daniel handed Sue Ann the two telegrams he had just entered into evidence. "These are telegrams from the proprietors of hotels in Macon and St. Joseph. Do you see that name on these as well?"

"Yes."

"They confirm that Alvis Purdy stayed at their hotels in Macon, Georgia, and St. Joseph, Missouri, do they not?"

"Yes."

"And the dates Alvis Purdy stayed there match the dates when the prostitutes in Macon County, Georgia, and Jefferson County, Missouri, were murdered?"

"Yes."

Daniel paused a moment, strictly for dramatic impact, then he asked her, "What did Alvis Purdy write on the registers of these two hotels and yours as his occupation?"

"Book and Bible salesman."

Pandemonium broke loose in court, and it took Judge Billings several minutes of gavel-pounding effort to silence the crowd this time. Alvis jumped up and ran for the door, trying to duck past Bobby Tom, but it was useless. The stalwart deputy cuffed him in plain view of the jury, and led him away.

Daniel rested his defense, and made his closing argument short and sweet. Hugh's closing argument was brilliantly crafted, excellently delivered, and made absolutely no difference. The jury convened at half past four that afternoon, and returned to give their verdict before five o'clock. "On the sole count of the indictment, murder in the first degree," the jury foreman intoned, "we, the jury, find the defendant, Amos Jefferson Boone, not guilty."

"Yes!" Daniel shouted, unable to suppress his exultation. He always loved to win. But when he turned around and saw Lily behind him with all the relief, happiness, and gratitude of the world in her eyes, he knew this was the sweetest win of all.

❖19❖

"I KNEW IT all along," Dovey said as she stood beside the counter in Rosie's Cafe and poured herself a glass of lemonade. "I knew all along he was innocent. Didn't I, Densie?"

"Oh, yes," her sister agreed, nodding so vigorously, the feather in her bonnet bobbed. "Yes, indeed."

Lily's and Rosie's gaze met across the counter, both of them trying—and failing—to suppress their smiles.

Dovey, however, was not the only person in Shivaree who had a faulty memory. Rosie's was crowded with townsfolk who were now singing Amos's praises, but who, a week ago, might have lynched him if they'd had the opportunity.

Sheriff Trusedale squeezed between two of the ladies gathered round the refreshments laid out on the counter, and Mary Alice laid a hand on his arm as he helped himself to a cookie. "That awful Alvis Purdy is safely locked up, isn't he, Sheriff?" she asked.

"Yes ma'am. Not a chance he'll get away. Your husband will be presiding at his trial, by the way."

Mary Alice shuddered. "To think, that man has been coming through here, selling his books, and behaving just like anybody else, and him a murderer the whole time. How horrible."

"Yes, ma'am," True agreed and turned to Lily. "If you wouldn't mind, Lily, I wanted to talk with you for a second."

"Of course," she answered, thinking perhaps he wanted to ask her questions about Alvis. She followed him around the crowd of ladies and through a pair of swinging doors into the kitchen.

True turned toward her, opened his mouth to speak, then shut it again. Obviously uncomfortable, he shifted his weight from one foot to the other, tugged at his collar, and cleared his throat three times. If he wanted to talk about Alvis, he sure was taking a long time to do it.

Finally he spoke. "Lily, I want you to know that I'm the one who put that note about the social club in your house."

Dumbfounded, she stared at him. With the murder of Corrine Hughes and Amos's arrest, she'd forgotten all about that note. "You did? You?"

"Yes, ma'am."

"But you're the sheriff. How could you, of all people, do such a thing?"

His gaze fell to the floor, and he looked thoroughly ashamed of himself. "A bunch of us got together that night, and we had a bit to drink . . . and, well, a few of us got all worked up about you and the ladies trying to stop us from having our fun." He let out his breath on a sigh. "I guess it's one of those things that seems like a brilliant idea at the time, but then you wake up the next morning and realize it was downright stupid."

She stared at him, and did not know what to say.

He must have mistaken her silence for censure, because his face reddened, and he refused to look at her. He continued to stare at the kitchen floor. "When Daniel brought that note to me and asked me to find out who had left it on your table, I just didn't have the guts to 'fess up."

He took a deep breath and lifted his head to finally look her in the eye. "Even though I was drunk when I did it, and didn't mean any harm, what I did was a crime. If you want to press charges against me for trespassing, tell Bobby Tom. You have every right to do that. And you have every right to set all the tongues in town talking about it, if you've a mind to. I'll bet you're mad as hell."

Strangely enough, she wasn't angry. Maybe because that note seemed ages ago. Or maybe because today was a day to celebrate, and she was in too good a mood to be angry with anybody. Or maybe because she had learned something very valuable over the last few weeks—how to forgive and forget.

"True, I'm not going to press charges against you." She waved a hand as if the note were of no consequence. "I appreciate that you've told me the truth, and I'm relieved. Now, let's just forget about it, all right?"

She could tell her words surprised him. He stared at her for a long moment, tense and skeptical, as if wondering whether or not she really meant what she said. Finally, a smile lifted the corners of his mouth. "I appreciate that, Lily. Thank you. And I am sorry, I truly am."

He tugged at the brim of his hat in farewell, then turned and left the kitchen. She waited a moment, then followed him, resuming her place at the counter. Conversation was still centered around the stunning events of that afternoon.

"How clearly Daniel laid out all the evidence," Mary Alice was saying. "Of course, Lyndon has said all along he's a brilliant lawyer. He certainly proved that today."

Lily glanced across the room at the subject of the conversation. Daniel, Samuel, and Judge Billings had their heads together, obviously discussing the intricate legalities of the trial, as Amos listened with an expression on his face that said he didn't have a clue what the other three were going on about.

Lily smiled at that. Ever since his acquittal that afternoon, Amos had been following Daniel around like a puppy. Hero worship had replaced fear, and now he and Daniel were the best of friends.

Suddenly, Daniel glanced in her direction, and their gazes met. He excused himself from the group of men surrounding him and began to walk toward her. Lily saw what was in his eyes. There was intimacy in the look he slanted her beneath his lashes—intimacy and intent—and Lily felt that odd, weightless sensation in the pit of her stomach. She took an involuntary step backward and hit the counter behind her. Suddenly unable to face that heated gaze, she turned her back and made a great show of rearranging Rosie's pies and plates of cookies.

"Evenin' ladies," he said, halting beside her. The other women surrounding the counter greeted him, but Lily couldn't choke out a single word. As talk of the trial swirled around her, all Lily could hear was Daniel's voice from a few nights ago.

When this trial is over, you and I are going to finish what we've started.

So much had happened since that night, and she'd had little time to dwell on it. But now, now when they were in a room full of people, people who could create a sensation out of the most mundane scrap of information, the extraordinary memory of how Daniel had touched her and called her beautiful came back with unrelenting force, and Lily was sure everyone in the room knew Daniel's intentions as surely as she did.

He reached for a cookie, and doing so brought his arm perilously close to her breasts. She gave a start and ducked her head as she felt the embarrassing heat rise in her cheeks. "I think we need more lemonade," she mumbled and made a hasty retreat to the kitchen. It wasn't until she got there that she realized she had forgotten to take the pitcher with her.

She pressed her hands to her burning cheeks and leaned back against the icebox. She knew what he wanted of her, and she wanted it, too. But that wasn't what turned her inside out, that wasn't what gave her this panicky feeling. No, what scared her was the certainty that as a lover, she was bound to be a disappointment. Jason had always thought so.

"You forgot this."

She jumped at the sound of Daniel's voice. She could not meet his eyes as he crossed the kitchen and handed the nearly empty pitcher to her.

"Thank you," she choked and grabbed the glass pitcher from his outstretched hand. As she turned to open the icebox, he followed her move, so close behind her, she could feel his breath against her cheek. "I think you should make me supper tonight," he murmured. "You leave first. I'll wait a discreet amount of time, then follow you. Leave the back door open. I'll come in that way."

He was gone before she could make the choice to consent or refuse, and she realized there was no choice to make. It was inevitable, and she was powerless to stop it. To her own shame, she was forced to admit that she didn't want to stop it. But it frightened her.

She had tried to be a good wife to Jason, and that had included the wifely tasks conducted in the privacy of their bedroom, but it had made no difference. Nothing she did had pleased him, and within a month, he had moved into a separate bedroom, sleeping in her room when and if he felt like it. Within a year, he had seldom visited her room at all. When he had, the lovemaking act had been quick and furtive, born of his lust and her duty.

Lily closed her eyes, hugging the lemonade pitcher to her breast. Daniel made her feel things Jason never had, and she could only hope that lovemaking with him would not be the empty, meaningless act it had been with her husband. Perhaps it was foolish of her, but she wanted it to be more, so much more than that.

When she had refilled the pitcher with lemonade, she returned to the dining room. Daniel had resumed his conversation with Samuel and Judge Billings. Around them, other men had joined in the discussion. Around the counter, the women were gathered, still chatting away. Lily set the pitcher on the counter and waited until there was a lull in the conversation, then she turned to Rosie, a grimace of pain she hoped looked genuine on her face. "I'm going home," she said, holding a hand to her head. "I've got a bit of a headache."

"Poor dear," Densie said and patted her arm. "You do look quite peaked."

"Ice," Dovey said decisively. "Only thing to do."

"Oh, no, I can give you something better than ice," Mary Alice told her. "I have some laudanum at home. I can have Lyndon—"

"No, no laudanum, thank you," she said. "Ice will be fine. What I really need is just to lie down. The past few days have been very difficult, what with worrying about Amos and all." She forced a wan smile. "I'm just going to go home and get some rest."

Everyone seemed to take her departure at face value, but Rosie gave her a searching glance across the counter as she picked up her reticule, and Lily knew she was not fooled. But she also knew that from Rosie she would receive no censure for engaging in a liaison with a man who was not her husband.

It was still daylight when she left the cafe, but she knew it would not be long before Daniel joined her, and that gave her very little time. When she arrived home, Lily unlocked the back door as he had instructed, then filled a washbasin and a pitcher and went upstairs. She bathed and she washed her hair as quickly as possible, but then spent twenty precious minutes agonizing over what to wear. What sort of dress was appropriate for an illicit encounter with a lover? she wondered wildly, pushing aside gown after gown in her armoire. Her wardrobe possessed nothing alluring or seductive. She also knew that Daniel didn't care for the flamboyant colors she used to wear, and she wanted to wear something he would like. She finally chose a willow-green dress of polished cotton. Her hair was still damp when she pinned it in a simple twist at the back of her head and secured it with a handful of pins and a pair of tortoiseshell combs.

She hoped that all of her efforts would make her feel more assured, less insecure, but with each moment that passed, she found herself more nervous than before. All she could think of was the extraordinary way he had kissed her and touched her, and those memories made her skittish as a colt.

Just as she was dabbing a bit of cologne behind her ears, she heard strains of Mozart drifting up the stairs to her room. Startled, she froze, listening, and she knew Daniel was downstairs waiting for her. He had put on the Victrola.

She glanced at herself in the mirror one last time, took a deep breath, and left her room. From the top of the stairs, she could see him standing in the foyer waiting for her, and she saw that he, too, had changed his clothes. In his black suit, white shirt, and pearl-gray waistcoat, with the late afternoon sun that poured through the transom window above her front door turning his hair every shade of gold and brown, he looked so devastatingly handsome that she froze, one hand on the rail, and simply watched him.

The music stopped, and Daniel looked up at her. For a moment, time seemed to stand still, and Lily felt again that glimmer of fear. But suddenly Daniel reached out and picked up the tiny pillow that rested atop the newel post. A wicked grin lit his face as he held it up. "Do you ever really use this thing?"

"Of course I do," she lied. "Every day."

"Show me." He tossed the pillow to her. "I dare you."

She caught the pillow, and she knew there was no way she could let a challenge like that pass. Acting as if she did this all the time, Lily positioned the pillow on the railing, sat on it, and let gravity do the rest. When she reached the bottom, momentum sent her flying off the railing and straight into Daniel's arms.

"Told you," she said, laughing to cover the nervousness she felt at the feel of his arms around her. "I slide down this banister every day."

"Sure you do," he answered gravely, and she knew he didn't believe it for a second.

He planted a quick kiss on her lips, then he let her go and turned his attention to the Victrola by his side. Lily watched as he removed the shellac disc recording of Mozart and returned it to its paper jacket. "I love this thing," he commented as he put the disc back in the Victrola cabinet and selected another. "Music on command."

He placed the disc on the machine, turned the crank to set it in motion, and carefully set the steel needle on the edge of the disc. Music poured from the Victrola, filling the house with the lush sounds of a Strauss waltz. He held out his hand to her. "May I have this dance?"

She looked up at him, and she felt an absurd desire to cry. He remembered what she had confessed to him weeks ago—that no man but her own father had ever asked her to dance. She could not believe he remembered that.

At that moment, Lily Morgan fell in love with Daniel Walker.

She took his hand. "I don't know if I even remember how," she whispered, but when he put his hand on her waist and began to move, the painstaking lessons of her girlhood came back to her, and she began to move automatically through the steps. She felt awkward at first, but Daniel danced well, and given the sureness of his lead, she soon found herself following him without hesitation, until it seemed almost as if they were dancing on air. When the music stopped and they came to a halt, she looked up at him with no idea how to tell him what this one gesture meant to her. One dance, and he made her feel beautiful, graceful, and most of all, desirable. Impulsively, she reached up and touched him, laying her palm against his lean cheek. "Thank you."

Suddenly a wicked gleam came into his green eyes, and he turned his head to press a kiss into her hand. "Don't thank me yet," he murmured against her palm. "We're just getting started."

Before she could reply, he pulled her hand away and cupped her face in his hands. Lifting her face, he bent his head and kissed her. His lips grazed her lightly until she opened her mouth in response, then he deepened the kiss, tasting her with his tongue.

Lily clutched at the lapels of his jacket and lost herself in the sensation of what he was doing to her with his mouth. She didn't have much experience with kissing, but as she had confessed to Rosie a few weeks before, she knew Daniel was good at it. So good, in fact, that when he broke the kiss and pulled away, it took her several moments to come out of the dreamlike state he had created. She opened her eyes and found him standing on the other side of the foyer beside the front door, watching her.

Bereft without his arms around her, and puzzled by his sudden withdrawal, she stared at him helplessly. "Why did you stop?"

"I want you to be sure about this," he said, his voice

slightly uneven. "I'm giving you the chance to change your mind."

She drew a deep breath, grateful for the choice, but for all her nervousness, backing out was something that had not even occurred to her. Daniel made her feel things she had never felt before, and she wanted more of that sweet passion. "I don't want to change my mind."

He studied her through narrowed eyes. "If I stay, I stay until morning."

"I know."

"You're sure about this?"

Slowly, she nodded her head.

"Prove it then," he dared. "Come over here."

Slowly, she began to walk across the foyer toward him. With every step, her heart pounded harder and harder, until she was sure he could hear it in the hot, silent room. She halted in front of him and felt herself completely at a loss. She did not know what she was supposed to do, she did not know what he expected.

Experience could not guide her, for her husband had never been this way. Lovemaking with Jason had been hasty and furtive, done in the dark and quickly over, the act as empty and loveless as their marriage had been. She wanted so badly for this to be right, and yet, she felt so inadequate to the task. She came to a halt in front of Daniel and looked up at him. "Despite my wicked reputation, I've never had a love affair before. I don't know how to begin."

"I'll show you." He wrapped an arm around her shoulders, then dipped slightly to slide his other arm behind her knees, lifting her into his arms as if she weighed nothing.

"But . . . but . . . I thought . . ." she stammered as she wrapped her arms around his neck, "Shouldn't we have some supper first?"

"What I'm hungry for right now isn't food." He carried her upstairs, finding his way unerringly to her bedroom. Once inside her room, he set her on her feet and took her hands in his.

"The first step, of course, is to get undressed," he told her as he brought her hands up to the lapels of his jacket. He looked at her, daring her with his eyes, his voice, his touch. "Go on. Undress me."

He curled her fingers around the lapels and pulled the jacket wide, guiding her hands to slip it off his shoulders. The jacket fell from her fingers, and she reached for his tie, her hands trembling so badly that she fumbled with the knot. She gave a shaky laugh. "I don't think I'm going to be very good at this."

"It's very simple," he murmured. "You just start at the top, and work your way down. I'll show you."

He grasped her shoulders and turned her around. In the mirror above her vanity table, she watched as he began pulling the pins out of her hair. Released, her hair tumbled down her back, and he reached around her to toss the pins into a crystal dish on her vanity. She stared at their reflection as he fanned out her hair and began playing with it, rubbing it with his fingers, tangling it in his fists. "I love your hair. God, what a glorious color."

"Like Georgia dirt?" she quipped to cover her nervousness.

"Nothin' wrong with that," he drawled. "After all, I am a native-born Georgia boy." He slid his arms around her from behind and reached to her throat for the top button of her dress. He unfastened it. Then he unfastened another. Then another.

Her breathing quickened as she watched him undo the buttons. The sight of his hands on her did strange things to her insides, and she trembled with the sweet aching sensation of it. His hands brushed against her breasts and her ribs as he slowly worked his way down to her waist. He pulled the edges of the gown away, then slipped the dress from her shoulders and down her arms. It caught on the flare of her hips, but he grasped the cotton in his fists, and one final tug sent the dress pooling around her ankles.

His fingers lightly brushed the nape of her neck, and she shivered as he pushed her hair aside. Bending his head, he kissed her there, just above the edge of her chemise, then tilted his head to place more kisses along the side of her throat. When she felt the light scrape of his teeth against her earlobe, all the strength seemed to drain out of her. Her knees buckled, and she would have fallen, but he wrapped one arm around her waist to hold her as he nibbled on her earlobe.

She leaned back against him and closed her eyes, as Daniel used his free hand to undo the hooks at the waistband of her petticoat. Within seconds, it joined the dress at her feet. Using the arm he had around her waist, he lifted her out of the tangle of fabric and kicked both dress and petticoat aside before he set her back down. Then he turned her around, wrapped his hands around her waist, and lifted her again, setting her atop her vanity table.

She watched as he sank to his knees in front of her, and she had no idea what he was going to do, until he took one of her feet in his hands and began to unbutton her shoe. She stared down at his bent head, astonished, as he removed her shoes. Never could she have imagined that a man did things like this; undressed a woman, kissed her, caressed her like this.

Tenderness unfolded inside her like a flower, and she reached out to touch him, tangling her fingers in his tawny hair. He turned his head to press a kiss against her wrist, but did not stop what he was doing. He removed her garters, then slid her stockings down her legs, and tossed them aside.

He rose to his feet in front of her. "See how easy it is?" he asked and reached for her hands. He brought them once again to his tie.

She unknotted his tie and pulled it away, then removed his cufflinks and began to unfasten his shirt. Beneath her hands, she could feel the thud of his heart and the rise and fall of his rapid breathing, and Lily made another startling realization. She was affecting him in the same way he affected her. He was feeling the passion she felt, and that knowledge gave her a heady sense of her own feminine power. After she had removed his shirt, she ran her hands up his chest and across his wide shoulders, staring, fascinated at the hard muscles beneath her fingers. Lord, he took her breath away.

He stood utterly still beneath her touch, but she could feel the tremors run through his body as she caressed him. She ran her hands back down his chest to the buttons that fastened his trousers. He sucked in a deep breath as she began to undo them, one by one. Her knuckles brushed against him with each button she unfastened, and she could feel the hard ridge of his arousal beneath her hands. With her newfound sense of power, Lily became bolder. She pulled back the flaps of his trousers and found the shape of him with her hands. He groaned with pleasure, and she found that to be the sweetest sound she had ever heard.

Daniel laughed low in his throat and grasped her wrists, pulling her hands away. "If you keep that up, this is going to be over before it's even begun."

He let go of her hands and reached for the hem of her chemise, pulling it upward. She raised her arms toward the ceiling, allowing him to pull the garment over her head. He tossed it somewhere behind him.

Her long hair was the only thing that shielded her breasts from his heated stare, but he did not allow her even that much modesty, for he swept her hair back over her shoulders to gaze his fill. Lily curled her fingers around the edge of the vanity to avoid covering herself, but she held her breath, still afraid of being a disappointment. Her breasts were too small, she knew that. *Not enough to even fill a man's hand,* Jason had once told her with contempt.

Daniel put his hands on her shoulders and gently pushed her back against the wall, then slid his hands down to her breasts, cupping them, shaping them with his palms. She closed her eyes and shuddered at the exquisite pleasure of it as his thumbs brushed back and forth across her nipples. Lost in the sensuous haze of his touch, she forgot all about feeling inadequate. When he lowered his head and took one of her nipples into his mouth, she arched against him, raking her hands through his hair as she sought to pull him closer. She wanted more, so much more.

But he did not give it to her. Instead, he teased and toyed with her until she was twisting beneath his touch like a leaf in the wind, helpless to stop herself. Just when she thought she could withstand the exquisite torture no longer, he pulled back slightly, resting his cheek against her ribs. His hand slid inside the waistband of her drawers to caress her tummy. "You are so lovely," he murmured, his breath hot and quick against her skin. "Lovely, passionate, like fire in my hands. I knew you would be."

He straightened and placed his hands beneath her thighs, lifting her from the vanity. Arms around his neck, legs around his waist, she clung to him as he carried her to the bed, the most intimate part of herself pressed flush against his arousal, everything inside her straining toward what she knew would come next.

He set her down on the edge of the bed, and his hands moved to her waist to untie the satin bow of her drawers. "Lift your hips," he told her, and she did, enabling him to remove her drawers. Then he slid her fully onto the bed, tugged off his boots and remaining clothes, and stretched out beside her.

She thought he would take her then, but again, he surprised her. Leaning on one elbow, he looked at her, and their gazes met as his hand slid boldly down her body from her throat to her hips. When he slid his hand between her thighs, she gasped in shock. His fingers brushed against her in a caress so shockingly intimate, that she cried out in protest, moving to push his hand aside. Men simply didn't touch women in such a way. She knew that.

Daniel, however, didn't seem to care about what men were supposed to do. He did what he wanted. "I want to touch you there," he said. "Don't stop me."

He grasped her hand in his long enough to move it out of the way, then returned to what he was doing. As his fingers began stroking her, the sensation was so exquisite, so delightful, Lily could no longer protest.

She felt as if she were on fire. She began to move with his hand, unable to stop the gasps of pleasure that escaped her with each relentless slide of his fingers. The pleasure built in her like waves rising to high tide, and her gasps turned to soft, shuddering moans as he took her higher, and higher still.

He pulled back slightly and she knew he must be looking at her, but all she could think about was what extraordinary things he was doing to her. Suddenly, the movement of his hand changed and he began tracing a tiny little circle against her with the tip of his finger. That one touch seemed to be what her body had been waiting for. Pleasure seemed to explode in a white hot flash inside her, and she could not stop the ecstatic, wordless cries that one magical touch tore from her throat.

She heard his reply—a low, masculine sound of urgency, just before he moved on top of her. She felt the weight of his long, lean body, heavy and hard against her, and she knew what he wanted from her. Her legs parted, and he settled his weight between her thighs, entering her with a sudden, hard push that sent the air rushing from her lungs and left her breathless.

This she knew, this was familiar; the weight of a man's body, the heaviness inside her. But what she felt was so different, the slide and thrust of him inside her was luscious, filling her with him, body, mind, and soul.

She caressed his back, felt his muscles flex and tighten beneath her hands as he moved within her. She pressed her face into his shoulder, kissing him as she matched his pace, a slow and deliberate cadence that made her ache for completion.

Lily felt it coming again, that building anticipation and glorious rush of release, and she cried out his name one last time before she shattered with the sheer pleasure of it. He sensed her reaction, and she understood he had been waiting for it, holding back until it came, for when it did, he quickened the pace until he was moving within her with the rough and frantic rhythm of passion finally unleashed. With a hoarse cry of purely male satisfaction, his body jerked with his own explosive release as he thrust into her one last time and was still.

Lily's arms tightened around him, and she lay beneath him, savoring the weight and strength of his body. Breathless, overwhelmed by what had just happened, she could not move, or even think. Five years as a married woman, and she had known nothing of this. Five years alone, and she had not realized the depths of her own loneliness, her longing for what Daniel had just given her. Passion and tenderness. A glorious feeling of joy welled up inside her, joy so potent and so powerful that she could only cling to him and revel in it for as long as it would last. She loved him, and there was nothing more joyous than that.

❖20❖

SHE WAS CRYING. Night had fallen, and in the darkness of the bedroom, he could not see her tears. Pinned beneath him, she did not move. She made no sound. But somehow, Daniel knew. He brushed kisses across her cheeks and tasted the salty wetness there. It unnerved him that something so pleasurable for both of them should make her cry.

"Lily?" He lifted his weight onto his forearms and nuzzled the base of her throat, inhaling the delicate scent of lilies that enveloped them both. "What's wrong?"

"Nothing," she whispered, her arms tightening around him. "Nothing at all. I'm just happy." She gave a tiny laugh as if unable to believe it herself.

"You're crying because you're happy?"

"I never knew." She laughed again and slid one arm between them to caress his face with her fingertips. "I never knew it was like this."

The realization came to him with a force akin to

hitting a brick wall. "Jesus," he muttered, "what kind of lover was Jason anyway?"

She was silent for a moment, then she said, "He was my husband, but he was never my lover. Until now, I never understood the difference."

Anger toward the man who had once been his best friend flared inside Daniel; sudden, savage anger that surprised even him with its intensity. "Damn Jason. He never took the time to make it right for you, did he?"

"I didn't even know he was supposed to," she confessed. "I thought the . . . the act of lovemaking was quite overrated, actually." He felt her lips curve into a smile against his neck. "I think you've just proven I was wrong about that."

Daniel didn't know what to say. He had pleasured her in a way no other man, not even her husband, ever had before. That knowledge rather awed him; it left him feeling both stunned and immensely gratified. "Careful," he warned her, as he began trailing kisses along her neck to her collarbone. "Compliments like that will force me to live up to them. I just might have to ravish you again." He pressed his lips to the pulse at the base of her throat. "And again."

"All right," she whispered as her body moved sensuously beneath him. "You twisted my arm."

He brought his mouth to hers and kissed her one more time, then lifted himself free and rolled onto his side. "You'll have to give me a little more time than that," he told her. "After that, a man needs a chance to recuperate. Especially when he didn't get any supper."

"Gracious," she exclaimed, turning her head to look at him, "we never did eat, did we? I can't expect you to live on passion."

He laughed. "Not if you expect such strenuous demonstrations of it."

"I'll make us something," she said, pulling the sheet with her to cover herself as she rose from the bed. Daniel grasped a corner of the sheet and yanked it back, leaving her without any covering at all.

"Daniel!" she cried, whirling around to make a grab for it, but he rolled across the bed away from her, balling the sheet in his hands. In the moonlight that filtered in around the closed shades, he could barely make out the outline of her form, but it was enough to rekindle the image of her body in his imagination. "Just as I thought," he said, deliberately keeping the sheet out of her reach. "A prude at heart."

"Give it back," she ordered in vexation, attempting to cover herself with one arm as she leaned across the bed to grab for the sheet.

"I don't know what you're so upset about. It's so dark in here, I can't see you anyway, more's the pity. Besides, I rather like the image of you naked in the kitchen, making me a meal."

Clearly unable to think of a clever reply, she took refuge in the oldest of all feminine arguments. "Isn't that just like a man?" she muttered in exasperation and walked away.

She pulled a robe from her armoire and put it on, then started for the door. "Are you hungry for anything in particular?"

"Now that's an interesting question." In the dark, he could not tell, but he just knew she was blushing.

"Daniel!"

He laughed. "I don't care what we eat as long as you don't go to a lot of fuss. Ham sandwiches or something like that."

"Ham sandwiches it is. I'll call you when they're ready."

"Uhn-uh." He shook his head. "Let's eat up here."

"What? Eat in bed?"

"Why not?"

She laughed. "I can't think of a single reason," she admitted and left him to go downstairs.

Daniel sat up in bed. He unfolded the crumpled sheet across the lower half of his body and settled pillows behind his back, then lit the lamp beside the bed. The room was a feminine one, pastel shades and vases of flowers, and he knew this was not the master bedroom. If Jason had been so callous that she had found no pleasure in his bed, it was no surprise that she no longer slept there.

He'd known Jason Morgan all his life, but Daniel was forced to admit that Lily had been right. He hadn't really known Jason at all. The only thing he knew for certain was that his best friend had been a selfish bastard. To Lily, he had been a bad lover and an even worse husband, and to Daniel, he had been no friend at all.

Even though Lily was not in the room, the scent of her lingered in the sheets and pillows—the delicate fragrance of her namesake. He inhaled deeply, closing his eyes, and the image of her came into his mind, an erotic image that rekindled his desire and heated his blood, that made him ache, made him want nothing more in the world than to pleasure her with his hands, his mouth, his body. By the time she returned with the sandwiches, food was the last thing on his mind.

"Supper," she announced as she came into the room with a tray. She crossed the room and bent to set the tray on the cedar chest at the foot of the bed. When she straightened, she caught his gaze, and she must have sensed something of what he felt, for she instinctively lifted her hand to clasp the folds of her robe together and her cheeks grew pink.

Daniel knew that her husband had done nothing to show her how beautiful she was, and how desirable. He wanted to show her that.

"I think we should eat later," he murmured. "Right now, I want something else." He lowered his gaze to the hand that toyed nervously with her robe. "I want you to take off that robe, come over here, and make love to me again."

"But the sandwiches—"

"They'll keep," he assured her. "Lily," he said gently, "Take off your robe."

She stared at him, wide-eyed, and he thought for a moment she was going to refuse. Her tongue passed nervously over her lips and her hands fidgeted with the sash that held her robe closed.

"Lily, I want to look at you."

Slowly, she untied the sash and parted the edges of her robe, then slid it off her shoulders. It fell in a heap at her feet. Daniel drew a deep, unsteady breath as he looked at her, his gaze moving up her body, from her long legs, across the flare of her hips and the sweet triangle between her thighs, along her slender waist and small, perfectly formed breasts, over the proud lift of her chin, around the coppery brilliance of her hair, to the pair of brown eyes that watched him, wide, unwavering, and scared to death he wouldn't like what he saw.

"God, Lily," he murmured, his voice a bit unsteady.

"You are so lovely." He slid down the bed onto his back, tossed the sheet aside, and held out his hand to her. "Come over here."

She walked to the bed, her steps agonizingly slow to Daniel. When she reached his side, he wrapped his arm around her and pulled her down on top of him. Grasping her shoulders, he pushed her back so that she was forced to sit astride him. He saw the expression of astonishment on her face, and he knew this was another situation beyond her experience. He flexed his hips upward and entered her, beckoning her to move with him.

His gaze locked with hers. "C'mon, Lily," he murmured and thrust his hips upward again, surging fully into her. "You know what I want." Instinctively, she followed his lead and began moving above him, tensing and tightening as she pulled upward, then opening herself to him as she came back down. "That's it," he groaned. "That's just right."

Daniel closed his eyes as their bodies began to rock with a rhythm as old as time. The slow, deliberate movements brought such intense pleasure, it nearly drove him mad as he held back, striving to wait, but when he opened his eyes and saw her above him so lush and erotic, he could wait no longer. Her fiery hair fell in long, tangled waves around her shoulders, her skin glowed with the delicate flush of a satisfied woman, and her lips had that mysterious half smile, so uniquely female, that told him she had just realized exactly what she was doing to him.

When she tilted her head back with a soft moan, Daniel knew he'd never seen anything more beautiful in his life, and he lost what little control he had left.

Grasping her hips, he increased the pace, thrusting deep, then deeper still, again and again. When he heard her startled cries of feminine release, he came in an explosive rush. Pleasure washed over him as she fell, panting, against his chest.

After a few moments, she lifted her head. "Daniel?" she whispered.

"What?"

"After that, don't you ever call me a prude again."

Daniel left her just before dawn, while it was still too dark for prying eyes to catch sight of him slipping out her back door and into Samuel's house. He knew if they were caught the consequences would be far more serious for her than for him, and he had no intention of ruining her reputation twice.

Some people, however, did not need to see him leave Lily's house in the wee small hours of the morning to know what was going on. Samuel's expression across the breakfast table told Daniel the older man knew perfectly well where he had spent the night, and he was not spared a lecture on the subject.

"I hope you know what you're doing," Samuel said darkly, as he buttered a hefty slab of cornbread. "This is a small town, remember."

Daniel gave him a pointed stare across the table. "And where were you last night, if I may ask?" he countered. "Do you really think I don't know where you spend many of your nights? Or what that cot in the back room of Rosie's Cafe is for?"

Samuel held up his hand, butter-covered knife pointed toward the ceiling. "I know, I know," he said, obviously irritated by the reminder. "People in glass houses and all that. But in some ways, I think of myself as a father to you, and I'm using a father's prerogative of Do as I say, not as I do." He set down the knife with a heavy sigh. "Lily's been bitterly hurt once before. She is also a divorced woman. And as far as I can see, there's no end to this situation that won't hurt her again. Unless you intend to give up your political ambitions by marrying a divorcée?"

"She doesn't want to get married," he countered swiftly. "She's told me that herself several times."

"Women often say that, but—"

He was interrupted by a loud knock at the front door. A moment later, Beatrice entered the dining room. "Telegram for you," she announced, handing it to Daniel.

He scanned it as Beatrice left the room. When he was finished, he looked up to find Samuel watching him. "It's from Calvin. He read in the Atlanta papers that the case here has been resolved, and he expects me back in Atlanta tonight. He wants to discuss strategies for my election campaign. He also plans to set up some kind of political fund-raising affair for early next week."

Samuel nodded. "It would probably be a good thing if you left town now anyway, before this thing with Lily goes any further. After all, there's no future in it for either of you."

Daniel did not reply, because there was nothing he could say. Samuel was right. No man's political ambitions could withstand a divorcée for a wife, so marriage was out of the question, and anything less would bring great risk to Lily's reputation.

He was reminding himself sternly of those uncompromising facts when he walked into the library two hours later to tell Lily of his imminent departure. She was upstairs on the mezzanine, her back to him as she stood high on a ladder putting away an armful of books. He crossed the library, mounted the stairs, and halted a short distance away from her, waiting for her to finish.

In a dress of butter-yellow, with the sunlight that poured through the windows glinting off her hair, she looked radiantly lovely, and he drank in the sight of her as he remembered the night before. He studied the line of buttons down her back and remembered each button he had unfastened last night. When his gaze moved to her waist, he remembered the shape of her in his hands, as slender and delicate as the flower that was her namesake. When she descended the ladder, he caught a glimpse of her shapely legs and remembered sliding off her stockings. When she turned and caught sight of him standing there, a blush lit her cheeks that made him know she was remembering all of that, too, and savoring it as much as he did. A glowing smile lit her face.

It did strange things to him, that smile. It wiped out his resolutions and his sanity. "I have to go back to Atlanta today," he blurted out, his voice low so that library patrons down below could not hear. "Come back with me."

"To Atlanta?" she whispered.

"Yes." He leaned closer to her, and caught the fragrance of lilies. Desire clawed at his insides, and he wanted to touch her. But people were watching, and he had to clasp his hands behind his back to stop himself from reaching for her. "I have to go. I have no choice. I want you with me."

"But Daniel," she whispered back, "I—"

"Hell, I just plain want you," he interrupted. "Say you'll come."

Her blush deepened at his frank confession. "But I have to run the library."

"Come down tomorrow. It'll be Saturday."

"I suppose I could do that," she murmured.

"You're in charge. Of course you can. Spend the weekend with me. We'll go to dinner. I'll show you my house. I'll teach you how to play poker. We'll go to the opera." He watched her intently, he saw her attempted resistence begin to melt, and he pressed his advantage. "You love the opera, Lily. Say you will."

"Oh, Daniel, I would love to go."

"Good," he said, drawing a deep breath of relief.

She lifted one hand in a gesture of futility. "But I can't. What on earth could I tell people here?"

Her wavering threatened to drive him insane. "Don't tell them anything."

She stared at him, clearly shocked by that suggestion. "I would have to have some reason to go to Atlanta. If I didn't, and I immediately followed you there, people would figure out why. There'd be no end to the talk."

"Then come tomorrow. The day after. Close the library for a few days and say you're going shopping in the city. Bring Rosie, I don't care. For God's sake, don't keep throwing objections in my face, Lily. Just say yes."

Her smile widened, and she whispered the sweetest word a woman could say to a man. She said, "Yes."

Daniel left for home on the afternoon train and met with Calvin that evening. The next day, Lily followed him to Atlanta, telling only one person of her plans. Rosie had misgivings and made them clear, but Lily refused to be deterred, and Rosie agreed to tell anyone who asked that she had gone to Atlanta to buy books for the library. It was a plausible excuse, since Alvis was in jail and she could no longer buy from him, but she knew no one would believe it. The ironic part of it was that she didn't care.

Lily knew there were risks to what she was doing, but when she saw Daniel waiting for her on the platform at the Atlanta train station, she knew the risks were worth it. Twenty-four hours apart from him had seemed like an eternity, and she knew that being with him was worth any risk.

He took her to his house, and as the carriage halted in front of the elegant Courtland Avenue mansion, Lily caught her breath in surprise. She had known Daniel had money, but she had not known how wealthy he truly was.

As he took her through the house, showing her everything from the cherry-paneled library to the luxuriously modern bathrooms, she could see how proud he was of his home and she could tell that he was even prouder of the success that it represented. In the dining room, he treated her to an elegant meal, and afterward, in the billiard room, he taught her how to play poker.

"But even if I hadn't folded, it wouldn't have mattered," she said, watching in despair as he swept yet another pile of chips to his side of the card table. "You had better cards and you would have won anyway."

"Maybe not," he answered as he shuffled the cards. "If you had continued to raise the stakes, I might have figured you had even better cards than I did, and I might have been the one to fold. Bluffing is part of the game."

Keeping that in mind, she tried again, but bluffing had never been her style, and in the end, he managed to take every single one of her chips. "I think dominoes is more my game," she told him as he put the cards and chips away. "Dominoes I can handle."

"But there's no real strategy involved in dominoes."

"Exactly."

Daniel laughed. "What about billiards?" he suggested and stood up. "That's a game you might like better."

She followed him across the room to the mahogany billiard table, and watched as he took a pool cue down from the rack on the wall. He used the cue to send a white ball rolling hard across the felt surface, breaking apart a triangular grouping of colored balls at the opposite end of the billiard table. Several of the solid-colored balls fell neatly into various pockets of the table, while several others remained scattered across the surface, along with all of the striped ones.

"That's called a 'break,'" he told her, "and it is the opening move in billiards." He explained the basic rules of the game, then handed the cue to her. "You try it."

She leaned over the table, holding the cue in her hands as she had seen him do, and though she hit the white ball, it completely missed the striped one she'd been aiming for.

Daniel brought the white ball back to its original position and moved to stand beside her.

"Try again," he told her, but when she moved to comply, he stopped her by placing his hand over hers on the table. He stood so close, she could feel the warmth of his body, and his palm against the back of her hand made her tingle at the memory of all the other incredible ways he had touched her as he moved her fingers over the top of the cue into the proper position.

He leaned even closer to her and brushed his lips against her ear. "Try it now," he murmured and stepped away, leaving her heart pounding as if she'd been running, and her wits so scattered she couldn't think at all. She missed hitting the white ball altogether.

"I don't think that was any better," she said, mortified to realize she sounded as breathless as she felt.

"Why don't I help you?" he suggested and moved to stand behind her. He slid his arms around her, curling his hands over hers where she held the pool cue. His hands were so much larger than her own, they covered hers completely. She could feel his breath against her cheek as they leaned over the table together.

A dreamlike sensation overcame her, as if she were no longer herself, but had somehow become part of him, and Lily molded herself against him, allowing him to move the cue within their hands to strike the white ball. It hit a striped one and sent it rolling neatly into a side pocket.

"Now that's the way it's done," he murmured, turning his head to press a kiss to her temple. They straightened together, but he did not let her go. With his arms still around her, he pulled the pool cue from her hands and set it on the table, then tightened his embrace, sliding his hands up and down her hips as he brushed kisses across the side of her face.

This was sweet torture, it truly was, and Lily could

not stand it. Impatient for more, she turned in his arms, her lips parting to receive his kiss as she entwined her arms around his neck.

They did not go upstairs to his bedroom until very late, because that evening Daniel taught her that a billiard table could be used for purposes far more pleasurable than playing pool.

❖21❖

THE FOLLOWING MORNING, as they had breakfast in bed, Daniel suggested that she might want to see some of the local sights, but he could tell from her expression that his idea met with little enthusiasm. "All right, then," he amended, deciding to put the choice in her hands, "what would you like to do today?"

She slanted him a speculative look from beneath her lashes. "Now that's an interesting question."

He shook his head, pretending censure as he leaned closer to her. "Insatiable," he accused in a low voice. "Absolutely insatiable."

She ducked her head, pretending to take great interest in buttering a muffin, but Daniel was not fooled. That adorable blush was in her cheeks, and he wondered if she would ever lose it. He hoped not.

"If you really want to take me sight-seeing, I'll go, of course," she said diffidently. "It doesn't matter to me what we do."

"No," he answered. "This is your day. You choose. We'll do anything you want."

"Anything I want?" she repeated. "Promise?"

When he confirmed that with an unsuspecting nod, she smiled a wide, satisfied smile, and Daniel felt a sudden hint of misgiving. When Lily smiled like that, trouble was brewing. "All right," she said. "I want to go shopping."

He groaned and quickly changed his mind. "Almost anything," he qualified, but it was too late.

She shook her head, still smiling. "Shopping. You promised."

Left with no choice, Daniel was forced into a day of dressmakers and department stores. His primary functions were as list-bearer and package-carrier, but after she held up a length of lurid tangerine silk with the unthinkable suggestion of making a Sunday-morning dress for church from it, he also insisted on acting as final judge, turning thumbs-down on the orange silk, the enormous stuffed finch she wanted for a hat, and several other outrageous choices.

He finally figured out she was deliberately provoking him. At Lady Elaine's, one of Atlanta's most prestigious dressmakers, a foulard walking dress was recommended in what Elaine proclaimed was the season's most fashionable color, a shade of brownish-green that Daniel felt matched what came from the south end of a northbound horse. He watched with growing dismay as Lily gave Elaine's suggestion serious consideration, but when her gaze met his briefly over the fabric counter and he saw the dancing mischief in her eyes, he knew he was being had.

"A lovely shade," he said gravely. "Perfect for you."

She made a face at him, and much to his relief, chose a ready-made evening gown of brandy-colored silk instead. For the remainder of the day it became a game between them, a joke on unsuspecting shop assistants, and he found himself enjoying it immensely. At one of the department stores, he pointed out to her the wide selection of corsets available, and even bought one for her; a particularly stiff one of whalebone and webbing that looked sturdy enough to truss an elephant. She was not amused, and promptly retaliated by purchasing a tie for him in that particularly detestable manure shade that was so fashionable.

They browsed through bookstores, had a midday meal at the Lexington, and rode in the park on a bicycle built for two. That night, as he had promised, Daniel took her to the opera.

Every year, he renewed his purchase of box seats at the Atlanta Opera House with every intention of going, but Daniel had seldom taken advantage of his membership. He had often found himself so inundated with work that he had usually ended up giving his seats away. When he saw Lily coming down the stairs that evening, he had to fight the impulse to toss the tickets in the trash and carry her back upstairs to his bedroom.

She was wearing the gown she had purchased earlier in the day. The brandy silk that skimmed her shoulders and dipped to a low vee just above her breasts brought out the delicate creaminess of her skin, and all he could think about was abandoning the opera altogether and getting her out of that dress again, as quickly as possible.

Something of what he was thinking must have shown in his expression, for she came to a halt at the foot of the stairs and eyed him in some uncertainty. "Is something wrong?" she asked. "You have the oddest look on your face."

"Do I?" He took a deep breath and blurted out in a choked voice, "Lily, you look so damned beautiful, I can't think straight. You leave me breathless."

Her response was a devastating smile that filled him with such pleasure, he was startled. He had always prided himself on his rigid self-control, and it was disconcerting to realize how easily she could strip that control away. Unnerved, he turned to pour himself a drink. He downed the whiskey in one swallow, and when he turned back to her, he felt considerably more in control. "We'd better go," he advised, glad to note his voice was steady once again, "or we'll be late."

He took her ivory silk wrap from her and draped it over her shoulders, offered her his arm, and they departed in his carriage for the evening's performance of Puccini's latest opera, something called *Madama Butterfly*.

Daniel's box at the opera house was one of the best, in an excellent location for seeing and being seen, and it was inevitable that at intermission acquaintances would stop by his seats. But when Calvin Stoddard's unmistakably hearty voice called to him from the doorway of his box, Daniel knew he had a problem on his hands. Calvin knew exactly who Lily Morgan was, and he wouldn't like the idea of Daniel squiring around that particular woman. He wouldn't like it at all.

When Calvin and his wife Abigail entered the box, Daniel stood up, his mind racing for a way to get out of this situation gracefully, but unless he found a way to avoid introductions, there was no way to escape Calvin's inevitable fury.

"I can't remember the last time I saw you at the opera," Calvin said with a laugh. "It's good to see you out enjoying yourself, for once." He glanced at Lily, and Daniel knew the moment of truth was at hand when Calvin looked back at him. "Aren't you going to introduce us to this lovely woman?"

Daniel knew he could lie about her name, but he refused to consider that an option. He was not ashamed of his involvement with Lily. He couldn't help how Calvin felt about that, and he'd just have to deal with the consequences of the man's anger later.

He performed introductions, and he did not miss the flush in the other man's cheeks at the mention of Lily's name. Never adept at hiding his emotions, Calvin stared at her in shock, and a thunderous frown clouded his face. "Lily Morgan," he repeated in disbelief. "Jason Morgan's former wife?"

The words were said with such blatant contempt that Daniel's own anger flared; white-hot, savage anger that surprised him by its intensity.

Beside him, he heard Lily's sharp intake of breath. He felt her stiffen, and all he could think of was to shield and protect her from any further cutting remarks Calvin might make. "The very same," he confirmed, meeting the other man's gaze head-on. Before Calvin could say another word on the subject, Daniel added in a soft, dangerous voice, "Be careful, my friend."

Calvin's fury looked about to erupt, and Daniel tensed, readying himself for one hell of a fight. But Abigail Stoddard, much more tactful than her husband, tugged at his sleeve. "The performance is about to resume, my dear," she pointed out in a soft murmur. "We should return to our seats."

Calvin allowed himself to be dragged away, but as he departed, he gave Daniel a hard stare over his shoulder. "We'll discuss this first thing tomorrow morning," he said, and Daniel knew there was no way to avoid the impending confrontation. He also knew there was no way to win it.

Daniel made love to her that night with fierce, sweet intensity, as if nothing on earth were more important than pleasing her, and Lily knew it was because of what had happened at the opera.

He did not discuss the issue with her, and she asked no questions, because in her heart she was afraid of the answer. He made love to her as if it were the last time he ever would, and she knew he did not even realize it.

The next morning, when she woke in his bed, she was alone. "Daniel?" she called, but there was no answer from the adjoining bath or dressing room. Sunlight peeked in around the shades that covered the windows, and Lily knew he must have already gone downstairs for breakfast. It was not like Daniel not to wait for her, and the fact that she woke alone reawakened the deep sense of foreboding she had felt the night before.

She flung back the sheet and got out of bed, dressed hastily, and went downstairs.

She was only halfway down the stairs when she heard Daniel's furious voice coming from the study and another man's equally furious response. Lily paused with one hand on the rail and stared at the open door leading into the study, unable to avoid overhearing the argument going on between Daniel and Calvin Stoddard.

"Are you out of your mind?" Calvin roared. "The opera, for chrissake! Throwing your mistress in the faces of everybody important in Atlanta society."

"Calvin, that's enough! The woman I choose to spend time with is my business."

"No, it isn't. It's mine. And Will Rossiter's. And every other man who had cast support for you."

"Why should you care? Why should any of them care? What difference does it make? I'm not a married man."

"And you won't be if you keep this up. What respectable young lady would have you, after seeing your willingness to take your mistress to a public function?"

"Despite my mistress, I'm sure any number of 'respectable young ladies' would be perfectly willing to marry me for the position and the money," Daniel shot back with unmistakable cynicism. "It happens all the time."

"But not if you insist on flaunting your mistress in public. If you must keep the woman, fine, but keep her out of sight."

She was a kept woman now, to be hidden away like a shameful, secret pleasure in the dark. Lord in heaven, the truth could hurt. Lily closed her eyes, trying to shut out the pain. But she could not shut out Calvin Stoddard's fury.

"I hope to hell the Morgan woman doesn't think you intend to marry her."

"She doesn't want to marry."

Her own declaration came back to haunt her. She had meant it at the time, but now it was a lie. Now, she was in love with Daniel, now she wanted to marry him, now she wanted to spend her life with him. Now, when Calvin Stoddard was making it plain that what she wanted was impossible.

"Thank God for that, anyway," Calvin said. "A

divorcée for a mistress is one thing, but a divorcée for a wife would be unthinkable."

Lily couldn't bear it any longer. She turned and fled, racing back up the stairs to the bedroom before she could hear Daniel's reply. Once inside, she shut the door and sank down on the edge of the bed, knowing that for the past two days, she had been fooling herself. For the first time since her arrival, she began to think about the consequences of what they had begun.

She had thought she could handle a love affair, but now she knew she could not. Now that their secret was out, vicious gossip and scathing condemnations would follow. The talk would not only wound her, it would wound Daniel, as well. She could not bear that.

She also knew he could never marry her. Marriage to her would destroy him and everything he wanted, and she could not allow that to happen. She could not do that to him.

She reached behind her for Daniel's pillow and wrapped her arms around it, hugging it tight and inhaling the scent of him. "What happens now, Daniel?" she whispered to the empty room. "What future is there in this for either of us?"

The answer to that question was that there was no future for them at all. If they stayed together in an illicit affair, it would erode her self-respect and his career, and there would come a time when the bliss of the past two days would change to bitterness and resentment.

The clock on the mantel of the fireplace chimed the hour of nine o'clock. The next train going north from Atlanta left at ten. Lily knew she had to be on it. She tossed the pillow aside and stood up. Without stopping to think, she dragged her trunk out of the dressing room and began flinging clothes into it as quickly as possible. Once she was packed, she called for a maid, informing the girl of her departure and asking her to have Hezekiah, Daniel's driver, hitch up the carriage, then come upstairs and fetch her trunk.

As Hezekiah carried her trunk downstairs a short while later, Lily followed in order to tell Daniel of her decision. The study door was closed now, she could hear no sounds of argument, and she knew Calvin must have left. She waited until Hezekiah had deposited her trunk in the foyer and gone out to the carriage house to bring the carriage around front, then she crossed the foyer to Daniel's study. Taking a deep, steadying breath, she knocked on the door.

When the door opened and she saw him standing there with his hair disheveled and wearing only a black silk dressing gown, she caught her breath. He was so devastatingly handsome, it made her heart hurt to look at him, and she had to fight back the desire to fling herself into his arms and abandon her decision altogether.

Daniel looked her up and down, taking in the fact that she was dressed for departure. When he glanced over her shoulder, he must have seen her hatbox and trunk in the foyer. He looked back at her through narrowed eyes. "Where do you think you're going?"

She had to stay strong. She had to hang on to her resolve. "I'm leaving," she said, gripping her reticule so tightly, her fingers ached. "I'm going home today."

"You're not supposed to be leaving until the end of the week."

"From Calvin Stoddard's reaction to my presence, I think it would be best if I left today."

"Hang Calvin!" he shouted, slamming a hand against the doorjamb. "You're not cutting your visit short because of him. In fact, you're not going anywhere. You're staying here for the entire week."

"Daniel, I can't stay a week, and it was foolish of me to think I could. I have a job, obligations. So do you." It sounded exactly like the pitiful excuse that it was, and she went on, "My life is in Shivaree, and yours is here, and Mr. Stoddard has made that abundantly clear."

He sighed, raking a hand through his hair. "How much did you overhear?"

"Enough to make me understand that there is no common ground between our lives."

"Then change your life. Make a new one, here, with me. Stay for good."

She caught her breath, her heart pounding so hard, she could not make sense of his meaning. "Move to Atlanta?"

"Why not? It isn't as if you had family to consider. Lily, I want you to stay."

"Stay where?" she countered gently. "Here, in this house?" She shook her head. "That would never work. Calvin Stoddard's reaction to my presence would only be the beginning. You know that as well as I do."

"Then I'll buy you a house of your own close by. We'll be discreet if that's how you want it. I want you here, with me."

"So that I can be your mistress? That's what you mean, isn't it? It doesn't sound as if you're offering me a marriage proposal."

He stiffened, staring at her. "I thought you didn't want to ever marry again."

The look of dismay on his face twisted her heart with pain. "I don't," she answered, and the moment she said it, she knew she had made the denial too quickly. It sounded hollow and false.

Knowing he might sense her words were a lie, that marrying him was a hope she had foolishly harbored deep down in her heart ever since she fell in love with him, she rushed on, "A marriage between us would never work anyway. Aside from being a divorcée, I would still make a horrible wife for a politician. I have absolutely no tact, and I'm no good at hosting supper parties, and I always hated having my name in the society columns."

She saw him open his mouth to argue with her, and to reinforce her point, she rushed on, "I wouldn't marry you even if you asked me. Jason married me out of obligation, and both of us suffered for it. If you married me, it would ruin all your aspirations. It would destroy your future, and there would come a time when you would resent me for it."

"I would do no such thing," he shot back. "I would never resent you."

"You would. Some time in the future, you would. And I could not bear to see that happen, to see what we have turn into something ugly and bitter."

"Dammit, Lily, I don't care about the future. All I care about is now, here, with you."

"Now is not enough."

"It's all I have to offer you."

"I know." She reached out to touch his lean cheek. "This has been the most wonderful two days of my life," she whispered. "Thank you."

"Lily, don't leave. Stay. I don't care what people say, I don't care. Do you hear me? I don't care. And if anybody says anything about you, I'll tear them apart. I swear it. Stay."

She let her hand fall. "What are you going to do? Fight with everybody?"

"If I have to."

Slowly, she shook her head. "You can't, Daniel. A fight for my honor is a fight you can't win." She took a deep breath. "I love you."

Stunned, he stared at her. "Now's a helluva time to be saying that, woman," he muttered through clenched teeth, "when you're about to walk out my door."

"Timing never was my strong point."

"God!" He tilted back his head with a laugh that had no humor in it. "I can't think of a single thing to say. What is it about you that can reduce me to a blithering idiot?"

Lily smiled, never loving him more than she did at this moment. "You're not a blithering idiot. You're a brilliant lawyer and a fine man. You'll make a great politician."

Before Daniel could reply, Hezekiah entered the front door. "The carriage is ready, ma'am," he announced.

"I'll be out in a moment, Hezekiah," she told him and pointed toward the trunk. "Take that, would you please?"

"Yes'm." The young man grabbed her trunk by the handles and hefted it onto his back, then departed to wait for her outside.

"Lily." Daniel reached for her, but she eluded his grasp and hastily reached for her hatbox, knowing she had to leave now, while she still had the strength to do it, before he could touch her, before he could persuade her to stay, before she could ruin his life. "I have to go," she mumbled. "The train leaves in twenty minutes."

"I'll come with you. Give me a moment to get dressed—"

"No," she said. "I want you to stay here. I—" To her shame, her voice broke, threatening to break her resolve as well. "I don't want you to go with me. I couldn't bear a train station good-bye."

She stood on her toes and pressed her lips to his for one last kiss, but when she felt his arms come up around her, she felt herself weakening, felt her resolve begin to crumble in his embrace. She wrenched free and stepped back, shaking her head. To her mortification, the tears she had been fighting back for the last hour hovered on her lashes, threatening to fall, and she turned away before he could see them. She walked out the door, then ran to the carriage as tears fell, unheeded now, down her cheeks.

"Lily! Lily, dammit, come back here!"

She stepped into the carriage as Daniel continued to call her name, and as the carriage rolled away, she had the sinking feeling she would hear his tortured voice in her dreams for many long days and nights to come.

❧ 22 ❧

Daniel had no doubt the party at Calvin Stoddard's house would be pronounced a glittering success. All the important people of Atlanta society were present as his candidacy for the state senate was formally announced, and tomorrow the papers would be filled with the news. The society columns would report even the most minute details, everything from the costly trims on Miss Elizabeth Granger's gown to how many times champagne glasses were lifted hailing Georgia's next senator, and they would miss the most vital fact of all: that the guest of honor was not celebrating.

Daniel put on a good show. He smiled, he shook hands, he danced with Miss Elizabeth Granger an appropriate three times. That particular debutante was the odds-on favorite to become the wife of Atlanta's most eligible bachelor, and Daniel was certain that by morning, the papers would have them engaged and picking out china patterns. The very idea revolted him.

There wasn't anything particularly wrong with Miss Elizabeth Granger, debutante, if a man could ignore that her lovely head was completely empty, that she chattered nonstop, and that she honestly believed President Roosevelt's greatest contribution to the world thus far was a stuffed toy bear. No, Daniel knew Elizabeth Granger's greatest flaw was that she was not Lily Morgan.

Lily. Just thinking about her brought intense pain, and Daniel had been thinking about her for the past thirty-six hours, ever since she had walked out his door. He hadn't realized how long one night could be, or how empty his house could seem without her.

Calvin saw him standing alone by the doors into the parlor and crossed the room to stand beside him. "Why is the guest of honor standing here all alone?" he asked. "This is your party, you know," he went on, waving a hand toward the guests that crowded the room. "You're supposed to mingle."

"Yes, I know."

Calvin noticed his lack of enthusiasm, but he misinterpreted it. "Daniel, even though the Shivaree Social Club was closed, you mustn't take it so hard. I know you feel like you lost, because you didn't do what you went down there to do and keep my club open. But I want you to know I don't blame you for that, and you mustn't blame yourself for it either."

Daniel felt an absurd desire to laugh. The closure of the club was the last thing on his mind just now. He missed Lily too much to give a damn.

"Everything is working out for the best anyway," Calvin went on. "I've sent Helen and most of her girls down to Savannah. We're opening a gentlemen's club down there, and it's going to make the Shivaree Social Club seem like a Texas crossroads whorehouse by comparison."

Daniel was suddenly struck by an overpowering disgust with Calvin, his businesses, his ways of making money. He had always been able to represent his clients despite any of his own personal feelings, but after everything that had happened during the past two months, he couldn't seem to walk that line anymore. "I don't want to know about it. Don't tell me any more."

"Sorry." Calvin held one hand palm outward in apology. "I forgot about those legal ethics."

His face must have shown something of what he felt, because Calvin tactfully changed the subject. He gestured toward Elizabeth, who was standing with a group of other young ladies. "She's the one for you, I think. Her father, Albert Granger, has a lot of influence, you know. And she would be the perfect wife for a senator."

"Yes, perfect," Daniel echoed, his voice grim. "But I have no intention of marrying Elizabeth Granger."

He set his empty champagne glass on the silver tray of a passing maid and grabbed a full one. He downed the champagne in one swallow. Perhaps he ought to get drunk. Daniel had always prided himself on his logic and reason, and getting drunk, in his opinion, was a logical and reasonable thing to do under the circumstances. He was, after all, supposed to be enjoying himself.

Everything he wanted, everything he had dreamed of, everything he had spent the past fourteen years working for was in his grasp. He was no longer the son of a poor white trash Cracker from the backwoods. He no longer had to prove himself to anyone. He ought to be savoring his success and looking forward to his future.

Samuel's words of two months ago echoed through his mind: *The love of a good woman is worth more than all the success in the world.*

Back then, he had laughed at that notion. Now as he looked around the luxurious parlor packed with influential people, he knew Samuel was right. None of it meant a damn thing, because he loved Lily. Without her, there was no success. There was no future. Daniel tossed his empty glass into a nearby potted fern, turned his back on everything he had always thought he wanted, and walked away.

"Daniel?" Calvin followed him across the foyer. "Where are you going?"

Daniel ignored him. "Have my carriage brought around," he told the boy who stood beside the door for that very purpose, and the child departed to follow his instructions. He accepted his hat from the butler and started to walk out the front door, but Calvin put a hand on his arm to stop him.

"What the hell are you doing?"

"What does it look like I'm doing?" he countered, turning to face the other man. "I'm leaving."

"What, now?" Calvin stared at him in shock. "You can't leave now. We're in the middle of a party, a party in your honor."

"Too bad." He met the other man's gaze. "It's no good, Calvin. I can't do this. I won't."

"What do you mean?"

"I mean, I'm calling it off."

Calvin's brows drew together in a furious frown. "Is this about that Morgan woman? For chrissake, Daniel, don't let lust do your thinking for you!"

Daniel ignored that advice. "For the first time in my life, I know what is really important. I know what really matters. Calvin, I'm not going to run for senate, I'm not going to marry the right girl, I'm not going to be the golden boy of the political scene, because none of that means a damn thing to me anymore. I'm giving it up. All of it."

"What? You can't quit now! I have a great deal invested in you."

"That's your misfortune."

Daniel walked out the door, knowing he was blowing all the bridges of his ambition sky-high, and he didn't care. He stepped into his carriage and let Calvin think up an excuse why the guest of honor had just left the party. Daniel figured Calvin ought to tell everybody the truth, that he was giving it all up for love. That would really give the society columnists something to write about.

Shivaree was always the same. Each day blended into the next with monotonous predictability, giving Lily a clear indication of what her life would be like from now on. Safe, secure, and loveless.

She was once more a welcome face in her community, she was invited to quilting parties and social events, she had friends again, but Lily had never felt lonelier in her life.

She picked up another law book from the pile on the floor beside her. She was typing cards for Samuel's law books to put in the card catalog, thinking it would be more of a distraction than dusting bookshelves, but it wasn't. She caressed the cover of the book almost lovingly, remembering all the nights she'd sat here with Daniel, reliving with aching sweetness every look, every argument, every caress, deliberately torturing herself with memories of nights that somehow seemed ages ago.

It had been only three days since she'd walked out of his house in Atlanta. Only three days since she had last looked into his eyes, only three nights since she had last felt his touch. Never could she have imagined that three days could be so dull and three nights so long.

Did he love her? Was he as miserable as she? Lily knew those were futile questions. She had no regrets about her decision. She had left for his sake, for his future, and she would do it again. But that didn't stop her from being totally miserable. She stuck another card in the typewriter and pecked listlessly at the keys, wishing for something, anything to distract her from thoughts of him.

As if in answer to her wish, Rosie entered the library. Lily straightened in her chair and resumed her typing, trying to look efficient and busy, so that her friend would not see the emptiness she felt.

Rosie sat down opposite her at the desk. "How are you feeling?"

Lily wanted suddenly to laugh. That was the kind of question a friend asked when you were getting over a cold, not a broken heart. But she knew her friend was asking out of concern and compassion. "Fine," she choked. "I'm fine."

Rosie didn't believe her. "Lily, what happened in Atlanta?"

She hadn't told her friend anything about the choice she had made, and she wasn't ready to tell her now. Maybe one day she would, but not yet. Not when she felt herself always on the verge of dissolving into stupid tears.

The opening of the front doors saved her from replying to Rosie's question. At that moment, Dovey sailed into the library, with Densie in her wake as usual. "Good morning," they chorused as they walked past Lily's desk, heading for the novels at the back of the library.

Rosie smiled. "So, Dovey and Densie are making use of the library, I see."

"Every day this week." Grateful for the distraction, Lily cupped her hands around her mouth and added in a whisper, "They're reading *Tom Jones*."

Rosie laughed and whispered back in mock horror, "That dirty book?"

"They won't check it out, but they've come in every day this week to read another chapter. They think they're fooling me hiding over there in the corner, but I know exactly what they're up to."

"How?"

Lily gestured over her shoulder to Amos, who was dusting bookshelves near the two older women. "Amos is my spy. He can't read the titles, of course, but he can recognize the covers. He tells me what books people are reading."

Rosie laughed. "It's almost impossible to keep a secret in this town."

Lily leaned forward in her chair. "I don't know about that," she whispered. "You've managed to do it."

A pink blush came into Rosie's cheeks. "Not for long," she whispered back. "It's going to come out very soon."

"What do you mean?"

Rosie glanced around to make sure no one was nearby, then she said in a low voice, "I'm going to petition Judge Billings for a divorce from Billy on grounds of desertion. I've finally managed to convince Samuel, and as soon as the divorce is final, we're going to get married."

"Oh, Rosie, that's wonderful. I'm very happy for you."

Rosie looked down at the reticule in her lap, nervously toying with the clasp. "I wanted to tell you myself because I didn't know how you would feel about it."

"Why?" Lily asked in surprise. "I'm certainly not in a position to give you a lecture on the subject of divorce."

"That's not what I meant." Rosie looked up and met her friend's gaze, took a deep breath, and added, "I want to have Daniel handle the divorce for me. I don't want Samuel to do it because he hasn't practiced law in years, and it would start people talking, and it would just be better if Daniel handled the whole thing."

"I see." Lily sat back, not knowing what to say. "If Daniel handles it for you, I'm sure everything will be fine."

"I didn't know how you would feel about it. I mean, he'll probably have to come back here. You might see him."

Lily tried to make her shrug casual. "He'll be back anyway from time to time to see Samuel. I'd better get used to it."

At that moment, Samuel walked into the library. As he crossed the room to Lily's desk, Rosie stood up with an exclamation of surprise. "Is it eleven o'clock already?" she asked him as he came to a halt beside her chair and nodded.

"Just after," he answered. "The eleven o'clock from

Atlanta pulled in a few minutes ago. We'd better go, or we'll miss the eleven-twenty going back."

Rosie turned to her. "We're going to Atlanta for the day." She blushed. "We're celebrating, even though it's still a secret."

"Did she tell you?" Samuel asked, looking across the desk at Lily, who rose to her feet, pasted a smile on her face, and offered them her congratulations. The pair accepted them, then started for the doors. With mixed feelings, she watched them go. She was genuinely happy for Rosie, glad her friend was finally going to have some happiness. She was also envious, and ashamed of herself for feeling that way.

She knew she had made the right decision. With marriage out of the question, there had been only one choice to make. She could not have lived as a mistress, getting only scraps of Daniel's attention, watching her love for him become an inconvenience in his life, waiting until the inconvenience became a burden and he set her aside.

"I did the right thing," she reminded herself in a whisper, but the words sounded as hollow and empty as she felt.

She watched Rosie and Samuel walk out the doors, but they had barely swung shut behind the pair before they swung open again. The man who strode into the library was the last person in the world she expected to see.

When he caught sight of her, Lily stiffened, unable to breathe, unable to think, unable to do anything but stare at him with bittersweet pain, hungrily, as if she hadn't seen him for months, studying every feature of the lean, handsome face that had haunted her for three sleepless nights. She could not look away, she could not seem to find any armor to shield her from his perceptive eyes. Never had she felt so utterly vulnerable.

He began walking slowly toward her desk, and she struggled against the impulse to turn tail and run. She'd known he would come back, sometime. She'd known that she would have to prepare herself for that, but she hadn't had time. It had been only three days. Three days wasn't long enough to toughen her heart, three days wasn't long enough to get him out of her mind. She was still raw, wounded, exposed. She was still in love with him. He should have waited until she was ready to face him again. Thirty years or so.

She wondered wildly what had brought him back so soon as he halted before her desk. His first words gave her an incredibly trivial explanation. "I want a library card."

Lily stared up at him blankly. Of all the things she might have expected him to say, asking for a library card was not one of them. "What are you doing here?"

Daniel sat down. "I told you, I want a library card," he repeated, gesturing toward the tin box on her desk. "Go on, Lily. You're the librarian. Issuing library cards is still part of your job, isn't it?"

She sank down in her chair. "Why do you want one?"

He looked at her with patient gravity. "Maybe I want to check out some books. Stop asking questions and type me out a card, please."

She fumbled with the card box, remembering the day she had refused him a card and how long ago that seemed, how different her feelings were now from what she had felt then. Lily removed a blank card and placed it in her typewriter. Her hands shook as she held them poised over the keys. She couldn't resist playing out the scene as they had done two months ago. "Name?" she whispered.

"Walker. W-A-L-K-E-R. Daniel Jeremiah Walker."

She typed with painstaking care and still misspelled Jeremiah. Too preoccupied with wondering what he was up to, she didn't stop to correct it. "Address?"

"Fourteen Harlan Road. Shivaree."

She automatically started to type the address he had given her, but when she realized what he had actually said, she froze and looked at him over the typewriting machine. "You've given me the wrong address."

He smiled, a smile so tender that it twisted her heart. "I don't think so."

"But Fourteen Harlan Road is the old Brody place. It's where you used to live."

"Don't worry. We won't have to live in the old shack. We'll build a house of our own—"

"Daniel," she interrupted, terrified that she misunderstood him. "What are you talking about?"

"I mean I gave it up, all of it." He pulled the newspaper from beneath his arm and tossed it on her desk. It was a copy of the *Atlanta Constitution* from the morning before, folded back to the society columns. "This is a library. Don't you read the newspapers?"

"It takes two additional days for us to get the Atlanta papers," she answered, staring at the story splashed across the page. Dazed, she picked up the paper and scanned it, reading how Daniel Walker, successful Atlanta attorney and candidate for the state senate, had walked out in the middle of a fund-raising party at Calvin Stoddard's house, declaring he was withdrawing from the race. Rumor had it he was planning to sell his Atlanta mansion and return to his hometown of Shivaree to practice law. Lily looked up at him over the top of the paper.

"You're not running for the senate?"

"No."

"You really walked out of Calvin's party?"

"Yes. Aren't you going to ask me why?"

Trying to stay calm, she took a deep, steadying breath. It didn't help. "Why?" she choked.

He rose from his chair, came around the desk, and took her hand gently away from the typewriter, then he pulled her to her feet. "It was a logical, reasonable decision, based solely on facts."

He lifted her hand and began kissing her fingertips as he listed each of those facts. "One: The world doesn't need another politician. Two: I'm thirty-four and it's time I got married. Three: I happen to be in love with a woman who wouldn't marry me any other way. Four: None of it means a damn thing to me without her. Five—" he paused and looked at her over the top of her trembling hand. "Have I made my case yet?" he murmured, his lips brushing her knuckles, "or does the judge need more information before she stops asking questions and agrees to marry me?"

"You don't mean this," she whispered.

"Oh, yes, I do."

With a sob, Lily pulled her hand free and entwined her arms around his neck. She buried her face against his chest with an unintelligible reply.

"Was that a yes I heard?"

She nodded against his chest.

He grasped her shoulders to push her back so he could look into her face. "Say it."

"Yes!" she cried. "Yes, I'll marry you."

"And I get my library card?"

"Yes!" She was laughing and crying as she curled her arms around his neck. "Yes, yes, yes."

He pulled back to look in her face. "Lily, ever since I was a boy, success has been the only thing I've wanted. Winning has been the only thing that mattered to me. But you've made me understand for the first time in my life that success without love is meaningless. Without you, I haven't won anything."

"I think you've made your case." She cupped his face in her hands. "Oh, Daniel, I love you."

"I'm sorry for what happened all those years ago." He turned his head into her hand and kissed her palm. "So goddamned sorry."

"Don't blame yourself for that. It was Jason. He used both of us."

"I know." Daniel pulled her hard against him. "Forget about him. Let's talk about something else— you marrying me, for instance."

She laughed. "Where are you planning to take me for our honeymoon?"

"Hell, I don't know. Where do you want to go? Italy? Paris? Athens?"

She was silent for a long moment, thinking it over. Then she took a deep breath, and said, "How about if you take me to Birmingham, Alabama?"

He lifted his brows in surprise. "Are you sure you want to do that?"

"I'd like to at least try to make peace with my family. But you have to come with me. I don't think I'd have the courage to face them alone."

"I don't believe that for a second." He pressed a kiss

to her forehead. "Besides, you'll never have to face anything alone again. Ever."

He pulled back and glanced around the room, then he looked at Lily. "Dovey and Densie are watching us over the top of a bookshelf with their opera glasses," he murmured. "In fact, everybody in the whole place is watching us." He gave her a wicked grin and tightened his arms around her. "Let's give 'em something that'll leave 'em breathless, sugarplum. Something they'll talk about for years. Kiss me."

She did, and it was a kiss scandalous enough to keep the people of Shivaree talking for a long time to come.

Read all of the thrilling romances from Sonnet Books

Linda Lael Miller

SPRINGWATER SEASONS

UNDER THE BOARDWALK

Linda Howard, Geralyn Dawson,
Jillian Hunter, Mariah Stewart,
and Miranda Jarrett

**A DAZZLING COLLECTION OF ALL-NEW
SUMMERTIME LOVE STORIES**

O **Under the Boardwalk**
Coming in July 1999

Kimberly Cates

☐ **Briar Rose** (now available) 01495-1/$6.50

Laura Lee Guhrke

O **Breathless** Coming in July 1999

Andrea Kane

☐ **The Gold Coin** Coming in August 1999

Tracy Fobes

O **Heart of the Dove** Coming in August 1999

Linda Lael Miller

SPRINGWATER SEASONS

Rachel

Savannah

Miranda

Jessica

The breathtaking new series....Discover the passion, the pride, and the glory of a magnificent frontier town!

Available now from Pocket Books 2043-01

SONNET BOOKS
PROUDLY PRESENTS

THE CHARADE
Laura Lee Guhrke

Coming soon in paperback from
Sonnet Books

The following is a preview of
The Charade. . . .

At dawn, North Square was seething with activity. Women with baskets stood amid the flimsy stalls of the marketplace, haggling with farmers or their agents over the high prices. Their arguments mingled with the crowing of live turkeys for sale, the beckoning calls of merchants, and the rattle of carts that rolled through the square carrying precious firewood, apples, and onions from the country.

Preoccupied with their own business, no one noticed the man who stood in the doorway of the inn on the edge of the square. Perhaps it was because the winter morning was bleak, and his long black hair and black cloak blended into the dark shadows of the doorway. Or perhaps it was because he stood utterly motionless, little more than a shadow himself.

His position commanded an excellent view of the square, and in the dim light of early morning, his gray eyes restlessly scanned the area. He was looking for one man, and that man would tell him that his call for a meeting had been heeded.

Ethan Harding's friends would have been astonished to see him skulking about in doorways in the wee small hours of the morning, since it was common knowledge that he never rose before noon. But then, they would not see him here, for they were fast asleep in their beds themselves, and it was unlikely they would have recognized him in any case. The dark clothing he wore was so unlike his usual wardrobe of colorful silks and lace, and his hair was not concealed by a powdered wig. The dandy of the Tory drawing rooms was completely unrecognizable in the serious man swathed in black who stood in the doorway of a second-rate inn on North Square. And that suited Ethan perfectly well.

A fishmonger's cart rolled into his line of vision and came to a stop. Ethan let out his breath in a slow sigh of relief at the sight of the driver, a burly, barrel-chested man who jumped down from the cart, crying, "Fresh clams today! Fresh clams!"

Colin Macleod's fish were often wrapped in seditious newspapers. Ethan smiled to himself, knowing perfectly well that Samuel Adams didn't mind if his fiery prose smelled of cod or plaice, as long as the public was kept informed of the British government's latest atrocities.

Ethan started toward Colin, but matrons and housekeepers eager for fresh clams swarmed around the cart, and he stepped back into the shadows, waiting for the women to depart. While he waited, he continued to observe his surroundings. After what had happened only a few hours before, Ethan knew there was a strong possibility he was being watched. Though he could not be certain his identity had been compromised, he walked with danger at his elbow these days, and it was always best to be on guard.

The baker, Matthew Hobbs, whose stall was beside Colin's cart, seemed to be doing a brisk business. A pity, since the man was a staunch Tory. Ah well, not everyone wanted liberty from England. What they didn't realize was that it was inevitable.

A young woman of perhaps nineteen or twenty paused beside the baker's stall, less than a dozen feet from where Ethan stood. Her clothes were rags, too tattered to make her the servant of even the meanest master. Even against the chill of the Boston winter, she wore no hat. Her hair, the color of amber honey, was cropped short, and Ethan guessed she had probably sold the rest of her hair to buy food or lodgings. She stood in profile to him, and although the long cloak she wore hid the lines of her body, Ethan could see hunger in the hollow of her cheek and the line of her throat. She was clearly a beggar, a common street waif that a man would seldom notice, unless it was with a wary eye and a hand on his purse. But when she turned his way, Ethan drew a deep breath of surprise and revised his opinion. There was nothing common about this girl. She had the face of an angel.

Ethan was not a man to be impressed by a woman's beauty. In truth, he seldom noticed women at all these days, which he considered rather a shame when he took the time to think of it. There had been a point in his life when women had been one of his major preoccupations, but suspicion was his only mistress now, and he knew all too well that treachery often hid behind a woman's charms. Nonetheless, he could not help staring.

Her wide eyes were the azure blue of a summer sky, with all the innocence of a child. Yet her thick, dark lashes and soft, generous lips had all the seductiveness of a courtesan. Her features were delicate, her flawless skin the color of cream. But it was her smile that fascinated Ethan. It was a smile that could make a man abandon his ideals, forget his honor, sell his soul. It was a smile that enslaved. It was magic.

He wondered what had brought that smile to her lips, but from this vantage point, he could not tell. She turned away and returned her attention to the baker who, like Colin, was preoccupied with a crowd of customers. Because he was observing her so closely, Ethan did not miss the apparently casual glance she gave her surroundings, nor the two meat pies that slipped from the baker's table into the folds of her cloak.

Well done, he approved, watching in amusement. Anyone who stole from a Tory deserved high praise indeed. She moved out of Ethan's line of vision, and he leaned forward so that he could continue to watch her, but she disappeared into the crowd.

Ethan leaned back in the comfortable shadows of the doorway to wait for Colin to be free of customers. Even though the two men would speak in trivial terms, Ethan never allowed his conversations to be overheard if he could help it. It was safer that way.

"Thief! Thief!"

The cry rose above the noise of the crowd, and Ethan once again leaned forward in the doorway, curious to see what was going on. To his surprise, he saw the angel girl again, but this time she was in the grip of a richly dressed merchant.

"I am no thief!" she said indignantly, trying to wrench her wrist free of her captor's grasp. "Unhand me!"

"You took it. I know you did." Keeping a firm hold on her wrist, the man looked around for a constable. Ethan watched as she shoved and struggled against her captor, and he caught the glint of silver as she slipped the man's watch back into his pocket.

Clever girl. Ethan grinned, knowing no one would be able to prove theft against her now. Unaware that his watch had been returned, the merchant continued to shout for a constable, but the only person who came forward to assist was a young redcoat officer. "What is going on here?" he demanded as he stepped forward out of the gathering crowd.

"This girl stole my pocket watch," the merchant accused, twisting the girl's wrist with enough force to make her cry out.

"I did not! It's a lie!" She looked up at the officer, her gorgeous eyes wide and pleading. She lifted her free hand in a helpless gesture. "A ghastly mistake has been made," she said in a voice that would have melted stone. "This man seems to believe I have stolen something from him, and I am unable to convince him of my innocence. Oh, Major, you seem such an able and intelligent gentleman. Please help me."

The officer, who was only a lieutenant, puffed like an arrogant peacock at her flattery. He smiled and patted her arm. "I'm sure everything will be fine," he said soothingly and turned to the merchant. "When did you lose your watch, sir?"

"I didn't lose it," the other man said angrily, scowling at the officer. "She stole it."

"Have you proof of this?"

"Proof? She'll have it on her, and that's all the proof you'll need."

The girl's expression was one of such martyred innocence that Ethan nearly laughed aloud. "By all means, search me if you must," she said with injured dignity. "I will gladly submit if it will convince you I am innocent. But, if you please, sir, ask this gentleman to search his own pockets as well, for I am sure he is mistaken."

The lieutenant would not have been human if he had not responded to such a plea. He turned to the merchant. "Sir, are you certain your watch is not on your person?"

"Of course I'm certain. Any fool can see she stole it."

Being called a fool did not sit well with the lieutenant. He frowned. "Would you mind verifying that the watch is missing?"

"Of all the ridiculous . . ." The merchant let go of the girl and patted his pockets, muttering impatiently to himself and scowling, but his irritated expression quickly changed to astonishment as he pulled the heavy silver watch out of his coat pocket.

"It seems you have falsely accused this young lady," the lieutenant said.

"I must have misplaced it," the other man murmured, and Ethan choked back his laughter only with a great deal of effort. Red-faced, the merchant bowed stiffly and walked away without another word.

The girl turned to the officer, her face shining with gratitude. "Oh, Major, I don't know how to thank you."

Now that the excitement had passed, the crowd that had gathered around them dissipated. After such a close call, Ethan expected the girl to beat a hasty retreat, but he found he had underestimated her. Instead of counting her blessings and going on her way, she lingered beside the officer, talking with him. One or two more flattering comments, a few moments of rapt, wide-eyed attention, and the lieutenant was completely captivated. He smirked and swaggered, too besotted by his bewitching companion to notice when one of her small, delicate hands slid into his pocket.

Tongue in cheek, Ethan watched her remove the officer's money purse quicker than the blink of an eye and slip it into her cloak. *By the devil,* he thought in admiration, *this girl could get through heaven's gates by stealing the keys.*

Impressed by her audacity, Ethan watched, certain that the officer would come to his senses and realize what had happened. But such was not the case. She touched the redcoat's cheek in a lingering caress of farewell and turned away, leaving the dazed young officer staring after her with an expression on his face similar to that of a bewildered sheep. Giving him one last glance over her shoulder that held all the promise a man could want, she melted into the crowd and disappeared.

Still grinning, Ethan watched her go, feeling a hint of regret. He couldn't recall witnessing anything in his life that had given him more pleasure than the past few moments. For wit, even a Molière play could not compare. That girl was one in a thousand.

With an effort, Ethan brought his attention back to the business at hand. He had dangerous work ahead of him, and he could not afford to be distracted by a clever street thief, even if she did have the face of an angel.

Had the pious ladies who ran the Benevolent Home for Unfortunate Girls in London known that Katie Armstrong would turn out to be a natural thief, a talented pickpocket, and an accomplished liar, they would have prayed harder for her soul and applied the willow switch to her backside with even more frequency. Had they known she would never suffer a guilty conscience for her sins, they would have sent her straight to a workhouse, dismissed her soul as a lost cause, and would never have bothered with her at all.

At this moment, Katie was nibbling the second meat pie of her stolen breakfast and trying to find the cheapest lodgings she could get with her stolen coins. Guilt was the furthest thing from her mind.

She needed a place to stay. Sleeping outdoors on one Boston December night had been enough to convince her of that. For lodgings, she had needed money. The handful of silver she'd taken from James Willoughby's strongbox had brought her all the way from Virginia, but that money was gone, Massachusetts winters were severe, and Katie had nearly frozen to death last night. She cursed herself as all kinds of a fool for heading north instead of south when she'd run away from Willoughby, but there was no help for that now.

She swallowed the last bite of her meat pie and decided she'd better settle for one of the cheap rooms she'd found earlier around Mt. Whoredom. With what she'd dipped out of that lieutenant's pocket this morning, she could have lodgings down there for at least a month. She knew many of those rooms had fleas, but she couldn't afford to be choosey.

She had to stay here for the winter, and it was harder to dip in a small city like Boston than it had been in London. Too much risk of getting caught and hanged. She had to make her stolen coins last as long as possible.

Preoccupied with her thoughts, she did not notice the carriage that halted beside her, nor the two soldiers who stepped down from it until a pair of hands closed over her arms and seized her.

Struggling against the grip of her assailant, Katie let fly with a string of angry curses as she was turned around and slammed back against the wall of the alley to face the pair of redcoats. Her heart thudded with panic, but neither of these men was the dolt-headed lieutenant she'd fleeced that morning.

The one who held her firmly by the shoulders nodded to his companion. "She's the one." Looking once again at Katie, he added, "We've been looking for you all morning, my girl."

They must have seen her stealing from their fellow officer. Or worse, they were friends of his, come to find her from his description. She thought of the miserable weeks she'd spent in Newgate two years ago before being transported to the colonies, and she struggled furiously to free herself. Better to die trying to escape than end up in prison living with the rats and facing the gallows again.

A vicious kick to her captor's shin loosened his grip and she jerked free, but her victory was short-lived. The two men easily overpowered her. Hurling every curse she knew at them, Katie struggled in vain as the soldiers dragged her into the waiting carriage.

During the brief ride, there was little chance for escape. Both soldiers kept a firm grip on her, and both were immune to her pleas, questions, and curses. When the carriage came to a halt, she made one last attempt to break free, but it was useless.

Her captors dragged her inside a tavern, past the doorway of a taproom empty at this hour of the morning, and up a set of narrow stairs. Still struggling, Katie was hauled into a large, sparsely furnished room. A man was seated at the head of a long table and he rose to his feet as she was brought in.

At the sight of him, Katie went still and her curses died on her lips. This was not the lieutenant. In fact he was not an officer at all. This man had pale skin stretched tight across his cheekbones, eyes that were dark and expressionless, and a smile that was coldly mocking. His face reminded her of a death's head.

He glanced to the soldiers on either side of her and gave a nod of confirmation. "Excellent work, my good men. You may let her go."

The two soldiers obeyed, and Katie gave each of them a resentful scowl before she turned her attention to the man at the other end of the room. He studied her as he came around the table and walked toward her, and she subjected him to the same careful scrutiny he was giving her. Whatever this was about, she refused to show fear.

He did not look like a magistrate. Too richly dressed, she decided, studying him from his powdered wig and white lace jabot to his silk hose and silver buckled shoes. He paused a few feet away from her, and without taking his eyes from her face, he spoke to the pair of soldiers. "Leave us."

The soldiers departed, closing the door behind them.

"I am Viscount Lowden," he said.

A British viscount? Katie was astonished.

"What is your name?" he asked. When she remained silent, he went on, "I can easily find out. You might as well stop wasting time and tell me."

"Katie," she answered.

"Your surname?"

She sighed, knowing a man like this would discover it anyway. "Armstrong," she answered in resignation.

"Well, Katie Armstrong, do you have any idea why you are here?"

Her mind raced frantically, but she could not figure out the purpose of all this. She didn't think she was officially under arrest. She shook her head in answer to his question.

"I summoned you here because I have a task for you to do."

She raised her eyebrows at those words. "Summoned? Dragged is more like it."

"I suggest you curb your insolence, girl." He took a step closer to her and grabbed her hand. Peeling back her tattered glove, he turned her palm upward to expose the T branded into her skin. The mark of a thief. "If you do not watch your tongue, I shall find another girl to suit my purpose, then I will find your master and return you to him."

Dread seeped into her bones at the idea of returning to Willoughby, and for the first time in months, she remembered what real fear felt like. *Steady,* she told herself and looked the viscount in the eye. She jerked her hand away and put just the right hint of defiance in her voice when she said, "I don't know what you're talking about."

He smiled, and Katie felt the hairs rise on the back of her neck. This man was no fool.

"Come, come, my girl," he said with a hint of impatience. "Let us stop the pretenses, shall we? I know you are a thief. I know this not only by your brand, but also because I myself witnessed your little escapade in North Square this morning. Though a thief, you are too young to have worked off a seven-year indenture. So, you are obviously a runaway bondswoman. I am no stupid fresh-faced lieutenant, and I didn't bring you here so I could have you hanged for something as mundane as stealing. Nor am I in the business of finding runaway servant girls for colonists careless enough to lose them."

Katie was fatalistic by nature. She knew when struggle was futile and lies became useless. Her only option was to cooperate and see what happened. She shrugged. "Very well, then. What do you want of me?"

He pulled a folded sheet of parchment out of his pocket. "This is an arrest warrant against you for stealing. It is signed by Lieutenant Weston, whose purse you lifted this morning in the marketplace."

"God's blood, you're a lying bastard," she ground out between clenched teeth. "You just said you didn't bring me here to have me hanged for theft, yet you have an arrest warrant!"

He was completely unperturbed by her rage. "Mind your tongue," he said softly. "Insult me again, and I'll not bother with warrants. Make no mistake, I could kill you right now, and no one would ever know."

She knew he spoke the truth. He was a man with money, title, and power. He could debauch her, or kill her, or both, and no one would ever know or care. She stiffened and glared at him. "I've faced the gallows before, and I got used to the idea of dying a long time ago, so your threats are wasted. I'm not frightened of you." The last was a lie, but she had her pride. By God, she'd not cower before any man. Katie held out her hand. "Let me see the warrant. I want to read the charges against me."

For the first time, she seemed to surprise him. "You can read?"

She gave him a bitter smile. "Don't expire from the shock, my lord, but yes, I can read. Let me see the warrant."

He handed her the document, and she read it all the way through. It was a detailed account of her escapade that morning. She handed it back. "All true," she said with a blitheness she was far from feeling. "Except about my hair. It's more blond than red."

"Better and better," he murmured to himself, ignoring her comment. He put the warrant back in his pocket. "The fact that you can read is an unexpected bonus. Can you write as well?"

"Aye."

"Excellent." The viscount drummed his fingers on the table beside him, staring at her thoughtfully. "Despite the fact that you curse like a sailor, you speak with a cultured voice. Despite your insolence, you seem to have some knowledge of manners and polite society."

"I am an orphan, my lord," she answered dryly, "not an animal."

He ignored that. "And you can read and write. How does a street thief develop such accomplishments?"

Katie knew from experience that whenever possible it was best to tell the truth, so one didn't get trapped in one's own lies. "For nearly a decade, my mother was the mistress of a wealthy gentleman. Most of my childhood was spent in his household. My mother taught me to read and write. As for the rest, I observed those around me and paid attention. My mother died when I was ten, and her paramour packed me off to an orphanage."

"You are fortunate it wasn't the workhouse," he commented.

That was one way of looking at it, she supposed, but she thought of Miss Prudence's thin, cruel lips and sadistic fondness for the willow switch, and she didn't quite see it as fortunate. "Why have you brought me here?"

"You're a very good liar, you know. I suspected as much when I saw you making a fool of that lieutenant."

She did not respond to that. She simply faced him in stony silence, waiting for an answer to her question.

"You are audacious," he continued, "clever, quite pretty, and completely unscrupulous. And that, my girl, is exactly what I want from you."

"I don't understand."

"Danger does not seem to bother you," he went on as if she had not spoken. "Death doesn't seem to frighten you. I have a mission for you that involves the possibility of both."

"Do I have a choice about this?"

"Of course." He smiled, but it was not a nice smile. "If you accomplish this mission, I will buy your indenture and set you free. I will also give you a gift of seven and six to start a new life. If you refuse my proposal, I will find your master and send you back to him."

A choice like that was no choice at all. "Whatever you want me to do, I'll do it, if you set me free."

"It is dangerous work. You may not live long enough to enjoy your freedom."

"I don't care. I'd rather be dead than indentured."

"Very well," he said, nodding as if he had not expected her to say anything else. "But know this. If you betray me, what I do to you will make indenture seem like heaven by comparison."

Katie looked into his dark, empty eyes and suppressed her shiver. He meant what he said. But if he was willing to free her, she didn't care how dangerous he was. "What is it you want me to do?"

"Doubtless you have heard of the Sons of Liberty?"

"The secret society?" she murmured. "Of course I've heard of them."

"Their headquarters is here in Boston, and I am here to arrest the ringleaders and demolish the organization. You are going to help me do that."

"I?" Katie stared at him in astonishment. "You want me to find the Sons of Liberty for you?"

"No. We already know who they are. However, confidential information is being passed to them by someone at the highest level. It is being given to the rebel leaders through a man named John Smith. We don't know very much about him. He appears to be a longshoreman, but he seems to have enough money that he can spend his Friday nights drinking rum at the Mermaid Inn, a rebel tavern in North Boston. Somehow, he is receiving information from someone close to the governor, and I want to find out who that person is. Discovering that will be your task."

"You want me to spy for you?"

"Exactly."

Katie frowned, thinking it out. "These Sons of Liberty would hardly allow a woman, a stranger, to become one of them. How am I to get to know this John Smith and find out the identity of the person from whom he gets his information?"

"I leave that up to you." He walked over to his chair and sat down, then took up quill and ink. "Find a way to become his mistress," he suggested, his quill making scratching sounds against the parchment as he wrote. "With your background, that should not be difficult."

Katie wanted to grind her teeth at the insult, but she remained silent.

"If you don't favor that idea," the viscount continued, sensing her resentment, "you might find a way to work at the Mermaid. Your cleverness is one of the main reasons I chose you. I'm sure you'll think of something." He blew on the paper to dry the ink, then rose and walked back to her side. He handed the paper to her.

Katie ran her gaze down the list of names. "These men are the Sons of Liberty?"

"The ones we know of, yes. Memorize this list, then burn it. Your main concern will be to find out who is giving John Smith information, but bring me anything you discover about any of these men, however unimportant it may seem."

She put the list in her pocket. "How am I to find employment without papers? The owners of the Mermaid won't hire me unless I can prove I'm a free woman."

He stared at her for a moment, then he said, "I'll have false papers drawn up for you to take with you. Wait for them downstairs in the kitchen."

"How do I report to you?"

"Come to the marketplace at dawn every Saturday, and one of my men will find you. I give you a week to get settled in your new situation, so you will meet one of my officers on Saturday next."

"I understand."

"If you learn something that cannot wait for a Saturday, you may leave a message for me here with the cook, Mrs. Gibbons, whom I trust absolutely." His eyes narrowed. "If I can arrest the traitor based on your information, I will have you set free and you will get your money. If you fail me, I will return you to your master. If you are found out by the rebels, you'll be tarred, feathered, beaten, and probably killed, and I will not be able to come to your aid. Should you disappear with the false work papers, I will find you. When I do, I'll use the warrant and have you arrested. You'll be tried and hanged for the theft of Lieutenant Weston's purse. Is that clear?"

"Perfectly clear."

"Good." He waved her toward the door. "Now go."

Katie followed his instructions. She sat by the fire in the kitchen of the tavern and waited, stunned by the odd turn her life had taken.

There would be no more looking over her shoulder, no more going hungry, no more sleeping in alleys and fields, and no threat of Willoughby in her shadow. Katie shuddered at the memory of him. Anything was better than returning to that lecher. She would be successful. She had to be.

Look for
THE CHARADE
Wherever Books
Are Sold
Coming Soon
in Paperback from
Sonnet Books